Thomas Barclay, George Lockhart Rives

Selections from the correspondence of Thomas Barclay

Thomas Barclay, George Lockhart Rives

Selections from the correspondence of Thomas Barclay

ISBN/EAN: 9783337281922

Printed in Europe, USA, Canada, Australia, Japan

Cover: Foto ©Andreas Hilbeck / pixelio.de

More available books at **www.hansebooks.com**

SELECTIONS FROM

THE

CORRESPONDENCE

OF

HOMAS BARCLAY

FORMERLY BRITISH CONSUL-GENERAL AT NEW YORK

EDITED BY

GEORGE LOCKHART RIVES, M.A.

LATE ASSISTANT SECRETARY OF STATE
OF THE UNITED STATES

NEW YORK

HARPER & BROTHERS PUBLISHERS

1894

PREFATORY NOTE

Of the voluminous correspondence of Thomas Barclay only fragments now exist. He kept few of the letters addressed to him, and none of a purely familiar or domestic kind. Copies, or sometimes rough drafts, of the letters he wrote were entered in letter-books, but none of his papers exist of a date earlier than 1790, and there are no letter-books later than 1818. Nevertheless, fragmentary as the collection generally is, the records of many of his public services are tolerably complete; and it has seemed to one of his descendants that the printing of portions of his correspondence would not only afford some memorial of a long and honorable career, but might also throw new light upon certain historical events.

New-York, Oct. 15, 1894.

TABLE OF CONTENTS

CORRESPONDENCE

OF

THOMAS BARCLAY

CHAPTER I

EARLIER YEARS

THOMAS BARCLAY was born in the city of New-York
on October 12, 1753. He was an active and zealous Loyalist during the Revolution, and at its close
sought refuge in the Province of Nova Scotia. In
1799 he returned to New-York as British Consul-General; and here, with brief interruptions, he resided
until his death on April 21, 1830. Nearly fifty years
of his life were spent in the public service of Great
Britain, and yet he was by descent and marriage, as
well as by birth and residence, essentially an American,
and not an Englishman. He was indeed a very typical
New-Yorker, of the pre-Revolutionary and loyal sort;
closely allied to the English Church and the Royal Government, but tracing his descent back through four gen-
erations to some of the earliest settlers in the colonies.

JOHN BARCLAY, the first of the name in America, was
a member of an ancient Scottish family, and settled
about 1683 in New Jersey, whither he had been directed through the influence of his brother Robert, the
well-known author of the "Apology for the People

called Quakers." It came about thus: the Duke of York, dividing up the great province granted him by his brother, had conveyed what is now New Jersey to Sir George Carteret and Lord Berkeley, whose shares were subsequently partitioned, East Jersey being set apart to Carteret. Carteret dying, East Jersey was sold to a company of twelve Quakers, who subsequently associated with themselves twelve other persons, mostly Scotch; and to these twenty-four the Duke of York, on March 13, 1683, made a new confirmatory grant. Among the twenty-four proprietors were the Earl of Perth, William Penn, and Robert Barclay. Barclay was appointed by the proprietors to be Governor of East Jersey; but he never visited the colony, administering its affairs in England. He sent out instead his younger brothers David and John. David came over in 1684, returned again to Scotland, and sailing from Aberdeen the end of August, 1685, died at sea. John had come over earlier, for he was back in London by the end of December, 1683, bringing letters from East Jersey. One may guess that he was then about twenty-five years old, for his parents were married on January 26, 1648, and his mother died in 1663, leaving five children, of whom John appears to have been the youngest.[1]

By the first of August, 1684, John Barclay was back once more in New Jersey, living at Elizabethtown, whence he removed to Plainfield, and finally settled at Perth Amboy.[2] About 1685 he married a lady whose name alone is sufficient evidence of her descent. She was Cornelia Van Schaick[3]—a member, it would seem, of the extensive Van Schaick family of Albany.

[1] Gen. Acct. of the Barclays of Urie. London, 1812.
[2] N. J. Arch., Vol. I, pp. 446, 459;
Whitehead's Con. to Hist. of Perth Amboy, p. 42.
[3] Holgate's Amer. Gen., p. 129.

In April, 1692, John Barclay was appointed surveyor-general of East Jersey, and later on became deputy secretary and register, clerk of the council, clerk of the courts, and a member of the Provincial Assembly.[1] He was not in favor during Lord Cornbury's turbulent administration; and being in fact in violent opposition, was denounced in 1702 as one "of the Scotch and Quaker ffactions concerned sundry years in y⁰ divisions, & incendiary Parties, that has brought these Provinces into such Confusion of Governmᵗ, Injustice to y⁰ Proprietors, and aversion to y⁰ Planters and Inhabitants."[2] In later years, and with a change of administration, he came to be on better terms with the colonial authorities; and he died in the spring of 1731, fully seventy years of age, generally respected and with the character of a good neighbor and a useful citizen.[3]

As we have seen, John Barclay was described as a Quaker in 1702. In point of fact he had by that time come over to the Church of England, being chiefly induced to that step by the influence of a very remarkable man—George Keith—who had himself been bred a Quaker, but had been united with the English Church, and, having taken orders, had been sent out to America by the Society for the Propagation of the Gospel. In 1718 John Barclay was named as one of the church-wardens in the charter granted for St. Peter's Church in Perth Amboy, and he contributed liberally toward the erection of the church edifice.[4]

Before the establishment of St. Peter's Church, ser-

[1] N. J. Arch., Vol. II, p. 81; Vol. XIII, pp. 200, 227, 262, etc.; Whitehead's Con. to Hist. of Perth Amboy, p. 42.

[2] N. J. Arch., Vol. II, p. 487.

[3] Smith's Hist. of N. J., p. 424.

[4] Whitehead's Con. to Hist. Perth Amboy, pp. 21, 211, 218; Churchman's Mag., Vol. VIII, p. 356; Keith's Jour., in Prot. Epis. Hist. Coll., Vol. I.

vices were occasionally held at Perth Amboy by an
English clergyman, who was expected to minister to the
whole region from Elizabethtown to Freehold. The Rev.
Thorowgood Moore had attempted for a while to perform that somewhat extensive duty; but in August,
1707, his plain-speaking having offended drunken Lord
Cornbury, he was thrown into prison, but escaped
thence to Boston, and sailing for England, was lost at
sea. Now this Mr. Moore, before coming to Perth Amboy, had been a missionary at Albany and among the
Indians, and we may well suppose that he did not fail,
when he found a likely young man with a vocation for
the ministry, to urge the noble work that might be done
on the wild frontier about the head waters of the Hudson River. Whether Mr. Moore did, indeed, find such
a young man at Perth Amboy, and whether he did influence the course of his career, must remain a conjecture; but certain it is that THOMAS BARCLAY, a son of
John Barclay, went early in the eighteenth century to
England, took orders, and was in due time sent, in his
turn, by the Society for the Propagation of the Gospel,
as missionary at Albany and among the Indians. He
seems to have reached Albany in 1707, or 1708, and
there we find him zealously laboring in September,
1710.[1] He had been there for some months, catechiz-
ing the youth, teaching Dutch children to make their
responses in the English tongue, marrying and baptiz-
ing in the absence of a Dutch minister, performing the
Church of England services both in English and Dutch,
shunning all controversies, and preaching once a month
at Schenectady—"a village situated upon a pleasant
river"—where there were about sixteen English and

[1] Doc. Hist. of N. Y., Vol. III, p. 540.
See, also, Hill's Hist. of the Church in Burlington, N. J., pp. 64-90.

one hundred Dutch families; in short, a very busy, earnest, sensible young man. "More of the Dutch," he writes, "would accept my ministry but that Mr. De Bois, minister of the Dutch Congregation of New-York, comes sometimes to Albany. He is a hot man, and an enemy to our Church, but a friend to his purse, for he has large contributions from this place." There was at that time no minister of any church north of New-York but Mr. Barclay, for the former Dutch ministers at Albany and Schenectady had died or moved away. The Dutch had converted some thirty Indians, who were communicants, "but so ignorant and scandalous that they can scarce be reputed Christians." The neighboring Indians were well disposed to receive missionaries, but—writes Mr. Barclay—"I am sorry to tell you, sir, that I am afraid the missionaries that are coming over will find hard work of it, and if the commander of that fort [Fort Hunter, at the lower Mohawk castle] be not a person of singular piety and virtue, all their endeavors will be ineffectual; these, here, that trade with them, are loth that any religion get any footing among them; besides, these savages are so given to drinking of that nasty liquor rum, that they are lost to all that is good."

In 1714 the Governor granted a patent for building an English church in Albany, named, like the church at Perth Amboy, St. Peter's, and Thomas Barclay was appointed its first rector [1]—the services having theretofore been held in the fort—and in Albany the remainder of his life was passed. We read, however, that he was for a short time in New-York, and assisted in the services of Trinity Church.[2] He died at Albany in the early part of the year 1722.

1 Doc. Rel. Col. Hist. N. Y., Vol. VI, p. 88.
2 Berrian's Hist. Sketch of Trinity Church, p. 34.

1A

Soon after settling in Albany he married Anna Dorothea Draeyer, or Drauyer, daughter of Andries Draeyer and Gerritje, his wife—who was, in turn, a daughter of Goosen Gerritse Van Schaick, of Albany,[1] and probably a relative of John Barclay's wife. Of this marriage there were born three sons—Thomas, Anthony, and Henry. Thomas died unmarried. Anthony married Helena Roosevelt, became a merchant near New-York, and left many descendants, with whom, however, we have here no immediate concern.

HENRY BARCLAY was born at Albany, probably about 1712, was entered at Yale College, and graduated at the head of his class in 1734. Returning to Albany, he was appointed, in 1735, catechist to the Mohawk Indians, in whom he seems at all times to have taken the liveliest interest. In later years he made some progress toward the translation of the Book of Common Prayer into the Indian language.[2] With youthful enthusiasm, he took a far more hopeful view of the possibility of effecting permanent results than his father had done. He believed the prospect of converting the Indians was " truly great," and he reported that he found them desirous of instruction. In 1737 he was recommended to the Society for the Propagation of the Gospel as a person of good morals and learning, who had many years applied himself with great diligence to learn the Indian language, and had made such progress as actually to instruct and catechize them in the Mohawk tongue. The society sent for him to England, and there, at the end of 1737, or beginning of 1738, he

---

1 Holgate's Amer. Gen., p. 145.

2 Doc. Rel. Col. Hist. N. Y., Vol. VIII, pp. 815–817; Doc. Hist. of N. Y., Vol. IV, pp. 206–217; Dexter's Yale Biog. Rec., p. 503.

was ordained.[1]   Returning to Albany, he resumed his pious labors among the Indians, and succeeded to his father's cure as rector of St. Peter's.   We find him writing on November 10, 1738, still hopeful, that there grew a daily reformation among the Mohawks, and an increase of virtue proportionable to their knowledge.

These rosy views and cheerful labors were destined to be soon ended.   On him, too, fell the evils caused by the wickedness of Frederick of Prussia; and when the whole world sprang to arms at Frederick's signal, and red men scalped each other by the great lakes of North America, that Frederick might rob a neighbor whom he had promised to defend, the quiet missionary in the valley of the Mohawk found that his dreams of Indian reformation and virtue were over.   The Indians of the Six Nations had been temporarily quieted by the treaty held by Governor Clinton at Albany in the early summer of 1744; but by 1745 northern New-York was aflame, and the French and Indians ravaged the country as far south as Saratoga.   In 1746 Albany had become the headquarters of a considerable army, and the Mohawks left their schools to enlist under the gentle influences of Sir William Johnson.

Such were the depressing surroundings at Albany when, on July 11, 1746, the Rev. William Vesey — for fifty years the rector of Trinity Church in New-York — finished his earthly course.   "He had," wrote the vestry, "the inward pleasure of leaving in peace and good order one of the largest and finest Churches in Amer-

[1] The Bishop of London, writing to Dr. Johnson, February 3, 1707–8, says of him: "As this comes by Mr. Barclay, I need not say anything of what has been done here with regard to him. By all the conversation I have had with him, he seems a truly valuable man, and to have both ability and disposition to do much good." — Churchman's Magazine, Vol. VII (1810), p. 311.

ica, with a considerable congregation, who, almost with one voice, named the Rev. Mr. Barclay to succeed Mr. Vesey as Rector." They would not, they added, have presumed to call him from his labors in the service of the Society for the Propagation of the Gospel, had they not been "well satisfied that, since the war with France he had met with insupportable discouragement, which rendered his mission and best endeavours fruitless, as well as the safety of his person precarious among those savages in the Mohawks' Country which, with many other parts of the County of Albany, being the frontiers of the province, is now deserted by the Christian Inhabitants, and almost laid waste by Barbarians and French." The call was not declined. On October 17, 1746, Mr. Barclay attended a meeting of the vestry, and formally accepted; and on the 22d of the same month, by authority of the Governor, he was inducted into the church with no lack of formal ceremonial.[1] The society which he had so zealously served very highly approved of his action under the circumstances of the case; but wrote requesting him to continue the Mohawk Indians under his care, as far as was consistent with his care of Trinity Church. The temptation to read the society a lecture on geography must have been great, but Mr. Barclay successfully resisted it, and gravely replied that he feared no missionary could reside among the Indians while the war should continue; that if he had had the least prospect of doing so himself, he would not have laid down his employment; and that he would do all in his power to keep alive and cherish that good seed which he had so happily sown among them.

Mr. Barclay had not only come by ecclesiastical pre-

[1] Berrian's Hist. Sketch of Trinity Church, pp. 68–76.

ferment, but his removal to New-York led him to a very prudent and fortunate marriage. In 1749 he married Mary, the youngest daughter of Anthony Rutgers — a rich brewer, whose death had occurred about the time of Mr. Barclay's call to Trinity Church.[1] Mr. Rutgers had married the widow of Robert Benson — Cornelia de Roos, her maiden name — and left sons and daughters of unmixed Dutch descent, who, in their turn, multiplied plentifully. Mrs. Rutgers, by her first husband, had three children; and of one of her grandchildren, Egbert Benson, we shall hear later on.

Of the marriage between Henry Barclay and Mary Rutgers — she pure Dutch, he one-fourth Scotch and three-fourths Dutch — there were born five children: Thomas, or Thomas H. Barclay, the eldest son, with whom we are here chiefly concerned; Anthony, who became a farmer at Newtown, L. I.; Catharine, who died young and unmarried; Cornelia, who married Stephen De Lancey; and Anna Dorothea, who became the wife of Beverly Robinson.

Henry Barclay's incumbency of Trinity Church seems to have been prosperous and peaceful. The growth of his congregation soon made it necessary to found a chapel of ease, and St. George's was established, to become in time a strong and independent parish. The New-York Society Library was founded, and Mr. Barclay was named as one of its first trustees. And in 1754 the long-cherished wish of many in New-York was realized by the granting of a royal charter for the founding of King's College — under the terms of which the rector of Trinity Church was to be always *ex officio* one of the governors. Columbia College to-

---

[1] His will is dated August 2, 1746, and was proved in New-York, September 17, 1746.

day owes much of its prosperity to the valuable grant from Trinity Church of a tract of land—then estimated to be worth £3000, and now yielding the college upward of $100,000 a year. This tract was conveyed upon the express condition that the president of the college should forever be a member of and in communion with the Church of England, and that the morning and evening service should be in the liturgy of that church. The same condition was in substance embodied in the charter, but this concession was only gained by the Church party after violent discussions, which gave rise to much angry debate in public and much anxious thought in the Trinity vestry. The Presbyterians, under the lead of William Livingston, were earnest in their opposition. The founding of a college under such sectarian influences was, they cried, but the entering wedge for bishops and tithes, and would surely end in the loss of religious freedom, " and even in persecution itself." For a time the issue seemed in doubt; but the Episcopalians remained firm and carried their point, and there is ample evidence that Mr. Barclay was a most active mover in the business, and steadfast to see that " a gift so valuable in itself, and so absolutely necessary," should "be a means of obtaining some priviledges to the Church." [1]

His zeal and diligence were rewarded by the honor of a degree of Doctor of Divinity, conferred by the University of Oxford about January 1, 1761, at the personal solicitation of the Archbishop of Canterbury.[2]

---

[1] Berrian's Hist. Sketch of Trinity Church, pp. 77, 101–105; Doc. Rel. Col. Hist. N. Y., Vol. VI, pp. 912–14; Jones's Hist. of N. Y., Vol. I, pp. 10–17; Beardsley's Life and Corr. of Samuel Johnson, p. 195.

[2] The letter from Archbishop Secker to the vice-chancellor of the University has been preserved. It is dated November 22, 1760.

After discussing the advantages to the cause of religion in the colonies

Dr. Barclay did not live long to enjoy his academic honors. On August 20, 1764, he departed this life, beloved and respected, leaving his wife and four children surviving.

"Last Monday morning," says the *New-York Mercury*, of August 23, 1764, "between three and four o' Clock, departed this Life, in the 53d Year of his Age, the reverend Henry Barclay, D. D. Rector of Trinity Church; in this City, and on the Tuesday following, his Remains, attended by the Clergy of the several Denominations, the Gentlemen and Chief Inhabitants of the City, preceded by the Charity Scholars, who sung a Psalm, suitable to the melancholy Occasion, during the Procession, were carried to Trinity Church, where an excellent Funeral Sermon, from Rev. 14, 13, was preached, by the Rev. Mr. Achmuty, to a prodigious large Audi-

from conferring the doctor's degree upon some of the principal clergy in those parts, the Archbishop prefers his request that that compliment be paid to Mr. Barclay, and continues: "It appears from the journals of the Society for the Propagation of the Gospel, that Mr. Barclay is the Son of a Missionary of that Society to the Indians on the frontiers of New York; that he was educated under Dr. Johnson at New Haven College; that in 1735 he was appointed by the Society Catechist to the Mohock Indians, and in 1737 ordained priest, and settled as a missionary among them; on which occasions the fullest testimonials were given in his favor by persons of the first rank and character, Clergy & Laity; that having learnt the language of those Indians, he preached to them in it with such success as to form out of them a Christian Congregation of 500 persons, 61 of whom, in all appearance were worthy Communicants; that he continued in this station till the year 1745, when the French Indians, falling on the Mohocks, obliged him to retire for the safety of his person; that in 1746 he was chosen Rector of Trinity Church, vacant by the death of Mr. Commissary Vesey, and hath continued there ever since. Dr. Johnson saith further, that he is a prudent and laborious man, an accomplished divine and an excellent preacher." On January 20, 1761, the Archbishop writes to Dr. Johnson announcing that the degree had been unanimously conferred on Mr. Barclay, and offering his congratulations on this well-deserved compliment. Dr. Johnson was then President of King's College. See Doc. Rel. Col. Hist. N. Y., Vol. VII, pp. 451, 454.

ence, who were extremely affected with the pathetic and moving Manner, in which they were addressed."

Dr. Barclay's will bears date June 19, 1764. He bequeaths his books in English to his eldest son Thomas; his books in Dutch and other personal effects to his wife; and the residue of his estate he gives, one-third to his wife and the other two-thirds to be equally divided among his four surviving children. He appoints as his executors his wife Mary Barclay, his brother Andrew Barclay, his brother-in-law Leonard Lispenard, and his friend David Clarkson.

THOMAS BARCLAY was not quite eleven years old when that moving funeral sermon was preached before the "prodigious large Audience," and the legacy of books in English came to him. No record remains to show what store he set by his books, or how he was taught, or where he went to school. One may easily picture him growing up in the little provincial town in the early days when George the Third was King; and one likes to think of his widowed mother encouraging him in a constant spirit of loyalty to his father's memory, and to the church and state of which his father had been in a manner the official representative. No doubt the boy, with the profound and assured conviction of youth, believed his father to have been the finest preacher in all the colonies, the Church of England the embodiment of all spiritual truth, the young King the ablest and best of rulers, and the system of government administered by Cadwallader Colden the perfection of human reason. One form of education was certainly not lacking. The divine right of kings and the rights of the people must have been debated in every boy's hearing often enough in the stirring days when the

Stamp Act Congress was sitting in New-York, and the province was pointing the way to independence.

In 1768 Thomas Barclay, not quite fifteen years old, was entered at King's College. His father, his uncle Leonard Lispenard, and his father's friend David Clarkson were among the original governors of the college. The two latter were still sitting in the board, and Lispenard was its treasurer. Dr. Myles Cooper, late a fellow of Queen's College, Oxford — a jolly, convivial gentleman, and an eager supporter of the royal authority — was president; Dr. Clossy, of Dublin, and Mr. Harpur, from Glasgow, composed the remainder of the faculty; but the classes were small as yet, and the instructors were thus "enabled to extend their plan of education almost as diffusely as any college in Europe." Diffuse was indeed the word. An appalling list of studies remains, drawn up by Dr. Cooper; and we find divinity, natural law, and Hebrew taking their place with Latin, Greek, and mathematics, and "whatever else of literature may tend to accomplish the pupils as scholars and gentlemen." To judge by results, the college system worked well. The best people in the place sent their sons, and the graduates were in good truth "scholars and gentlemen." Richard Harison, John Jay, Egbert Benson, Robert R. Livingston, John Watts, and Gouverneur Morris were among the most recent alumni. In the list of those who were fellow-students with Thomas Barclay we find the names of Pell, Knox, King, Ogden, Bogert, Philipse, Auchmuty, Robinson, Jauncey, Nicoll, Rapelje, Troup, Remsen, and Livingston — familiar to every student of the local history of New-York.

The college influence was of course in a direction favorable to the crown. While the College of New Jersey was in the hands of the Presbyterians and the college at New Haven was reckoned "a nursery of sedition, of faction and of republicanism,"[1] King's College was under the shadow of the Church, and governed by a board which included not only the principal officers of the province, but such earnest Loyalists as John Watts the elder, Frederick Philipse, Oliver and James De Lancey, Charles Ward Apthorpe, Thomas Jones, Jacob Walton, and John Harris Cruger. Indeed, of the college graduates down to 1776 a greater number were to be found in the King's troops than in the service of the Continental Congress.

In the spring of 1772, when the long-threatening discontent of the colonies was daily gathering force, when Samuel Adams was preaching sedition in Massachusetts, and the men of Rhode Island were burning the *Gaspee*, Thomas Barclay was graduated. The commencement was held at Trinity Church on Tuesday, May 19th, in the presence of "a numerous and respectable Audience," which included Governor Tryon and General Gage. After prayers, and "an elegant Latin Oration" by Rev. Mr. Inglis, Mr. Ogden delivered the salutatory oration "with great propriety of Pronunciation and gracefulness of Gesture." The audience was next agreeably entertained by Mr. Bowden, "whose elegant Composition and animated delivery did him much Honour." Then Mr. Skene "discovered much Brilliancy of Fancy and Refined Taste"; Mr. Winterton and Mr. Muirson maintained a "Forensic Dispute"; Mr. King "gain'd much Applause by an animated Latin Oration"; and Mr. Roebuck made fun of the "Bold Hypotheses of Presumptuous Philosophers and the Ridiculous consequences of Confidence and Dog-

[1] Jones's Hist. of N. Y., Vol. I, p. 3.

matism " in a manner which " occasioned much mirth."
The degrees having been conferred, "the Exercises of
the Day were then concluded with a very sensible Vale-
dictory Oration on Sociability by Mr. Barclay, whose
judicious Observations and modest Address gave him
universal Approbation. The Attention," adds the honest reporter, " paid by the Audience and the Satisfaction
they expressed during the Course of the Exercises did
much Honour to themselves, and the Speakers; and must
give pleasure to every Lover of Literature, and every
true Patriot, who wishes to see the Sciences dissemi-
nated and widely flourishing in this happy country."[1]

Barclay made choice of the law for his profession,
and it is the tradition of his family that he became a
student in the office of John Jay. In due course he
was admitted to the bar—probably about 1775, when
he was just of age. It was not a favorable time for a
young lawyer to enter upon his profession. Even in
the city of New-York, distant as it was from the fields
of actual conflict, the laws were silenced in the clash of
arms. The news of the battle of Lexington brought
turmoil and confusion. The Provincial Congress met
(Leonard Lispenard and David Clarkson among them),
and began raising troops and fortifying at Kingsbridge
and along the Hudson. Washington passed through
New-York for the eastward, stopping at Lispenard's
house. Zealous Dr. Cooper, roused at midnight and
huddling on a few of his clothes, jumped from a back
window of King's College to escape a party bent on
shaving his head and cutting off his ears; and never
stopped till he found safety in a snug living in England. Governor Tryon withdrew from the town and
prudently took refuge upon the *Asia*, man-of-war,

[1] N. Y. Jour., May 28, 1772.

where he transacted all his business and held his councils. The courts were still sitting, but no business of a civil nature was transacted in them. Open outbreaks occurred between the people of the town and the crews of the King's ships, and on August 24th the *Asia* fired upon the city. Early in September one-third of the citizens had moved away. "Every office shut up almost," wrote John Morin Scott, "but Sam Jones's, who will work for 6/ a day and live accordingly — All Business stagnated, the City half deserted for fear of a Bombardment."[1] Surely an unfavorable prospect for our young attorney.

But dark as the future might seem — and it doubtless appeared darkest to those who believed most firmly in the courage and constancy of the revolted colonies — young gentlemen of Tory families were not to be frightened away from assuming new duties and responsibilities. Marrying and giving in marriage went on, although Montgomery and Arnold were marching into Canada, and Washington was drilling his minutemen under the elms at Cambridge. Were not ships coming across the sea to set the world right once more? And so, on October 2, 1775, Thomas Barclay and Susan De Lancey were married at West Farms, near New-York.[2]

---

[1] Lamb's Hist. of N. Y., Vol. II, pp. 21-49; Jones's Hist. of N. Y., Vol. I, pp. 39-63.

[2] At the same time Mrs. Barclay's sister Jane was married to John Watts, the Recorder of New-York. The double marriage was thus announced in Rivington's Gazetteer:

"This evening were married at, Union Hill, in the borough of Westchester, New-York, John Watts, Junior, Esq., recorder of New-York, to Miss Jane De Lancey; and Thomas H. Barclay, Esq., to Miss Susanna De Lancey, daughters of the late Peter De Lancey, Esq.

'Round their nuptial beds, Hovering with purple wings, th' Idalian boy
Shook from his radiant torch, the blissful fires
      Of innocent desires,
While Venus scattered myrtles.'"

It was a singularly happy union. For more than fifty years this husband and wife were to live together in evil fortune and in good, secure in a most earnest and constant affection. Home and land might be lost, but from early youth to extreme old age they remained true and faithful to each other. In the dark days of exile no shadow of dissension seems ever to have come between them, and their later years were prosperous and happy.

Susan (or Susanna) De Lancey was the fifth daughter of Peter De Lancey, and one of eleven children. She was born September 15, 1755, and was therefore not quite twenty at the time of her marriage. Her maternal grandfather was Cadwallader Colden, the sturdy old Scotch doctor who, as Lieutenant-Governor of the province, had so long contended against Stamp Act congresses and sullen assemblies and turbulent committees of safety, and who was now living retired in his new house at Flushing. Her paternal grandfather was a Huguenot refugee of a good Norman family, who had drifted from France to Holland, from Holland to England, and from England to New-York, and had here married a Van Cortlandt of the old Dutch stock. The family is famous in the local annals of New-York as the stanchest supporter of the royal authority and the Church of England. One of Susan De Lancey's uncles—James De Lancey—had been Chief Justice of the province, and Colden's predecessor in the office of Lieutenant-Governor. Another uncle—Oliver De Lancey—was a General in the British service. A cousin — Stephen De Lancey—who had married Cornelia Barclay, was a Colonel in the King's troops; and their eldest son was Wellington's chief-of-staff at Waterloo, where he lost his life. One of Mrs. Barclay's brothers—James De Lancey—raised a loyal regiment in Westchester

2

County. Another James, a cousin, the Lieutenant-Governor's son, was the agent for the Loyalists in England after the peace, and so lost his great estate in the heart of the city of New-York. Oliver De Lancey, the General's son, succeeded André as Adjutant-General of the British forces, and died a Lieutenant-General. With few exceptions, the men of the family were strenuous in their support of British authority to the very last, and died in exile; but one or two of them, and notably one of Mrs. Barclay's brothers, courageously refused to take arms against the country of their birth.

The city of New-York, as we have seen, had so clearly become an undesirable residence for professional gentlemen, that our young married couple took up their abode in Ulster County, "at the Wallkill," near Coldenham, in what is now a part of Orange County, where grandfather Colden owned large tracts of land. But Ulster was no place of repose for Tories, or even for those who were willing to be neutral in the great contest just beginning. The committees of safety in the various counties were not content with anything short of open and unqualified adherence to the Continental cause, and were only too willing to find occasions for discovering enemies to the State. The powers of these committees were as vague as they were extensive, and were often exercised harshly and unjustly. It was the common course of procedure to summon individuals who were suspected of a leaning to the British cause and to tender them the oath of allegiance to the State, or the "general association," which included a pledge to take up arms against the King; and arrest, imprisonment, and banishment followed a refusal. To speak disrespectfully of the Congress, or to refuse to take Continental money at par, were good grounds for arrest. All who were not known to be well affected became objects of silly suspicion; and nervous people imagined conspiracies and secret treachery to be hatching all about them, and worried and bullied their neighbors, until they were like to drive into opposition many of those who had previously been not very unfavorable to the cause of the colonies.

In the rough county of Ulster we may well imagine that the farmers and woodmen were not delicate in dealing with suspected Tories, and that dissent from the views of the majority — and much less open opposition — was intolerable and not to be endured. And so in the year 1776, when the battle of Long Island was fought, and Sir William Howe was slowly driving the Americans back from New-York, Thomas Barclay laid his law-books aside, set his face southward, and joined the British army as a volunteer.

For the next seven years he was a soldier, and, as we shall see, a very active and efficient one — marching and fighting in New-York, New Jersey, Connecticut, Virginia, and the Carolinas. On April 10, 1777, being twenty-three years old, he was commissioned a Captain in Beverly Robinson's Loyal American Regiment, and was soon promoted to the rank of Major for gallant service at the taking of Forts Clinton and Montgomery.[1]

Beverly Robinson, his Colonel, was a Virginian by birth, and a son of John Robinson, who had been a member of the council, and Acting Governor of Virginia in 1749 and 1750. Beverly Robinson's wife was Susannah Philipse, of Yonkers — a sister of General

[1] His commission as Major bears date August 2, 1778; but he is to rank from October 7, 1777, the date of the capture of the forts.

Washington's Mary Philipse,—and through her Robinson had acquired large tracts of land bordering the Hudson River. His residence opposite West Point acquired a tragic notoriety as the headquarters of Benedict Arnold; and, indeed, Colonel Robinson was himself actively concerned in events of September, 1780. He had accompanied André on that disastrous journey up the river, and from the *Vulture*, "off Sinsink" (Sing Sing), he wrote to Washington, recalling their early friendship, and demanding in peremptory fashion André's immediate release. At the close of the war Colonel Robinson retired to England,where he died.

The Lieutenant-Colonel was Beverly Robinson, Jr., the Colonel's son. He was born in New-York in 1755, graduated at King's College in 1773, and returning long after the peace, died here in 1816. As we have seen, he had married a sister of Thomas Barclay.

From 1776 to the late summer of 1781 Barclay was constantly employed in active service. The long period of negotiation followed, to be terminated in the spring of 1783 by the announcement of the ratification of the provisional treaty of peace. The Loyalist troops were disbanded, their officers were placed on half pay, and the wave of British invasion began to recede, sweeping away in its retreat prodigious numbers of American loyalists, who were scattered to England, to Canada, to Bermuda, and to Nova Scotia, to begin life again under another sky. Tens of thousands of these unhappy people sailed away into exile during this year of 1783, and with them went Thomas Barclay, accompanied by his wife and four little children — the eldest not seven years old.

Under the act of the New-York Legislature of October 22, 1779, he had been attainted and convicted of high treason; his property was declared to be forfeited to and vested in the people of this State; he was forever banished; and it was provided that if he should be at any time found within the State, he should be declared guilty of felony and should suffer death without benefit of clergy. He was just thirty years old when New-York was evacuated, and except his half pay he had little left but a sturdy frame and a stout heart.

Writing nine years later to his friend Brook Watson, in London, he thus recounted his services to the British crown:[1]

TO BROOK WATSON.

Annapolis, 20th Oct[r] 1792.

DEAR SIR: I have now some Business of my own I wish to trouble you with, and I have no doubt of success should you find yourself at liberty heartily to unite with two or three of my other friends in England. It has only wanted a person of some Interest and Activity to obtain it these three years, for I am certain if the facts were known to the Minister or Lords of the treasury it would not be denied. Of your wish to serve me from your past favors and Professions I can and have no doubt,—I have only to request if it is in the least inconvenient or militates with any other object you may have in view, you will by no means comply with my request.

The application I wish my friends to make is for a pension in lieu of the professional Loss I stand reported for by the Am[n] Commissioners and which my half pay by the act of Parlia-

---

[1] Brook Watson had a singular and adventurous career. He was of humble origin, and had sought his fortune in all parts of the world. He was for a time Commissary-General of the British forces in America. He became a leading merchant in London, a Member of Parliament, a Baronet, and Lord Mayor of London. A sketch of his life will be found in Nova Scotia Hist. Coll., Vol. II, p. 135.

2A

ment excludes me from receiving.[1]   It is improper and useless
to urge any argument against the exception in the act of Parliament, but it strikes me as extremely obvious that Gentlemen
who bore an active part during the War and hardly earned
their pay, merit some thing more than those drones who remained inactive, and were a dead weight on Government receiving an allowance of money and provision without doing
any thing for it.   The professional Compensation includes
most of the latter description and very few of the former.
However I neither could expect or would I apply for a pension
were there not several Instances of them, and as I conceive myself equally entitled with any officer who served and have as
ample certificates of my behavior and Services as can be
penned, I deem it but Justice to my numerous family to request the aid of my friends to obtain that we so much want
and others under similar circumstances enjoy.—I shall name
only three Gentlemen who receive these pensions altho' there
are many more.   They are Gentlemen of family Character and
every way deserving of the attention of Government.   The
first, Col. Cruger,[2] merits it also on the Score of important
Services and spirited behavior.   The two others, majors Van
Cortlandt[3] and Bayard[4] can have no claims from Service, having seen but very little if any.   It is disagreeable for me to say
anything on the Score of my own, but as I am writing to you
what to urge in favor of my pretensions, you will not I trust
look on it as proceeding from vanity or savoring of Egotism.

[1] The act referred to is 23 Geo.
III., Chap. 80, passed in July, 1783,
under which a board of three commissioners was created "for enquir-
ing into the respective Losses and
Services of all such Person and Persons who have suffered in their
Rights, Properties and Possessions,
during the late unhappy Dissentions
in America, in consequence of their
Loyalty to His Majesty, and Attachment to the British Government."
The final statement of the commissioners was presented to Parliament
in March, 1790.

[2] John Harris Cruger, Lieutenant-
Colonel of De Lancey's First Battalion.   Best known for his brilliant
defense of the fort at Ninety-Six, in
South Carolina, June, 1781.

[3] Philip Van Cortlandt, Major of
the Third Battalion, New Jersey
Volunteers.

[4] Samuel Bayard, Major of the
King's Orange Rangers.

In the spring of the year 1776 I was driven from my home by the Americans and joined the Royal Army, wherein I acted as a volunteer during the Campaign of that year.[1] In the beginning of 1777 I joined Col: Robinson in raising a Corps and was that Summer at the storming of Forts Clinton and Montgomery. My Behavior there met the approbation of Sir Henry Clinton and he promoted me to the Majority of the Regiment. At that time I went out for him on a feigned flag of truce in order to discover General Putnam's & Parson's Situation,— Sir Henry being apprehensive the latter had marched to attack the Lines at Kings Bridge then very weakly defended. This I effected at the risque of my Life, having been detained a day and a half on Suspicion of being a Spy, and brought Sir Henry at Verplanks Point agreeable and positive Information. In 1778 I served on Board the *Carrysfort* Frigate with 100 of the Reg^t as Marines while the French fleet were at Rhode Island and at the Hook near New York.[2] In '79 was in Connecticut under General Tryon,[3] and during

[1] The "spring" of 1776 seems to be an error. Lord Howe only reached Staten Island July 12, 1776, so that Barclay could not have joined the Royal Army before that time. He may, however, have left Ulster County earlier and gone to Queens County, which was a much more congenial locality. His first child was born at Flushing, December 3, 1776. A week earlier, on November 27, 1776, the Committee of Safety, sitting at Fishkill,— having before it "an inventory of the personal Estate late belonging to Thomas Barclay of Ulster County," who had "some months since gone over to the enemy on Nassau Island,"— ordered William Duer to take all the hay, forage, and grain from Barclay's farm for the use of the army, and directed that the live stock be sold at pub-

lic auction — reserving only so much as might be needed for the support of Mr. Fowler, the overseer, and his family, and the slaves on the farm. Journals Prov. Cong., Vol. I, p. 721.

[2] The *Carrysfort* was a frigate of twenty-eight guns, commanded by Captain Robert Fanshaw. On August 18, 1778, we read in Montresor's Journal that she was lying, with the *Camilla* and the *Zebra*, near Flushing, and that on the 20th "the Regiment of New York Loyalists embarked on board the frigates at Flushing" were ordered to land "and take up their old ground." N. Y. Hist. Soc. Coll., 1881, p. 510.

[3] This was in July, 1779. On the night of July 4th and the morning of the 5th, 1779, Governor Tryon

the remainder of the Season composed one of the Garrison at
Verplanks Point (opposite Stony Point) under Lt Col. Webster [1] who commanded from May to Aug^t, during which period
I had the care and command of the right hand redoubt which
from having it in the magazine sustained the whole of the
cannonade and bombardment of the Americans for four days
from Stony Point which they had gained.[2]   About the last of
August the 33 Rg^t & Col Webster left Verplanks Point when
the Commander in chief appointed me to the command on the
Recommendation of Col. Webster, with a Garrison of 600
men two thirds of whom were ill with Agues and fevers.   I
maintained the Post until ordered to evacuate it in Nov^r,[3]
notwithstanding Mr. Washington and his whole army were
within a days March and reconoitering our Works and attack-
ing the Picquets daily.   During the Winter of 79 & 80 I was
twice in the Jerseys in command, once with a detachment of
the Guards, the second time with German Troops.   In 1780 I

landed near New Haven. A stand
was made by the defenders at West-
bridge, on the Milford road, and the
British were forced to turn from their
path. At Thompson's Bridge, on the
Derby road, another skirmish har-
assed the British, but New Haven
was entered, plundered, and sacked.
The President of Yale was among
those maltreated.   Leaving New
Haven, the fleet sailed to Fairfield.
Little resistance was made, and the
town was plundered and burned.
Green's Farms was the next object
of the vengeance of Tryon, and was
almost utterly destroyed.   On the
11th Norwalk was entered and destroyed. Tryon was then recalled
to New-York.

[1] James Webster was the son of
a Scotch clergyman of Edinburgh.
He came to America as Major of the
Thirty-third Foot, was promoted to
be Lieutenant-Colonel, and was
killed at the battle of Guilford, North
Carolina, March 14, 1781. Lee, in
his Memoirs of the War, p. 292, declares that Webster was the first
among the officers of Cornwallis's
army.

[2] General Wayne retook Stony
Point on the morning of July 16,
1779, and held it for only a few days.
That post, and the works at Verplanck's Point on the east side of
the river, had been captured by Sir
Henry Clinton in May.

[3] Barclay, writing from memory,
is not quite accurate in his dates.
Verplanck's Point was evacuated on
the morning of October 21, 1779,
when the British set fire to their
buildings, and, embarking on transports, sailed down to New-York.
See Memoirs of Maj.-Gen. Heath,
p. 220.

was attached to the provincial Light Infantry,[1] served with
General Leslie in Virginia where I commanded the advanced
Post,[2] and afterwards in Carolina under Lord Rawdon. In
Carolina we were frequently in Action, in one of which (at
Kanty's house) I received two wounds in the same charge.[3]
When Lord Rawdon resigned the Command in Carolina I was
requested by him to carry his Dispatches by Sea to Lord
Cornwallis at Yorktown in Virginia, and was taken at the
Enterance of the Capes by the French fleet in attempting
to make my way through them to his Lordship, was a Pris-
oner with the French during the Action off the Capes under
Ad. Graves and Count de Grasse,[4]—obtained my parol in a
few days after, and arrived at New York in time to give the
Commanders in Chief by Sea and Land very full and necessary information. From that period the offensive part of the
War ceased—Lord Dorchester[5] arrived and yourself with
him—you therefore my dear Sir can say what Character I
had at New York as an officer and have therefore only to add
that after the War instead of going to England to prosecute
my claims and obtain a pension as many officers did,—I came
to Nova Scotia at Lord Dorchester's & your request to locate
the Lands for the provincial troops in company with Col. D.

[1] This was the Corps of Provincial
Light Infantry, made up of fragments of several Loyalist regiments,
and placed under the command of
Lieutenant-Colonel Watson. Watson was an Englishman by birth,
and a Captain and Lieutenant-Colonel in the Third Foot Guards. His
corps was very constantly and actively employed in the Carolinas.
He rose eventually to the rank of
General, and died in France in 1826.

[2] General Leslie, with about 3000
men, was sent by Sir Henry Clinton to meet Cornwallis in Virginia
in October, 1780. Leslie occupied
Portsmouth without opposition; but
Cornwallis, in consequence of the

defeat at King's Mountain, abandoned his march to Virginia; and
on November 22, 1780, Leslie reëm-
barked his detachment and sailed
for Charleston.

[3] This affair was probably a skirmish between Watson's Light Infantry and Marion. Canty's house is
shown on the map prefixed to Tar-
leton's Letters, etc., and lies about
fifteen miles east of Nelson's Ferry
on the Santee, on the road to Georgetown.

[4] September, 1781.

[5] Lord Dorchester, better known
in our history as Sir Guy Carleton,
arrived in New-York as Sir Henry
Clinton's successor, in May, 1782.

L.[1] & Ed. Winslow.[2] How well we executed this trust I leave you to speak.—This I may safely add, the Province of New Brunswic owes its present existence to our exertions and representations to you.

From this detail you will observe I have been on actual Service and in action more or less every campain from 1777 to 1781. The copies of Certificates inclosed will prove how well I served. The originals have been delivered into the Treasury. If more were necessary Generals Leslie, Vaughn and Mathews—Cols. Watson, Small and Balfour and all the officers of the Guards 63 & 64 Regts. who served in Virginia and Carolina would cheerfully certify—Lady Southampton (who is a cousin German of Mrs. B's) has promised her Lords Good offices in my favor.[3] I have given you as full a Statement as I think requisite. My recommendations are ample. My Presence in the County of Annapolis has contributed more to its improvement, and retaining the Loyalists here than any other person, and the Henly settlement in Wilmot exceeds any new one in either province. Those pursuits, which dearly benefit the parent state have been the obstructions to my coming over to London—I conceived it a duty incumbent on me at the close of the War to attend those who had faithfully served their king and see them comfortably setled — Had I gone home in 1783 or any subsequent year by my personal attendance, added to the Interest of my friends, I should have procured a temporary support and a pension afterwards. In case you my friends should not succeed this Winter, I must cross the Atlantic and try my own exertions. I have a family of ten Children and find my half pay and practice unequal to their maintenance even with studied Economy,

[1] James De Lancey, Mrs. Barclay's brother.

[2] Edward Winslow, Jr., born in Massachusetts about 1745, graduated at Harvard, 1765. He was a Colonel in the King's service, and in 1782 was Muster-Master-General of the Loyalist forces. He died in New Brunswick in 1815.

[3] Lady Southampton was the daughter of Admiral Sir Peter Warren, whose wife was Susan De Lancey, Mrs. Barclay's aunt.

and when I have made this last Attempt I shall set down satisfied that I have left nothing untried.—

Copies of Certificates which accompanied Major Barclay's Application to the right Honble the Lord Commissioners of His Majestys Treasury.

I Certify, That I always considered Major Barclay of Colonel Beverly Robinsons Regiment of Provincials as a very zealous active officer, and in every respect intitled to the Attention of Government

H: CLINTON L^t GEN^l.

I Certify, That Thomas Barclay Esqr Major to Colonel Robinsons Regiment of Provincials served under my command in Carolina, and merited much praise for his activity, courage and conduct on every occasion. His zeal was equally conspicuous in the earlier Period of the War, I, therefore, beg leave to recommend him Strongly to the Commissioners tho' he is not here in Person to make his application.

RAWDON.
London Feb^ry 5th 1790.

I do Certify, that as Inspector General of the late Provincial Forces in North America, I had an opportunity of being personally acquainted with the Character of Major Thomas Barclay of the Loyal American Regiment commanded by Colonel Beverly Robinson; and can give the most ample Testimony of his Zeal, Spirit and Loyalty, from the earliest period of the Rebellion, and of his Worth and good Conduct as an Officer.

ALEX: INNES,
(late) Insp^r Genl of P. Forces.

I do hereby Certify, that Major Thomas Barclay, late of Colonel Beverly Robinsons Regiment of Loyal Americans, served during the War in a very distinguished manner — I think his Zeal, Bravery and good Conduct, which has been shown on so many occasions, give him the fullest Claim to the

favour of Government; I therefore beg leave to recommend
him in the Strongest manner to the Commissioners of American Claims, as worthy of every Indulgence that can be shown
to him.

OL: DE LANCEY
late Adju^t Genl N° Am^a.

I do Certify, that I was intimately acquainted with Major
Thomas Barclay, late of the Province of New York, many
Years before the Late dissensions in America. That he was
bred to the Profession of the Law, and had entered into the
practice of that Profession before the Troubles began.— That
he purchased an Estate in the County of Ulster on which he
was Settled, was very much respected by all Ranks of People,
and had as fair and promising prospects of success as any
young Gentleman in His Line of Business.

That he took an early and active part in the cause of Great
Britain, by opposing the proceedings of the Americans, for
which reason he became so obnoxious to the Leaders in Rebellion, that he was obliged to quit his Estate and business, and
fly to the Kings Army in the Latter part of the year 1776.

That in March 1777, He joined the Loyal American Regiment as Captain, and by his great exertions and activity was
very serviceable in raising that Corps, in which he served
as Captain till the Month of October following, when he was
for his Bravery and good Conduct at the Attack and taking of
Fort Montgomery on the Hudson River, and for other essential Services, during that Expedition, Promoted to the Rank
of Major in the Sd Regiment; That he continued with the
Regiment from this time to the summer of 1780, and was
always on active Service either with the whole Regm^t or De-
tachments from it, and on every occasion gained Credit to
himself and the approbation of His superior Officers.

That in the year 1780, when Sir Henry Clinton ordered a
Corps of Light Infantry to be formed from the Provincial
Line, under the command of Colonel Watson, Major Barclay
desirous of being employed in the most active Line of duty, of-

fered his services to Sir Henry Clinton, and requested he
would appoint him second in command to Colonel Watson,
which Sir Henry was pleased with, and gave him that Appointment; with this Corps he went to Virginia under the
command of General Leslie, and from there to South Carolina. In both these Provinces he served with great Credit and
Reputation, and to the Approbation of the different Commanders under whom he did serve.

Bev. Robinson.

Wilmot, to which our exiles had retreated at the
close of the war, lies on the railway near the head of
the pleasant valley of Annapolis, and about half-way
between the villages of Annapolis and Grand Pré. It
is even at the present time a remote and thinly settled
region, with a few scattered hamlets and farm-houses
strung along the course of the little river, and the deep
forest stretching away from the hills on either side.
But in 1783 the forest primeval and the murmuring
pines and the hemlocks stood untouched through the
entire valley, except where the clearings reached out
under the walls of the deserted French fortress of Port
Royal. The long and desperate struggles between the
English invaders on the one side, and the Acadians and
their Indian allies on the other, were indeed at an end.
The banished Loyalist found no worse enemies than
winter and rough weather, but the forces of nature
were in their fullest vigor of resistance and were not
easily to be subdued.

Of the bitter struggles of those first years of banishment in the heart of the wild forest of Nova Scotia
only a scanty record remains, and we can but dimly
picture the daily recurring dangers and privations to
which these unwilling pioneers were subject; but with
a brave spirit difficulties were met and overcome, and

children were born and grew into vigorous manhood amid those discouraging surroundings. Major Barclay, we are told, "with his own hands levelled the forest on his new possession, which gratefully rewarded his toil and perseverance; while he converted the settlement of troops into a respectable society of which he soon became physician, pastor, counsellor and judge. By his industry in farming, he supported a large family, until finding his colony in a prosperous and orderly state, he removed to Annapolis Royal about the year 1789, to pursue his profession at the bar, which he exercised with great success through the province of Nova Scotia."[1]

As a successful country lawyer, he naturally entered the public service, and in 1785 was elected a member of the General Assembly of the province. On March 20, 1793, he became speaker of that body—a post which he retained until 1799, when he removed to New-York.

For a time his old military experience came again into demand. At the outbreak of the French Revolution fears were entertained of an invasion of the maritime provinces, and militia regiments were raised both in New Brunswick and Nova Scotia. Major Barclay became Lieutenant-Colonel of a regiment, and for a time was Adjutant-General of the provincial forces.[2]

---

[1] Curwen's Journal and Letters, edited by G. A. Ward, p. 598.

[2] Writing in 1817 to the Foreign Office, in reply to an inquiry as to his rank in the army, Barclay said: "In the year 1793 His Majesty was graciously pleased to appoint me Lieutenant-Colonel to the Royal Nova Scotia Regiment, which situation I held only a few months, as Sir John Wentworth, then Governor of Nova Scotia, agreed in opinion with me, that I could render His Majesty more essential Service by raising a Corps of fencible militia in Nova Scotia, which I did without incurring any expense to Government. My rank therefore is that of a Provincial Lieut.-Col., but when I draw half pay, I receive that of Major of the late Loyal American Regiment. It is however now upwards of eighteen years since I have drawn half pay."

These varied activities are but slightly reflected in the following correspondence. Such letters as have been preserved deal mainly with matters of current business, and rarely touch on questions of public interest; but his allusions to the condition of the Loyalists in Nova Scotia and the prospects of the colony are perhaps not unworthy of preservation.

TO LIEUT. FENWICK, CHATHAM, ENGLAND.

27 October, 1790.

SIR:

Mr. Cutler on his arrival in this Province delivered me your favor of the 31st of August with Letter Attorney inclosed. I shall most chearfully undertake the agency you request, having a fellow feeling for those whose property is remote from their residence and whose situation prevents their personal attendance. Since the peace in 1783 my mother died in the State of New York in North America, and devised a fourth part of her Estate to my Children (being myself from attainder incapable of inheriting) and altho she has been dead more than four years and I have written innumerable Letters to the Executors, still I have never been able to bring about a division or Sale.[1] . . .

Should you incline to sell [your farm] you may let me know the lowest price you wish it to go at as I will set it up at that and if any one gives more let him have it. I shall want a

---

[1] "Four years" is a mistake. Mary Barclay died on Sunday, June 8, 1788, only a little more than two years before the date of this letter. "The hearts of all who knew Mrs. Barclay," said the New-York Daily Advertiser, in announcing her death, "will testify to her worth. From a long and intimate acquaintance with the precepts of Christianity, she fulfilled its duties with uniformity and zeal, the reward of which she is now reaping, while her children must deplore the loss of a most tender parent, the poor a cheerful contributor, and all her acquaintance a pleasing friend." Her executors were Egbert Benson, Samuel Bayard, and John Watts, Jr.

Letter of Attorney ennabling me to sell either together or by divisions, as it is possible it may fetch more in parcels.

In Countrys like this it is impossible to say whether lands will increase in value superior to the money at interest. Since the year 1786 they have greatly decreased in this Province, owing to the immense number of Loyalists returning to the united States. At present they are rather on the rise. My own opinion is that money at use here is preferable to Lands; and ever will be in this frozen Zone.

TO WM. STURGE MOORE.

Annapolis, 7th June, 1791.

DEAR SIR:

Your favor of the 6th April came to me the 31st of May. I am sorry to find you still undetermined about coming out, and at your Silence in answer to mine of the 27th of Dec'r wherein I requested you to let me know how much I should bid at Auction for you on the Sale of the Parrsborough Estate—The two other Trustees and myself were of opinion it would be more satisfactory to Captain Moore, yourself and the Creditors that White Hall should be sold at Publick Auction to the highest Bidder, than to you at the Price I offered, to wit £400. As soon therefore as we came to this determination I wrote you and begged your orders how far I should bid for you at the Auction. I was aware it was possible some person or other knowing your demand might run it up to a Considerable amount, and tho' far Short of the balance due you, sell more than its present value. I declined therefore having the Auction until I had your order to what amount I might bid— You are now therefore to make up your mind whether you will remove to Nova Scotia and of course take White Hall or whether it shall be sold and brought in for you or not as it may happen. This my dear sir to you is a question of moment and I should advise you not only seriously to Consider it your Self but also to take the advice of your friends at home on the Subject. Nova Scotia is neither like Great Britain or even Pensylvania where lands bring in a certain an-

nual profit and expences may be ascertained to almost a farth-
ing; was I to consult my own feelings and Inclinations I would
advise you to come, but as your friend who wishes your Interest it is my duty to give you a faithful detail and leave you to
make up your own mind — Parrsborough is by no means a
flourishing settlement, most of the half pay officers settled
there deeply involved and no prospect of any success in the
mercantile Line — If your views are agricultural, I am satisfied you had better make a present of White Hall and purchase a farm already cultivated than to undertake the Clearing
of new lands — I speak from experience that the cultivation
of new lands in Nova Scotia is attended with Double the expence that you might purchase a good farm for — To set
down at Parrsborough for the sake of a Good house, is like a
hungry man setting down to a table well set out with a variety
of empty plate and Dishes. The house at Parrsborough however is not finished and will cost at least £200 pounds to compleat it. No Gentleman in this Province can farm to advantage. I speak from experience and I believe I managed as
well as most persons, what your Situation at home is I know
not, but if you can live there in a Comfortable retired manner
without losing your Capital, never remove to this Country —
I have Given you my Opinion with a Candour I conceved necessary and which to you I hope will not be disagreeable. I
beg however you not rely on it solely, but take the advice of
friends able to give it you. Let me know your Determination
and what Sum I am to go to for you. Should you determine
to remain in England I would advise you if £400 is bid for
Whitehall to let it go, and even loose a part rather than be en-
cumbered with inproductive place, and a house which time
every day renders less valuable.

3

TO RUFUS CHANDLER.[1]

Annapolis, 6th Nov., 1791.

MY DEAR CHANDLER:

Your favor of the 11 Aug and its duplicate I have duly rec'd and am greatly obliged to you for your Attention to my troublesome commissions and the affectionate Chearfulness with which you transact them. Your Letter I have shewn to the Gentlemen of this place who Desire me to return you their best thanks and to request you will send them out an Engine of the size of No. 2 made in the best and most substantial Manner. Also the extra 21 feet Suction Pipe.

I had seen Kinyons determination about assigning half pay in an English News Paper.[2] I can not say it meets my approbation, nor do I think it tends to preserve *bonos mores* in Society. Half pay is as Clear a Chattel as a man can be possessed of; neither can I subscribe to any of the Arguments adduced in favor of those who oppose its being assignable — The Half pay is the property of the Officer as long as he lives (unless he commits an act that excludes him from it — that however is out of the question) it is a certain half yearly income that is ascertained to a fraction. It is the reward of past Services and his exclusive property. If this is the case surely he has a right to do with it as he pleases. A man possessed of a lease for a term of years or of an Annuity has a right to Assign them to any other person and to direct the rents Issues Profits or money to be paid him. When once his Assignment is made the Assignor is bound and cannot make his Act. Why then shall not a half pay officer have the same power?

[1] Rufus Chandler was born at Worcester, Mass., in 1747; graduated at Harvard College in 1766, and practised law until the outbreak of the Revolution, when he removed to Nova Scotia. He subsequently took up his residence in England, and died in London in 1823.

[2] Lord Kenyon's decision in *Flarty v. Odlum*, 3 *Durnford & East*, 682, is doubtless meant; in which he held that half pay could not legally be assigned, as it would be highly impolitic to permit creditors to reach emoluments of this sort, as they "are granted for the dignity of the State and for the decent support of those persons who are engaged in the service of it."

It is because he is a fool — a madman — or a Spend thrift —
To call us all so is paying us a very bad compliment.—The
determination has only one Effect, to wit: to give Men of that
Class an Opportunity of being Rogues if they please and of
Spending their pay in a dissolute Gaol to the Injury of their
Creditors and the ruin of their own healths and Morals.

Mrs. Barclay desires her best regards to you and requests
you will purchase her two pieces of fashionable Ribbon to
wear on her head round a Cap — She is fond of plain colours,
and wishes it rather broad. *Consult the taste of some fashionable acquaintance of yours.*

The Wesley Locusts have entered this province and are rav-
aging the County of Annapolis. In particular Cozins, the
Bennetts, Seabury, and many others have joined them. They
have erected a handsome meeting house in the rear of Cozin's
Lott facing the street wherein Worthy Lake lived. One of the
Preachers, a little diminitive limping fellow, has so charmed
Miss Henny Cozens (as she is called) that she has married him.
I am told he and all his family before him were beggars in
Shrewsbury, New Jersey. His name is Cooper — possibly Col.
Lawrence may know him — I never heard him, some Com-
mend, others speak lightly of his Abilities. I Should however
suppose him clever from having preached himself into Cozen's
good Graces and Fortune and into his Daughter —

For the Honor of Massachusetts be it made known that his
Majesty's Attʸ General at Halifax[1] in a late affair of Honor
has come off with flying colours, and that the Solicitor General that worthy descendant of fair Hibernia[2] was obliged to

[1] Sampson Salter Blowers, born in
Boston in March, 1742, graduated at
Harvard College, 1763, and died at
Halifax, October 25, 1842, at the age
of over 100 years. He was associated
with John Adams and Josiah Quincy
in the defense of the British soldiers
tried in 1770 for their part in the
Boston massacre. He was imprisoned as a Tory during the Revolution, but soon liberated and sent to

Halifax. In 1795 he was made a
Judge, and in 1801 Chief Justice of
Nova Scotia.

[2] Robert John Uniacke was Soli-
citor-General from 1785 to 1797. At
the date of this letter, he was also
Speaker of the Assembly, an office
he held from 1789 to 1793, and again
from 1799 to 1805. He succeeded Mr.
Blowers as Attorney-General.

make a humble apology to him. The dispute was about a
Negro Man whom Uniacke had dismissed and Blowers took
into Service. On this occasion Uniacke said some rude things
—Blowers challenged—the Chief Justice interfered and
bound them both over in £1500, notwithstanding which
Blowers wrote Uniacke he was ready to break his Bonds and
meet him,—that Satisfaction he would have sooner or Later.
This determined Conduct so frightened Uniacke that he
begged pardon.

We are very gay here this Winter—Assemblies once a fortnight and a Weekly Club. Annapolis is still the seat of Harmony and friendship, I wish I could add wealth.

I have written this in a small hand to comprehend all I had
to say on a sheet. Give my sincere love to your father, may
you and he enjoy many years of uninterrupted health and
happiness is the sincere wish of

your very affectionate
and faithful
THO BARCLAY.

TO BROOK WATSON & CO.

Annapolis, 13th January, 1792.

GENTLEMEN :

In an accidental conversation I lately had with my Brother
in Law Mr. Stephen De Lancey, I discovered that Col. Dundas
and Jeremy Pemberton Esquires the Commissioners appointed
to examine into the Losses &c &c of those Loyalists who were
resident in this and the other Provinces, had after examining
me and hearing Witnesses on my claims, struck out a part by
mistake or misinformation to which I was most justly entitled
and for a loss exactly similar to which they allowed Mr. De
Lancey—The case is this—Mrs. Barclay (who was a daughter of the late Mr. Peter De Lancey) and her brother Mr.
Stephen De Lancey were with the other Children of Mr. Peter
De Lancey possessed of an Estate at the Whitehall in the City
of New-York consisting of Dwelling Houses Store Houses and
Stables—In 1776 that part of New York was burnt and it was

generally believed by the Americans, the fire happening the very night or night after the Kings Troops took possession of that City [1] — I clearly proved Mrs. Barclay's title and the value of the Property and should as you will see from enclosed Letter have rec[d] a Compensation therefor, but for some misinformation given the Commissioners, or their not properly understanding the merits of the Claim — The expression used by the Commissioners in their Letter (written by a pro tempore Secretary of theirs) is "They find Major Barclay disposed of his Ground right after the division of the Property" — I have ever lamented in investigating the Claims of the Loyalists the Commissioners had not devised a better mode to ascertain the justice of each Loyalists Claim than what they adopted. It is true they first gave each of us a fair candid and impartial hearing, but from this alone I am convinced their Judgements were not made up, but that they from time to time procured private information and that ex parte — This must have been the case in the instance I now represent to you; and I lament the Gentlemen had not when they rec[d] this information, complained to one of the Crown officers and had me indited for Perjury, for I should have been liable to the Pains thereof if found to have sworn to demands I had no claim to — The reverse however would have been proved, I should have rec[d] my compensation, their informer would have been treated with proper contempt and perhaps such an instance would have been an end to all future private information — The least the Commissioners could have done on this occasion would have been to have given me notice and told me unless I disproved the information I should receive no compensation for that loss — I take the Liberty to request you will endeavor to have my claims reviewed by some mode or other as to this point — It is

[1] The fire broke out at one o'clock on Saturday morning, September 21, 1776. It began near Whitehall Slip and spread fast before a strong southerly wind up the westerly side of the town as far as the College grounds. An account is given in Lamb's Hist. of N. Y., Vol. II, p. 135, where the original authorities are fully referred to, and a map is given showing the extent of the burned district. Cadwallader Colden, Mrs. Barclay's grandfather, died the same day.

3*

a matter that may easily be seen from looking over my claims
in the reports from Halifax there the whole will appear; and I
trust the Lords of the treasury will when once they find I have
by mistake been deprived of a sum the Commissioners intended to report me; generously order me payment — In 1776
the property at White Hall I claimed for was burnt; for you
are to observe I only claimed for the buildings not the Ground
— It was impossible to suppose I could conceive that could be
burnt — Now admitting I had sold the Ground after the fire,
does it follow from thence I was repaid for the Loss sustained
in the buildings, or could the selling of the Ground oust my
claim for compensation of the buildings — The fact however
is otherwise. I never disposed of the ground until the last of
the war. In 1780 or 1781 I do not recollect which Mr. John
De Lancey another Brother of Mrs. Barclays asked me to sell
him my Wife's share — I told him I did not know what it was
worth, but that he might take the Possession and give me
whatever he gave the other Brothers & Sisters — Nothing more
ever passed than this and altho he might in 1783 at the peace
have lent Mrs. Barclay some money on an expectation of a
purchase of her share, it never was compleated until this last
Autumn — I now send you only a copy of the Secretaries Letter in order that you may lay it before the Lords of the treasury and if the original is necessary and my own and Mr. John
De Lanceys affidavit to prove when I disposed of the Ground
and how many years after the Loss was incurred — Let me
know and they shall be sent — I feel myself much hurt at this
part of the Claim being rejected as it in some measure reflects
on my veracity and Candor; which except in this instance
has never been doubted — If it can be ascertained the Commissioners have been guilty of a palpable mistake, I trust the
treasury will ever be ready to rectify it —

FROM JOHN WATTS.[1]

New-York, 20 August, 1792.

DEAR SIR:

I lately was favored with your Letter of the 2nd. July last and delayed answering it till I could inform you that the sale of your Jersey Land, which was then pending, should be carried fully into execution, tho' I had taken for granted that Mr. Creighton to whom you had written in respect to that Business would have made you acquainted from time to time of the State of it. This land has been sold for £110. The money rec'd by Mr. Creighton & paid by him to Childs, who has executed a Bond of Indemnity in the manner you desired.

The Corps you are now raising will not I presume make it requisite for you to leave Home and in course you will derive every advantage without much inconvenience.

The People in general of these States are much attached to the Cause of France, altho' the excesses committed there in the prosecution are much lamented. However our Government as well as the People in general are for a strict Neutrality consistent with our existing Treaties. We have for a fortnight past had a large french fleet in our Harbour, in which many of the unhappy people from the Cape have come Passengers who are in the most distressed Situation and must be provided for at the Expense of the Publick. The Crews of the fleet have conducted themselves in the most peaceable manner towards the Citizens.[2]

The Lots in this City have, as you mention, risen greatly in Value, much beyond what I had any expectation of, I own no property in the City except the House I live in.[3] House Rents & the expences of Living in this City have for some

---

[1] John Watts had, notwithstanding his close connection with the chief Loyalists, maintained a neutral position during the Revolution. At the date of this letter he was Speaker of the New-York Assembly. From 1793 to 1795 he was a member of Congress. He died in 1830, aged eighty-seven.

[2] For an account of the arrival of the French fleet bringing refugees from Cape François (Hayti) see McMaster's Hist. of U. S., Vol. II, pp. 123-125.

[3] No. 3 Broadway.

time past been constantly on the Rise and it is unaccountable How People afford to live in the manner they do. However so it is, that we see no Diminution of the Style of Living and hear of no Failures.

My family are all well, I have been (but not with my good will) in town the whole summer which hitherto has been uncommonly hot. As I am not in Business It would not only be Agreeable but an object of œconomy to me (which you know is material in a large family) to reside in the Country, which my wife does, about 6 or 7 Months in the year.

I have not heard from my Brother Stephen [1] for two years past, but frequently hear of him and that he is well. I am in the bad Habit of not writing any one, unless Business makes it requisite, in course our Correspondence is very much Interrupted.

I am etc.
JOHN WATTS.

TO MR. FINDLAYSON.

Annapolis 28 Aug 1793

SIR

The Rev[d] D[r] Brown of Halifax has advised me to write you on the subject of procuring from Scotland a Gentleman as a private Tutor to my Children, and has been so good as to promise to send this under Cover to you stating the Conversation and describing what kind of Person I wish.— Convinced that Cultivation of the human mind, is one of the first Objects of your Wish, I trust you will not deem this troublesome or impertinent, altho' it comes from a person who nei-

---

[1] Stephen Watts was Major in Sir John Johnson's Royal Greens, a detachment of which he commanded at the battle of Oriskany, where he was desperately wounded and left for dead. He was found alive two or three days after the battle by some Indian scouts, and carried to the British camp. He subsequently went to England, where he married a Miss Nugent, and where the rest of his life was spent.

ther has or probably ever will have the pleasure of your Acquaintance.—

In Nova Scotia we have two public Seminaries, one at Halifax the other at Windsor, both of which are tolerably well fitted with Professors and tutors. The Expense however of send ing a number of Children to either of those places, exceeds my limited Circumstances; and in this Village we have not even a decent School, where the younger Children can receive the principal of Education—I have 10 Children, six of whom are of Ages fit to receive Instruction, and the two eldest of them tolerably advanced in Lattin, Geography, Arithmetic &. &. and am anctious they should have their education compleated under my own Roof, as being less expensive and at the same time affording me a better opportunity of establishing their morals and improving their manners—Dr. Brown thinks it very probable you may procure me a Gentleman agreeable to my wishes.—The utmost sum I can go to will be thirty pounds Sterling per Annum with washing bord and lodging in my family—The English, Lattin and French Language if possible, I wish my Children to be well founded in, together with a good Mathematical, Geographical, Astronomical and Historical Education, If therefore you can provide for me a person duly qualified to teach my Children as above mentioned; and who is willing to come at the salary mentioned you will do me a favor.— The Gentleman must be at the expense of his own passage, but as it may not be convenient for him to advance the money I now enclose you a draft on my agent in London for £25 Sterling which you will have the goodness to pay him in advance if necessary—This however you may add by way of inducement that in case the Gentleman remains four years with me, I will repay him his passage money. —Dr. Brown thought it might be an additional inducement to promise my interest in any Church or Professorship Promotion—The Gentleman may at all times depend on my Little Interest and every exertion in my power in his favor. I should however be wanting in Candor if I did not at the same time observe, I at present saw very little Prospect of either in this Province;—and to intreat him not to let any such promises be the preponderating weight in his determination to come out.   Ships belonging to the House of William Forsyth & Co of Halifax Merchants sail every Spring and Autumn for Halifax and New Brunswick from Glascow and Greenock, the Gentleman had best take passage in one of them being cheaper and more convenient than coming up to London for a conveyance and crossing to St. Johns New Brunswic will be preferable to Halifax; Annapolis being only twelve leagues water carriage from St. Johns and Halifax a distance of a near one hundred and forty Miles land Carriage and double that by water—I shall only add that your good Offices in procuring a Gentleman of Genius and Ability agreeable to the above description will greatly oblige

Sir

Your very obedient and

most humble Servant

THO BARCLAY

CHAPTER II

THE TRUE RIVER ST. CROIX

NOTWITHSTANDING the definitive treaty of peace between the United States and Great Britain had declared that all past misunderstandings and differences were forgotten, and that the intercourse between them was so established as to secure perpetual harmony and peace, scarcely ten years had elapsed before the two countries were again almost at war. Perhaps the real cause of the bitterness of feeling lay rather in the tremendous possibilities suggested by the French Revolution than in the ostensible grounds of controversy; and yet these were numerous and serious enough to furnish out a formidable quarrel. The English complained that the debts due them had not been paid, and that confiscated estates had not been restored; the Americans complained of the carrying away of their negroes, of interference with their commerce, of the impressment of their seamen, and of the failure to surrender Detroit, Buffalo, and Oswego and other western posts; while the parties differed as to the very starting-point for the boundary between their respective possessions. With what we must now regard as great moderation and good sense, the United States agreed to a treaty which gave them but a part of their demands, and left other questions to be settled when their increasing strength should compel a more attentive hearing. The general settlement of the question of neutral rights and the impressment of seamen was postponed. The disputes as to boundaries, British debts, and illegal captures were submitted to arbitration. The western posts were given up. Temporary regulations for commercial intercourse were adopted.

The treaty was concluded on November 19, 1794, and was entitled a "Treaty of Amity, Commerce and Navigation"; but it has been generally known as Jay's Treaty, from the name of the American negotiator. It met with extreme disfavor in the United States. Washington hesitated before submitting it to the Senate; the Senate ratified it only after long debate and with the suppression of one of its articles; and it was not until October 28, 1795, that the ratifications were finally exchanged.

The controversy as to boundaries, which was to be partly settled under this treaty, was destined to last for nearly a century, for it was not until 1873 that the line between the British possessions and the United States was at last adjusted in its full extent. Beginning at the eastern end, the line was marked out from point to point by a series of interesting compromises and arbitrations; and with the earlier stages of this long process of adjustment Thomas Barclay was intimately concerned.

The only question with which Jay's Treaty dealt was the starting-point of the line on the Atlantic coast. The treaty of 1783 had attempted a precise definition of the boundary. It was to begin at "the north west angle of Nova Scotia, viz., that angle which is formed by a line drawn due North from the source of the St. Croix River to the Highlands"; and it was to run thence "along the Highlands which divide those rivers that empty themselves into the river St. Lawrence from those which fall into the Atlantic Ocean." The eastern boundary of the United States was to be a line "drawn along the middle of the river St. Croix, from its mouth in the bay of Fundy to its Source, and from its Source directly North to the aforesaid highlands." And the first point to be settled was: "what river was truly intended under the name of the river St. Croix?"

On the western shore of the bay of Fundy, west of the St. John's River, two considerable streams fall in from the north. The easternmost still bears the Indian name of Magaguadavic, and it was this which the American Government claimed as the true St. Croix. The westernmost, known in its various parts as the Schoodic and Chiputneticook, was the one on which Great Britain insisted; and the matter was further complicated by the fact that this river branches out into a tangle of smaller rivers and lakes, so that if this was indeed the St. Croix it was no easy matter to fix its source. The difference of opinion involved an extensive territory. The mouths of the two rivers are some nine miles apart, while the northerly lines to be run, according to the extreme pretensions of the two parties, lay full fifty miles distant from each other. The territory involved in this dispute covered six or seven thousand square miles.

By the fifth article of Jay's Treaty the question was referred to the decision of three Commissioners — one to be appointed by the King, one by the President, and one by agreement between the two first named; and in case they were unable to agree the third Commissioner was to be selected by lot. The Commissioners were to make a written award, deciding which was the River St. Croix intended by the treaty of 1783 and describing it throughout, and particularly fixing the latitude and longitude of its mouth and of its source. The Commissioners were to meet at Halifax, and were empowered to appoint a secretary and employ such surveyors or other persons as they should judge necessary. And both the United States and Great Britain agreed " to consider such decision as final and conclusive, so as that the same shall never thereafter be called into question, or made the subject of dispute or difference between them."

Under this article of the treaty, the King appointed Thomas Barclay; General Washington appointed David Howell;[1] and the two agreed upon Egbert Benson[2] as the third Commissioner. The Commission met for the first time at Halifax on August 22, 1796. A unanimous agreement was finally reached, and the award of the Commission was signed at Providence, R. I., on October 25, 1798.

FROM LORD GRENVILLE.

Downing Street, March, 1796.

SIR

Herewith you will receive, a Commission under the Great Seal appointing you His Majesty's Commissioner for the pur-

---

[1] David Howell was born in New Jersey, January 1, 1747, and was graduated at Princeton in 1766. He became Professor of Mathematics and Natural History at Brown University in 1769, and subsequently studied law and lectured upon it. He was a member of Congress from 1782 to 1785, and Attorney-General and Judge of the Supreme Court of Rhode Island. He died in 1826.

[2] Egbert Benson was born in New-York, June 21, 1746, and was graduated from King's College in 1765. He was the first Attorney-General of New-York, member of Congress from 1784 to 1788, and afterward Judge of the U. S. Circuit Court and of the N. Y. Supreme Court. He died in 1833. His father, as we have seen, was a half brother of Thomas Barclay's mother; so that he and Barclay were first cousins of the half blood.

pose specified in the fifth article of the Treaty of Amity, Commerce and Navigation concluded with the United States of America on the 19th of November 1794. I likewise transmit you His Majesty's Instructions for the regulation of your conduct in the situation in which you are to be employed.[1]

I am, etc.,
GRENVILLE.

TO LORD GRENVILLE.

New York,[2] 30th May, 1796.

MY LORD

I have the Honor to acknowledge the receipt of your Lordships Dispatch of the 6th of March last with His Majesty's Commission under the great seal appointing me His Majestys Commissioner for the purposes specified in the fifth article of the Treaty of Amity Commerce and Navigation concluded between His Majesty and the united states of America on the 19th of Novr. 1794; and the Royal Instructions under His Majestys privy Seal for my guidance and direction in the execution of the said Commission.

I intreat your Lordship to lay at His Majestys feet my most humble acknowledgements for this instance of his gracious Favor, and beg I may be permitted to assure your Lordship that I shall by a punctual and diligent attention to the duty committed to me endeavor to merit this mark of His Majestys Confidence.

Private Business has led me to this City; at which place I received your Lordships dispatch by the march pacquet on the 10th of this Month, and conceiving an interview with Mr. Liston his Majestys Plenipotentiary residing in Philadelphia necessary previous to my departure for Halifax, I immediately took post for that purpose. Mr Liston had nothing particular

[1] These instructions are purely formal; they bear date March 5, 1796.

[2] By an act of the New-York Legislature, Chap. 68, Laws of 1792, all the persons named in the act of attainder of 1779, and who had thereby been banished from the State, were permitted to return and reside within it.

missioner my being at present in this City, and agree on some place for a meeting before my return, conceiving it might expedite the completion of the object committed to our determination and in the hope that I might have the pleasure of his Company to Halifax. I shall therefore the moment I am made acquainted by you of M[r.] Howell's acceptation of the appointment, write him respecting my return to Nova Scotia and proffer him an interview either here or at Rhode Island which ever to him may be most agreeable.

Whatever my own sentiments may be respecting the construction of that part of the fifth Article of the treaty which directs Commissioners therein named to meet at Halifax; I find myself so limited by the Instructions from his Majesty, that I cannot officially proceed on the Commission, before I meet the American Commissioner at the place agreed on in the fifth Article of the Treaty. Indeed it would be improper for many reasons. The interview therefore that I shall propose to Mr. Howell, will be of a private nature; in which we will freely communicate, and in all probability chalk the outlines of our future proceedings, and come to some determination respecting the nomination of a third Commissioner, Secretary, Surveyors &c. &c.

TO MR. HAMMOND.[1]

Annapolis, Nova Scotia 12 July 1796.

(*Private.*)

DEAR SIR

I wrote you from Philadelphia on the 25th and from New York on the 30th of May acknowledging the receipt of your very friendly letter of the 6th of March and requesting your acceptance of my warmest acknowledgment for recommending me to his Majesty and Lord Grenville for the appointment

[1] George Hammond — at this time Under-Secretary of State for Foreign Affairs. He had been Hartley's secretary during the negotiations in Paris, and British Minister to the U. S. from 1791 to 1795.

wherewith through your friendship I have been honored. In discharge of the trust reposed in me in addition to every other consideration, I shall endeavor to merit your approbation and to afford you the pleasing satisfaction that your good offices have not been improperly exerted in my favor.

A Delay has been occasioned on the part of the Americans by General Knox who was originally named by the President as the Commissioner on the part of the united states declining to accept the office. I am told he assigned many forcible reasons, among which was his being interested in the question. In consequence of his declining to serve Mr. Howel of the State of Rhode Island was appointed, and it was not until the 16th of June that I was informed through Mr. Liston of his acceptance. It was Mr. Listons wish as well as the American Secretary of State that Mr. Howell and myself should have an interview previous to my return to Nova Scotia. This I readily assented to, and accordingly met him at Boston on the 27th of June. At that meeting several persons were named as a third Commissioner. Mr. Howell alleged ignorance of the Characters of the Gentlemen I proposed. Amongst those he named there were three either of whom I told him I would agree to nominate, Judge Benson of New York who I fancy you recollect when he was a member of Congress—a Mr. Milledge of this province, and Mr. Antil of Lower Canada. Mr. Howell however declined the nomination, until he had consulted the American Ministers. He also informed me as his appointment was unexpected, he would not be prepared to meet me in Halifax before the 15th of August. I really fear from what I discovered at the interview we shall be compelled to leave the appointment of a third Commissioner to the accidental determination of a draft. We have therefore agreed to name three able and respectable Characters on each side out of which the opposing party respectively is to strike the names of two from each list and the two remaining names to be put into a box and one drawn out for the third Commissioner. I conceived this the least exceptionable mode in the event of our not mutually agreeing on a Commissioner.

I am apt to think there will be a necessity of procuring some

documents from England. I shall not however trouble his Majestys Ministers until I find them absolutely necessary and that they cannot be procured on this side of the Atlantic. Mr. Chipman the Solicitor General of the province of New Brunswick I am informed is appointed Agent on the part of Great Britain.[1] I have written him to come to me, and expect his arrival hourly. After we have consulted, we shall be able to know what proofs are wanting to substantiate our claims.

Accept my best wishes for the health and happiness of yourself and Mrs Hammond and family.

FROM MR. BOND.[2]

Philadelphia 27 July, 1796.

(Private and confidential.)

MY DEAR SIR,

I repaired to New York, as I told You I should, previously to the Departure of the Packet, of this Month, and was not a little disappointed to find You had set out for Boston, a considerable Time sooner than You expected.

It will occur to You, at once, upon examining the Documents produced, on the Part of the United States, that, in the Execution of Your Duty in ascertaining the true River St. Croix, you will have very little Difficulty. It is only necessary to recur to the Extract I gave You, from the Act of Parliam^t and to compare it with the Notes of *our* Historiographer, to be satisfied that there is not the least Ground to suppose, the Pretensions of the United States are founded in Justice.

[1] Ward Chipman was a native of Massachusetts, and graduated at Harvard in 1770. He left Boston with the King's troops in 1776, went to England, and returned to America about 1778, when he served in various military capacities, and doubtless formed Barclay's acquaintance. At the peace he removed to Nova Scotia. He subsequently filled important offices in New Brunswick, and became chief justice and president of that colony. He died at Fredericton in 1824.

[2] Phineas Bond, British Consul-General for the Southern States.

I have convinced the Gentleman who furnished me with the material Paper, of which You are in Possession, that so far from impeaching our ancient Boundary, all that He has collected, serves manifestly to confirm it.

It seems the Objection, first, originated in a Suggestion made by Gov[r.] Sullivan,[1] that the true River St. Croix was much to the Eastward of the River, which had been considered as the Boundary of the United States. In order to establish this Idea, the learned Gentleman, in a Book, He has lately published, has prepared a Map in which He has given a new & unheard of Name to the *real* River St. Croix, & has called a little Inlet, on the East Side of Passamaquaddi Bay, St. Croix River.

The Fallacy of all this is, easily, detected, by examining all the ancient Maps, which designate the Situation of St. Croix River, to be on the *West* side of Passimaquaddi, (which Situation the Act of Parliament, which established the Boundaries between the Provinces of Massachusetts Bay, and Nova Scotia, expressly recognizes,) whereas Gov[r.] S., to favor his Purpose, has placed the River St. Croix on the East side of that Bay. This, of itself, appears to me to be conclusive. I have not been able to get his Book here. I saw it for a Moment, and think it is called the History of the Province of Maine. It was published last Year; — I think You ought to have it, and shall direct the King's Consul, at Boston, to procure it, and send it on to you, by the Gentleman, who conveys this Letter to You.

I have some Reason to believe that the Government of the United States begins to be convinced there is no Meaning in the Claim it has instituted, & does not intend to urge it, *very* violently.

Our *Historiographer*, is a little anxious about his Notes; — I

<hr/>

[1] James Sullivan, then Attorney-General of Massachusetts. The book referred to is Sullivan's History of the District of Maine, published in 1795. Bond's error in referring to Sullivan as "Governor" was pro-phetic, as he was elected to that office in Massachusetts in 1807. As to Sullivan's share in this business, see Chap. xiv of Amory's Life of Sullivan.

have assured him that they can, in no possible Event, ever be brought to Light; and that they are only to serve, to furnish References to those Documents He has compiled, which so irrefragably, decide the Justice of our Pretensions.

I have a Chance of collecting some other Information, very shortly, of which I shall apprize You by the first *safe* Conveyance.

I shall be happy to hear you have received this Letter.

Mr. Liston is not returned from the Southward,—I write in Haste.   I am, &c.

P. BOND.

FROM MR. BOND.

Philadelphia, 18 Aug*t*., 1796.

(Private & Confidential.)

MY DEAR SIR:

Inclosed I send You duplicate of my Letter of the 27th Ult: — tho' I, sincerely, hope the original may have, long since, reached You; as, with it, you would probably have received Judge˘ Sullivan's famous History of the District of Maine which I requested the King's Consul at Boston to forward to You, by the Gentleman to whom I committed the Care of that Letter.

From the Suggestions of this Author, as I have told You, all this Difficulty respecting the true River St. Croix has arisen. In the Map He has prefixed to this Notable Work, He has, not only, changed the Position of the River — but it's name;— giving to the true river St. Croix, situate on the *West* side of Passimaquaddy Bay, the Name of Schoodic River, and to a little Inlet, on the *East* side of the Bay, the Name of St. Croix River.

As the Author has been nominated by this Government Agent of the United States in the pending Negotiation, to ascertain the true River St. Croix, He will, independently of interested Motives, which may, perchance, have warped his geographical Judgment, be now influenced by Pride, & a nice

Sense of literary Honor, in maintaining his visionary Positions: But there seems to be no Chance of his succeeding, since, exclusively of other Means of Refutation, with which You will be furnished, I take it for granted, an actual Survey of the spot, must fix the River we contend for, as the true River St. Croix, namely, that River, which empties itself on the *West* Side of Passimaquaddy Bay:—The original Description of the Island, & River St. Croix, seem to be so accurately defined, as to leave no Particle of Doubt upon the Subject. After various Delays & Disappointments, I am, at Length, in Train of obtaining, shortly, a very accurate Detail of every historical Fact, which can serve Us, upon this occasion; which is also extended to a Refutation of all Judge Sullivan's material Positions.

The Purpose of my troubling You, now, is, to intimate to You, that unless You shall see Your Way, perfectly clear, in ascertaining the grand object, which so much affects the Interests, as well as the Credit of His Majesty's Government, it will be expedient to suspend Conclusion upon the Point, until You shall be in Possession of such Documents, as will, speedily, be completed here: For this purpose, it will be advisable, previously to your leaving Halifax, (if that should happen this Autumn) in order to explore the geographical Situation of the two Rivers, to fix some mode by which a safe Correspondence can be maintained with You, from hence, which appears to me to be most practicable thro' the Medium of the King's Consul, at Boston, with whom You will be pleased to make the proper Arrangements, seasonably:—As far, however, as I can calculate, at present, You may count upon having the expected Detail, forwarded to you, at Halifax, by the first Mail:—any other Mode of Conveyance might be hazardous.

In conversing with the Gentleman, who prepared the material Paper I delivered to You, I soon found He had gone upon a mistaken Idea that we meant to carry the Western Boundary of Nova Scotia, as far as Kennibeck River, according to the former Pretensions and Claims of the French upon Acadia—who in Virtue of Sir Wᵐ Alexander's Grant of the Province of Nova Scotia, endeavor'd to engross not only the Province of Nova Scotia, but also that portion of the Plimouth Grant, which was allotted to Him, as an Individual Member of the Company, which Portion it so happened, was bounded on the *East*, by the St. Croix River; — His observations, therefore, tended to defeat this Westerly Extension of the Boundary of Nova Scotia by showing that Portion of the Plimouth Company Grant assigned to S^r. Wm Alexander, and bounded on the *East* by St. Croix River, was, as well by the Terms of the original Grant, as from prescriptive Recognition, within the Province of Massachusetts Bay.   I am &c.

P. BOND.

FROM MR. BOND.

Philadelphia 29 Augt 1786.

(Private and Confidential.)

MY DEAR SIR,

I write to You by a Conveyance, upon which I place but little Reliance — & therefore I shall say *but little.*   Since I wrote to You on the 18th curr^t I have procured the *material* Paper, I contemplated, & in my Opinion it clearly establishes all we contend for; so that if the Commissioner, on the Part of the United States should not accede to our Claim, in it's full Extent, You will find ample Means to establish it: In *that Case* an actual Survey seems indispensable, which, however it may be attended with some Fatigue, will, in the result of it, most amply repay all our Labours.   By the next mail You are to expect all the Communications, You are to look for from *hence.*

I am &c.   P. BOND.

TO LORD GRENVILLE.

Halifax 30 Augt 1796.

MY LORD —

I have the honor to inform your Lordship that on Monday the 22nd Instant I met at this place David Howell Esqr the

Commissioner appointed on the part of the united States of America to settle the boundary between the united States and His Majestys Province of New Brunswic under the fifth article of the Treaty of Amity Commerce and Navigation between His Majesty and the united States of America and that upon perusing his Commission I find it differs from His Majestys Commission to me as your Lordship will see by a copy of it which I have the Honor to inclose. In the Commission to Mr. Howell the President of the united States expresses himself in these words "and thereupon with the other Commissioners duly sworn to proceed to decide the said question and exactly perform all the duties conjoined and necessary to be done to carry the said fifth Article into compleat execution"; while in His Majestys commission to me it is declared, "We will give and cause to be given full force and effect to such final decision in the premisses as by our said Commissioner together with the other two Commissioners above mentioned or the Major part of the said three Commissioners shall duly be made according to the Provisions of the said Treaty."—Upon discovering this variance I communicated with Mr. Howell and requested he would report to the President of the united States the construction given to the fifth Article of the Treaty in my Commission from His Majesty and that his Commission might be so amended as to comport with mine.—He observed that his Commission was framed in the words of the fifth Article and that he did not feel himself at liberty to suggest an alteration to the President, neither did he think the president would make any; he at the same time assured me he believed it the intention of the contracting powers that a declaration under the hands and Seals of a Majority of the Commissioners should be final and conclusive, that this was not his opinion alone, but of every man in office in the united States with whom he had conversed on the subject.[1] After this declaration and from a

[1] Notwithstanding Mr. Howell's emphatic assertion, it was a fact that the Attorney-General of the United States entertained the opposite opinion. Under date of July 23, 1796, Mr. Lee wrote that the decision could not be made by a majority of the Commissioners. See Opinions of Atty.-Gens., Vol. I, p. 66.

conviction that the very words of the Article strongly favor such a construction, I have determined to proceed on the subject referred to our determination. If the intention of the contracting parties had been that the whole of the Commissioners should agree in order to make the declaration valid and binding, they would have named two or four Commissioners, indeed the very naming of a third Commissioner imports that the acts of two shall prevail where the three are not agreed. Should your Lordship differ in Sentiment with me my commission may be restricted, as Mr. Howell has agreed not to require a copy until the declaration is engrossed and ready to be executed. He has written to the American Secretary of State for a certified Copy of His Commission which shall be forwarded to your Lordship the first Pacquet after I receive it.

The American Commissioner and myself after several Communications have this day agreed in the choice of Egbert Benson of the City of New York Esq' as the third Commissioner —A Gentleman of Ability, Candor and Integrity and in whose impartiality I have the utmost confidence. His appointment will be forwarded to him by a conveyance which sails to-morrow. The Agents on the part of Great Britain and the united States that no time may be lost will proceed immediately to Pasamaquaddy to effect accurate Surveys of the two Rivers in dispute the Scoodiac and the Magaguadavic.

I have industriously exerted myself since I had the honor of receiving his Majestys Commission in procuring for the Consideration of Mr. Chipman his Majestys Agent such papers proofs and documents as could throw light upon the subject in controversy, but I find his zeal and industry in the fulfillment of the duties of his appointment, and his thorough knowledge of the subject will relieve me from every apprehension that anything will be omitted in procuring or arranging the evidence in support of the Claim of the British Government which can in any degree tend to elucidate their justness or force — I understand from him that he has expressed to Governor Carleton his wish to be furnished with Champlains Voyages, Purchases Pilgrim or Collection of Voyages, and

L'Escarbot as in them or some of them is contained a particular description of the Isle of St. Croix resorted to and named by the Sieur de Monts in 1604 from whence the river in question took its name and which island Mr. Chipman is confident from the description of it in some extracts from L'Escarbot with which it has fortunately been in my power to furnish him, he has discovered upon viewing the place to be actually situated at or near the mouth of the River which is claimed on the part of His Majesty to be the River St. Croix truly intended by the treaty of Peace.[1] He informs me he has also requested to be furnished with Copies of the Acts of Parliament of Scotland the records of which are kept in the Castle of Edinburgh by which the two Provinces of Alexandria and Caledonia into which the Country of Nova Scotia granted to Sir William Alexander are established and confirmed, as he conceives it probable that in those Acts the River St. Croix may be ascertained by a more particular description than the Grant to Sir William Alexander contains — As a hearing of the Agents upon the question will be deferred until the Surveys are compleated of the Rivers claimed as the boundary on the part of the respective Governments there will be time without creating any additional delay, to cause him to be furnished with these Documents, and I have taken the liberty to men-

[1] " Quittant la riviere Sainct Iean, ils vindrent suivant la côte à vingt lieuës de là en vne grande riviere (qui est proprement mer) où ils se camperent en vne petite ile size au milieu de cette riviere, que ledit sieur Champlein avoit esté reconoître. Et la voyant forte de nature et de facile garde, joint que la saison commençoit à se passer, et partant falloit penser de se loger sans plus courir, ils resolurent de s'y arréter. . . . Et d'autant qu'à deux lieuës au dessus il y a des ruisseaux qui viennent comme en Croix se déchargor dans ce large bras de mer, cette ile de la retraite des François fut appelée SAINCTE-CROIX, à vingt-cinq lieuës plus loin que le Port-Royal. . . . Ladite ile a environ demie lieuë de tour, et au bout du côte de la mer il y a vn tertre et comme vn ilot separó, où estoit placé le canon dudit sieur de Monts, et là aussi est la petite chappelle batie à la Sauvage. Au pied d'icelle il y a des moules tant que c'est merveilles, lesquelles ou peut amasser de basse mer, mais elles sont petites."
Lescarbot, Histoire de la Novvelle France, Liv. IV, Chaps. iii and v.

tion it for your Lordships Consideration lest Governor Carletons letter should not be forwarded in season to go by this Conveyance.

FROM MR. BOND.

Philadelphia 6 Sept'. 1796.

(Private & Confidential.)

MY DEAR SIR,

Inclosed I beg leave to forward to You, Duplicate of my Letter of the 29th Ult; sent by a Cartel Ship, & written at the Moment of her Departure. Having now a much safer Conveyance by the Packet, I can with more Propriety, enlarge upon the Nature of the *other* material Paper I have procured, of which Mr. Liston has been in Possession some days. It is rather a tedious Compilation, but it, undoubtedly, discovers a very extensive Knowledge of Historical Facts, applied to the Subject, confirming, by a vast variety of Documents & Observations, the *Location* of the River St. Croix — and clearly refuting all that has been said, upon the Point, by a certain *Author*, who is raised to the High Station of Agent for the United States, in the pending Negotiation.

Judging from the vague & fallacious Positions which this Author, under the Effect of rooted Prejudice, or of Interest, has thought fit to advance, we have little to expect from the Candor of the Man, in executing the Duty assigned to Him. It is not perhaps too much to impute the Dispute as to the true River St. Croix, to the Author of the History of the District of Maine, encouraged by Persons, who have sinister views to gratify, by extending the Eastern Boundary of the United States beyond the river St. Croix, which Great Britain has uniformly considered, as the Western Boundary of the Province of Nova Scotia; and whose Features are so well designated in ancient History, (without resorting to the Acquiescence of the Inhabitants of the Vicinity,) as not to admit of a Doubt on this Point, at this late Day.

My best wishes always attend You—may Success and Reputation result from Your present Efforts

I am &c.   P. BOND.

TO MR. TURNER.[1]

Annapolis 18th October 1796.

MY DEAR SIR—

An application having been made to me by Mr Schuyler Livingston for my assent to his being married to my daughter, who had for several years resided with her Aunt at New York for the purpose of completing her education—I determined notwithstanding my friends had assured me the connection was advantageous and every way agreeable, to go and judge for myself, previous to giving my consent.[2]

As soon therefore as the Governor had adjourned the house of Assembly (about the middle of April last) I embarked for the States, on board the Earl of Moira, with which Sir John[3] had politely accommodated me and arriving at Boston in four days, went from thence to New York by land.—Having on particular enquiry ascertained the connection requested to be every way eligible, I consented to the Union, and on the 17th of June in order that I might be present, the marriage of my daughter and Mr Livingston was solemnized at her Aunts Seat about 16 Miles from New York—Ten days after this I set out on my return for Nova Scotia and got home about the 5 of July.—As soon as Messrs Fouman and Grassie heard of my arrival they forwarded me your favor of the 21 of March last, inclosed with a pacquet from Mr Watson & another from the house—My time has been ever since so totally occu-

[1] John Turner was a partner in the house of Brook Watson & Co.

[2] Schuyler Livingston was born September 24, 1772. He was the son of Walter Livingston, who was the son of Robert Livingston, the third proprietor of the manor.

Schuyler Livingston's mother was Cornelia Schuyler. The wedding took place at the house of Mrs. Cox, who was Anne De Lancey, Mrs. Barclay's sister.

[3] Sir John Wentworth, Governor of Nova Scotia.

pied in and about the execution of the Commission wherewith
His Majesty has been pleased to Honor me, that I have not
really had a leisure moment to attend to my private concerns.
— I am now but just returned from St Andrews Passamaquady where the Commissioners have held their first meeting
on the question referred to them, it appeared the most proper
place, being part of the territory in dispute and contiguous to
the two rivers respectively contended for as the true S^t
Croix

The judicial capacity in which I am to act renders it improper for me to discuss the subject, or express my Sentiments in any manner relating to the dispute, except in the
presence of my brother Commissioners and officially — Indeed
if these Objections were removed, the length of the case in
order to give you a just idea of the controversy would too far
exceed the limits of a letter to admit of it — After a Weeks
communication at Halifax in August last, the American Commissioner and myself agreed in the Choice of Egbert Benson
of the City of New York Esqr as the third Commissioner — A
Gentleman of undoubted Ability and Integrity, and who from
being a near relation was brought up in my fathers family,—
I found it impracticable for Mr Howell the American Com^r and
myself ever to agree on any other person, and that unless I
joined in the appointment of Judge Benson, we must proceed
to the unpleasant alternative of balloting for the third Commissioner — To this I am extremely averse, from a conviction
that by this measure the question would be decided rather by
lott, than on its merits — I was convinced of the Justice of His
Majestys Claims, and the indisputable authorities that could
be adduced to support it — To leave it therefore to a ballot,
would be putting what I looked on as a certainty in hazard,
a game I by no means conceived myself authorized to play.—
It is true the American Commissioner gave me the names
of two or three Gentlemen in England, one of whom he was
willing should be opposed to Mr Benson, but these Gentlemen,
I learned were warm minority men, and I did not conceive it
probable they would leave their pursuits and cross the Atlantic, on such a question and under our nomination.— Thus cir-

cumstanced I judged it most for His Majestys interest to give up the only possible objection to Mr Benson, that of his being an American, under the hope of having a cool, sensible, and dispassionate third Commissioner — His future conduct I trust will prove the propriety of my determination —

To say I am much obliged to you for your exertions in my favor respecting the application for a pension, would too faintly express my feelings — Permit me therefore to offer you my most grateful thanks and to assure you the impressions your kind interference has made will never be effaced from my recollection — Mr Hammonds observations were so just as to carry conviction with them, and I feel equally obliged to him for the remark and you for adopting it — For the present therefore we will drop the pursuit, and wait an event more favorable —

I am happy I can assure you that before the first day of January next the Province of Nova Scotia will be totally disincumbered of Debt — It was a load that lay heavy on my mind, from the first day I became a member of the house of Assembly; and my principal exertions have bent to free the Province from such chains. You may rest satisfied that the same principles will induce me to oppose every measure tending to incur similar embarrassments —

TO MR. BOND.

Annapolis 24th Octr 1796.

(Private & Confidential.)

MY DEAR SIR

The paper you allude to in your dispatch of the 7th of Sepr. came safe to hand, and your directions respecting it have been obeyed — Accept my sincere thanks for your industry and zeal in furnishing me with what you can collect and conceive of consequence to be communicated — And permit me to intreat a continuance of your good offices — I hope you and Mr Liston approve of the nomination of Judge Benson as the third Commissioner, who I know to be a man of Candor, Integrity and Abilities and with whom I believe from his intimacy with Mr. Hammond you are acquainted.

I cannot conclude without cautioning you against——. He who betrays faith reposed in him even by a villain, is not to be trusted by an honest man. His Character at this day is the same my worthy father gave me of him upwards of 30 years since. That he was a man of duplicity and not to be trusted.[1]

TO LORD GRENVILLE.

Annapolis 24th Octr. 1796.

MY LORD—

In my dispatch No. 3 dated Halifax the 30th of August last past, a duplicate whereof is enclosed, I informed your Lordship that the American Commissioner and myself had agreed in the choice of the third Commissioner and that a vessel was sent to carry him his appointment. The American Commissioner and myself being of opinion that the meeting of the Commissioners at St. Andrews in the County of Charlotte Passamaquady (a part of the lands in dispute) would facilitate the business, and prevent the Agents removing from a place where their presence was necessary, we accordingly adjourned to St. Andrews and notified Mr. Benson the third Commissioner to meet us at that place on the 3rd of October. — On the 4th of October the three Commissioners having met at that place were sworn, agreeably to the 5 article of the treaty by Robert Pagan Esqr His Majestys first Justice of the Court of Common Pleas for that County, after which the Board of Commissioners appointed Edward Winslow of Fredericton in the Province of New Brunswic Esqr their Secre-

---

1 The person here alluded to seems to have been Mr. Bond's historiographer, who furnished a copy of the American case and other information. He was presumably a New-Yorker, and must have been employed in the State Department; but it does not seem possible now to establish his identity.

tary and received the claims of the respective Agents copies of which I have the honor to inclose to your Lordship. The 5th we made an attempt to proceed up the River Scoodiac claimed by the Agent of His Majesty as the true St. Croix, but the Wind failing we were compelled to return to St. Andrews; after which the board met, confirmed the surveys commenced under the mutual agreement of the Agents and taking the future operations of the Surveyors under our control established rules and orders for their direction and government; ascertained their pay per day and that of the chainmen and laborers under them &c &c. On the 6th the Commissioners attended by the Agents went to view the mouth of the River Magaguadavic claimed by the American Agent as the St. Croix intended in the treaty of Peace and the Island which he said had been named by the Sieur de Monts in 1604, *Isle de St. Croix*. The 7th we had a view of the Isle de St. Croix in the River Scoodiac as shown us by His Majestys Agent with the small Island in its front and as much of the River as he said he conceived necessary to be seen to evince that the Islands and River corresponded with the description given by L'Escarbot and Champlain french Historians, who attended the Sieur de Monts in his Voyage to that part of North America in 1604,[1] and on our return we examined under oath in the Evening a number of Indians produced on the part of the united States — On the 8th the board established rules and regulations for authenticating Records and other public documents to be given in Evidence, with several other necessary orders and resolutions, particularly one directing a survey to be made of the bay of Passamaquady, the Islands therein, the Brooks and Rivers that discharge themselves into it and all the Mountains, high lands or head lands which present them-

[1] "Il nous faut dire que l'Ile de Saincte Croix est difficile à trouver à qui n'y à esté, car il y a tant d'iles et de grandes bayes à passer devant qu'on y soit, que je m'étonne comme on avoit penetré si avant pour l'aller trouver. Il y a trois ou quatre montagnes eminentes par dessus les autres aux côtez; mais de la part du Nort d'où descend la rivière, il n'y en a sinon vne pointuë eloignée de plus de deux lieuës."
Lescarbot, Liv. IV, Chap. v.

5

selves to view in proceeding up the bay to either of the rivers in question, representing their Shapes and appearances respectively as they make or appear in proceeding to and up each of the Rivers in question.

Having examined the Surveyors as to the probable period when their surveys would be completed and finding they could not be effected until late the next Autumn and the Agents having stated by a joint memorial that it would be out of their power to deliver in the Arguments on which their claims were founded until they were possessed of these Surveys, the board adjourned to the second Tuesday in August next, then to meet at Boston in the State of Massachusetts for the purpose of examining witnesses and to adjourn from thence to such place as his Majesty's agent should think necessary for examining any other witnesses he might wish to produce. The weather from the 20th of September to the 8th of October was so unfavorable as to prevent the Gentlemen employed from ascertaining the longitude of the mouth of either of the Rivers and the Season being far advanced we gave up the pursuit until next Spring. The Surveyors will probably continue at Work to the 10th of November, at all Events they will remain in the field until driven in by Snow and extreme cold.

Private. I take the liberty of suggesting to your Lordship a circumstance which probably will be laid before you by His Majestys Agent through Governor Carleton, but as an accident may happen to his dispatches and no time ought to be lost, I presume to suggest to your Lordship, what certainly with more propriety would come from him. The Agent of the united States has related to His Majestys Agent that the Plenipotentiaries who concluded and signed the definitive treaty of Peace between His Majesty and the United States of America at Paris in the year 1783, had in contemplation and believed that the River called the River St. Croix in the treaty was the first River to the Westward of the River St. Johns in New Brunswic, that they had Mitchels map before them at that time, which lays down the eastermost river in the Bay of Passamaquady as the River St. Croix, and that Mr. Jay and Mr. Adams the surviving American Plenipotentiaries and Mr.

Hartley the British Plenipotentiary, together with Lord St. Helens[1] and a Mr. Whitford[2] who were then present will attest to the above representation, and aver that the River next to the River St. John in New Brunswic was the one by them intended as the point from whence the dividing boundary between Great Britain and the united States should commence, and that he should next August examine Mr. Jay and Adams on the subject. What weight such testimony will have with the Commissioners is not for me to suggest. I have given your Lordship the above information, that you may if you conceive it necessary examine Mr. Hartley, Lord St. Helens and Mr. Whitford or any other persons who were present at the forming and executing of the treaty, and advise His Majestys Agent what they will declare under oath respecting the same — Also whether Mitchels map was or was not the chart by which they governed themselves — The American Agent further states, that the Source of which river shall be decided to be the River St. Croix truly intended, cannot be extended beyond the flowing of the tide, and that he shall establish this position by the decision of the King and Council, on the source of the Merrimac river in setting the boundary line many years since between the Provinces of Massachusetts Bay and New Hampshire, and a similar determination respecting the source of the Piscataqua river.— The absurdity of the position is too gross to admit of a moments hesitation — It may not however be improper to possess His Majestys Agent with authenticated copies of all papers on file, & the opinion of the King and Council on the question of the last above mentioned rivers.

Although Mr. Chipmans abilities are unquestionable and his application intense, still he wages a very unequal War with the American Agent, who has two of the Council, two of the Senate and one of the most eminent of the Law Counsel in the State of Massachusetts assigned to assist him in collecting documents and evidence and preparing a case and arguments on this important question; on which a territory of not less

[1] Alleyne Fitzherbert, raised to the Irish peerage as Lord St. Helens in 1791.

[2] Caleb Whitefoord, Secretary to the British Commissioners who negotiated the preliminary treaty of peace.

than 6 or 7,000 Square miles depends, part of which is invaluable to His Majesty for the masts and yards it will furnish for the Navy.— Under these circumstances I am extremely anxious, and have therefore been the more readily induced to communicate the above information to your Lordship, that His Majesty's Agent may in time be informed of the facts and furnished with every necessary map and paper that may elucidate the question, or enable him to oppose and confute the arguments and suggestion of the opposing party—

FROM MR. CHIPMAN.

St. John, 9th Nov' 1796.

MY DEAR SIR,

I feel myself under peculiar obligations to you for the very interesting and friendly communications in your letter of the 3ᵈ instant. I perfectly agree with you that the mode you have adopted with regard to my concerns, bids much fairer for success than any other, and whatever the event may be, I shall ever very gratefully recollect your kind interference upon this occasion. I am rejoiced that you have met with Popple's Map, as I believe from the description I have of it, it will be of great use.—There is another point which I am endeavoring to ascertain, which if it turns out as I have reason to believe it will, must be decisive in our favor.—The line from the Source of the St. Croix you will recollect, is by the Treaty of Peace to run " due North to the Highlands which divide those Rivers which fall into the *Atlantic Ocean* from those which fall into the *River St. Lawrence.*" Now by an inspection of Capt. Sproules Map it appears to me, that a line drawn due North from the source even of the Cheputnaticook will strike the River Restigouche which runs into the Bay of Chaleurs, and of course *falls* into the *Gulph* of Saint Lawrence ; such a line therefore will not answer the description in the Treaty, much less will a line drawn from the Source of the Magaguadavic or any other source eastward of the Source of the Cheputnaticook,—but a line drawn due north from the Source of the Scoodiac will run to the westward of the sources of all the Rivers that *fall into the Gulph of St. Lawrence*, and will of course extend to the Highlands mentioned.—The idea was first hinted to me by Mr. Owen. I have communicated it to Governor Carleton, and requested that he will have the line run this winter due North from the source of the Cheputnaticook to see where it will strike and that we may have evidence of the fact if it proves to be in our favor:—and if it should not, I think such a line must be run hereafter from the Source of the Magaguadavic, as I am satisfied that it will upon this principle, clearly show that this cannot be the river. Let me know your opinion of this hint. I think we should at present keep it secret, I have intimated as much to the Governor.

I thank you for your attention respecting the Cyder. Make my best compliments to Mrs. Barclay and affectionate regards to your little Flock, and believe me,   &c.

WARD CHIPMAN.

TO MR. HAMMOND.

Annapolis, 20th Nov., 1796.

MY DEAR SIR:

The inclosed is a duplicate of what I wrote you in Oct. last. Two things have since occurred which I think of moment to communicate; the first of which I intreat your attention and that by the earliest conveyance you will have the goodness to inform me what Governor Franklin recollects on the subject. Cap⁺. Moody the well known secret Service man under Sir Henry Clinton during the American War, tells me he was in London when Mr. Hartley returned from Paris after executing the definitive treaty of Peace in 1783. That he called on Governor Franklin to pay him a visit, who informed him that Mr. Hartley had just left the room, with whom he had had a long conversation respecting the territory ceded the united States. That he (the Governor) had asked Mr. Hartley why the Plenipotentiaries had not made the river Penobscot the beginning

5A

boundary between Great Britain and the United States. To which he answered, that Doctor Franklin had so clearly demonstrated that the River St. Croix was a preferable boundary being the dividing limit formerly existing between Nova Scotia and Massachusetts, that the Plenipotentiaries acceded thereto. To this the Governor replied that the loss of the intermediate Country was of consequence to Great Britain, and that he was afraid his father the Doctor had been too cunning for Mr. Hartley. Captain Moody is certain Governor Franklin will recollect this conversation, as he appeared much interested and told him, he and Mr. Hartley had conversed near an hour before his arrival. As Doctor Franklin is dead, it may be of moment to refresh Mr. Hartleys memory by what the Governor recollects.

By the treaty of peace the line from the source of the St. Croix is to run due north to the Highlands which divide those rivers which fall into the *Atlantic Ocean* from them which fall into the River St. Lawrence. Mr. Chipman His Majestys Agent has hinted to me, and from examination I am apt to believe it will prove so, that a line drawn due North from the Source even of the Chiputnatcook, (the North branch of the Scoodiac) will strike the River Restigouche which empties into the Bay of Chaleurs and of course *falls*, into the Gulph of St. Lawrence; such a line therefore will not answer the description in the treaty, much less will a line drawn from the Source of the Magaguadavic or any other source eastward of the Source of the Chiputnatcook. But a line drawn due North from the Source of the Scoodiac will run to the westward of the Source of all the Rivers that *fall into the Gulph of St. Lawrence* and will of course extend to the Highlands mentioned — I shall unite with Mr. Chipman in an application to Governor Carlton of New Brunswic to have a line run this Winter due North from the Source of the Chiputnatcook to see where it may strike, and that we may have evidence of the fact if it proves in our favor. Should it not, then to run the north line from the Magaguadavic. If it turns out as I expect, our cause will be essentially strengthened, indeed the question will be at an end. The result you shall be informed of by the first conveyance after it is ascertained. I have taken the liberty to hint to Lord Grenville the propriety of furnishing Mr. Chipman with Champlain, L'Escarbot & Purchase[1] with all authentic maps and a copy of the acts of Parliament of Scotland which are kept in the Castle of Edinburg by which the two provinces of Alexandria and Caledonia into which the Country of Nova Scotia granted to Sir Will[m]. Alexander are established and confirmed, as they are material and as he is want of them.

FROM MR. BOND.

Philadelphia 29 Nov[r] 1796.

(Private.)

MY DEAR SIR

I am now to acknowledge the Receipt of Your very interesting Letter, with the Inclosures, which accompanied it, dated at Annapolis Royal on the 23rd Ult: for which I thank You exceedingly.

It appears to me that You have analysed the Business, to which Your Commission relates, with all the Precision which was to be expected from Your Ability & Zeal:—there seems little, to apprehend.

For the present, I have only to remark to You, that I have from long Experience, dearly bought—formed, precisely, the same Opinion of the Man, which You entertain of the Person from whom many copious Details, relative to the Subject in Dispute, have been obtained. In the present Instance, however, let me do Him the Justice to observe, that in the Communications He made to me He did not conceive He betrayed any Confidence, which had been placed in Him: on the con-

---

[1] The books referred to are: "Voyages et Descovvertes faites en la Novvelle France. Par le Sieur de Champlain, Cappitaine ordinaire pour le Roy en la Mer du Ponant." (1619.) This book contains a map of the Island of St. Croix. "His-toire de la Novvelle France. Par Marc Lescarbot." Published in three editions, 1609 to 1618. "Purchas his Pilgrims," the well-known collection of travels by Samuel Purchas, an English divine; published in 1613.

trary, He professed that Truth, alone, was the Object of his Investigation, and if that End were eventually realized, it was of little Consequence to Him, what the Issue of the Examination, to either Party, might be.

Knowing Him as well as I did, there was little Danger that our Cause should suffer by a *Surcharge* of Confidence.

I am &c.   P. BOND.

FROM LORD GRENVILLE.

Downing Street, Dec' 9ᵗʰ, 1796.
SIR   .

Your several dispatches to No. 3 inclusive have been received and laid before the King; and I have the satisfaction of informing you that His Majesty has been graciously pleased to approve of your conduct in having proceeded to execute the trust committed to you, notwithstanding the variation which appears to subsist between your commission and that which has been given to Mr. Howell by the President of the United States. That variation is indeed extremely unimportant in itself, and it is still more so when it is considered that the general sense of the two contracting parties upon the subject is so clearly to be ascertained by a reference to the two succeeding articles of the treaty which relate to the appointment of Commissioners for other purposes and to the mode which is prescribed for deciding the questions submitted to them. In order however to remove all doubts upon this point, Mr. Liston is instructed to state the variations between Mr. Howell's Commission and yours to the American Ministers, and to propose to them the interchange of declarations, purporting that His Majesty and the United States will consider as final & conclusive the decisions of the three Commissioners or of a majority of them, as to the river, which was the River St. Croix intended by the definitive treaty of Peace between His Majesty and the United States. It must however be observed that in order to render the proceedings under this Commission comformable to the principle established for the others, no such decision nor indeed any other proceeding can take place but in the presence of the three Commissioners.

Although I understand that the books and papers specified in the concluding part of your dispatch No. 3 have been already transmitted from the Duke of Portland's Office to Mr. Chipman His Majesty's Agent, I nevertheless, in order to guard against the effects of any accidents happening to the Packet by which the other copies were sent, enclose to you those extracts of the Acts of Parliament of Scotland which you consider as likely to be of importance in the investigation of the question which you are appointed to decide.

I am &c.   GRENVILLE.

TO LORD GRENVILLE.

Annapolis, 8th Sept., 1797.

MY LORD

I have the Honor to acquaint your Lordship that the Commissioners for setting the disputed Boundary of the River St. Croix met early in August at Boston to which place they had adjourned. Judge Benson's ill health prevented his travelling with expidition from New York to Boston and occasioned a delay in the meeting of the Board of seven days.

In my dispatch No. 4 I suggested to your Lordship, that the principal inducement for the Adjournment to Boston was founded on the representation of the American Agent that he had a number of witnesses to examine amongst whom were Mr. Adams the now President of the United States and Mr. Jay the present Governor of New York, both of whom were Plenipotentaries for effecting the definitive treaty of peace between Great Britain and the United States of America at Paris in 1783, and a conviction on the part of the Commissioners that it would save time and expense to meet the witnesses at that place. On perusing the Affidavits of the major Part of the witnesses his Majestys Agent agreed to their being filed de bene esse conceiving they can take little or nothing material to the present Question. Your Lordship will recollect my having hinted that the American Agent had said he should be able to prove by Mr. Jay Mr. Adams & Lord St. Helens that at the execution of the treaty of Peace in 1783 the Plenipotentiaries intended by the River St. Croix (the beginning point of delineation of the Lines which were thereafter to divide the United States from His Majestys Possessions in America) the first River to the Westward of the River St. Johns, and of course that the first River to the Westward of St. Johns was the river truly intended in the treaty.

It is impossible for me to say whether such testimony would have been received by the Commissioners had it been offered. I am however happy to add the Case has not occurred and consequently no question on that point has been agitated. Mr. Jay on being requested by the American Agent to attend at Boston for the purpose of giving testimony wrote the Agent a letter stating that he would not depose any thing material to the present question. That all that he knew was that Mitchels map was the only one the Plenipotentiaries had before them or used in setting the boundaries and that the river described on that map as the river St. Croix, having been taken for granted as correctly laid down by the Geographer it was named as the commencing boundary. That as to any error in the Map, or there being several rivers of the name of St. Croix, contiguous to each other; it never was suggested, and of course no provision made in such case by the Plenipotentiaries. That this was all he could possibly depose, yet if the American Agent wished his attendance, on notice he would immediately set out for Boston.

Mr. Adams' deposition was taken before the Commissioners, it amounts to little more than Mr. Jays statement, and I think I may very safely say that it makes me more in favor of the British than the American claims.

He swears that on his arrival from Amsterdam at Paris, he found the other Plenipotentiaries had already held several communications on the subject of the Boundaries. That on the part of Great Britain the river Kennebec and afterwards Penobscot had been urged as proper bounds, while the American Plenipotentiaries Mr. Jay and Mr. Franklin contended for the River St. John. That he candidly told both parties he differed with them; and his brethren the American Plenipotentiaries, that they pressed as much too far to the North East, as the British were short of the real commencing point of division. That the original North East boundary of Massachusetts in his opinion was the line which ought to be adopted, and that it stood limited by the River St. Croix. That having Mitchels Map before them, he then traced out the boundaries on the same, and he thinks marked them with a period. In every other particular his testimony agreed with Mr. Jays information.[1]

The Surveyors are busily employed on the respective rivers. Those on the Magaguadavic will compleat their surveys this fall, but whether the Survey of the St. Croix will be effected is a great Doutt. Artists are also engaged in taking the Latitude and Longitude at the mouths of the two Rivers. The instant the Surveys are finished a general map is to be made of all Rivers and Bay of Passamaquady, by Mr. Sproule the Surveyor General of New Brunswic, copies of which are to be delivered the respective agents to enable them to perfect their arguments and replies. The Commissioners have adjourned to the first Monday in June next, then to meet at Rhode Island, for the purpose of deciding the Question, at which period they trust the general Map will be compleated and the Agents ready to deliver their respective replies.

His Grace the Duke of Portland having forwarded to Mr. Chipman His Majestys Agent Extracts from Champlain and Copies of his Maps, particularly of the River St. Croix and the Island on which the French built and wintered in 1604; and that map having represented the situation and extent of the Buildings on the Island; Mr. Chipman immediately sent to a Gentleman residing near that place a copy of the map, and requested him to dig agreeably to the positions laid down. On removing the young growth of Wood, which covered the

1 The statements of Adams and Jay are printed in full as Appendix 4 to the statement presented by Great Britain to the King of the Netherlands in 1824.

face of that part of the Island, and digging a very little way
under the surface, the foundations of the french Buildings
were found in an almost perfect state also the Brick of which
the oven was made. An old metal Spoon, Iron spikes nearly
destroyed by rust, peices of earthen and Iron pots, and char-
coal in an apparently perfect state, but which on being exposed to the Air slaked and crumbled into dust. This discovery identifies the Island, and River, named St. Croix by the
French. I take the liberty to remark to your Lordship that
as the question now stands, and I know of no other testimony proposed to be adduced, there can be no doubt of a decision favorable to His Majestys claims. One thing however
is absolutely necessary; to wit that the Agent Mr. Chipman is possessed of that edition of Champlain, and the maps
from whence the extracts and fac similies were made, which
have been forwarded. The American Agent has opposed admitting the certified extracts and maps above mentioned in
evidence; and I doubt the Commissioners receiving them,
while the originals can be procured. Permit me therefore
to request your Lordships attention to having this Edition
of Champlain forwarded during the Autumn or very early in
the Spring.

I have been so fortunate as to procure a very excellent
french Atlas published in 1755 which lays down the Rivers in
the Bay of Passamaquady very correctly, and gives the name
of St. Croix to the Western Branch of the River. Also a
french Map stated to be a correction of Mitchels. D. Anvills
Map, and several other very favorable descriptions of the
River; all of which I have delivered to Mr. Chipman.

FROM MR. LISTON.

Philadelphia 30th October 1797.
SIR,

I have had the pleasure of receiving your letter No. 6 of the
12th of last month (accompanied with a private one of the

same date) and have to thank you for the satisfactory account you have given me of the State of your proceedings.

I had some weeks ago prepared a dispatch to His Majesty's Agent, which I meant to have accompanied with a copy of a couple of maps published by authority of the British Government at the time of the disputes with the Court of France concerning the boundaries of the respective Crowns on this side the Atlantick, which ultimately led to the war of 1756; but I was prevented from sending my packet by a report early spread here, that the Commissioners were not to enter on the business till next year, and that your stay at Boston would be extremely short.[1] I have now resolved to forward the packet I allude to, together with Mitchell's map, by some one of His Majesty's Ships of war that may be bound to Halifax: and as I propose to set out in a few days on an excursion to Norfolk in Virginia, I think of carrying it with me, and delivering it myself into the hands of some of the Captains who I think will take proper care of it.

His Majesty's Secretary of State communicated to me the observation made by you on the difference between the terms of your Commission, and those of the one given by the President of the United States to Mr. Howell, and His Lordship directed me to request an explanatory declaration on the subject on the part of the American Ministry. On executing this commission, I perceived that Colonel Pickering was a little hurt as well at the imputation of inaccuracy or insufficiency thus cast on an Instrument which had been carefully drawn up by himself, as at the surmise that appeared to be started respecting the sincerity and good faith of the Government of the United States. I did not therefore insist upon any changes being made in Mr. Howell's Commission, and contented myself with a general declaration, made to me by authority, that the President would give the decision of the Commissioners full force and effect. I do not indeed entertain the smallest apprehension that any difficulty will occur with regard to the exe-

[1] Colonel Barclay's return to Nova Scotia was hastened by the illness of his youngest child, Clement, who died about the 20th of September, 1797, soon after Barclay's arrival at home.

cution of the award of the majority of the Commissioners, whatever it may be. I have &c.

ROB. LISTON.

TO MR. LISTON.

Annapolis, 23 Dec' 1797.

SIR,

I was favored with your letter of the 30th of last month a few weeks since. Mr. Chipman and myself will be greatly obliged to you for the Copies of the maps you propose sending by Captain Cochrane.— It is necessary His Majesty's Agent should be in possession of everything that has been published on the Subject to which his agency extends: and admitting all the maps which have hitherto been published of that part of the River Scodiac and its branch the Chiputnaticook beyond the falls to have been merely ideal or at best taken from Indian information, still the general prevailing opinion of the direction of that River will operate forcibly in the decision of the question.

It was my duty to communicate to Lord Grenville the variance between Mr. Howells Commission and mine for His Majestys information and to remove from myself all responsibility respecting it — In doing this my intention was the reverse of imputing inaccuracy or insufficiency to the instruments you mention as having been framed by Mr. Pickering, on the contrary my letter plainly imports that the American Commission was drawn up in the Words of the fifth Article of the treaty, and that His Majestys Commission to me went beyond the expressions used in that Article. Previous explanations on points which admit of doubt are all ways proper and particularly necessary where responsibility attaches; nor ought constructions to be left open for future argument, when the present moment admits of an explanation. I am really sorry Mr. Pickering could suppose my letter above alluded to carried with it the most distant hint of a suspicion of the Sincerity and good Faith of the Government of the united States.

Inclosed is a copy of it, and you will do me a favor by explaining it to him, who assuredly at the present very much misconceives what I had represented.

FROM MR. LISTON.

Philadelphia, 4th April, 1798.

SIR, .

Since the date of my last (which was of the 30th of October) I have not had the pleasure of hearing from you.

On the 4th of December I forwarded from Norfolk (in Virginia) a letter to Mr. Chipman, which I flatter myself he has received, since Captain Cochrane, to whom it was entrusted, had a very favourable passage to Halifax. It was accompanied with Mitchell's Map of North America, with the correction, and a copy of the maps published by the Courts of Great Britain and France, to illustrate their reciprocal pretensions on the subject of the limits of Acadia and Nova Scotia, prior to the war of 1756. These are the only materials that have come in my way which appear to me to deserve notice; and I have only to repeat what I have already observed on the subject, that Mr. Chipman seems to be already in possession of so much information, and to treat the subject with such superior ability, that he scarcely stands in need of any assistance whatever.

I have received orders to negotiate and conclude an additional article to the Treaty of Amity Commerce and Navigation, with a view to liberate you from the obligation of fixing (with a precision perhaps impossible to obtain) the longitude and latitude of the source of the St. Croix, and to stipulate some other method of ascertaining the question respecting the disputed boundary between the two countries. The American Minister is willing to proceed as soon as may be to this business with me (although he had at the same time authorized Mr. King to manage the affair in London); but the attention of this Government has for some time past been so completely engrossed by their dispute with France, that it has been impossible for Colonel Pickering to find leisure to give the necessary consideration to the subject. As soon as it is in my power, I will transmit to you and to Lieutenant Governor Carleton a draught of the article we may think likely to answer the purpose, that you may favour us with such alterations and amendments as shall in your opinion be expedient.

I have &c   ROB. LISTON.

P. S. Since writing the above, I find by letters from Lord Grenville that the additional article alluded to in my letter is to be negociated in London.   R. L.

TO MR. LISTON.

Annapolis 2nd May, 1798.

(*Private.*)

SIR,

Mr. Thornton [1] by the last Post from Halifax forwarded me your dispatch, No. 1 of the 4th of April. Before this, I hope my letter of the 23 of Dec' has come to your hands. It was put on board a Brig which was to have sailed from Digby about the latter end of December for Philadelphia; the severity of the weather and violence of the Gales induced the owners to postpone her departure until March, when she sailed for Baltimore. I now enclose a duplicate, and hope you will be able to remove the unfavorable impression Mr. Pickering through mistake entertains of my suggestion to Lord Grenville.

The letter and the maps you some time since forwarded by Captain Cochrane have been transmitted to Mr. Chipman, who is not a little flattered with the favorable opinion you entertain of his industry. I have no doubt you will be pleased with the case he has made out on the part of His Majesty; it was my wish to have forwarded a copy for your and Mr. Bonds perusal; the Secretary however has not yet had leisure to make me one.

The Commissioners and Agents conceived it unnecessary,

---

[1] Edward Thornton, the British Secretary of Legation.

and a measure that would greatly retard the conclusion of the question, to ascertain the Latitude and Longitude of the Source of the River; because the taking the latitude and Longitude at the mouth of the River and giving a minute description of the Courses and distances from thence to its source would completely answer every purpose intended and identify the source beyond the possibility of future doubt. Under these impressions the Agents were permitted to apply to their respective Governments, that that part of the directions in the fifth Article of the treaty might be dispensed. By your favor I find that in addition to this "a new Article is to be negotiated in London whereby some other method will be adopted for ascertaining the question respecting the disputed boundary between the two Countries." Ignorant of the particular object this article is proposed to embrace it is out of my power to give an opinion of its expediency; still I consider it my duty to state for your and my Lord Grenville's information the probable issue under the present Commission admitting it is proceeded on according to their original instructions.—The River Magaguadavic contemplated by the Americans as the S⁺· Croix, can never be confirmed as such. Its only support is Indian tradition, while every document, description, actual survey and representation prove the reverse.—The Scoodiac therefore will be the river comprehended in the decision of the decision of the Commⁿˢ·—But as this River divides itself into two Branches some distance above the falls, the one the Chipatnaticook tending very nearly north, the other the continuance of the Scoodiac West North West; it will become a question with the Commissioners which of these two Branches are to be considered as the S⁺· Croix intended in the treaty of 1783—Printed and written evidence are in favor of the latter, to which I may add that on comparing the actual Surveys of these two Branches with the most correct maps extant, the resemblance will be found to operate strongly in favor of the western Branch, particularly at the Sources. It follows from hence that circumstances are in favor of the Question being determined to the extent of his Majestys claim, and even under the most unfavorable Event

6

that an offset of upwards of 20 miles West will be gained between the Magaguadavic & Chipatnaticook.

The course of the Chiputnatecook from its mouth to its
source is very nearly north. By examining the maps, you will
readily discover that a line drawn due North from the mouth
of this River to the Highlands will leave a large part of New
Brunswic to the Westward of this line and cut off the communication between that Province and Canada; whereas a North
line drawn from the Western extremity of the Scoodiac, if it
did not leave new Brunswic entire, would take but a very
small portion from it. If therefore the new Article in contemplation goes to confirm the Western Source it may be an object
of moment. In the negotiation however the Magaguadavic
must be removed even from the back ground, and the Chiputnatecook and Scoodiac spoken of as the only possible streams
in question. I have taken the liberty to give you my sentiments, least Lord Grenville might be induced to consider the
question of the two rivers as still involved in doubt and from
thence be led to yeild a greater equivalent than he otherwise
would do. In negotiating this new Article it is of moment to
comprehend the Islands in the Bay of Passamaquady which appertain to his Majesty beyond contradiction, some of the best
of which are now in the possession of the Americans.

The Agent on the part of the United States during the last
Winter applied through Mr. Chipman for my consent to a
farther adjournment of the meeting of the Commissioners,
which stood for the first Monday in June, suggesting as his
motive the survey, not being completed and the impracticability of his finishing the case on the part of the United States
before he was in possession of a copy of the survey. To this
application I gave a negative. He has since repeated his request and in addition to his former reasons, added that in case
the board met in June, he would be compelled to protest
against delivering in his argument in an unfinished State and
to pray a further day. Previous to the receipt of this, Sir John
Wentworth had requested me in pointed terms to postpone if
practicable the meeting of the Commissioners until the latter
end of July, that I might attend the next Session of the House

of Assembly. I have been therefore induced to acceed to Mr. Sullivans proposal, and acquainted the other Com" if they had no objection, I was willing to extend the time to the 23rd of July.

From the communication in your letter I have reason to suspect Mr. Sullivan to be at the bottom of "the proposal for the additional article" you mention. I am led to this opinion from the very particular manner in which he stands pledged to confirm the Magaguadavic as the St. Croix, not only in his History of the Province of Maine, but the general Language he has held for years past in public and Private; He must now be fully convinced that the Event will be unfavorable to his position and wish to avoid the Odium and censure that inevitably will follow an adjudication unfavorable to his assertions, and the only method of doing this is by suspending the present question and altering the nature of the issue.

TO MR. LISTON.

Annapolis, 10th May, 1798.

SIR.

I did myself the Honor on the second of this month to reply to your favor of the 4th of April, since which Mr. Chipman has enclosed me a copy of Lord Grenvilles letter to you under date the 9th January last, from which I find I had given too extensive a construction to your expressions "and to stipulate some other method of ascertaining the question respecting the disputed boundary between the two Countries"; and that you intended nothing more, than that this new Article should, in addition to exonerating the Commissioners from expressing in their declaration the Latitude and Longitude at the Source of the River, prescribe some particular mode for perpetuating the boundary between the North East Bounds of the State of Massachusetts and the North West Angle of Nova Scotia, the terminus a quo the North line deducted in the treaty of 1783 is to commence.

It is unnecessary for me to remark the difficulty that attends astronomical, or indeed any other observations in uncultivated Countries, and Climates subject to fogs and cloudy weather, that a variation of a few minutes will create a greater difference in the Longitude, than perhaps the nearest collateral stream is really distant from the River St. Croix, and that if at a future period the Latitude and Longitude should be again taken, the degrees expressed in our adjudication, may be found to correspond with the source of a stream, other than the one intended. To prevent these difficulties, it was the wish of the Commissioners that they might be authorized to omit in their declaration the Latitude and Longitude at the Source of the River; to supply which it was our intention to annex to the Declaration, as his Lordship very properly advises a correct map of the Bay of Passamaquady with all its rivers, particularly the St. Croix from the mouth to the source thereof, designating every stream or fork that empties its waters into it. A map thus compiled from accurate surveys, whereon the courses and distances are minutely laid down, and every collateral stream represented on a proportionable Scale will inevitably place the Source of the River beyond the probability of future doubt. The Comm^{rs}. in establishing the point which is hence forward to be considered as the Source, will naturally take the upper most lake, or some other prominent feature near the Source, and from thence give the bearings and distances to the Source. It may possibly not be amiss to erect a stone column on the Spot, as a monument, and to have it revisited every third year; I cannot however say I think it a measure either safe or necessary.

The present dispute owes its origin to the want of correct maps of the Rivers in the bay of Passamaquady, and definite names to the river of all which the Americans in 1783 were equally ignorant with his Majestys subjects. The dispute is not as to the Source, but which is the River, and I take it for granted, the river once established, the source will readily be ascertained. With all deferance therefore to his Lordships opinion, I am led to believe the map intended to be annexed to the declaration, will prove a more safe guide, to find the source of the River St. Croix; than any monument that Art can erect. If a monument is erected the map and declaration will in future be con-trouled by that land mark, because it is composed of matter, and place is the very object and essence of its foundation, whereas the descriptive part of the declaration will be founded on the map, which is no more than an ideal representation, protracted from a measurement. Between individuals cases frequently occur whose landmarks are basely transposed, the same sinister motives may lead persons owning lands in North eastern parts of Massachusetts to remove a national boundary solemnly erected by the consent of the two nations. Admitting some of the Inhabitants of Massachusetts were induced by interest to remove this structure, to the next eastern stream; how easily and privately might it be effected, in a desert upwards of seventy miles from any settlement? This done, it would only be necessary to secure the testimony of one of the persons appointed to inspect, and the whole question would again be open for negotiation or controversy, with the additional onus on the part of Great Britain to prove the removal of the monument; a fact not easy under common circumstances, and perhaps impossible, if the person who inspected it on the part of Great Britain, was dead. I admit such a case to be highly improbable, still while it is within the degrees of possibility, is it not evident that a natural, notorious object near the source of the river, which nothing less than a convulsion of nature can injure or destroy, and will be a preferable Guide, for the information of succeeding Ages, to a pillar of stone, which may as easily be removed, as raised, and which by removal would only change its place, but not its form or effect. Extend this Idea, and suppose engraved on this Pillar an inscription, purporting it was erected by order of His Majesty and the united States of America to identify and perpetuate, the place hereafter to be considered as the Source of the River St. Croix; what would the consequence be, if it was removed to the head of the next eastern stream. The persons sent to inspect it at the expiration of three years, might never have been there before, and of course consider it as standing in its original position; but admitting they suspected it had been removed, neither the declaration of the Commissioners

6A

or the Map subjoined could effect its locality, nor could it be reconveyed to the original Station without at least the interposition of the two powers, a measure dependant on the good understanding then subsisting between them.

FROM MR. LISTON.

Philadelphia, 11 June, 1798.

SIR,

I have been favored with your letters No. 1 and 2 of this year, from Anapolis, enclosing a duplicate of your No. 7 of last year, the original of which has not yet come to hand.

With regard to the terms made use of in the full powers of the respective commissioners, which gave rise to an application by me to the American Government in consequence of orders from home, the fact is, that I did not, on reading Lord Grenville's letter on the subject, rightly comprehend the difference that had struck you. It never once came into my head that there could be any doubt with respect to the validity of the decision of A MAJORITY of the three commissioners; so that I merely copied what Lord Grenville had said to me, blindly obeying my orders, without understanding the reasons of them. And I believe the American Secretary of State comprehended them as little as I did. I shall now take an opportunity of explaining the matter to Colonel Pickering; through the distance of time is so great and the dissatisfaction shewed by him was so slight, that it is hardly worth while to return to the subject.

The additional article with regard to the ascertaining of the source of the River St. Croix having been concluded in London, and ratified by His Majesty and by the President, I take an opportunity of forwarding a copy of it.[1]

[1] It was signed in London, March 15, 1798; and its ratification advised by the Senate, June 5, 1789. It provides for erecting " a suitable monument " at the source of the St. Croix, instead of ascertaining the latitude and longitude of that spot.

I think with you, Sir, that a monument of stone is liable to
be removed by ill-designing persons, unless indeed it were
constructed at a large expence; — such for instance as an
Egyptian obelisk,—(an immense column of one piece of stone,)
— which could not be placed upright without a great union of
force and skill, an operation that must make a great impression on all the neighborhood, and that individuals could not
afford to undertake. Since it has been determined on however, I suppose it must be erected. At the same time there is
surely no reason why the additional evidence,—to be derived
from a map or chart of the course of the river,—should not be
rendered as precise and authentick as possible. Natural objects, of great size, of a particular kind, might be designated
in the map, and in the declaration or award of the commissioners. It is right, and it is essentially necessary, that no possible doubt should be left remaining.

I propose soon to take an opportunity of sounding the
American Ministry concerning the Islands in the Bay.

I remain, &c   ROB. LISTON.

FROM MR. CHIPMAN TO MR. LISTON.

Providence 23^d Oct. 1798.

(Private.)

SIR,

I have the honor to inform you that the proposed decision
and declaration of the Commissioners before whom I have been
appointed to manage the business as Agent on the part of His
Majesty, have been communicated to me by which it appears
that the River Scudiac claimed on the part of his Majesty to
be the Source of its Western branch is to be decided to be the
River St. Croix truly intended under that name in the Treaty
of Peace the Source of this Branch is however in this decision
particularized to be where it issues from the Lake Genesaga-
rumsis the Easternmost of the Scudiac Lakes and distant about

five miles and three quarters on a direct course from where the Cheputnaticook falls into it. Altho' this decision is very flattering to me, as it establishes every principle upon which the claim on the part of his Majesty was founded, and is fully accordant with the prayer of that claim, still in it's consequences I fear it will prove very inconvenient if not injurious to the Interest of the Province of New Brunswick, as a North line from this Source will intersect the River St. John so as to leave the Military posts at Presque Isle, and the Grand Falls and every part of the River St. John above Presque Isle, which is about Eighty miles above Fredericton within the territory of the United States. Some inconveniences will at the same time result to the United States from this decision, as the North line from this Source will leave in His Majesty's dominions a considerable tract of Country lying between this line and the River Cheputnaticook which has been granted to Individuals by the State of Massachusets. These inconveniences are considered so great by the Agent of the United States as to induce him to propose to me an accommodation between the two Governments, by an Agreement to recommend to the Commissioners to decide the Northernmost Source of the Cheputnaticook to be the Source of the Saint Croix, in lieu of the Source above mentioned. By such a decision the North Line from this Source will run Nine Miles to the Westward of the Post at Presque Isle and upwards of four miles to the westward of the Grand Falls and will intersect the River St. John one hundred and thirty five miles above Fredericton as you will perceive by the Maps accompanying this Letter. Not only therefore a very great tract of country will be gained by the alteration of the place to be particularized as the Source of the River but the communication with Canada by the River St. John will remain to a much greater extent unbroken. Had I any authority to enter into a negotiation of this nature I should not hesitate to accede to this proposal and to endeavor to effect a decision in conformity to it, but such as an undertaking is beyond my duty or powers as his Majesty's Agent. I consider it therefore extremely fortunate that I have an opportunity of consulting you Sir upon this occasion, by your accidental arrival at this place at a moment so critical, as the final declaration is expected to be signed this day.

I have been given to understand that nothing has induced Colonel Barclay to assent to the decision now in contemplation, but the consideration, that the Commissioners would otherwise separate without coming to any determination, and that it is so dissatisfactory to Mr. Howell the American Commissioner originally appointed that he will not sign it, as he contends for the Cheputnaticook River and that its Source should be particularized to be, where it issues from the first or most eastern lake connected with that Branch; he is therefore averse to the proposed alteration, but will accede to it, if recommended by the Agent on the part of the United States. I am aware that difficulties may arise in carrying the proposed agreement into effect, as the other Commissioners have not been yet consulted upon it, but if I have your approbation and sanction of the measure, I shall feel myself justified in attempting to avail myself of an opportunity, which may perhaps never again present itself of effecting upon so easy terms a settlement of this Boundary line in a manner so favorable to His Majesty's interests, and at the same time an event so desirable as an unanimous decision of the Commissioners in the present cause.

I shall hope for an answer to this Letter as speedily as may consist with your convenience and the urgency of the occasion.

I have, &c.

W. CHIPMAN.

FROM MR. LISTON TO MR. CHIPMAN.

Providence, 23ᵈ Oct. 1798.

(*Private.*)

SIR,

I have considered with attention your Letter of this day, and it appears to me evident, that the adoption of the River Cheputnaticook as a part of the Boundary between his Majesty's

American Dominions, and those of the United States in preference to a line drawn from the Easternmost point of the Scudiac Lakes, would be attended with considerable advantage. It would give an addition of territory to the Province of New Brunswick, together with a greater extent of Navigation on St. Johns River, and above all a longer stretch of natural frontier calculated to prevent future difficulties and discussions between the two countries.

If therefore by assenting to the proposal of the American Agent you can bring about the unanimous concurrence of the Commissioners in this measure, I am of opinion that you will promote His Majesty's real interests; and I will take the earliest opportunity with a view to your justification of expressing these my Sentiments on the Subject to his Majesty's Secretary of State.   I have, &c.,

ROB. LISTON.

TO LORD GRENVILLE.

Annapolis, Nova Scotia, 10th Nov., 1798.
MY LORD,

I have the Honor to inform your Lordship that I returned to this place on Saturday last from Providence in the State of Rhode Island, having on the 26 of October compleated the Commission with which his Majesty has been pleased to honor me; the event of which I trust will meet His most Gracious approbation.

A copy of the Declaration of the Commissioners is herewith inclosed to your Lordship, an original of which with a map of the Territory in dispute has been delivered to his Majesty's agent.[1] Your Lordship will observe that the Event has been very favorable, the River claimed on the part of His Majesty as the true St. Croix having been confirmed as such by the

[1] The award of the Commissioners will be found in American State Papers, For. Rel., Vol. VI, p. 921, where various other documents relating to this matter are printed.

Commissioners. It was not, however, in their power to extend
the Western Limits of the late Province of Nova Scotia to the
extreme point claimed by His Majesty's Agent, to wit, "ad
scatureginem sive fontem ex occidentali parte ejusdem, qui se
primum praedicto fluvio immisset," the words made use of in
the Grant of King James to Sir William Alexander. Had the
boundaries contained in the Commissions to the Governors of
Nova Scotia from the year 1763 tallied with those in Sir William Alexander's Grant, Mr. Benson the third Commissioner
would readily have gone with me in establishing the most remote Western spring on the Scoudiac, as the Source of the
River St. Croix, but as those Commissions use only the expression of *to the Source of the River St. Croix*, Mr. Howell conceived the Chiputnatucook from its superior magnitude to be
the branch, we were to follow for the Source; while Mr. Benson and myself were of opinion that the continuation of the
Scoodiac was the real St. Croix, because it had ever retained
the same Indian name with its waters, below this ramification
of the River. Mr. Benson, however, could not from the words
of the treaty of Peace in 1783; or the boundaries of the Province of Nova Scotia as expressed in the Commissions to the
Governors from the year 1763 find himself authorized to proceed farther up the River Scoudiac for the Source, than where
the waters issue from the lake Genesagaragum-siss into the
Scoudiac, a distance of not more than five miles from the
mouth of the Chiputnatecook, as your Lordship will observe
by reverting to the map annexed to the declaration. The following were his objections. That previous to the year 1763
the only bounds to the Province of Nova Scotia were those
expressed in the Grant to Sir William Alexander, the then
Western limits of which "were the most remote Source or
Spring on the Western side of the said River (the St. Croix)
which first mingles its waters with the aforesaid River." That
this most Western Source or fountain, was from a literal translation of the words, a stream of water different from the St.
Croix, and at all Events could not ex vi termini merely be considered the Source of the River St. Croix; that the Commissions to the respective Governors of Nova Scotia from the

establishment of the Province to the year 1763 were general
and without expressing any particular bounds. In 1763, when
the French ceded Canada to Great Britain, the Northern limits
of Nova Scotia were narrowed and confined to the Highlands,
&c., &c., a commission to Montague Wilmot as Governor of
Nova Scotia issued soon after in which commission new bounds
were given to Nova Scotia in the Words following, " bounded
on the Westward by a line drawn from Cape Sable across the
enterance of the Bay of Fundy to the mouth of the River St.
Croix, by the said River *to its Source* and by a line drawn due
North from thence to the Southern boundary of our Colony of
Quebec."

These same boundaries are expressed in several Subsequent
Commissions. That the Words *to its Source* in these commissions and in the treaty of Peace in 1783, are very different
from those of " most remote source or Spring on the Western
side of the said River which first mingles its waters with the
aforesaid river" made use of in Sir William Alexanders Grant.
That a chain of Lakes could not be called a river, in proof of
which Mr. Benson referred to the second Article of the
Treaty of Peace between His Majesty and the United States
of America, wherein the River St. Lawrence is considered to
cease at the Lake Ontario, and all the Waters that connect the
lakes from Ontario to the lake of the Woods are called water
communications and not the River St. Lawrence. That the
lake in the Woods was as much the Source of this River, as
the most remote western lake of the Scoudiac was of the St.
Croix. He therefore could not with propriety go beyond the
first lake in the Scoudiac for the Source of the St. Croix — so
far he could consistantly go, beyond it, all was uncertain, and
mere conjecture. Mr. Howell adopted a similar mode of
arguing for the Source of the St. Croix on the Chiputnatecook. After much debate between Mr. Benson and myself
as to the source of the River, His Majesty's Agent, with the
advice of Mr. Liston the Envoy Extraordinary requested me
to acceed to the Chiputnatecook provided I could obtain the
northwest Source of that River. To this point Mr. Benson,
as a matter of negotiation and accommodation between the

nations, readily assented.[1] Mr. Howell declined being a party
to the declaration; until it was engrossed and ready for execution. He then reluctantly directed his name to be inserted
in the Declaration, which he eventually signed. By taking
the Northwest Source of the Chiputnatecook, instead of the
Scoudiac where it joins the lakes, we gain a very considerable
addition of territory, and the line to be drawn from thence
due North will intersect the River St. John very high up,
some distance above the Grand falls. Whereas a North line
from the lake Genesagaragum-Siss would have crossed the
River St. John to the Southward of the Post at Presque Isle.
By the present decision all grants under the Crown are secured. The mast country preserved and about nine-tenths of
the Lands in dispute confirmed to the King; in addition to
all which the Chiputnatecook putting the Grant of Alexander
out of the Question, is beyond all doubt the principal feeder
of the River St. Croix, and of course the Branch on which the
Source is to be found and from its direct course an infinitely
preferable national boundary to the upper part of the Scoudiac. I shall leave to His Majesty's Agent to explain the
effect our decision will have on the Bay of Passamaquady
and the Islands therein; adding only this remark that the
Commissioners could not find the mouth of the River St.
Croix (agreeably to the treaty of Peace) in the Bay of Fundy,

[1] Judge Benson's views as sum-
marized in this letter, were preserved more at length in a MS.
memorandum, a copy of which was
filed in 1817 with the Commissioners
under the 4th Article of the Treaty
of Ghent. It is published in Rec.
Mass. Hist. Soc., Oct., 1887. In regard to the compromise concerning
the point to be selected as the
source of the St. Croix, he says:
"The reference, as it respected the
Source of the River being as it were
an appeal to mere judgment or
opinion, is in that view analogous
to cases of assessment of damages,
not capable of being liquidated by
calculation or *definite* Rule, and
therefore to be assessed according to *discernment* or discretion; a
latitude of arbitrament is in such
cases supposed to be permitted to
the Jurors, but as they must at the
same time agree in a *precise* sum,
accommodation of sentiment among
them to a degree is necessary and
consequently justifiable." This ex-
plains Benson's readiness to assent
to the selection of the northwest
branch of the Chiputnaticook "as
a matter of negotiation and accommodation."

but at a Point near St. Andrews at the head of the Bay of Passamaquady.

I have repeatedly observed to your Lordship that the surveys of the Rivers were the sole cause of procrastinating the decision. The Arguments also of the Agents have been diffuse in the extreme. These were closed on the 22d of September, and the maps compiled from the Surveys by the Surveyor General of New Brunswic arrived at Providence the 15th of October. The Commissioners on that day entered on their decision and the declaration was executed on the 26th of that month. It has been my constant study to promote His Majesty's Interest by every means within my power consistent with my duty as a Commissioner; and if my conduct happily meets the approbation of my Sovereign, your Lordship and His Majestys other Ministers, it will afford me infinite satisfaction.

CHAPTER III

THE question of the River St. Croix being thus happily disposed of, Colonel Barclay,— after a brief
visit to New-York,— returned to Nova Scotia in the latter part of the year 1798 to take up again his duties at
the bar and in the legislature, and to go on with the development and sale of his lands. His children were
fast growing up, and their settlement in life was beginning to claim his constant care and thought. Of the
three eldest, Eliza was indeed happily married; but
Henry was almost out of his apprenticeship as a clerk
with Hartshorne & Boggs, of Halifax, and money would
be wanting to establish him in business; while De Lancey was loitering away his time as an officer in a fencible
regiment.

To support a family of ten children — to marry the
daughters — to buy commissions and partnerships for
the sons — was no easy task upon the income and with
the opportunities of a lawyer in a Nova Scotia village.
But their stay in the British provinces was nearly at
an end. Barclay's report on the boundary had hardly
reached the Foreign Office when he was appointed
British Consul-General for the Eastern States of America in the room of Sir John Temple, deceased.[1]

[1] Sir John Temple Bart. was the
son of Robert Temple of Boston,
Mass. On the death of his distant

relative, Sir Richard Temple, of
Stowe in Buckinghamshire, in 1786,
he succeeded to this ancient baron-

On June 15, 1799, Barclay and his wife arrived once
more in New York to find again the home which they
had lost nearly sixteen years before. He was now just
forty-six; she a year younger. Their daughters were
all with them, but of the sons, only Henry and Beverley
accompanied their parents to New-York. George and
Anthony, the two little boys, were at school at Windsor, N. S.; for the gentleman of genius at £30 a year,
whom Colonel Barclay had wished to import from
Scotland, had never been discovered. Thomas the
younger had also been left behind at school; but on
September 1, 1799, being then nearly sixteen, H. M. S.
Boston received him aboard as a midshipman, and
he sailed away for his share of glory and prize-money.
De Lancey, too, was soon to leave Nova Scotia, for on
January 11, 1800, he was appointed an Ensign in the
Forty-first Regiment of Foot, then stationed in Canada.

The summer of 1799 was probably passed by Barclay
and his household near Flushing; but in the Autumn of
that year he hired the house No. 142 Greenwich street,
at what he considered the extravagant rent of £250,
New-York currency, or $625 a year. His salary was
nominally £1500 a year, but it was paid with the
greatest irregularity and was subject to heavy deductions for taxes, office fees, and other impositions. Barclay entertained largely, seeing, as he says, more company in a month than Sir John Temple in a year. But
writing a couple of years later to his sister Cornelia in
England, he complains that neither he nor his wife
"relish the mode of life which we are compelled to

etcy. He married, January 20, 1767, Elizabeth, daughter of Governor Bowdoin, of Massachusetts; was appointed British Consul-General in February, 1785, and died in New-York, November 17, 1798. A monument erected to his memory stands in St. Paul's Church on the north side of the chancel. His successor's commission bears date January 26, 1799.

from my situation; and yet," he adds, " we are far from entering into the gay circles of dissipation. In two years I have been only to one assembly and two plays, to private balls probably eight or ten. Both of us grow old, are fond of early hours, and have lost all relish for those gay Scenes that once afforded pleasure." About this period (for the date is not quite certain) Maria Barclay, the second daughter, was married to Simon Fraser, a gentleman of the name and family of that Lord Lovat who "suffered" in 1745. Mr. Fraser settled in British Guiana as a planter, living on the river Berbice, and so Maria disappeared henceforth from the family circle.

Public affairs for the first three years after Barclay's return to New-York wore a doubtful aspect. The Federalists went out with Adams and the Republicans came in with Jefferson. The troubles with England were temporarily ended, but no man could tell when they might break out again. With France we were actually at war. In Europe there was no peace. Marengo and Hohenlinden were fought on land, and the battle of Copenhagen at sea. England took Malta and Minorca and drove the French from Egypt. Pitt fell from power, and Addington succeeded him—to make peace with France and imperil relations with the United States. And some echo of these great events found its way into New-York, where peace reigned and merchants were growing rich upon the profits of the neutral trade.

TO LORD GRENVILLE.

Annapolis, 11th May, 1799.

MY LORD:

I was last Evening honored with your Lordships dispatch of the 19th of January last, informing me of your having had

7

the Goodness to submit my name to His Majesty, as a proper person to succeed the late Sir John Temple, as His Majesty's Consul General for the Eastern States of America, and that His Majesty had been graciously pleased to confer upon me that appointment. Also that my commission would be transmitted to Mr. Liston by the next Packet, and that it was His Majesty's pleasure I should remove to New York with as much expedition as the situation of my private affairs will allow.

Permit me to intreat your Lordship to lay at His Majestys feet, my most humble acknowledgements for this repeated instance of His Royal Favor, and with all due submission to assure His Majesty I shall by an unremitted attention to my duty endeavor in some degree to merit this most gracious testimony of His Royal confidence, and I earnestly request your Lordship will be pleased to accept of my most grateful thanks for your kind offices, and I trust my conduct will in no instance afford your Lordship occasion to regret the favor you have conferred on me.

I shall with all possible expedition arrange my private affairs and hope within a month from this day to leave this Province for New York, of which I shall acquaint Mr. Liston by the earliest conveyance.

FROM MR. BROUGHTON.

Downing Street, July 2d, 1799.

SIR:

I was favored with the receipt of your Letter on Saturday last inclosing a Power of Attorney to enable me to receive your Appointments as His Majesty's Consul General to the Eastern States of America. I lose no time in returning you my thanks for this mark of your Confidence, and I shall not fail immediately after the receipts of any part of your Allowances to pay the Balance over to Messrs. Brook, Watson & Co. after deducting the usual Treasury and Exchequer Fees and the Agency of 6:6:0 per Quarter. The Particulars of

which I shall not fail to transmit by the first Mail after such
Payment has been made.

It may be proper to inform you that the Civil List is now
Five Quarters in Arrears; so that it will in all probability be
some time in April or May 1800 before the Appointments due
5th. Jany. 1799 are issued at the Exchequer.

I send you the Morning Herald, which altho' by no means
a favorite Paper of mine with regard to Politics, yet as it certainly gives the News and Lies of the *Day more in detail* and
in a more lively manner than any other Journal, I have
selected it under the idea that it will prove the most enter-
taining.

                          I am, &c
                                CHAS. R. BROUGHTON.[1]

TO LORD GRENVILLE.

                                    New York, 8th August, 1799.
MY LORD:

In my dispatch of the 16th of June, I stated to your Lordship the objection that lay to the issuing of my exequatur as
His Majesty's Consul General for the Eastern States of America
in consequence of my commission not having arrived, since
which, on a personal interview with Mr. Pickering, the American Secretary of State at Philadelphia, the exceptions have
been so far obviated that letters Patent have issued from the
President of the United States recognizing me as His Majesty's Consul General and granting all the Priviledges appertaining to that office. I at the same time received a letter from
the Secretary of State, requesting me to forward my commission as soon as received that it might be inrolled and an exequatur be made out. The situation, my Lord, of His Majesty's
Ships of War, Packets, and Merchant Vessels coming to this
and the other ports in the United States of America is very

---

[1] The writer of this letter was a
clerk in the Foreign Office, who was
employed by various consular officers as their agent to settle accounts in London.

unpleasant and truly detrimental to the Service. Captain Douglass of His Majesty's Ship Boston who convoyed a number of American Merchantmen safe to their respective ports, arrived at New York about the 20th of June. The crew of the Barge that rowed him to shore were in his presence invited by a number of persons who surrounded the Barge, to desert the Service, with promises of better pay and protection. In consequence of this several of Capt. Douglasses best men left the barge. He complained to the Mayor of this City who replied that if he could identify the persons that seduced his men he would have them apprehended. This was impracticable, being a total stranger in the City. His Majesty's Packet boats invariably lose a part of the Crews by desertion, who the instant they get on shore are at Liberty, or what is still worse and more provoking are supported by men whose employment it is to procure Seamen for American Merchant Vessels. If a captain of a packet was to meet any of his absconding Seamen and attempted to carry them by force on board, it is more than probable they would be rescued by a mob, but admitting he succeeded, a habeas corpus would again set them at liberty, the Crimps being ever ready as bail. If the Captain of the Packet is either Plaintiff or Defendant, he must remain in this City with his witnesses until the Cause is tried, a measure which is inconsistent with the Service. Of course he is compelled to give up the pursuit. The Packets frequently leave this with little more than half their compliment of Men, and trust to Halifax for the remainder. I recollect in May last one of them was detained several days in Halifax for want of men, and if I am not mistaken, Admiral Vandeput eventually furnished her from his own ship. Merchant ships are in a similar situation, and complaints to me are daily. The enormous pay allowed by the Americans to Seamen is too great a temptation for our Sailors to resist. I have taken the liberty to state the above to your Lordship possessed of the facts. An additional article to the treaty, authorizing the issuing of a warrant for apprehending British Seamen deserting, with an Act of Congress inflicting pains and penalties on persons seducing or even taking into their Service British Seamen, would effectually remedy the Evil. Mr. Liston informs me that he has had several conversations on the subject with the American Secretary of State, and has hopes that something will be agreed on this year for the preventing of these evils.

The expense of living in this City is so enormously extravagant and the number of strangers resorting to it, who naturally expect invitations and attention from His Majesty's Consul so great, that the Salary graciously allowed me by His Majesty will fall infinitely short of my annual expenses when contracted by the strictest Oeconomy. Under these circumstances, my Lord, I shall in future presume to take, from Foreigners only, fees for granting certificates until your Lordships pleasure is known. The annual amount may at the utmost pay my house rent in this city. I consider it for the Honor of my Sovereign and the Interest of the Nation, that I should live genteely and hospitably so as to secure a good understanding with the official Characters of this Government and all respectable strangers who may visit this City, a measure indispensibly necessary to promise early information and to facilitate business.

TO CAPT. BARRON, UNITED STATES SHIP CONSTELLATION.[1]

Hallitts Cove Long Island 1st Oct' 1799.

SIR:

Captain Champion of the private armed British Merchant ship the ——— acquaints that since his arrival in the port of New York, many of his Seamen have deserted and left the Ship in violation of their shipping articles, and that some of them have been entertained at your recruiting rendevous in the City and eventually entered and received on board the united

---

[1] The Constellation was built at Baltimore and launched in 1797; in 1812 she was rebuilt, and technically is still afloat; but she has been repaired so much from time to time that there can be but little left even of the ship of 1812. From August 2 to November 11, 1799, she was commanded by Captain Samuel Barron, who is not to be confounded with his brother, the unfortunate *James* Barron.

7A

States Frigate under your Command. I have acquainted Captain Champion of my having no doubt but you would on a personal application from him, deliver up such men as belong to his Ship, for which purpose he now waits on you. He will inform you of the very special condition on which he is chartered and the very probable serious consequences which will follow to his owners in consequence of the loss of these Men.

In addition to the treaty existing between Great Britain and the united States of America; I am convinced the delicate situations wherein those two powers stand each to the other with respect to seamen, will have that weight with you which the present case demands.

From the very handsome and honorable manner in which you have ever been represented; I anticipate a favorable issue to this application.

As the present, from the Constellation being under orders for sailing the day after tomorrow, will probably be the only opportunity I shall have of writing you on this Subject previous to your return; I am reluctantly compelled to add, that in case men are not given up I shall be under the necessity not only of representing the case officially to your Government, but of transmitting an authenticated Statement of Facts to be laid before His Britannic Majesty, a measure you must be sensible fraught with the most serious consequences.

TO MRS. GRACE KEMPE, LONDON.

New York 2d Oct' 1799.

MADAM:

Your favor of the 3ᵈ of June came to hand only a few days since by the July Packet the Marquis of Kildare. Accept my best thanks for your polite and very friendly congratulations on my late appointment as His Majestys Consul General for the Eastern States of America.

I am gratefully sensible of this testimony of Royal confidence and favor; and Mʳˢ Barclay and myself much grati-

fied in being once more united in the same circle with many
of those relations and friends we so reluctantly parted with
at the close of the American War.—An interval, however, of
fifteen years has made an astonishing alteration in this City;
so that I feel myself almost a perfect stranger in the place of
my nativity.[1]—By removing to Nova Scotia, new connections and acquaintances were formed to whom from their
amiable manners and sterling worth we became particularly
attached & of course the parting with these in a great
measure damped the pleasure a removal to this Country
would otherwise have produced; in addition to this the
healthy and charming climate of Nova Scotia was reluctantly
resigned by us for that of New York which never was healthy
and latterly has become every Summer really pestilential.
New York at this moment is nearly deserted owing to the
prevalence of the yellow fever. I have not been in it for upwards of a fortnight, nor shall I enter it again until the fever
is removed.—All the Gentlemen of the Law have also removed into the Country, so that at present it is not in my
power to sanction with their opinion, that which I shall give
you of my own.

You are undoubtedly entitled Madam to your dower in the
Lands whereof my worthy friend, your husband, was possessed.[2] This dower will be valuable in proportion to the
Lands, and the State of Cultivation they are in—at all Events
your dower is worth some thing and you may safely make the
experiment, because you will receive more than the trifling
costs you will be put to. The State of New York I understand
have appointed Commissioners to enquire into claims of dower
and to report what they consider as an equitable equivalent.
This in your Situation will be better than being put into the
possession of wild or remote lands for life, because whatever
they report is given you as a satisfaction for your dower.

[1] The population of New-York in
1783 was estimated at 24,000; in
1799 it was upward of 60,000.

[2] John Tabor Kempe was a native
of England, but came to New-York
when a boy. He was for many years
Attorney-General of the Province.
Having been attainted by the Act of
1779, he removed to England, where
he died.

The Season will be too far advanced before this will get.to hand for you to transmit me any original papers, so that you had better postpone sending them until March next, either in a packet or Man of War, the latter is the most safe. In the mean time forward by the first conveyance your letter of Attorney with a memorandum or description of the lands Mr Kempe possessed and in which you claim a dower — Situation, boundaries, and number of Acres, together with the title under which he held them; and if there is any indorsement on the Grants or Deeds of their inrolment or recording, annex an exact copy of it that we may refer to the Registry.

It will afford me real pleasure in this and every other instance to render you or any of the family every service in my power. Mrs Barclay unites with me in sincere regards to your daughters and yourself.

TO MR. GREENWOOD.

New York, 2ᵈ Octr 1799.
SIR :

Inclosed is an extract from a letter I received from His R. H., the Duke of Kent, by the packet from Nova Scotia,[1] in which he advises me to apply to you on the Subject of procuring a Lieutenancy for my son De Lancey Barclay with as little delay as possible in order that he may the sooner have permission to purchase a Company. To effect this as there is not a Lieut^y in the Royal Fusiliers vacant at present, it is necessary my Son commences with the first step, that of an Ensign, and his R. H. points to one you have the disposal of at the regulation — he then proceeds to observe that Lieutenancys are daily to be had on similar terms, and recommends me to apply to you in his name for your interest and good offices in

[1] The Duke of Kent had resided at Halifax as Commander of the Forces from 1794 to 1798, during all of which time Colonel Barclay was Speaker of the Provincial Assembly. The Duke had at this time just returned to Halifax after a short visit to England. He was the father of the present Queen of England.

favor of my son. The directions of his R. H. to me will, I trust, be a sufficient apology for my commencing thus abruptly a correspondence, and requesting your assistance in effecting my wishes.

At the commencement of the present war, and under the erroneous opinion that its continuance would be but of short duration, I was induced to put my Son De Lancey Barclay at the solicitation of Col. Sir John Wentworth into the Royal Nova Scotia Regiment, wherein he has served five years in the respective ranks of Ensign, Lieut., and Captain, Commanding the Grenadier Company upwards of a year on a detached Command at Cape Breton. When he first entered the service it was not my intention he should continue it as a profession; he, however, appears fond of it, and in compliance with his request I now wish him in a regular old Reg'. He has entered his 20th year, is well grown, has had a liberal education, is a very handsome young man, and free from every vice or fashionable dissipation.

FROM COX & GREENWOOD.

London, 6th. Feby, 1800.

SIR:

We have the pleasure to acknowledge the receipt of your favor of the 2nd. Oct. to Mr. Greenwood respecting the Purchase of a Commission in the Army for your Son whom you are desirous of attaining the Rank of Captain for as soon as possible.

In this we shall be particularly happy to forward your wishes when it can be done; but you must be apprized that from the late Regulations of the Commander in Chief an Officer cannot be permitted to Purchase a Company until he shall have served two years as a Subaltern.

There being an opportunity of purchasing an Ensigncy in the 41st. Regt. lately gone to Quebec we conceived it would be more agreeable to you to have your Son in one in America than any where else, especially as he goes into that Regiment very advantageously there being other vacancies and we believe he will be first or second for the Purchase of a Lieuty. when one falls vacant in the Regiment; which is the only chance of his obtaining a Lieuty. as they are become now very scarce and difficult to be had.

We have also the pleasure to acquaint you that the Ensigncy was purchased under the Regulation, having been got for 350 Guis. Ensign Barclay's Commission is Dated the 11ᵗʰ January.

It will be necessary for you to write to the Commanding Officer of the Regt. Lieut. Colonel Thomas, stating when Ensign Barclay will join.

We have etc.
Cox & Greenwood.

TO HIS MAJESTY'S POSTMASTERS-GENERAL.

New York Consul Generals Office 15 March 1800.

My Lords:

His Majestys Packet Boats and Merchant Vessels having ever since my arrival at this place suffered great inconvenience and occasional delay in consequence of the desertion of their Men, and the impracticability of regaining them unless by the tedious and ordinary process at Common Law; induced me to represent the grievance to some of the leading members in the House of Representatives of this State, and to request them to procure a Law for the summary trial of deserting, or absenting Seamen; A measure founded in Justice and due to all Nations in alliance with the United States of America.

I am happy to acquaint your Lordships that my application has succeeded and have the honor to inclose your Lordships a Gazette containing the Act passed for that purpose.

Your Lordships will observe from the words of the Act that the Agreement by the Seamen to perform a Voyage must be made in writing, I take the Liberty to suggest this, from the Captains of Pacquets having repeatedly informed me that it was not customary for seamen employed in that Service to sign Articles. Permit me to add it will advance his Majestys Service in these parts, to direct that the Seamen in future employed in the Pacquets shall on entering sign articles, and that the Articles of Agreement in future to be used be correctly and explicitly drawn by a professional Gentleman.

TO LORD GRENVILLE.

New York 15 March 1800.

MY LORD:

I have the satisfaction to acquaint your Lordship that I have through the intervention of some of the leading Characters in the house of Representatives of this State procured an act for the summary trial of Seamen deserting or absenting themselves from the Ships to whom they are articled to perform a voyage; a copy of which act is inclosed.

The grievance had become almost intolerable to His Majesty's Subjects and the Pacquet service in many instances delayed. These Evils I had stated to Mr Liston as well as your Lordship, and finding from him that it was improbable any immediate general remedy would be administered, I considered it advisable to effect, if in my power, a partial one confined to this State. I hope the measure will meet your Lordships approbation.

By this conveyance I write His Majesty's Postmasters General on the Subject, inclosing them the Act, and recommending the Seamen in that Service, being in future under Articles, to enable me to recover them in cases of desertion.

TO MR. BROUGHTON.

New York 6th May 1800.

DEAR SIR:

Your favors of the 24 & 31 of January I received by the Earl Gower Packet. The letters accompanying them addressed to persons in this City were immediately delivered, and those for Canada forwarded the first Conveyance. I am much obliged to you for the purchase of my two half Lottery tickets and your attention in forwarding the numbers; pray favor me with their fate.[1] Will you do me the favor to send me a hand Bill of the Rates for Life Insurance and Endowment of Children at 21 years old. I will thank you to discontinue my London paper, as we generally have later European news by private Conveyances than by the Packets. Instead of these send me the Antijacobin Reviews and any political Pamphlets of merit from time to time published.

TO LORD GRENVILLE.

New York 7th May 1800.

MY LORD:

I did myself the Honor of writing your Lordship by the last Packet on the Subject of an Act of the Legislature of this State; a printed copy of which I took the Liberty to inclose to your Lordship.

It is with no small degree of disappointment that I am under the necessity of acquainting your Lordship that I was premature in the Communication, and that the Bill after having passed the house of Representatives and Senate of this State, was rejected by the Council of Revision. Permit me, however, in my own Justification, to remark that previous to the meeting of the Legislature I had recommended the Bill to two or three of the leading members who promised to bring it forward, and that I not only had the public prints of this City as the Channel of information that the Bill had passed, but also the Mayor of the City who read me an extract from M[r] Rigg's letter (a member of the Legislature) wherein he desired the Mayor to congratulate me on the subject. With such testi-

---

[1] Barclay was constantly buying State lottery tickets in London either through Mr. Broughton or David Barclay, of Bury Hill. These ventures seem to have been uniformly unsuccessful.

mony, I considered it a matter beyond all doubt, and accordingly gave it to your Lordship, as I was convinced it would afford you Satisfaction.

The Bill was rejected by the Council of Revision upon a principle that it was a commercial regulation which appertained to the Congress of the United States. At the next meeting of Congress I shall endeavor to get an Act of this kind passed.

TO MRS. MARGARET DE LANCEY,[1] BATH, ENGLAND.

New York 8th Nov[r.] 1800.

MY DEAR MADAM:

I wrote you a hasty line by the Lady Arabella Packet, being at that time very unwell with an intermitting fever, from which I am now happily recovered, though much reduced. In that letter I acknowledged the receipt of your favor covering the letter of Attorney, and my readiness to render you any Service in my power. I at the same time Stated to you my having retained M[r] Harison[2] as your Council, and acquainted you that M[r] Hoffman being the Attorney General of this State rendered it improper for him to act for you. I took the liberty at the same time to give you my opinion re-

[1] Margaret De Lancey was the widow of the James De Lancey who was Agent of the American Loyalists in England. She was the daughter of Chief Justice William Allen of Pennsylvania, the friend of Benjamin West and Benjamin Franklin. James De Lancey died at Bath, 1799. He had been attainted by the Act of 1779, and his property in the city of New-York had been sold at various times prior to February, 1787. A full account of these sales will be found in Mr. E. F. De Lancey's notes to Jones's Hist. of N. Y., Vol. II, pp. 540–559. His widow, of course, became entitled to dower in all the lands sold.

[2] Richard Harison was born in New-York, January 23, 1748, and died in the same city, December 7, 1829. He was graduated from Kings College in 1764. He married first, Catharine, daughter of Dr. Jones of Long Island; second, Frances, daughter of George Duncan Ludlow, one of the Judges of the Supreme Court of the Province of New-York, and afterward the first Chief Justice of New Brunswick. Harison was inclined to the Tory side, but in 1789 he was chosen one

specting the mode of obtaining your dower or compensation in lieu of it; and Mr Harisons opinion on the same subject. I shall repeat these, least by an accident to the Lady Arabella you may be deprived of my former letter.

Having fully considered your claim of dower,—the very great number of Tenants of the freehold who must be sued—the probable delay before you will be put in possession. The forcible reasons why the Major part of the Proprietors will prefer your having the actual possession of one third of the Lots and houses. The enormous expense attending a litigation, where there will probably be not less than three or four hundred Suits, your own costs of which, you must defray. The immense number of vacant lots, which altho' they are valued at about £100 this Currency each, do not, nor would they at any future period in your hands, produce any annual rent. The precarious tenor of life—The loss your Children would sustain by your dying at the earliest within fifteen years. The length of time it would require to make the rents issues and profits of your third part of this Estate, after deducting six hundred per annum as Interest for the Capital, net you a clear principal of £10,000 this Currency. The impossibility of your renting unimproved lots and parts of Lots, from the uncertainty of your Life—The difficulty of obtaining tenants, to occupy a third part of a house, containing not more than two small rooms on each floor and those houses generally not more than two Stories. The defalcations in rents, where Tenants are poor and the expense of employing

of the delegates from the city of New-York to the Poughkeepsie Convention that ratified the Federal Constitution, his colleagues being John Jay, Richard Morris, John Sloss Hobart, Alexander Hamilton, Robert R. Livingston, Isaac Roosevelt, James Duane, and Nicholas Low. He was for many years one of the leaders of the New-York bar, and counsel in a large proportion of the more important cases reported in the early New-York reports. Upon the organization of the Federal Government he was appointed by General Washington U. S. District Attorney. From 1798 to 1799 he was Recorder of the city. For forty-one years — 1788 to 1829 — he was one of the Trustees of Columbia College, and in 1823 was Chairman of the Board. He also held the office of Comptroller of the Trinity Church Corporation.

an Agent to take care of the Property and receive the rents—
With numberless other serious objections; I say after having
maturely weighed all these, it was my decided opinion that
you had better take up with a compensation from the State
of New York, attended with but little expense and which you
would almost immediately receive, than to involve yourself in
Litigation, and place a very handsome Sum on the casual
Event of your Life admitting, as I consider it, to be, equal to
that of any other person for fifteen years to come. It would
take up too much time, and tire your patience was I to give
you at length my reasons, on each of the objections mentioned. I shall therefore only say they are admitted as
natural by Mr Harison.

A combination or conspiracy very probably may also be
entered into by the Proprietors to dissuade persons from becoming your Tenants, and to threaten them with innumerable
unpleasant incidents in case they do it. Their side of the
Question, however equitable yours may be, will be the popular one; in a Country where the Claims of Loyalty are considered by the vulgar as usurpation.

You may perhaps think I write in strong terms, and that
my apprehensions are unreasonable. The greater part of
what I have stated will inevitably come to pass, and the
remainder is founded on probabilities approaching to cer-
tainties. I have measured all these on the Scale of your
Interest, and by opposing the one to the other, have no hesitation in saying, that a Sum far short of what might fairly
be calculated from the rents of the Estate, admitting solvent
tenants could be procured, will be preferable to the uncertain
amount you will receive in consequence of being unable to
obtain tenants, and the losses incurred by many of them being
unable to pay their rents—With regard to lots on which there
are no buildings it will be difficult to find Persons who would
even be at the expense of inclosing them, when they know
their possession depends on your life. Was the property
situate in a valuable part of the City and vested in decent
houses, the annual rents might be calculated to almost a fraction—But your lots are in the Suburbs, which may be said

to be half town half Country.[1] It is impossible to say what the State may allow you: but at the lowest valuation I should suppose not less than 25,000 Dollars, and possibly more than double that Sum. On this occasion I should strive to get the most for you. But every thing considered I really think even 25,000 dollars in hand, better than a general litigation.

M[r] Harison differs in Sentiment with me; and thinks you will advance your interest by applying to or prosecuting the Individual Proprietors. Having his opinion and mine, it remains for you to decide and to send me your orders without loss of time, providing duplicates and triplicates of letters.

If we are to prosecute it will be indispensibly necessary for you to send me out all the Title deeds for any part of the Estate, not only in the Bowery, but in broadway opposite the Estate M[r] DeLancey gave to his brother John.[2] I think there was also property in other parts of the State. Let regular and correct copies of them be made and taken to the Lord Mayor of London to examine and certify, and leave them with him until the Event is known, whether the originals have come safe to my hands or not. Should a treaty of Peace be entered into between the States and France, it will be most safe to send the papers out in some good safe American Ship, delivered to a Gentleman Passenger, or to the Master, if a decent Man. It may be necessary also to prove M[r] DeLancey's death. Furnish me, therefore, with the name of the Parson who can attest to his person and demise. It will be best to have this testimony also taken by the Lord Mayor of London. Inform me if the Witness can attend before him. Proof of your Marriage will be required and of your being alive at the time that proof was taken. Was your Brother, M[r] Andrew Allen, present at your marriage, or who was.

I have employed Beverly Robinson, Grandson of the late Col. Robinson, a young Gentleman of merit and abilities, rec-

[1] They lay east of the Bowery, between Division and Stanton streets, in what is now perhaps the most densely populated spot in the world.

[2] These lots were at the corner of Broadway and Little Queen (Cedar) street. Brother John was John Peter De Lancey, of Mamaroneck, father of the Bishop.

ommended to me by Mr Harison as your Attorney. And I think it will be most for your Interest to engage Mr Cadwallader Colden, the Assistant Attorney General of the district,[1] as Council with Mr Harison, he having prosecuted several claims for dower and compounded to great advantage with the State. He informs me of what Mr Harison was ignorant, that the State will agree in settling of the Sum to be paid you, to my nominating two; and the Commissioners, one Appraiser, who will value the property at what it is at present worth; from whence, after making a small deduction of ten or at the utmost fifteen per Cent., they will calculate the Sum total by the London tables on Lives and allow you whatever sum these tables direct. Mr Harison told me the Commissioners would only take the Sum for which the Estate sold, which was about £100,000 this Currency. Now I suppose the Estate fairly valued could not come short of £500,000; of course your compensation, allowing the Commissioners deducted even a fifth, would be far above what I have stated it.

TO MR. HARTSHORNE, HALIFAX.

New York 5th Decr 1800.

MY DEAR HARTSHORNE:

I am at this moment favored with your most kind letter of the 11th of November and shall reply to the latter part without delay in the hope of getting it on board a vessel bound for St. John, New Brunswick, being more than anxious to remove from Sir John Wentworth's mind any unfavorable suggestions which must tend to lessen me in his good opinion.

You are no stranger to my Sentiments with regard to Sir John, or of the grateful Sense I entertain of his uniform friendly behavior towards me and of the many essential favors

[1] Cadwallader D. Colden, a grandson of the old Lieutenant-Governor, and therefore a first cousin of Mrs. Barclay's. He was at this time Assistant District Attorney of the U. S., and was afterward Mayor of the city.

8

received at his hands. I will therefore thank you candidly to declare what I have repeatedly remarked in confidence to you respecting him and the obligation I felt myself under for his marked predilection towards me. I am satisfied I have always been regarded by him as a confidential friend, and I have the satisfaction to feel that my conduct has generally met his approbation, and that in no one instance have I ever behaved to him or any other Man living with duplicity. He possesses my utmost regards, and there is no person to whom I should more readily apply for advice had I an object in contemplation; indeed, I consider myself in some measure bound to do so, having on former occasions consulted him, and always obtained his ready aid and interest. From these remarks it is scarce necessary for me to contradict the report mentioned at the foot of your letter, to wit, "*that I was trying to obtain the Government of Nova Scotia.*" Accept my thanks for the reply you made the Governor when he mentioned the report. You will, I hope, continue your friendship in contradicting on any future occasion suggestions tending to my injury until you have reason to alter your opinion of me.

I have never made any application directly or indirectly for the Government or the reversion of it in case of Sir Johns removal or demise. Neither have I in writing or verbally expressed a wish or sentiment on the Subject to any person. Had such a measure been contemplated you would have been the most probable person to whom I should have communicated my Sentiments. This report is similar to that you mentioned to me last Winter respecting the Government of New Brunswick. I received on that subject not less than twenty letters, several of which were congratulatory of the appointment having taken place, and I have little doubt but Governor Carleton imagines that I really did apply. Many of my friends, and some of the first consideration in Nova Scotia and in England have in their letters lamented my leaving Nova Scotia, and hinted that they hoped yet to see me filling an office of responsibility in that Province. I had no doubt they meant the Government; still, so little did I think of it, that I have in no one instance ever noticed the latter part of their remarks. It is not impossible but they or some other persons may have written that on the demise of Sir John it was probable I would succeed to the Government, and from such an hint, it may have grown into a confirmed report of my soliciting for it. Assure Sir John he will ever find me to be his zealous friend, incapable of doing an act incompatible with honor or candor. That it would be doing violence to my feelings to accept of any appointment at the expense even of a stranger; and of course that I am incapable of soliciting the removal of any person from office to make way for myself. If these are my principles, judging of my affection by that he bears to me, he will be readily satisfied that the report was without foundation.

TO LORD GRENVILLE.

New York 5 Decr. 1800.

MY LORD:

I have the Honor to inclose your Lordship Quarterly returns of the Imports and Exports to and from this Port from the first of September to the 30th of November last past.

It may perhaps not be disagreeable to your Lordship to be informed that it is more than probable Mr Adams and Mr Pinckney will be elected President and Vice President of the United States. Which of the two will, by having the Majority of Votes be President is uncertain, I however suspect Mr Adams will be reelected.

TO MR. BOND.

New York 29th Decr 1800.

DEAR SIR:

Vice Admiral Sir Wm Parker commanding his Majestys Ships in America has written to me that an armed Ship named the Faustina which sailed from New York some time in April last, had on a former Voyage captured and destroyed certain Merchant Vessels belonging to His Majesty Subjects, that he was apprehensive she would commit similar depredations during her present Voyage — That she has long been engaged in a contraband trade with His Majestys Enemies; and that tho' she is well adapted to all the purposes of Commerce, she is in every respect equipped for War; and on meeting with British Vessels regulates her Conduct by the Force they display, by hoisting the Colours of the United States of America in the presence of our Ships of War or armed Vessels of superior or equal force and those of Spain when she meets Merchant Vessels or small Privateers and acts as such — He wishes to know the real Character and Pursuits of this Ship, particularly the object and destination of her present Voyage.— From the best information that I can obtain in this place, from public and private Channels, a ship of the name of Faustina has not cleared out from this Port during the present year; nor can I discover that there is a ship of that name owned in this State. A Spanish armed ship named the Astiganaga or Aristazaraga sailed from hence in April last (nominally) to Montevideo in la Plata, but as was generally suspected to cruize on the Coast of Africa for some time for British Vessels.— I am of opinion this is the same Ship the Admiral enquires after, and it is possible she may have a false set of papers, purporting her to be an American Ship named the Faustina.— Should this be the case I can give the Admiral the best information existing here respecting her, and he will be ennabled to judge whether it is the same vessel, by the list of British ships she captured on her leaving this and previous to her departure from the Coasts of the United States —

Least however I may be mistaken in my conjectures, permit me to request you will make enquiry at Philadelphia, if there is a ship of that name belonging to that Port, or if any ship of that name has cleared out from thence answering the above description, also the owners name, her pursuits and present destination — where she is now supposed to be, and the earliest probable period of her return.

It is unnecessary for me to add that the utmost caution and secrecy are necessary in investigations of this nature, where the fears and suspicions not only of the owners, but the underwriters are all alive from the sailing of each ship until her safe return into port—Should it be necessary to expend a small Sum to effect the above purposes I will readily pay it, as I can have no doubt but the Admiral will readily repay the same.

FROM DE LANCEY BARCLAY.

Montreal 26th, January, 1801.

MY DEAR MAMMA:

I cannot let another opportunity pass without writing to my best of Mothers. A description of my very disagreeable and tedious Journey here you undoubtedly have seen in my letters to my dear Papa. I asure you the cake you or my dear Maria put in my Portmanteau was very acceptable to me and my fellow travellers the night I spent in the woods; it is impossible for me to express my feelings while I was eating it; gratitude, with my dear Parents &c. &c. occupied my mind, and thinking how unhappy you would have been had you known my situation, while I was only a little uncomfortable. I am living at Sir Johns which Lady Johnson has insisted on I shall make my home, she has frequently told me the time she spent at West Chester with you was the happiest part of her life, she made me a present of three black martins for a Cap which I suppose would have cost me a Guinea a piece; I receive the greatest attention both from her and Sir John.[1] I am sorry to say Lady Johnson intends going home in the spring I am sure she will be much missed in this place You know not how anxious I am to hear from you as I have had that pleasure but once since I left New-York. Remember me

[1] Sir John Johnson was at this time Superintendent of Indian Affairs in British North America. Lady Johnson was formerly Mary Watts, sister to John Watts of New-York. Lady Johnson's arrest and detention in 1776 by the American authorities, as a hostage, is vigorously related by Judge Jones in his history of New-York, Vol. I, pp. 74-81; and further details are given in Mr. De Lancey's notes. When released she selected Barclay's house at the Walkill as her residence. See Journals Prov. Con., Vol. I, p. 761.

8A

to my dear Brothers and sisters, with my aunts Cox and Watts, and all other friends, with Griser and other servants, and believe me my dear Mamma your very sincere and affectionate son

D. BARCLAY.

MY DEAR PAPA:

Although I have little or nothing to say having wrote you not long since I should feel unpleasant did I let a conveyance slip without a line to my dear Father I have not yet been able to obtain a french master, though in the mean time I think I am losin nothin while I am making myself master of the Grammar, and writing french, and frequently having an opportunity of speaking it. It is now after two o'clock therefore I shall bid you good morning and retire to my bed, as I rise at six. I shall write you again by the first good opportunity. Believe me ever your very sincere and affectionate Son

D. BARCLAY.

Should the gentleman who takes charge of this and with whom I dined a few days since whose name is Mr. Leith come to New York (of which he is not certain) and call on you I will thank you to pay him some attention, not to put yourself out of the way, should you have a party while he is there invite him — he is in the fir trade.

TO LORD GRENVILLE.

New York 12th March 1801.

MY LORD:

I have the Honor to inform your Lordship that the President of the Chamber of Commerce of Philadelphia a few Weeks since, wrote an official letter to the New York Chamber of Commerce wherein after remarking the immense number of american Ships captured by His Majestys Ships of

War, he acquainted the New York Chamber of Commerce of the determination of the Philadelphia Merchants, to petition the President of the United States to grant in future convoys under certain regulations to merchants ships that their property might be secured against British depredations.[1] The chamber of Commerce of this place have not co operated with the Philadelphians under a conviction that their proceedings were too high toned and that it was probable the President of the United States might remedy the evil complained of by a more conciliatory line of Conduct. They have therefore reported to the President the Captures of Ships from this Port by British Ships, and subjoined the facts respecting each individual Ship leaving the President to adopt such measures as he conceived would best remedy the evil.— M[r] Bond His Majestys Consul General at Philadelphia will probably furnish your Lordship with the particulars of the proceedings at Philadelphia. I have not yet learned whether any thing has been done to the Eastward : but consider it certain that application equally violent with that from Pennsylvania will be made by the Merchants of Baltimore, Virginia and the Carolinas. I am happy to inform your Lordship that the respectable part of the Mercantile Interest in this City are federal and warmly attached to G Britain; and that altho' few of these Characters ordinarily attend the meetings of the Chamber of Commerce; I had influence sufficient to procure their attendance on this occasion, and to them and a few others, the lenient measures adopted are to be attributed. I intreat your Lordship will pardon me for obtruding this unsolicited, but zeal for His Majestys Service compels me in this instance to break through all rule; under an impression that it is probable your Lordship may be ignorant of what the Americans, with I fear some justice, complain of.— There are few if any instances of captures in Europe, or decrees in the Courts of admiralty in Great Britain that are considered otherwise than equitable

[1] In American State Papers, For. Rel., Vol. II, p. 347, will be found a letter from Thomas Fitzsimmons, Chairman of the Philadelphia Chamber of Commerce, to the Secretary of the Navy, dated Feb. 17, 1801, which is evidently the "petition" referred to.

and fair by the Americans; and I have scarce ever heard our Courts in England spoken of by them except in terms of the highest respect.— But the cry is universal from one end of the Continent to the other that the Cruizers in America and the West Indies send every American Vessel they meet, into one of his Majestys Colonial Ports for adjudication and that the Judges of the Provincial Courts of Vice Admiralty too generally condemn, and in cases where an acquital would have been decreed in England.   To appeal they remark is so nearly allied in its consequences to a total loss, that it is not worth the pursuit.   First from the length of time that elapses before a decision takes place — and secondly the immense expense attending appeals.— I am satisfied my Lord that not a little of Enemies property is covered by the Americans and that articles contraband of War are frequently exported from the States: but I am equally certain that bona fide American property is too often improperly condemned in the Provincial Courts of Admiralty.   From hence it is that the Americans feel injured, and unless a remedy is applied, I fear we shall not long continue on a friendly footing with them.— The Eastern States are at the present moment more firmly attached to G Britain than at any period since the year 1783, and would be perfectly satisfied if the least alteration was made by Government for the protection of lawful American Property from capture and condemnation.— What I have stated to your Lordship is in perfect confidence and I hope will not be considered by your Lordship out of place.   Permit me to intreat that my name may not be made known as the author of this communication.[1]

[1] The subject treated of in this letter had already engaged the attention of the Ministry. By a letter from Lord Grenville, dated January 22, 1801, the King directed the Lords Commissioners of the Admiralty to revoke all the prize commissions which had theretofore been granted to the numerous Vice Admiralty Courts in the West Indies and in other British Colonies. The irregularities which had prevailed in these Courts had long given occasion for complaint; and the Government "thought proper, by lessening their number, by extending their jurisdiction, and by increasing the salaries of the judges, to give them greater consequence and dignity, and to induce gentlemen acquainted with the

TO MRS. MARGARET DE LANCEY.

New York 3ᵈ May 1801.

MY DEAR MADAM—

Your favor of the 15ᵗʰ of Decʳ and 26ᵗʰ of January I have had the satisfaction to receive; and had flattered myself that it would before this have been in my power to have given you the pleasing information of the settlement of your dower with the State of New York. For which purpose, as I informed you last Autumn, it was necessary to have an accurate list and valuation of each lot, by appraisors, appointed by the Commissioners of this State — Through Mʳ Cadwallader Colden your Attorney for this purpose, I therefore presented the Commissioners with twelve respectable names and desired to nominate three out of that number — They directed the first three to be taken; who with great attention and industry, aided by Stanton & a Surveyor, completed the return in February last; the total value of the Estate, computed at 604,707 dollars & the annual value thereof at 30,831.— With these documents and a petition drawn up by me in your name Mʳ Colden proceeded immediately to Albany, and laid them before the Commissioners — The Legislature of the State was then sitting in that City. The Commissioners having examined the valuation, made by Gorman, Russel & Carmer the appraisers, were of opinion, that it was an equitable appraisement; but as your demand amounted to a Sum infinitely beyond what had ever come before them, they considered it their duty, altho vested with full powers to purchase your release of dower, to report the facts to the Legislature, and to pray

---

law, and the practice of the Courts in England, and particularly some of the advocates of the civil law, to accept of these judicial offices." Accordingly by an act of Parliament (41 Geo. III, Chap. 96) courts were established at Halifax, Jamaica and Martinique only, and salaries were authorized to be paid of £2000, besides perquisites not to exceed another £2000 a year. Martinique having been given up by the Treaty of Amiens, a Vice-Admiralty Court was established at Barbadoes. See Introduction to Stewart's Adm. Reports. American public opinion was no better satisfied with the decisions of the new courts than with those of their predecessors.

their orders thereon—A committee was appointed to take the same into consideration and report. Mr Colden attended them and they some days after made a private report, which I understand from good Authority amounted to this — That the appraisement was consistent and rather under than above the value of the Estate — Yet that it would be improper for the House of Assembly to sanction the Commissioners in paying so large an amount as you would be entitled to, on the Scale used on former occasions by the Commissioners; for if they allowed you an annuity during your life, it could not be less than 8000 dollars per Annum and if a sum in gross it would amount to near 80,000 dollars.— Such compensations to Widows of Loyalists, they imagined would make no little noise in the State and prove injurious to their political Interest — They therefore recommended that the Commissioners should not for the present offer you any compensation but that Mr Hoffman the Attorney General, be directed to defend every suit commenced for the recovery of your dower, create every possible delay, and endeavour so to perplex and exhaust your patience, as to induce you to a second application, and then that the Commissioners might pay you 30,000 dollars for your release in full — I relate the above in confidence and intreat you will not let it be known, as it might injure me —

Under these circumstances we have now no alternative but to commence Suits — In this, I shall use every possible discretion; for if the Court should determine, that you are to pay your own Costs, which I fear will be the Case, a large proportion of the property will not be worth suing for — I mean vacant lots, and those whereon small tenements are erected.— At the same time, it will be necessary to sue all the Tenants of the Freehold, who possess property to any amount, and to hurry on these suits, in order to render them anxious on their own account, and compel them in turn to become Petitioners to the Legislature during their Session in February next — If we can effect this we shall turn the tables on them and obtain a better compensation.— Of this rest assured that I shall act for you as if the stake was my own, and that neither attention or industry shall be wanting on my part — By the advice of M[r] Harison I have retained General Hamilton the ablest Council in this place to assist him and in July next, it is more than probable that your claim to the property in Broadway will be brought to a decision.

In the mean time I intreat that by the earliest good American conveyance you forward me, every paper relative to the Estate of your deceased husband, for property in the city, or elsewhere — The wild lands you mention, have probably been sold by the State, are now under cultivation and worthy your attention — Send me also the affidavits requested by M[r] Colden —

It was stated in the house of Assembly that M[r] De Lancey had given long leases for a part of this Estate, and that you had joined in these Leases — Also that he and you had conveyed Mount Pit to Judge Jones[1] — Pray answer me particularly as to these suggestions — Stanton tells me M[r] De Lancey had repeatedly said to him, that as M[r] Jones had not any Children, he did not intend to give him a deed for the property —

TO LORD HAWKESBURY.[2]

New York 12 May 1801.

(Private.)

MY LORD

I consider it my duty to acquaint your Lordship that it is generally reported in these States, and I suspect not without truth, that the Government of the United States are resolved to refuse complying with the increased demands of the Dey of Tripoli; in consequence of which it is supposed the Tripolitan Ships will have orders to capture all American Vessels.— To protect the American Commerce in the Mediterranean it is

1 "Mount Pitt" was the town house of Judge Thomas Jones, the Tory historian of New-York. It lay not far from Corlear's Hook on the East River. Mrs. Jones was Anne De Lancey, a sister of James.

2 Lord Hawkesbury had been appointed to the Foreign Office February 20, 1801, on the formation of Mr. Addington's Ministry. He is better known by his later title of Lord Liverpool.

said that a Squadron of five Frigates and two Cutters are to be sent to cruise in those seas, with orders to act defensively only for the present.— The Ships are to rendezvous in the Chesapeak without loss of time, and will probably sail in a month from this.

I subjoin the names and force of the Ships to be employed on this Service

	Guns
United States	44
Constitution	44
President	44
Congress	36
Essex	32

TO LORD HAWKESBURY.

New York 5th June 1801.

My Lord —

Complaint has been made to me that two officers who served in the Provincial Corps during the Amn War and who are now in the receipt of half pay, have taken the oaths of allegiance to the United States of America, and in that oath in positive terms and by name, abjured our most gracious Sovereign.— Gabriel V Ludlow Ensine in Brigr General De Lanceys Brigade — and a Mr Thomas Carpenter, at present of Saratoga in this State, but to what Provincial Corps he belonged I cannot learn; are the persons who have taken these oaths.

It is not for me to make any remark on the Conduct of these persons, or to observe that prudence dictates that the allowance of half pay, should be with held from Characters of the above description; but it is a lamentable fact that there are at this moment a great number of half pay officers, who have become subjects of the United States; and many of them violent in their principals and Conduct in opposition to His majesty and the interest of the united Kingdom —

TO VICE-ADMIRAL PARKER.

New York 8th June 1801.

SIR:

The inclosed letter will give you in substance the latest accounts that I have received from Virginia respecting His Majesty's ship the Boston and the french Frigate the Semillante. By a schooner that left Hampton roads on Tuesday last, I am informed that the American Squadron and the Semillante lay there apparently ready for Sea. Should the Semillante wait the sailing of the American ships, it is probable she will not be out in some days. Captain Douglas has almost a daily communication with Col. Hamilton the Consul at Norfolk.

Monsieur Pichon chargé des affaires from the french republic to these States called on me a few days since on the subject of a flag of truce, which he wished and I had declined. In that conversation I drew from him that he had sent sixty people of colour who had been prisoners to the Americans to Boston to assist in manning the Berceau. These men have gone most reluctantly and although exchanged were kept in Gaol until embarked for Boston. I suspect the Berceau has sailed by this — her destination I have not been able to ascertain.[1] The news from Egypt is the more pleasing, as it contradicts the french reports.[2]

TO VICE-ADMIRAL PARKER.

New York 24 June, 1801.

SIR

I have the honor to inform you that early this morning the French armed Brig the Mutine of 16 Guns, with an armed

[1] The Berceau was a French corvette captured in November, 1800, by the U. S. Ship Boston. She was restored to the French Government in accordance with the third article of the Convention of September 30, 1800. The U. S. S. Boston is not to be confounded with the British frigate of the same name. The American vessel was built at Boston in 1799, and came to an ignominious end in 1814, being burned at the Washington Navy Yard to avoid falling into English hands.

[2] The "news from Egypt" was Abercromby's victory at Alexandria, March 21, 1801.

Merchant Ship of ten Guns from Cayenne came to an anchor about four miles below this City. I have not yet been able to learn precisely their object or destination, a confidential person was on board both of them last Evng on entering the Hook, but as he did not speak french, and found only one man on board the Brig who could speak English, he obtained but little information. It appears that the Ship has a number of exiles from France on board who had permission to leave Cayenne, but I have not yet ascertained whether they are to go to France or settle in America. On Board the Mutine the men and officers were very inquisitive to learn whether there were many British Ships in Port, how many had lately sailed, and if there were any nearly ready for Sea —

I have sent back the person above mentioned, with another equally trust worthy who speaks french; but as it is uncertain whether they will return in time for the New Brunswick Vessel, which leaves this in an hour or two, I have determined to forward this imperfect Statement. About two hours after the above vessels came to an anchor, His Majestys armed Brig the Serpent commanded by Lt Dwire came up to Town. He informs me that he was ordered on a Cruize by Admiral Duckworth with orders to proceed as far as 35 North Latitude and if possible speak one of the Ships belonging to your Squadron, to inform you that on the 23 of May two french Frigates of 48 & 44 Guns had got in to Guadeloupe from France. Near that Island they were met with by His Majestys Ship the Andromacke who exchanged a few broadsides with both of them, but the french frigates avoided the action and got into Point Petre.— That the Admiral was suspicious they would endeavour to get out, and probably come on this coast. Lt Dwire adds that there is a chain of Privateers from Guadeloupe extending from Longitude 60 to Newfoundland— That one of these had captured the Duke of Kent Merchant Man ladened with fish, which he recaptured in sight of Guadeloupe — Lt Dwire put in to this place in distress, having sprung a leak and making so much water as not to be able to keep his ship free with one pump — The Carpenters go on board the Serpent early in the morning and I hope in two or three days she

will be ready for sea.— I am very apprehensive L' Dwire will
lose many of his men — He however thinks otherwise, as they
have been some time on board the Brig, and have upwards of
£80 per man due them for prize money.— In case the Mutine
attempts to put to Sea while the Serpent remains here, I will
procure him as many volunteers as he needs to pursue her —
The Serpent he assures me sails remarkably well, and he assures me he is equal to both these ships — He passed in coming up within half a cables length of both of them, and tells
me the Mutine has very long six pounders, so that they must
be loaded out side — On Saturday the Berceau was still at
Boston ready for sea. She has shipped 50 American Seamen,
discharged from the Amⁿ Frigate the Constitution, at 200 dollars per man for the run to France — This is correct, should
she therefore fall into our possession you will of course take
care of these men amongst whom it is to be feared you will
find British Seamen — Accept my best thanks for your polite
and friendly answer respecting my Son on board the Boston, and
for your assent that Mʳ Izard my nephew may join the Boston
until you have a proper ship whereon to hoist your flag.[1]

I intreat you to pardon this hasty letter, written under
great distress of mind, my dear little infant being dangerously
ill —

TO MR. THORNTON.[2]

- New York 30th June 1801.

Sir —

I am this moment honored with your letters of the 27 & 28
Current, the former accompanied with copies of regulations es-

[1] "My son" was Thomas Barclay
the younger, then a midshipman
aboard H. M. S. Boston. "Mr. Izard
my nephew" was a son of Ralph
Izard of South Carolina, whose wife
was Alice De Lancey, a sister of
Mrs. Barclay's. Young Izard must
have been a guest of the Admiral's,
for none of Ralph Izard's sons were
in the British service. Perhaps this
is Ralph Izard, Jr., of the U. S. Navy,
who distinguished himself three or
four years later at Tripoli.

[2] Thornton was at this time in
charge of the British Legation in
Washington, Mr. Liston having returned to England about a year
before.

tablished by the American Government in 1794 & 1795, to. which particular attention shall be paid — I received about a fortnight since from Mr Maston of Wilmington, Delaware, who arrived at Boston from Halifax Nova Scotia information that the British Vessel he was in, had been chased and fired upon near Cape Cod, by a small french privateer Schooner — on his arrival at Boston and making mention of the Circumstance, it was generally supposed she was the Borguine, Dallas Master, who had entered and cleared as a Merchant Vessel and after leaving Boston, mounted Guns, concealed in her hold — I learn from a Captain Stewart, a few days since from the Bay of Fundy, that close in with Marthas Vineyard, he was hailed and spoken to by a stout armed french Brig; and which from dates could not be the Mutine now in this Port — of all these circumstances, I have informed Admiral Parker, by two Conveyances the last of which sailed on Sunday — I have likewise made him acquainted with the french armed Vessels being in this Port, and what Admiral Duckworth, directed Lieut Dwyer to communicate to the Commanders of any of the Ships appertaining to the Halifax Station —

I have not seen Lt Dwyer, since the day of his arrival owing to the distressed situation of my dear infant, who lay in Convulsions from Thursday until Sunday, when it expired[1] — I however not only urged him to hasten her being ready for Sea, but desired Mr Shanyon, who superintends the repairs to furnish as many Carpenters, as could work to advantage.— I shall see him in a day or two, and if necessary press his stay, if consistent with his instructions —

TO LORD HAWKESBURY.

New York, 8 July 1801.

MY LORD,

A number of national french armed vessels and some privateers have within the last six weeks made their appearance on the American coasts and I am very apprehensive will injure

[1] Cornelia, born May 23, died June 28, 1801.

the British trade, not only to these States, but His Majesty's
colonies on the Continent. The Halifax Squadron under Vice
Adm! Sir W:ᵐ Parker is very weak, consisting at present of
only three frigates and two sloops. Of these the Cleopatra is
detached to Jamaica for Specie for the pay office at Halifax.
The Boston is and has been since the 26 of April at the Capes
of Virginia blockading the Semillante a french frigate laying
in Hampton Roads, and the Andromache sailed about a fortnight since for Virginia to relieve the Boston, who wants repairs not having been in port since last Autumn. The Pheas-
ant sloop is off Boston waiting the Berceau, a stout french
corvette, captured some time since by the Americans, and
lately restored to the french. The Lilly is either at Halifax or
cruising — Your Lordship will perceive that the Lilly, a miserable sloop, is the only ship, that can at present be detached
to protect the trade from Cape Breton to West Florida — and
there can be no doubt, but the numbers of french ships of war
and armed vessels will increase in proportion, as it is discovered, that these shores are unprotected —

TO LORD HAWKESBURY.

New York 3 August 1801.
MY LORD.

Your Lordship is undoubtedly fully informed of the immense emigrations that have taken place during the present
season from G Britain and Ireland to these States. Of the
cause however I suspect His Majestys Ministers are ignorant,
under this impression I take the Liberty to state, that there
are several Societies formed within the United States consisting principally of persons who have either from political or
religious principles left Great Britain and Ireland, who keep
up a constant correspondence with his Majestys Subjects, and
by every conveyance send over to England, Scotland, and Ireland, seditious inflamatory publications for the express purpose of rendering His Majestys Subjects dissatisfied with their
present situation and the measures of Government — Describ-

9

ing their own envied situation in America in the enjoyment of Liberty and equality, free from taxation; and painting these States as a field where wealth is reaped with care and moderate industry.— Of these mischievous societies some are headed by dissenting Clergymen, who were obliged to leave G Britain on account of political violence, these men in addition to the above mentioned arguments, urge fanatical persuasions and have deluded most of the Welsh that have emigrated this year.—

Part of my information I have from the unfortunate Wretches who have come over, and from finding themselves deceived, are more anxious to return, than they originally were to come out.— Near one hundred have at different periods made application to me for passages home, which was not in my power to grant; I have however given three Welshmen passages in the Prince Earnest Pacquet, in the hope, that on their return they will by their representations effectually prevent any more of their Countrymen from giving faith to these wicked representations.

About two months since I received correct information that a society was established in this City for the purpose of communicating with His Majestys Subjects in Great Britain & Ireland, in order to render them dissatisfied with their situation, to encourage them to attempt a revolution and in the event of that not succeeding to draw these over to this Country. Cheetham [1] an Englishman, the Editor of a newspaper, John Woods,[2] who had taught drawing in the University at Edinburgh, and a John Thomson, Scotchman were at the head of this junto.— About this period I received a note from a person who signed himself " an Englishman "; and wishing to give the person the information he desired, I advertised requesting him to call on me.—Woods instantly took the alarm, and suspecting that I had discovered the designs of his Society; got himself introduced to me, by a person who taught

[1] James Cheetham, at this time editor of the American Citizen and Watchtower.

[2] John Wood was born about 1755; emigrated to America in 1800, and died in 1822. He is best known as the author of the scurrilous History of the Administration of John Adams.

my children. His confession was full as to the original design of the institution, but he assured me, it was discontinued — For the moment I suppose it was, but I have no doubt it is again in operation and with increased violence and malignity against His Majesty and the Government. I take the liberty to inclose your Lordship two news papers, the consequences of Woods calling on me. The representations contained in the first with respect to myself are generally devoid of truth. Your Lordship will observe that Cheetham altho' he denies the Society having ever commenced their operations, fully avows what was intended.— These publications as well as private letters on political Subjects are forwarded in Ships bound to different Ports in Scotland. And I should suppose that a mode might be adopted by Government to possess themselves of some of them.—

TO BRIGADIER-GENERAL FULLER, GOVERNOR OF THE
ISLAND OF ST. CROIX.

Consul Generals Office 17 Septr 1801.

SIR.

In reply to your favor of the 16th of August delivered to me by Mr Farrell, I am sorry to inform you that I have not been able to discover the Person who carried to the Printers the Extract of the Letter from St Croix and which was published in the New York Gazette of the first of July.[1]

[1] The publication referred to is a Letter to a New York Gentleman from a Friend in St. Croix. " Since I left you at New York," says the friend, "we have had a great change in our Government. On the British fleet taking possession, I was in hopes that they intended to act with moderation; but (it seems) it was only to find out the real state of people's property, so that they might the more promptly fall on a plan to deprive every person of as much as they could lay their hands on. The General has been committing one act of violence after another for several weeks," etc.

St. Croix was taken by a British fleet under command of Admiral Duckworth on March 5, 1801. Being very ill prepared for resistance, the island was surrendered without opposition. It was restored to the Danish Government under the Treaty of Amiens in 1802.

Upon interrogating Mr Lang the Editor he told me that the Gentleman who gave him the extract was a Stranger and supposing it contained nothing peculiarly offensive, but rather matters of dispute under the treaty, he had published it. Mr Lang added that the person who brought the extract was attended by a lame Gentleman as I take it for granted this must have been Counsellor Benson, or Nelson, I never could distinguish the names between him and the Judge who both came from St Croix to this place —

I have spoken very severely to the Printer, and assured him it was more than probable he would be prosecuted as he either would or could not ascertain the Author. He is not a little alarmed, and has promised me to be more guarded in future.— I do not however think either a private action or an indictment against Lang would be attended with damages which would afford any satisfactory pecuniary punishment.—

The American presses are licentious in the extreme and the spirit of the Constitution tends the reverse of a check on them.

TO VICE-ADMIRAL LORD HUGH SEYMOUR, JAMAICA.

Consul General's Office for the
Eastern States of America 23 Septr 1801.

MY LORD —

It is always with extreme reluctance that I make application to any of His Majestys officers of the Navy for the discharge of American Seamen impressed through mistake into service, from a conviction that where we have one American in our Service there are fifty British Seamen serving in American Ships—

Instances however occur where humanity pleads so strongly in favor of persons impressed, that it would be doing violence to my feelings not to state their case, and intercede in their Behalf—The favor I am now to ask of your Lordship is of that description.

Jonas Hamilton a native and Citizen of the United States of America, a ship carpenter by trade and a resident in this

City, was advised for the recovery of his health to take a voyage, and being a poor man shipped as a Sailor on board the Ship Hercules, William Sutherland Master then bound for Curaçao — On the second August Hamilton was taken from on board the Hercules at Curaçao by a party from His Majestys ship the Quebec, carried on board her and detained as a Seaman when Cap' Sutherland came away — Hamilton has an aged Mother a Wife and two infant Children, dependent on his labor — he is 29 years of age, about five feet ten or eleven Inches in height and has a small Wen on one Ear and of a fair Complexion — Was born at Braintree, in the State of Massachusetts.

Permit me my Lord to intreat in behalf of the mother Wife and Children that you will have the Goodness to order that he may be discharged His Majestys Service, and that should he have been transferred to any other ship under your command, you will have the Goodness to direct the order to the officer Commanding for his release.[1]

TO H. R. H. THE DUKE OF KENT.

New York, 10ᵗʰ Oct' 1801.

SIR, ·

I intreat your Royal Highness will be pleased to accept my grateful acknowledgements for your most gracious and friendly letters of the 13ᵗʰ and 18ᵗʰ of July received a few days since by the Lady Hobart packet. Permit me at the same time to assure your Royal Highness that I am duly sensible of the interest you take in my son's promotion, and of your co-operation with Lord Hawkesbury in effecting His Majesty's permission for my coming to England and leaving my eldest son to transact the Business of my office.— I have for many

---

[1] A very large part of Barclay's correspondence was taken up by the ever-troublesome question of impressment. Only a few of his many appeals on behalf of Americans un- lawfully seized are here printed, for he was always ready to urge the release of any man who could produce evidence of being a native-born American citizen.

9*

reasons resolved not to avail myself of His Majestys leave of absence until the Month of March, when I shall embark for England. The possibility of a peace before that period is one of my reasons for not coming more early.[1]

I sincerely congratulate your Royal Highness on the recovery of His Majesty and am happy to hear from your pen that his health is better than it has been for some years past.— May God long preserve him a comfort to his family and a blessing to his Subjects.

The Vice Courts of Admiralty beyond all doubt required a great reform and under this impression I took the Liberty to communicate my opinion last Winter to Lord Grenville on the Subject of the captures and condemnations of American Vessels.— It is true the American merchants by contraband trade, and conveying Enemy's property, have given just cause to suspect that every one of their Ships were laden in part or the whole contrary to the Law of Nations and the existing treaty; still suspicion alone was not a sufficient cause for capture and detention, much less of eventual condemnation. By the present act of Parliament[2] these courts are now placed on so respectable a footing that while His Majesty's rights and those of the officers and men of the Navy are amply secured; the property of foreigners will be preserved sacred so long as they continue to remove it conformably to law.— Dr. Cook[3] whom your Royal Highness names as the Gentleman appointed for Halifax, I take for granted is an able civilian and one who will give universal satisfaction.

I sincerely lament that my amiable and worthy friend Sir John Wentworth is to be removed from his Government. The measure I fear will break that good man's heart.— A more zealous faithful Subject never existed; but I fear he may have been as inattentive to the expenditure of public money as of

---

[1] The preliminaries of peace were signed in October, 1801, the Treaty of Amiens, March 25, 1802.

[2] 41 Geo. III, Chap. 96.

[3] Alexander Croke, LL. D., is the person intended. He was a man of great ability and force of character, and exercised his powers with unsparing severity in condemning American vessels brought before him as prizes. His decisions are collected in Stewart's Reports.

his own.— His natural Benevolence has ever rendered him a dupe to designing men; and I have more than once intreated him to give an absolute negative in the first instance to improper applications.— His interference with the Maroons I protested against in the warmest terms, and if Sir John will revert to my letters when the maroons arrived in Nova Scotia he will find that what I then predicted has actually come to pass.— Still I believe his hands are clean, however negligent he may have been as to expenditures; and although I condemn the measure of his ever having had anything to do with them; I am satisfied, the location was judicious for their establishment.[1]

I took the Liberty to forward to your Royal Highness by the last Packet, a political Pamphlet, which I considered well written. I have now the Honor to inclose you the answer to it under the signature of Leonidas —— You will scarce have patience to run over this miserable performance. It is supposed to be the production of a Scotchman of the name of Wood, who was obliged to fly Great Britain to avoid a prosecution.

Mrs. Barclay requests your Royal Highness' acceptance of her most respectful regards, and desires me to add that she feels herself greatly flattered by finding you still hold her in remembrance.

TO GENERAL DE LANCEY.

New York 2nd Decr. 1801.

MY DEAR SIR,

By the promotions Stated in the London Gazette of the 5th of Septr. I learn that my son De Lancey Barclay has been re-

---

[1] Barclay's fears for Sir John were unfounded, for he continued Governor of Nova Scotia until 1808, when he was retired upon a pension. The Maroons here referred to were removed from Jamaica in 1796. They were at first lodged in tents near the City of Halifax and employed by the Duke of Kent in working upon the fortifications, where the Maroon Bastion still commemorates them. They were then colonized at Preston, where they were supported at very great expense by the Government of Jamaica; but this aid being withdrawn they suffered great privations during the cold winters of the province, and were finally, in 1800, removed to the more congenial climate of Sierra Leone. See Haliburton's Nova Scotia, Vol. II, p. 282; Dallas's History of the Maroons.

moved from the 41 Regt. to a cornetcy in the 17ᵗʰ Light Dragoons.[1] I am satisfied he owes this promotion wholly to your kindness, and am gratefully sensible of this continued testimony of your friendly disposition to me and mine. He is at present at Montreal in Canada with the 41ˢᵗ Regᵗ I have written to him informing him of his promotion and to Lᵗ General Hunter, requesting that he may have leave to come to New York in his way to England to join his Regiment. He will therefore leave this in February or March; not a moment shall be lost.—I can confidently assure you my dear Sir, that an acquaintance with my Son, will satisfy you that your good offices have not been improperly bestowed on him.— I hope to embark with him for London. By this conveyance I send you two Barrels best Newtown pippins, which I hope will arrive in good order—They are addressed to Brook Watson Esqʳ & Co.— Present Mrs. Barclay's and my best regards to Mrs. and Miss DeLancey.

TO MR. BROUGHTON.

New York, 13ᵗʰ Decʳ 1801.

Sɪʀ.

Your favor of the 11th Decʳ covering the bill of laden and accᵗ of the Statutes at large, which you have had the Goodness to ship me, also the certificates of the two half tickets in the State lottery I recᵈ by the Harlequin Packet—Accept my thanks for the trouble you have taken—I shall make no remarks on the quarterly amount you receive for me, waiting your answer to my letter on that subject, farther than to observe it appears less than my predecessor's, while my situation requires at least the same; for two reasons—First because the price of every article of Life is greatly enhanced and secondly from my seeing more company in a month, than Sir John Temple did in a year.—The latter is not from inclina-

[1] General De Lancey was Colonel of this Regiment. De Lancey Barclay's Commission as Cornet bears date August 29, 1801, and he was promoted to be Lieutenant in the same Regiment on July 9, 1802.

tion, but with a view to further His Majestys Service — of the propriety of which every days experience convinces me—I will thank you to hint this to Mr Hammond, in the Event of my present allowance being less than Sir John Temples. I do not under the present circumstances of the Nation wish it more. But rest assured my annual expenses exceed £2200 Sterling per annum; and yet economy presides in my family.—

Mr. Jefferson as you will perceive is President — The federal party, I mean the moderate ones are much pleased with his Speech, and augur a happy administration.—I wish their expectations may be realized — The better informed consider it vox et preteria nihil—

TO DANIEL COXE, LONDON.

New York 4th February 1802.

MY DEAR SIR

By the Brothers I replied to your favor of the 14th of October. I at the same time informed you, that I had consulted with all my Law friends in this City, who agreed in opinion with me, that there was not the most remote possibility of any success to an application of M^m Beverley Robinson for a compensation for her right of Dower in Lands in this State; or for lands which she owned in fee.— M^m Robinson, as well as many other feme coverts were attainted with their Husbands in the Act of this State passed in 1776,[1] and the disposition of the Legislature has ever been not to open a door for claims under that Act.— In addition to this M^m Kempes and M^m Margaret De Lanceys present claims (with those of many others) have so alarmed the people of this State, as to render it a subject worthy of notice in the Governors speech at the opening of the

---

[1] The act of October 22, 1779, is intended. Mrs. Beverly Robinson, her sister Mrs. Roger Morris, and Mrs. Inglis,—wife of the then rector of Trinity Church,—were attainted under this act. This is believed to be the only case, here or in England, in which women were attainted of high treason, and banished and threatened with death.

present Session of the Legislature.[1] What the event will be I
dare not predict — I hope favorable, but both M[rs] Kempes and
M[rs] De Lanceys Council advise a composition at almost any
rate rather than proceeding with our suits at Law and now at
Issue. They apprehend that when these causes are brought up
before the Court of Errors that the Senate will reverse the
Judgement of the Supreme Court, and declare that a Wife of
an attainted person cannot recover her Dower. We have also
ascertained that the Attorney General has Legislative orders
to throw every possible obstacle in the way, and to contend
inch by inch with us.— I hope before I leave this, which will be
by the next Packet, that something will be done by the Legislature, and on reasonable principles. I send you the paper
containing the Governors Speech. Have the goodness to communicate the purport of this to your amiable Sister. I would
write her by this Packet, but I dread the task, as I should be
under the necessity of mentioning the loss of my worthy
friend Captain Church. Whose memory will ever be dear to
many of his friends in America, as well as in Great Britain.

TO MRS. MARGARET DE LANCEY.

New York 6th February 1802.
MY DEAR MADAM

By the advice of your Council M[r] Harrison and General
Hamilton (as mentioned in my letter to you of the 4th of Dec[r])
M[r] Colden proceeds for Albany to make one more attempt for
an amicable composition with the Legislature of this State

[1] " The claims of dower by widows of attainted persons have assumed so serious an aspect, that the
commissioners appointed by law for
their liquidation and settlement,
deemed it expedient at the last session to submit them to the decision
of the legislature; and as nothing
was definitely arranged at that period, a great number of suits have
been commenced against persons
deriving title from the state. While
the honor of the state demands that
all proper claims should be satisfied,
an attention to public economy
equally requires that the treasury
should be guarded against improper
or fraudulent demands." Governor
Clinton's speech, January 26, 1802.

now sitting in that City; previous to our inquiring the amount of your Dower in the trial of the issues now joined between you, and several of the tenants.—Inclosed is the Governor's speech at the opening of the session—; in which he makes specific remarks on the claims and suits now made and depending by widows of attainted persons for lands in this State. It is impossible from the mode in which he expressed himself to ascertain whether it is his opinion that an equitable allowance should be made in extinguishing the claims for dower. Gentlemen in this place think he is inclined to an opposite line of conduct—Mr Colden however proceeds with every necessary instruction, and letters to many of the leading members on both sides in the house.—

I lament that Mr Brockholst Livingston[1] has vacated his seat, by accepting the appointment of Judge in the Supreme Court, as he had promised me his interest in obtaining you justice—He will however deliver his sentiments to the leading Members and recommends their making reasonable compensation—

I hope to have it in my power to write you in a few weeks that your business is terminated satisfactorily, but I cannot say I am sanguine in my expectations.—

FROM MR. COLDEN.

Albany 17 February, 1802.
My dear Sir

On my arrival at this place I found that the Legislature had anticipated the application I was about to make to them, and have by a resolution originating with Mr. De Witt Clinton in the Senate almost shut out every hope of compromising with the State on any Terms whatever—By the resolution I have mentioned the Senate have directed the Attorney General to bring before them by writ of error any judg-

[1] Appointed this year a Judge of the New-York Supreme Court. In 1807 he was appointed one of the Justices of the Supreme Court of the United States.

ment that may be pronounced in favor of the claims of Widows.—We may say that Mr. Clinton was lost to all kind of delicacy when by an order of this sort he shewed his anxiety to pass judgement on the point to be brought before him—We may say that this resolution discovers an eagerness very inconsistent with the dignity of a Senate, and with an intention to be upright and impartial judges—Mr. Clinton might be told that by resisting the judgement of the Supreme Court in favor of the Widows he was persecuting the inocent for the sake of his ambition, and to purchase an infamous popularity by the few thousand dollars that may be saved to the state thro his machinations—But all those reproaches would be in vain. I think that Mr. Clinton and the majority of both houses which he governs absolutely, are men utterly void of feeling and honor—Is it right? or wrong? are questions that never occur to them in the consideration of a measure—when it is ascertained whether it will be popular or otherwise, it is determined—

Finding that the board would not move a step in the business of Mrs. De Lancy I yesterday presented a memorial to the house of assembly—In which I stated that she was desirous of compromising with the State on terms the most favorable to them, and I endeavored to rouse the sympathy & justice of the house and a concern for the honor and reputation of the nation, as well as of the individual members who compose its Legislature—Yesterday, altho it was introduced in a very handsome manner by my friend Mr. Henry, nothing was done with this. What will be its fate it is difficult to say but I think there is hardly anything to be hoped—

I am &c CADWALLADER D. COLDEN.

FROM MR. COLDEN.

Albany 17th. February 1802.

MY DEAR SIR:—

Since I wrote to you yesterday the business that I am upon I think wears a more favorable aspect—I have had an opportunity of conversing with most of the influential members in the Legislature on either side and hope I have made an impression on their minds propitious to our cause — A committee has been appointed before which I have appeared and I am again to meet them to-morrow — And I have reason to hope that they will make a report more favorable than I a few days since expected to obtain — Tho it will by no means meet the justice of the claim — If such a report should be made, and should meet with serious opposition in the house, I have instructed my friends to ask permission for the claimants to be heard by counsel at the Bar.

Notwithstanding all I have said you must not be too sanguine as to my success — If you could know of what strange materials our present honorable legislature is composed you w^d easily believe that it is difficult to calculate upon their acts — Yet I verily believe that unless the Widows are successful in this mode, they can not expect it by other means. For the resolution of the Senate which I mentioned to you yesterday is too sure an evidence of the spirit with which the Court of Errors would hear their cause.

FROM MR. COLDEN.

New York March 25th, 1802.
Dear Sir:

Agreeably to your request I proceed to give you some account of what I have been doing at Albany in relation to the claims of Mrs. Kempe and Mrs. Delancy.

The releases which I herewith send you to be executed by Mrs. Kempe will sufficiently explain the bargain, I have made in her behalf with the State. It is to be understood however, that Mrs. Kempe has it entirely in her power to agree to this offer on the part of the State, or not as she may think proper. If she does not agree the various suits that have been instituted may be prosecuted — It must also be remembered that the costs of these suits are to be paid out of the sum mentioned in the release.

By far the greater part of the lands mentioned in the paper entitled a Schedule of the real estate of the late John Taber Kempe, Esquire are situated in the State of Vermont.

Taking this into consideration and also the disposition of our present rulers I think Mrs. Kempe certainly ought to accept this sum. Altho I am perfectly satisfied that it is not more than ⅓ of the real value of her dower.[1]

As to Mrs. Delancy's affairs I wish the information I have to give you was more satisfactory than what I can now offer you.

It will be unnecessary for me to repeat a detail of the circumstances that occurred last winter. It will be sufficient to say that what was then done satisfied us that all application to the board instituted for the purpose of Extinguishing Claims of this sort would be in vain. They have said that the amount Mrs. Delancy demanded was far beyond what the legislature had in view, when the power of this board was delegated And therefore they refused to act and referred us to the legislature. Of course all my applications this winter have been to that body. I was not a little surprised soon after my arrival in Albany to find a resolution brought forward in the Senate requiring the Attorney General to bring before the Court of Errors all judgments that had been or should be rendered in favor of the right of Dower of the widows of persons whose estates had been confiscated. You know the Court of Errors is composed of the very persons who as Senators passed this resolution. And it is a sufficient indication of what would be the event of the Causes which they manifest such a desire to have before them.

I presented a memorial to the Assembly which was committed to three Gentlemen two of them leaders of the political parties in the Legislature. After an attendance on this Committee of more than four weeks, in which time I made it a point to meet them or at least to see one of them every day, I was, after an absence from my office and family so much longer than I expected when I left them, obliged to return be-

---

[1] The sum for which Mrs. Kempe's claims were released, after deducting all counsel fees and expenses, amounted to $5713.39.

fore I could bring them to make any report upon the subject. I however had made them several propositions and obtained a promise that they would report in a few days.

I left the business in charge of Mr. Emott who is a partner of Mr. Henry one of the Committee. I am convinced Mr. Emott will attend to the business. And I hope I shall hear from him before you leave us.

I am &c.   CADWALLADER D. COLDEN.[1]

TO LORD HAWKESBURY.

New York 2d April, 1802.

MY LORD,

By the Packet which arrived last Evening I was honored with your Lordships letter of the 13th of February, in which you request my opinion, whether in the present state of the commercial intercourse between His Majestys Dominions and the United States, it is expedient to make a permanent Establishment of a Vice Consulship at New Port in the State of Rhode Island.—

Rhode Island is the second smallest state in the Union, possessed of but few seaports, and carrying on a very limited Commerce when compared with most of the other States; the appointment therefore of a Vice Consul to that State appears to me far from necessary taking the official duty simply into consideration. The Eastern part of the State of Connecticut,

[1] Here we take leave of Mrs. De Lancey and her claims. On April 5, 1802, the Assembly passed a resolution in favor of a compromise; and as Barclay was then on the point of sailing for England, he procured a letter from Harison advising a settlement. While in England Barclay succeeded in persuading Mrs. De Lancey to accept a moderate sum, and on January 31, 1803, while he was still abroad, $34,000 was offered. This amount was fixed by a report of the Commissioners,—the Comptroller, Attorney-General, and Surveyor-General of the State,—and was duly approved by the Governor. Mrs. De Lancey gave a release of all her claims and accepted the money, though not without vigorous grumbling at Mr. Colden's bill, which was only paid after the matter had been submitted to the arbitration of General Hamilton and Mr. Harison.

would be a preferable situation for the residence of a Vice Consul, within the Limits of whose Jurisdiction Rhode Island may be included — New London should be the place of his residence, a central position in the State, distant only sixty miles from Providence in Rhode Island, and one hundred and forty from this City.— I cannot however my Lord add that I even consider a consular appointment necessary for Connecticut.— In a political point of view there can be no question, but that Consuls or Vice Consuls in both these States, if Men of Prudence and engaging manner, might forward His Majestys Interests, and predispose the Inhabitants in favor of the British Government. In this point of view if only one Vice Consul is appointed, Rhode Island is the State, and New Port the place for his residence — During the Summer Season New Port is crowded with the most fashionable influential Characters from Maryland to Georgia, who go thither for the recovery of their health or to avoid the prevailing summer epidemics of a southern climate. A consul therefore resident in New Port would have an opportunity of becoming acquainted with the first Characters in America : and by gaining on their confidence naturally lead them to think favorably of the country he represents —

CHAPTER IV

CONSUL-GENERAL, 1803-1804

ABOUT April 10, 1802, Colonel Barclay, with his son De Lancey, embarked on the packet for England, touched doubtless at Halifax, and in due season reached his destination. It was his first visit to England, and it must have been full of pleasure and interest. He had many old friends and connections among the American loyalists who still survived; he was favorably known to the official world; and he met with a warm welcome from his distant relatives, the Barclays of the well-known banking and brewing firms in London. Unfortunately his correspondence for this period has not been preserved, but we get one glimpse of him through the official correspondence of the American minister. Madison, writing to Rufus King in June, 1802, had instructed him to endeavor to negotiate a treaty for settling the remaining questions relative to the boundary between the two nations, and especially those in regard to the islands in the Bay of Passamaquoddy. On February 28, 1803, King wrote from London that by Lord Hawkesbury's desire he had conferred with Colonel Barclay on the subject, and as the result of the conversation saw nothing to impede a settlement.[1]

On April 4, 1803, Barclay left London, and on May 21, after "an ordinary passage of six weeks," reached

[1] Amer. State Papers, For. Rel., Vol. II, p. 590.

New-York, and found his wife and such of his children as were at home all in good health. But they were anxiously awaiting the return of Beverley, the fourth son, who had gone South to avoid the rigors of a New-York winter. He had developed during the previous year serious symptoms of a pulmonary complaint, and had now been spending several months in South Carolina,—probably with his aunt, Mrs. Izard. The change of climate had, however, come too late. On June 5th he arrived in New-York in the last stages of consumption, and died on the 15th of the same month, being then not much more than sixteen years of age. "He was," said Barclay, writing to a friend, "one of the most amiable and promising of children, who never had rendered censure or admonition necessary, and whose application to his studies, added to more than ordinary natural abilities, gave me every reason to hope he would have made a distinguished literary character. You who are a Parent and blessed as I am with the best and most lovely of Children can feel for Mrs. Barclay and myself under this severe affliction."

The threatening aspect of the relations between England and the United States, however, soon came to divert Barclay's thoughts and claim his most serious attention. On May 16, while he was still at sea, war had again been declared between England and France, and Napoleon at once began his preparations for an invasion of England. The war was, however, mainly carried on at sea, and especially in the West Indies, where St. Lucie, Tobago, and Dutch Guiana were taken by the British forces, and the French islands were blockaded. The export of French sugars and other colonial products was a trade which the British government particularly sought to break up; and their courts held that such goods, if found in transit on a neutral ship, rendered the vessel as well as the cargo liable to condemnation. British squadrons were therefore kept constantly cruising off the coast from Massachusetts Bay to the capes of Virginia, searching one American vessel after another in the effort to find some pretext for putting a prize crew aboard and ordering her off to the Admiralty Court at Halifax. Above all, the impressment of seamen went on more vigorously than ever.

Under these circumstances, the post of British Consul in New-York became every day more delicate and important. Hardly an American vessel came in but had been searched by an English frigate, and had had men taken from her decks. On the other hand, every British ship that entered the harbor lost men by desertion. The great majority of the population openly sympathized with the French cause, and the authorities made no pretense of trying to assist in recovering deserters. As yet there was no open outbreak; but with every English frigate that took up her station off the Hook,—or, worse still, that came up to the Narrows,—there was the hourly chance of some provoking insult or reckless act of violence, that might bring about an actual collision.

Jerome Bonaparte's presence in the United States added another object for the watchfulness of the English naval force, and was another source of anxiety to the British Consul.

How Barclay steered his difficult course in these troubled times may be judged from the letters which follow.

He continued to live in New-York; but from August 20 to October 31, 1803, the prevalence of yellow fever

compelled him to remove with his family to Westchester. On the very day that the family removed to the
country, Susan, the third daughter, was married at St.
Mark's Church to Peter Gerard Stuyvesant,— a young
gentleman of excellent family and a genteel fortune.[1]

TO VICE-ADMIRAL SIR ANDREW MITCHELL.

New York 22 July, 1803.

(Private.)

It is with regret that I am under the necessity of informing
you that the Pilots of New York are to a man inclined rather
to favor the french, than the English, being of the description
termed in the Politics of America, democrats and not federalists. I mention this that you may caution the officers under
your command in the event of their being off this place not to
give credit to anything they may say, but to act from their
own Judgment and discretion.— There is a man of the name
of Daniel, lately dismissed the Service of Pilot, under the pre-
tence of his Having run the American Frigate Boston on
Shore, but in reality because he was a federalist and much attached to our Government — He was the oldest and best Pilot
in New York, and I think may be of Service if employed to
obtain private information by associating with the Pilots —
The Spanish Brig and French Ship which arrived here at the
time the Lilly was off the Hook, have sold their Cargoes in
this City, and the Ship is up for sale — I have not yet been
able to ascertain whether the other French Ship will after
she is repaired take in her cargo and proceed for France. Of
this I will give you the earliest notice —
Several Seamen have engaged with me to join your Squad-

[1] He was directly descended from
the last of the Dutch governors; and
his mother was Margaret Livingston,
a granddaughter of Robert Livingston, the first Lord of the Manor.
Mr. Stuyvesant was born in 1778,
graduated at Columbia College in
1794, and died without issue in 1847.

ron, and if they continue of the same mind they shall be sent in the Earl of Leicester Packet — I have desired Captain Sharpe of the Packet to send his Boatswain and a few good men on shore to endeavor to recruit Seamen.

TO LORD HAWKESBURY.

New York 29ᵗʰ July, 1803.

My Lord.

I have received correct information of Jerome Bonaparte having arrived from the West Indies to these States, and that he was in Baltimore on the 27ᵗʰ Instant; his wish is to get to France; he travels under an assumed name, and is very apprehensive of being taken by some of our ships of War in his way home.— He has talked of coming on from Baltimore to this city in order to embark; but the well known Commodore Barney [1] having taken him to his house in Baltimore, it is suspected that he will persuade him to take his passage from thence; at all Events it is uncertain from what port he may sail.—

I take the Liberty to give your Lordship a description of him and his companions and attendant, that you may if you think it of moment have it communicated to the officers of the Navy should they fall into their hands.— Jerome Bonaparte appears to be from twenty to twenty three years of age,[2] of a slender make and sallow complexion, about 5 feet 6 or 7 Inches in height.— His hair is cropped black and smooth, but at times he adds a que and powder. There are two Gentlemen who travel with him. The first about 30 years of age, dark complexion, short curly dark hair, marked a little with the small pox and has bad upper teeth, in height about 5 feet 9 or 5–10. The second is of the same stature fair complexion thick, bushy, sandy or reddish hair, marked also a little with the small pox;

---

[1] Joshua Barney was born in 1759, and died in 1818. He was in the United States Naval Service during the Revolution, was at times a privateer, and was accused by the English of piracy. From 1794 to 1800 he served in the French Navy.

[2] He was born November 15, 1784, and was therefore not quite nineteen years old.

has on his left ear a remarkable mole, immediately where an ear is perforated for a ring.— They pass under feigned names. Jerome Bonaparte— assumes that of Dalbert, or D'Albert. The first described of his Companions calls himself Armand, and the other is styled Alexander. I should not however be surprized if they again changed their names. A Servant of about 24 years, 5 feet 8 or 9 Inches attends them, his complexion and hair dark, the latter long and worn in a que. He wears Earrings.[1]

Should they come to this City, I will exert every nerve to find out the precise time of their sailing, and lay a plan to have them taken.— The above information shall be forwarded to Sir Andrew Mitchell at Halifax.

TO MR. HAMMOND.

New York 3ᵈ October, 1803.
SIR.

I have the Honor to lay before you the following statement for the information of Lord Hawkesbury, and in the event of his considering it of sufficient moment, that he may transmit the same to the Lords Commissioners of the Admiralty.

Nathan Haley an American citizen,— Master of the American Ship Hare sailed from London in the year 1797 for New York; but instead of proceeding for that place, he fraudulently carried the Ship into Dieppe, in the hope of having her condemned to him as a prize, he being at that time invested with a commission in the French Service. The Cargo and probably the Ship was insured in London, and there is reason to suppose Mʳ Isaac Classon the owner of the Ship was not ignorant of Haleys intention. The Underwriters in London have long since paid the amount assured.

[1] Jerome at this time had with him M. Meyronnet, a Lieutenant in the French Navy; a private secretary, M. Le Camus; a physician; and a young man named Rewbel, who afterward rose to the rank of General in the French Army. See Ducasse, Les Rois Frères de Napoléon I.

Haley is now on the point of sailing in a small ship named the Brutus; her description is inclosed, and it is generally supposed with a view to capture British merchant ships — It is given out that she is bound for the West Indies, but if Tom Paine goes a Passenger with him, I am rather apt to think they will proceed to France, and after landing Paine, that Haley will cruize on the English coast to be near a port to send his Prizes. From the construction of this Ship, Haley can have no other object in view, because as a Merchant vessel, she carries very little, and her expenses are great. Haley is a Native of Stonington Town in Connecticut. His person can easily be identified here and in London, and the original letter from him to Isaac Classon (a copy whereof I have the Honor to inclose) is in the possession of the Underwriters at Lloyds, their attornies, or the agents of the assured on that Ship and Cargo, as it was sent home to enable the assured to recover from the Underwriters.— The ship is supposed to be Nathan Haleys property, altho' the Sea letter is taken out in his Brothers name. It is not yet ascertained whether Haley will command her or not, but he will assuredly go in her.—Should she be met by any of His Majestys ships of War, on examination I trust she will be found a lawful Prize; at all Events Haley and Thomas Paine should be made Prisoners & committed for Trial. The former as an American Subject, having a french commission in 1797, and by virtue of that carrying British Property into an Enemies Port; the latter as a British Subject in the Service of France in the last War.— I have communicated the preceding to Vice Admirals Sir Andrew Mitchell, and Sir Thomas Duckworth.—

Permit me also to submit for the consideration of His Majestys Ministers, the propriety of prohibiting during the present war the exportation of Gun powder to these States as an article of merchandize; three fourths of which is sent from hence if not direct, at least through the Danish and Spanish Islands to the french settlements in the West Indies. A Pilot boat is now on the point of sailing for Saint Croix ladened with powder, with one tier of flour over it.

TO VICE-ADMIRAL SIR ANDREW MITCHELL.

New York, 5 Nov' 1803.

SIR.

I regret that some of our cruizers are not more often in and out of this port, or rather off and on it, communicating with me. Col: Hamilton[1] expresses the same Sentiments with respect to the Chesepeak.—The French Ship which came into the hook early last Summer at the same time with His Majestys Ship the Lilly, sailed about six days since for Bourdeaux with a very valuable cargo, under an American certificate of ownership as the property of a M' John Juhel her name the Eliza, Smith master.—I can prove the reverse of this, and she would have been a safe prize.—A schooner named the Niad will sail the first fair Wind for the West Indies, ladened with a valuable Cargo, and is to be converted into a privateer on her arrival. She is owned by a person named John Cauchois, a frenchman, made a citizen of these States; and a large french Ship now nearly loaded will sail in all next Week for Bourdeaux precisely under the same circumstances. A valuable french Brig and a Schooner have arrived within a few days from the West Indies.

Jerome Bonaparte appears at home in these States, and it is reported that he is soon to be married to a Miss Patterson a Lady of Baltimore with a large fortune.[2]—This City is once more restored to health. Had the Packet sailed on Wednesday, she might have carried my letter giving an account and description of the Eliza for Bourdeaux; but M' Thornton has detained her until this day, and now the Wind is Easterly with every appearance of foul Weather.

---

[1] British Consul at Norfolk, Va.

[2] His marriage-license was issued October 29, 1803. The ceremony was postponed in consequence, it would seem, of the efforts of Pi- chon, the French chargé d'affaires, who pointed out to all parties the invalidity of the proposed marriage under French law. Les Rois Frères de Napoléon I", p. 178.

TO CAPTAIN COCKBURN.[1]

New York 15th November 1803.

(Private.)

DEAR SIR.

I am much pained to learn of the desertion of eight of your men, and of the villainy of the caulker sent down from hence, to work on the Frigate, who shamefully enticed them to desert.—The Lieutenant who came up last Evening with your Letter to the Mayor [2] has reported to you my opinion on this subject. I am from mature reflection confirmed in what I desired him to say to you, towit that the only Measures to be adopted against the caulker, will be at law, as a misdemeanor in attempting to interrupt the Harmony which at present exists between the two Nations. Indeed I am not perfectly clear that even an Indictment will lay.—Mr Harison the ablest Counsel in America, and a Gentleman much attached to Great Britain coincides in opinion with me.—

The best mode to be adopted is to state the facts officially to Mr Merry, and request he will apply to the American Government for a redress of this act of sedition & Conspiracy committed by an American Citizen on board your Ship.—When you have done this, you have performed your duty, and it is more than probable the President will direct the Attorney General to prosecute this man; you will be obliged to have the Quarter Master here as the Witness.—I understand the Mayor will do every thing in his power to recover the deserters and send them to you.

My advice is that you put the Caulker at Liberty without Loss of time. Whatever his Conduct may have been, his detention can be punished.—The Treaty of Amity Commerce & Navigation is silent on this Head.

[1] Afterward Admiral Cockburn, notorious for his share in the burning of the public buildings in Washington. He was at this time in command of H. M. S. Phaeton, in which Anthony Merry, the new British minister, had come over, landing at Norfolk, Va., on November 9th. The Phaeton reached New-York November 10th, in need of extensive repairs.

[2] De Witt Clinton, who had just been appointed upon the resignation of Edward Livingston.

TO VICE-ADMIRAL SIR ANDREW MITCHELL.

New York, 22ᵈ Novʳ 1803.

SIR.

The Prince Adolphus Packet brought me your respective Letters of the 12ᵗʰ and 17ᵗʰ of October.—Jerome Bonaparte arrived here on the 19ᵗʰ current, with an intention, as it is said, of passing the Winter; a circumstance far from improbable, as he appears in full pursuit of matrimony.   While at Baltimore he was twice on the Eve of marriage, unfortunate however for him both matches were broken off either by the Ladies or their friends.   Such are the best accounts from thence.   Inclosed is an anecdote respecting him.[1] — Your letter for Mʳ Stewart has been forwarded to him, he not having yet returned to town owing to the indisposition of his Lady.—

His Majestys Ship Phaeton Capᵗ Cockburn which brought out Mʳ Merry to Norfolk in Virginia, arrived here about ten days since to refit.   Capᵗ Cockburn has lost fourteen men by desertion.   Her destination is secret, at least too much so to trust it in a letter going by a common conveyance.[2]   She will not leave this under ten days, possibly double that period.—

Captain Bradley of His Majestys Ship Cambrian was off this place, the last of September ; and dispatched a Pilot Boat to me with a letter, requesting to be informed, whether the report was correct that the Andromache Capᵗ Laurie was on shore at Cape Hatteras.   I next day returned him an answer, that it never had been credited, and from the period elapsed without further confirmation could not be true.   We have not any news at present.   The French Ship covered by an American Certificate sailed from Bourdeaux on Saturday, her present name the Jane.

Captain Bradley in the Evening of the 1ˢᵗ of October impressed from on board the Ship American Packet, Solomon

---

[1] No copy of the "anecdote" was preserved. It may probably have been a newspaper cutting.

[2] He was to carry out a part of the money payable by the U. S. to Great Britain. See the letter to Merry of December 9, 1803. A part of the money was shipped to Calcutta in the Sir Edward Hughes, belonging to the East India Company.

Swain Master, a Seaman named Thomas Cook, a Citizen of the
States, born at Shrewsbury in New Jersey, or near that place.
He is well known here as a real American Citizen, and I will
thank you to order him to be discharged.

TO LIEUT. GENERAL HUNTER.[1]

New York 2ᵈ Decʳ 1803.

SIR.

Jerome Bonaparte, brother of the first Consul has been some
months in these States, particularly in Maryland.   He arrived
at New York about the 20ᵗʰ Ult° and left it the day before yesterday professedly to return to the Southward.   I have however been informed that it is his intention after passing a few
days in New Jersey, privately to go to Albany, and to communicate with the French in Canada; it is also suggested that
he may probably go to the American Line near Lake Champlain, where a french man named Rous lives, and who is notorious for aiding and harbouring British Deserters from Canada.   MacLean who some years since was executed in Canada
was particularly intimate with Rous.   I have given you this
information to ennable you to keep an attentive Eye on the
Southern limits of Canada.   The information comes from
a Gentleman; who I am confident believes it, yet I confess I
have my Doubts.   Should I learn that he has really proceeded
Southward, you shall have the earliest notice; on the other
hand, if he arrives at Albany you will have advice from
thence.

TO MR. MERRY.

New York 9ᵗʰ Decʳ 1803.

SIR

I have the Honor to acknowledge the receipt by this days
mail of your Letter N° 2 dated the 5ᵗʰ Current, enclosing a bill

[1] Peter Hunter, born in Scotland, 1746; died at Quebec in 1805. He was
Commander of the Forces in Canada.

at sight dated 3[d] December 1803 for eight hundred and eighty eight thousand dollars drawn by Th T Tucker Treasurer of the United States on Jonathan Burrell Esq[r] cashier office Discount and Deposit New York payable to your order, and by your endorsement made payable to me.[1] I have presented the Bill for payment, and the Cashier is ready to make it in the current Money of the United States, whenever I may apply for it. He assures me however that it will not be in his power to convenience me with more than four hundred and fifty or at the utmost five hundred thousand Dollars. The remainder must be in British and Portugal — or French and Spanish Gold by weight. At present Spanish milled Dollars bear a premium of one and one half percent, but admitting that I was authorized to pay the same, I am satisfied that four hundred thousand dollars could not be procured from Philadelphia to Boston at that advance, and that the instant it was known the premium would rise to two and one half percent.— The obtaining of Dollars therefore to the Northward of the Chesepeak, other than from the Bank is out of the question.— I have communicated not only to M[r] Burrell the Cashier but also to M[r] Ray the President my disappointment in the information that the amount of the Bill could not be paid in Spanish milled Dollars, and I learn from them that they have not received any orders or directions, mediately or immediately from the Secretary of the Treasury on this Subject. I suspect an order, or strongly worded request from M[r] Gallatin, would effect the purpose of a payment of the whole in Dollars. —I shall therefore wait your further instructions. The money when received shall be paid over as you have directed, towit four hundred and forty four thousand Dollars to Captain Cockburn and the remaining four hundred and forty four thousand dollars to the Captain who may arrive here duly authorized to receive it.— Equal attention Sir shall be paid to every other part of the directions contained in your letter.—

[1] This was the first instalment of the £600,000 payable by the U. S. to Great Britain under Rufus King's Convention of January 8, 1802, which fixed the indemnity for the debts due to British subjects they had been prevented from collecting in consequence of the Revolution.

The Cashier of the Bank acquaints me that, I may tell the money out at my leisure, and that it may from day to day be redeposited in the Vaults of the Bank, the Boxes under my Seal, but that all sums told and so deposited must be at the risque of His Majesty. This I think but reasonable, I however wish your opinion thereon.

TO DE WITT CLINTON.

New York 29th Dec' 1803.

SIR.

I have the Honor to acknowledge the receipt of your letter yesterday respecting the Seamen of His Majestys Ship Phaeton George Cockburn Esq' Commander now confined as Vagrants in the Bridewell of this City, together with the determination of the Justices of the Police on the subject of their being delivered up to Captain Cockburn — There would be an end to all subordination in His Majestys Navy if Captains were compelled to come to such terms as are proposed by the Justices of Police, as a preliminary promise before the Seamen can be delivered; but this much Sir I can assure both you and them that Captain Cockburn will not bring the men to a general Court Martial, or have them severely punished on board his Ship. I trust therefore as the Men are willing to join their Ship, that the Justices of the Peace will order them to be delivered to Captain Cockburns order.

TO WILLIAM BRAMSTON, CANTON, CHINA.

New York 27 April 1804.

SIR.

M' Waters late Purser in the India Companys Ship Britannia, but now of the Sir Edward Hughes, arrived here in December last to take money on board for Calcutta — On my complaint to him that the Teas in America were of very inferior quality, he tendered me a letter of introduction to you, assuring me that you would have the goodness to send the best to be purchased at Canton — The letter from him I take the Liberty to inclose, and Mr Isaac Bell who goes from hence in the Ship Triton as Super Cargo will deliver to you two hundred and fifty Spanish Dollars — Will you do me the favor to apply one hundred or near that amount in the purchase of a set of table china, a list of which is inclosed — The remainder lay out in equal quantities of black and Green Teas of the first quality to be purchased — I must give you the additional trouble to intreat that a proportion of the black and green tea to the value of fifty dollars may be put up in separate Boxes, being for an old Lady my particular friend, the remainder for my use — Should the China or tea amount to a few dollars more, Mr Bell has my orders to pay it to you.—Mr Bell is a worthy honorable American Gentleman, any attention you may have it in your power to shew him will be doing me a favor.—

If I can render you any Service here it will afford me pleasure — I trust you will pardon the Liberty I have taken.

TO MR. MERRY.

New York 12th May 1804.

SIR,

Captain Douglass of His Majestys Ship Boston left this the day before yesterday at noon, to go on board his Ship at the Hook and proceed to Norfolk in Virginia. I this day received a letter from the President of the marine insurance Company in this City, stating a French Cruizer being off Georgia and South Carolina, committing depredations on British and American ships. Of this I have notified Capt. Douglass. At the same time I was informed of another French Privateer being on the Banks of Newfoundland — By a vessel going to Halifax I shall communicate the above to Vice Admiral Sir Andrew Mitchell.[1]

[1] See letter to Mr. Neilson, September 7, 1804, below.

TO MR. MERRY.

New York 25 May 1804.

SIR,

The Sybille and Dido French Frigates of 44 Guns each arrived here last Evening from Guadeloupe and anchored at the Quarantine Ground about nine miles below the city — I have not yet been able to learn their Business, probable stay or future destination. The moment I am possessed of either you shall receive information —

I have dispatched a letter to Boston, to be from thence forwarded to Sir Andrew Mitchell at Halifax, and will endeavour to hasten the sailing of a vessel for St. Johns, New Brunswick; but both these are circuitous routs.— It is much to be regretted that I am neither authorized by Lord Hawkesbury, or Sir Andrew Mitchell to hire a dispatch boat on such occasions. Perhaps your Excellency may think it proper to direct me to incur the expence on future occasions of moment.

TO MR. MERRY.

New York 1ˢᵗ June 1804.

SIR.

In answer to your letter Nº 12 of the 28ᵗʰ of May, permit to observe that I cannot learn that the Commander of the two French Frigates now in this Port, had any particular object communicated to him for coming here: although I think it probable he had either dispatches for Mʳ Pichon, or directions to receive orders from him. I procured a sensible young Gentleman to get acquainted with the Officers of these Ships, by taking his lodgings in the same hotel where they staid — From them he obtained the following particulars. That the Dido and Sybille Frigates had laid some time in Rockfort ready for Sea before an opportunity offered to escape the vigilance of our Cruizers — That they at length escaped, each ship having 350 Soldiers on board besides Seamen & Marines, also about 40 French men apprehended by order of the first

Consul and privately put on board. Amongst these were three Generals, and other Officers of various Ranks, and a number of editors of newspapers. These were landed at Cayenne as exiles — The Frigates then proceeded to Guadeloupe where about one-half of the land forces were disembarked, and the remainder put on board Privateers and sent to Martinico to reinforce that Garrison. The Ships immediately overhauled their Rigging, took in their water &c. &c and prepared with all haste apparently to return to France — That the officer Commanding gave passages to upwards of a dozen Gentlemen of Guadeloupe to go home in one or other of the Frigates. Having sealed orders on board to be opened on arriving in a certain Latitude, it was found on opening them, that the Ships were to repair to New York for further orders, but what those orders are I cannot learn. The Commanding officer on his arrival proceeded to the Southward and as I suppose to Washington — he is not yet returned. It is said their stay will be short, and I have reason to believe Bonaparte and his Lady will embark on board one of them.[1] The Winds for the last ten days have been unfavorable for the Vessels carrying my letters to Sir Andrew Mitchell — I however hope he will receive them in a day or two. The Frigates are very fine large Ships, particularly the Dido — They have fifteen ports on each Side, carry 18 pounders on the Main, and it is said 18[lb] Carronades on their fore castle and Quarter Deck, in my opinion their Carronades must be heavier. The officers complain of their Men not being expert Seamen, but the Pilot who brought up the Dido, assures me they are better than french Seamen ordinarily are, and that both Ships were worked up in a handsome seaman like manner.

It is not General Ney, but General Rey who has arrived here as Consul General. He is a native of Brittany, and commanded at Rennes — Was universally disliked both by the Civil and Military where ever he had a command — He is represented to me, by a person who knows him well, as a man of a ferocious disposition, violent temper, imperious manner, and much addicted to Liquor — He has brought his Wife, and

[1] Jerome Bonaparte and Miss Patterson were married December 24, 1803.

two or three Children with him and the opinion of the French here is that the first Consul gave him this appointment in order to get rid of him.— He springs from the Dregs of the nation.[1] His Chancellor is said to be a Gentleman of honor, abilities and amiable manners, who was at the head of one of the Civil Tribunals in St. Domingo, and his Secretary is represented in equally favorable colors.

TO MR. MERRY.

New York 5th June 1804.

SIR.

It is generally believed as you will observe it stated in the Gazette of this day that the Dido and Sybile French Frigates are on the point of Sailing, their destination unknown, tho supposed to be for some part in France. I have some reason however to doubt their leaving this place so immediately, or if they should it will be only for a cruize because the provisions ordered by the Agent for those ships were not delivered last Evening — You will also perceive a statement in this days paper that a line of Battle Ship supposed to be the Leander [2] has been seen off and on this port, I learn this report has been circulated in order to detain the Frigates a few days, while a Ship bound on a Contraband Trade to St Domingo made her escape from hence. From the Set of the Winds since I first

---

[1] Antoine Gabriel Venance Rey was born September 22, 1768. He entered the French army as a private in a cavalry regiment some years before the Revolution, obtained a commission in 1791, rose to the rank of General of Brigade in 1793, and after sharing in the defense of Mayence and displaying the greatest vigor against the Vendeans, was made a General of Division. He subsequently commanded in Italy, where he was accused of peculation, but was acquitted by a court martial. He was unfavorable to the Revolution of the 18th Brumaire, and so fell into disgrace, left the army, and accepted the post of Consul-General to the United States. He returned to France about 1808, reëntered the army, served in Spain with some credit, and died in 1836.

[2] Although the Leander played an important part in the battle of the Nile, she was not, strictly speaking, a line-of-battle ship. She was rated at 50 guns.

11

wrote to Sir Andrew Mitchell of the arrival of these Ships, it is improbable that the Letters have more than reached Halifax and impossible he could have sailed from thence and arrived off this Port.

TO VICE-ADMIRAL SIR ANDREW MITCHELL.

New York 15ᵗʰ June 1804.

SIR.

I have the honor to inform you that the Dido and Sybile French Frigates are still in this Port, altho I suspect they are on the point of sailing for France.

Jerome Bonaparte and his Lady arrived a few days since from Baltimore and avow their design of going in one of them probably the Dido as she is the best Ship and infinitely the fastest. I have done every thing in my power to prevent their sailing, by circulating Reports that Ships of your Squadron had been seen off in different directions; and causing persons living on the South side of Long Island to say that two Men of War generally stood in every Night and soon after day light hauled off again. They certainly are much alarmed, and as you will see by the paper inclosed have now two pilot Boats out to ascertain the truth. They have lost a number, upwards of forty of their men by desertion, and I understand the Crews are composed of men of almost every Nation — I was told yesterday by a Person who had it from the pilot, that the Crews were not only sickly, but that many within the last week had been taken Ill of the small Pox. Should this be the Case, I doubt their being able to go to Sea, until they are recovered — Their Ships are very dirty and officers and Men under great fear of meeting our Men of War.

TO MR. MERRY.

New York 18ᵗʰ June 1804.

SIR.

I have the Honor to inform you that His Majestys Ships Cambrian and Driver arrived at Staten Island late in the afternoon of Saturday last—Yesterday I saw Captain Bradley the officer commanding, who informed me he was under orders to proceed to sea the first fair wind.— I received late last Evening a letter from the Mayor of this City, a copy whereof I have the Honor to inclose you, requesting me to detain the Cambrian and Driver for twenty four hours after the departure of the two French Frigates now in this Port and who are ready for Sea.— I have sent Captain Bradley a copy of this Mayors letter, but I apprehend he will not feel himself authorized to remain here a moment after it is practicable for his Ship to go out of the Hook; Vice Admiral Sir Andrew Mitchell having directed him to leave this port the first fair Wind, and to cruise on this coast for the protection of the Merchants Ships belonging to His Majestys Subjects. I wait your directions with respect to the answer I am to send to the Mayor.

TO DE WITT CLINTON.

New York 18ᵗʰ June 1804.

SIR,

I have the Honor to acknowledge the receipt of your Letter of last Evening, informing me that you had received official notice that the Frigates Didon and Cybele belonging to the french Republic, and which arrived in this port the 4ᵗʰ Instant intended to Sail with the first fair Wind and requesting me to detain His Majestys Ships Cambrian and Sloop of War Driver, now also in this port for the space of twenty four hours after the departure of the French Frigates. By this days post I shall forward copy of your Letter to Mᵣ Merry His Majesty's Envoy Extraordinary and Minister Plenipotentiary to these States, and who is now at Philadelphia, and will on the receipt of his answer immediately communicate to you his directions on the Subject. I am however apprehensive that Captain Bradley the Officer commanding His Majesty's Ship of War will not feel himself authorized to comply with any requisition either from Mᵣ Merry or myself respecting his remaining a moment in this port after the Wind will admit of his departure, because his Orders from Vice Admiral Sir Andrew Mitchell direct him to proceed from here on the delivery of his Dispatches, on a cruize for the protection of the trade not only of his Majesty's Subjects, but of that of the people of these States, and which has lately suffered much from the depredations of several French Privateers on this Coast. I am led to believe the Admiral was induced to send these Ships for the above purpose, in consequence of my having transmitted to him the copy of a Letter which I lately received from the President of the Marine Insurance Company in this City stating the Injury the American Commerce had sustained from the predatory Corsairs; and requesting that measures might be taken to protect the American as well as British Commerce from farther Loss.[1] You will from this Statement naturally perceive the urgent necessity Captain Bradley is under to get from hence the moment the Pilot will undertake to carry his Ship down and as Captain Bradley had communicated his intentions to me, prior to the receipt of your Letter, I am of opinion he is entitled to a preference in point of time as to his departure. The French Frigates can avail themselves of the first fair Wind after the sailing of His Majesty's Ships. I am perfectly Sensible of the delicacy of your situation and that of the United States, when Ships of War of contending Nations enter your friendly Ports; and it will at all times afford me pleasure to lessen as much as lays in my power and the good of His Majesty's Service will permit, any embarrassments there may occur by the Ships of War of Great Britain and France lying at the same time in this Port.

' TO MR. MERRY.

New York 19ᵗʰ June, 1804.

SIR.

His Majestys Ship Boston arrived yesterday afternoon at Sandy Hook—In consequence of Captain Bradleys answer to

[1] An extract from this letter having been published in the newspapers, Mr. Neilson, the president of the insurance company, wrote to Colonel Barclay contradicting the assertion that protection to American

me on the subject of the Mayors requisition that His Majestys
Frigates might be detained in this port for the Space of twenty
four hours after the sailing of the French Frigates with the
first fair Wind, that he could not comply being under orders
to go to Sea immediately — The Wardens of the Port have issued an inhibition to the Pilots to carry out either of His
Majestys Ships, a copy of this order I have the Honor to inclose—I have to intreat you will give me your advice and
directions on this point.

TO CAPTAIN BRADLEY, H. M. S. CAMBRIAN.

New York 19th June 1804.

SIR.

The inclosed letter of complaint has this moment been delivered to me — You will observe that the Mayor considers your
boarding the Ship Pitt and impressing from on board that Vessel 18 Men, as an act of illegal violence committed within the
Jurisdiction of the United States.[1] He also complains of the
officers of your ship having obstructed the Lieutenant of the
Revenue Cutter and the Health Physician from doing their
duty; and adds that he has transmitted a statement of facts
to the Government of the United States, in order that they
may take the necessary measures.— I consider it necessary
that you and the officers of your ship make a candid representation of the transaction in order that I may lay the same before His Majestys Minister Plenipotentiary to these States,
who naturally will receive a letter of complaint from the
American Secretary of State.—

I am of opinion that you ought not to have boarded the Ship
or impressed any men out of her.— Having said this it follows

commerce had been asked. Barclay
admitted his mistake (see letter of
Sept. 7, 1804, below), but the erroneous assertion has been perpetuated
to this day. McMaster's Hist. of the
U. S., Vol. III, p. 246.

[1] The Pitt was a British vessel,
and was boarded and searched in
the lower bay by boats from the
Cambrian. The details of this notorious affair fully appear below.

that the men should be restored. What renders this measure the more necessary is that the Quarantine Officer will not deliver the Ship Pitt to the Captain until he musters on board of her all the men who navigated that Vessel.— For your security and my own satisfaction I have taken the opinion of a very able law character in this City, well attached to our Government, who agrees in sentiment with me.— The Language made use of by some of your officers to the Lieutenant of the Revenue Cutter was to say the least highly indecorous — Captain Campbell of the Ship Pitt will deliver you this letter, my advice to you is that the men are delivered up to him.

TO VICE-ADMIRAL SIR ANDREW MITCHELL.

New York 22ᵈ June 1804.

SIR.

His Majestys Ships Cambrian and Driver arrived in this port on this day week, and Captain Bradley unfortunately came up to Staten Island very near to the French Frigates before I knew of his arrival. Early on the following morning I went on board the Cambrian, and recommended his dropping down and coming to an anchor without the Bar and beyond the Jurisdiction of these States, being apprehensive attempts would be made to detain His Majestys Ships until the departure of the French. The Wind at the time was so much a head that the Pilots declined taking charge of them. On my return that evening to town I received an application from the Mayor of this City requesting the detention of the Cambrian and Driver for twenty four hours after the sailing of the French Frigates; provided they departed with the first fair Wind. In reply I informed him that I would lay his request before Mᵣ Merry his Majestys Minister Plenipotentiary and wait his directions, and added that I was apprehensive Captain Bradley, to whom I should transmit a copy of his, the Mayors, letter; would not feel himself authorized to comply with the request, having your orders to proceed to Sea, on the delivery of your dispatches. On Monday the Pilots received by order of the Mayor an injunction from the Port Wardens a copy whereof I now inclose — On that day also Captain Douglass arrived at Sandy Hook with His Majestys Ship Boston, and the next morning the Cambrian and Driver altho' the Wind was a head went down and anchored near the Boston. The French Frigates had unmoored in the hope that a want of Pilots would prevent His Majestys Ship from getting to Sea, but when they perceived them in motion they desisted, and about noon came up nearer to this City where they now lay.— It is suspected they will attempt a passage through Hell Gate and the Sound. But I cannot yield to this opinion from the many difficulties attending it, and from the certainty that our Ships will always have ample time to meet them to the Eastward. Their only chance would be to go to Newport Rhode Island, and thence wait a favorable moment.— Bonaparte had embarked with his Lady and baggage on board the Didon, and both the Ships would have gone to sea the first Wind, had not the Cambrian and Driver arrived. Such however were the apprehensions of the french, that for several days preceding they had officers in two Pilot Boats to the Eastward and Southward of the Hook on the lookout.— If you should resolve to watch their motions, I fear it will prove a tedious blockade. They never will stir while our ships are in sight, and I am led to believe the French Officers are not over anxious to return to France. Their Agent pleasantly remarked a day or two since that he would recommend their being laid up, and providing quarters for the Men during the succeeding Winter.— I have strongly urged Captain Bradley to remove from Sandy Hook Bay his present situation, without the Bar and at least a league from the Shore, to prevent future complaints of a violation of neutral rights.— This remark leads me to a painful and serious subject, on the Evening of Sunday the 17th Instant the British Ship Pitt from Greenoch arrived at Staten Island, which is the quarantine Ground — On her approach she was boarded by the Cambrians Boats, brought to an anchor and fourteen Men impressed from her. While the Cambrians Boats were thus employed the officers of the Revenue and Health officer came alongside of the Pitt to examine her, but they were prevented by the officers and men of the Cambrian.— The next day I received a letter from the Mayor on the subject, a copy whereof I have the Honor to inclose.— You will perceive he has transmitted a copy to his Government, and I have made Mʳ Merry acquainted with the facts. Captain Bradley assuredly has acted imprudently— It was my wish that the men should have been restored, in which event every other matter might have been got over, but in this particular he declines complying with my advice. The consequence is that the Pitt remains at the Quarantine Ground because the Health Officer will not muster the Ships company until these men are returned or give a certificate to entitle her to an entry. On the first of July an additional duty of 2 ¹/₂ per Cent takes place, to which the cargo of the Pitt will be liable unless entered previous to that day, and I fear I shall not hear from Mʳ Merry in time to prevent this inconvenience and expense.— I regret these untoward circumstances, particularly as the accident has happened to a character attached to His Majesty.—

TO MR. MERRY.

New York 23ᵈ June 1804.

SIR

I yesterday received a letter from Mʳ Thornton dated at Philadelphia wherein he informs me of his having received at that place my letters Nᵒˢ 14, 15 and 16 addressed to you, that he had opened them, and forwarded them to you at Washington, where you still remain owing to bad weather and worse roads, and where you would at least continue until the beginning of July.—

With this I have the Honor to inclose you copies of Captain Bradleys letters to me of the 20ᵗʰ and 21ˢᵗ current, and a certificate of the officers of His Majestys Ship Cambrian who boarded the Ship Pitt on Sunday last to impress men. This certificate is intended as a reply to the affidavit of the Lieutenant of the Revenue Cutter, who has deposed that some of the officers of the Cambrian, cursed him and damned the Revenue Laws.

I sincerely regret that Captain Bradley brought the Cambrian and Driver within the Jurisdiction of these States, and particularly that he came up to the Quarantine Ground within half a mile of the French Frigates. The instant I was apprised of it, I went down and begged him to drop without the Hook the moment the Wind would allow — I have also the Honor to inclose you a copy of my letter to the Mayor in answer to his letter requesting the detention of His Majestys Ships for twenty four hours after the departure of the French Frigates, provided they sailed the first fair Wind. I trust you will approve of what I have done, and of the Ships going down to the Hook notwithstanding the Mayors letters to me, or the prohibition of the Port Wardens to the Pilots. His Majestys ships were taken down by their own officers and at a very great risque.— The strong measures taken by the Mayor are I consider as wholly extra official, and pertaining only to the general executive Government of these States; and I am also of opinion that as Captain Bradley had signified his intention of departing to me, many hours before I received the letter of requisition from the Mayor, that he was entitled to a preference in point of departure to the French Frigates. Had the French Ships by accident got under way and passed the Cambrian and Driver I should have held it an infraction of the laws of neutrality for our Ships to have followed them, and had strongly impressed this on the mind of Captain Bradley.— The British Ships are at anchor within the Hook, the French as near this as the Laws will permit. I have pointedly recommended to Captain Bradley his going without the Jurisdiction of these States, and hope whenever wind and weather will permit that he will do it —

It is with pain that I am under the necessity of informing you that he declines complying with my advice to return the impressed men. By the Laws of these States the officers of the Customs cannot enter a ship, until she is regularly inspected by the health officer and has a certificate. The health officers refuse to examine the Ship until all the persons are on board who came in her. She therefore remains at the Quarantine Ground, and must continue there, until either Captain Bradley returns the men, or you obtain an order from the American Government for the Ship Pitt being admitted to an entry — You will perceive that one of the two ought to be done without loss of time, because in addition to every other inconvenience and expense attending demurrage, the prevalence of the yellow fever before the departure of the Pitt might prove a very serious obstruction to her return to Greenoch. I shall address my letters to you until further order to Washington.

TO CAPTAIN BRADLEY.

New York 23ᵈ June 1804.

I received the inclosed Letter from Philadelphia which I have the honor to inclose you. It comes from a Gentleman on whom every dependance can be placed, and may operate as a clue to useful discoveries, because it is probable Jerome Bonaparte will carry with him dispatches from the french Minister, all his own private correspondence his Journals and remarks. I have reason to believe his being made a prisoner by the Officers of His Majesty's Navy would be considered an agreeable circumstance by the Government. Should any Vessel proceed without documents from me you may rest assured there is great cause for particular search and almost a certainty of his being on board. The Trunk so particularly described in the Letter inclosed may be deep in the hold or else where concealed, but the mulatto Boy and Baboon are sure prognostics by which you may know his being on board. You will recollect his Lady goes with him, I should be sorry he escaped us, and I know their utmost cunning will be exerted to do this.— On Monday I hope it will be in my power to give you additional Marks by which you may develop this man. I think I shall have knowledge of every motion he makes. The marshall of the District court called on me about two O Clock P. M. this day and told me he had process against one of your Officers — I advised him to be cautious how he approached your Ship, and after some further Conversation I promised him a letter to you, which letter I inclosed to Captain Douglass and desired him to take it on board the Boston, and let Captain Douglass communicate the purport of his Business to you — I have this moment had my letters returned as he declined going to the Boston before he approached your Ship, and he is gone down — I hope Nothing unpleasant may occur, because I am certain he means well, and to offer no Insult.— The sooner you get beyond the Jurisdiction of these States by anchoring more than a League from the Hook, the better, but while you remain where I left you, every day will produce some unpleasant circumstance. It is hinted to me that the French Frigates intend attempting their way through Hell Gate and the Sound. If they do you shall have early Notice, and your laying over the Bar will enable you always to go to Sea. The attempt to Serve process on your officers through the Marshall of the District Court, is ample proof of the intention of the Mayor and other officers of the Government in this City.— It is a measure I trust which will meet the disapprobation of the American Government.— Let me beg you to admit no one alongside of your Ship, but he who has a letter from me, and then not until you have first read the Letter. When the Boats also come down with your Beef or Water, have them examined before they are permitted alongside of your Ship, too much caution cannot be used. I should not after your determination again touch on the Subject of the Seamen impressed from the Pitt, did I not apprehend that you are ignorant that on the first of July an additional duty of two and an half per Cent will attach on all Merchandize entered at the Customs in this City.— This the Freighters of the Pitt will have to pay, unless she is entered before that day — The more I reflect on the measures of Sunday last respecting the Pitt, the more I am confirmed in my opinion already expressed to you by Letter, that Prudence and Propriety dictate your restoring the men. — Mʳ Merry has been prevented leaving Washington, to this circumstance

the not having answers to my Letters is to be attributed —
To morrow I shall certainly hear from him.

TO MR. MERRY.

New York, 28th June 1804.

SIR.

I have not yet had the Satisfaction to receive an answer
from you to my Letters. I attribute this to the State of the
roads and Bridges rendered by the late violent rains as I am
informed impassable.

By a Clause in the Laws of the United States, a Penalty of
four hundred Dollars is laid on any person who shall be convicted of obstructing the officers of the Revenue in their duty.
Under this Act the Judge of the District Court of the United
States for the State of New York, has granted a warrant or
attachment against Lieut Pigot of His Majesty's Ship Cambrian, and the Marshal went down on Saturday last to serve
it. Captain Bradley received the Marshal, but the process
was not served, owing to Mr Pigot not being on board the
Ship. I understand the Marshall intends making another attempt, of which I have given Captn Bradley Notice — I shall
make no comment on these measures.

The British Ship Pitt from whom the men were impressed,
has at last been released from Quarantine and admitted to an
Entry — Captain Bradley has not however returned the Men,
and the Americans are very warm on this infringement within
their territory.

TO MR. MERRY.

New York 30th June 1804.

(*Private.*)

DEAR SIR —

I could have wished that you had expressed yourself in
stronger terms in your letter to me of the 25 Instant, respecting the necessity and policy of Captain Bradleys returning the

men taken from the Pitt, because it certainly is the only improper act intentionally committed by him and his officers in this unpleasant affair, and I have reason to hope that on the restoration of the men, and a full assurance on the part of Captain Bradley and his Officers that if the Revenue and health officers were obstructed by them in the execution of their duty, it was owing to the opposition they met with from the Passengers on board the Pitt, and that they are sorry for it— Should you agree in opinion with me that the impressment was illegal, having been made in the Port of New York, permit me to request you will urge the restoring of the men in your next letter — Captain Bradley is nearly complete in his Ships company.

With all deferance to your opinion, allow me to say, that let the deficiency of His Majestys Ships with respect to men have been ever so great, it is not a justification for the impressing of men within the Jurisdiction of this State, because by these means their naval powers would be increased, a measure inadmissible in a neutral port; and contrary to the Laws of Nations — Captain Bradleys answer therefore on this point, I trust will be considered by you as irrelevant; and of course that you will not urge the argument with the Secretary of State at Washington — You will pardon me for the Liberty I take in giving you my Sentiments.

Should you however differ in opinion with me, and think proper to urge the necessity of the measure, you may to strengthen your position remark that when the french republican Ship Ambuscade some years since was in this port and prepared to go out to meet His Majestys Ship Boston, that she was publicly permitted by the Governor of this State and Mayor of New York to increase her establishment of men at least one third, by recruiting seamen in this port for that purpose, and that no notice was ever taken of it by the American Government — After the action, the Ambuscade returned into this port, and then extra Seamen were discharged.[1] I shall continue to address my letters to you at Washington until further

[1] The action took place off Long Branch, August 1, 1793. An account of it will be found in McMaster's Hist. of the U.·S., Vol. II, p. 123.

notice — The french Frigates have Cut new Sails and taken pilots on board — still I fear they have no intention of going out — Strong suspicions have been entertained that Bonaparte would embark for Nantz on board the Brig Rolla — of this Captains Bradley and Douglass have notice, with ample private information respecting baggage and other incidental minutia.

TO VICE-ADMIRAL SIR ANDREW MITCHELL.

New York 3ᵈ July 1804.

SIR.

I yesterday had the honor to receive your private letter of the 8ᵗʰ and your public letter of the tenth of June — Herewith is a certificate from me on the points you requested respecting the blockade of Martinique, which I trust will prove satisfactory. Every measure in my power was taken immediately on the arrival of the French Frigates to give you the earliest Notice, but the easterly winds continued without intermission for ten days immediately after their arrival — Captain Lyall's meeting with the American Ship Mary was very fortunate, I regret he did not detain the french Prisoners because from his Statement their conduct was more than suspicious.

My letter to you of the 22ᵈ of June did not get down to Sandy Hook in time for the Driver, I mention this circumstance because you naturally must be surprized at not hearing from me by so direct a conveyance — The Ship Pitt has been admitted to an entry; but the American Government are warmly complaining to His Majestys Minister of the infraction of the Laws of Neutrality and violation of their own Laws by Captain Bradley and his officers — Mʳ Merry has also strongly remonstrated against the violent and illegal measures of the Mayor and Port Wardens by inhibiting the Pilots from taking His Majestys Ships to Sea — A Warrant has issued against Lieuᵗ Pigot from the district Court of the United States for obstructing the Revenue officer in the Execution of his duty — On Friday last[1] as His Majestys Ship Boston was

[1] The 29th of June.

working out to Sea having a Pilot on board, she took the ground (by shooting too far ahead as the Pilot says in his Justification in going about) — It was fortunately low Water, and she again floated in a little more than an hour, without sustaining the least injury — This accident was particularly unfortunate, having acquainted Captain Bradley of the sailing of the American Brig Rolla, in which I had reason to believe two of Bonapartes Servants, were, and did embark with dispatches and probably property — The Rolla went to Sea while the Boston was aground — The Boston has been ever since cruizing off and on this Port, and the Cambrian has probably gone out to join her this day — The french Frigates have Cut new sails, and taken Pilots on board, still there is no appearance of their going out — Their friends suggest that as these Ships were charged with a secret mission to the French Minister to these States, and have now his dispatches on board — they would not be justified in risquing an action — a miserable subterfuge.

Captain Lyall on his way from this impressed some Seamen, amongst whom is a man named Robert Kelly, who I understand is an uncommon fine Seaman and a respectable man — He is from Ireland — His Wife who appears a very decent Woman applied to me to endeavor to effect his discharge — This I refused; she then begged I would intreat you to permit her to come to her husband — I was so pleased with the manners and appearance of the Woman that I assured her I would request for her this indulgence; if therefore you can with convenience transfer this man to your flag ship and permit her to come on board you will do me a favor — She is accustomed to the Sea, and has been more than a year on board with him.

TO CAPTAIN BRADLEY.

New York 25ᵗʰ July 1804

MY DEAR SIR.

Your letter of yesterday with a dispatch for Mʳ Merry I received early this Morning from Peacock's Man — The latter will go to Philadelphia where Mr Merry now is by this day's Post.— Since my last to you, I have consulted with Daniels, formerly the oldest and most experienced Pilot for this Port, but who has been dismissed for his attachment to Great Britain, as I before mentioned to you. He agrees with me that the only sure method to give you at all times early Notice in the Event of the French Frigates going through Hell Gate, will be to have Stevenson below the Narrows between Coney and Long Island where he can lay in safety.— No one need know his business, and he can go and return every tide from Quarter flood to Low Water, because the French Ships if they intend passing Hell Gate must get under way the last of the Ebb, so as to be at Hell Gate at slack Water, or if there is a fresh Westerly Breese it is most safe for them to pass that place the very last of the Ebb.— Thus Stevenson may be away eight or nine hours every day and all Night, of consequence he can continue to pass from you to me, so that no additional expense will be incurred.— You can consider of this and resolve on what you think best.— I am promised the earliest Notice should they ship Pilots for Hell Gate : still it may so happen that I may be disappointed.— Everything appears very quiet amongst them.

The Complaints against the officers of His Majestys Ships under your Command you will observe are now become the Subject of National Enquiry. A Regular Complaint has been made by the American Secretary of State to Mr Merry His Majesty's Representative to these States, who from your answer, will make a reply to the Charges, and will naturally transmit Copies to Lord Harrowby the Minister for foreign affairs.— In saying that I hoped you would not again come up above the Narrows, I assuredly alluded to the avoiding any more Complaints that might be made in consequence of another application to detain His Majesty's Ships until the French had sailed : and I confess it is with Reluctance that I understand from your letter you intend coming within the Hook to Water.— The American Government already charge His Majesty's Ships with hovering on their Coasts, with a view of capturing Ships of other Nations in alliance with

them. Your coming in and going out will confirm the Charge.
The Weather is so very fine I should suppose you might be
watered over the Bar, from the Schooner that last watered
Capt Douglass.— I merely suggest this, you are the only and
best Judge.   I will see the man and either hire him, or a large
Vessel for you and send her down whenever you order it. At
all events she may go out and take your Empty Casks.— Let
me know the day you wish her sent down, how many casks
you have to fill.

TO MR. MERRY.

New York 13th July 1804

Sir.

I have the Honor to inclose to you, a copy of Captain Bradleys letter to me of yesterday in answer to mine in which
I forwarded to him an extract from your letter to me — What
Captain Bradley notices respecting the conduct of the officers
of the French Ship of War Poursivant in the Chesepeak, I suspect is correct, having not long since seen a very particular
statement of the Facts in a paper from Norfolk in Virginia —
Mr Moore communicated to me, the cause of your present detention at Baltimore — I regret the accident, as you will not
find it easy to replace the loss of a good coachman in America — By the public papers you will be informed of the unfortunate death of General Hamilton, one of the most respectable
characters in these States, and a gentleman of eminent Talents [1] —I consider him even as a loss to His Majesty and our
Government, from the prudence of his measures, his conciliat-
ing disposition, his abhorence of the French Revolution, and
all republican principles and doctrine, and his very great attachment to the British Government — The cause of the duel
originated in General Hamilton having repeatedly and publickly expressed his opinion of Mr Burr; particularly at the
late election for Governor of this State, and his endeavoring
to dissuade the Federalists from co operating in favor of M^r
Burrs election.

---

[1] The duel was fought on the 11th, and Hamilton died on the 12th of July.

12

TO MR. MERRY.

New York 18th July 1804.

SIR

Your letter of the 16th Current, I received this morning, together with a copy of a letter from the American Secretary of State to you under date of the 7th Instant. Copies of these are now making and will be forwarded this Evening or tomorrow morning to Captain Bradley of His Majestys Ship Cambrian and Capt Douglass of the Boston — It will not however be in their power to reply before I possess them with the remainder of the Documents you was from want of time prevented sending to me.

The Driver went to Sea on the 24th of June, the instant it was advisable for any ship to go out after the 19th from which day to the 24 it had blowed a gale from the Eastward, not a ship of any description had put to Sea in the interval. It is possible in her way off the Coast, she may have boarded several vessels, and impressed some men — The facts Vice Admiral Sir Andrew Mitchell will enquire into and every man not a subject of His Majesty will be discharged — But the charge of the Driver hovering on the confines of these States is incorrect — She most assuredly proceeded with all reasonable expedition to the place of her destination, Halifax — On her passage and near this place she met the young Factor and Diligence Ships from Ireland from whom she took some subjects of His Majesty. If any Americans were impressed through mistake they will be restored — From an intimate knowledge of Captain Lyall I can safely assure you, it was not done intentionally — you may safely, Sir, assure the American Secretary of State, that His Majestys Captains are very delicate on this Subject. I have never heard nor do I believe that either of His Majesty's Ships the Cambrian, Boston, or Driver boarded any ship or vessel from their arrival within the Jurisdiction of these States to the Day of their Departure the British Ship Pitt excepted. Neither have I heard of their boarding and impressing any men from Ships outward bound, even beyond the Jurisdiction of these States which to them was lawful and if any of the men on board were Subjects of His Majesty to take them from thence.

While the three Ships lay in Sandy Hook bay, they did not intermeddle with any vessel coming in or going out The Driver being only a Sloop of War went to sea on the 24th June at a moment when the two large Ships could not. In the same manner the Boston a ship of three and an half feet less water than the Cambrian went to Sea on the 30th of June when it was impracticable for the Pilot to take the Cambrian out — you will however recollect, that the day before from anxiety to get out the Boston made an Attempt with the Wind ahead, and took the Ground — On the 3rd July the Cambrian went to Sea — It is unnecessary for me to notice the remark made by the Secretary of State, that the Port of New York is virtually blockaded by our Ships — They are far beyond the Jurisdiction of the United States of America, where the Sea appertains to His Majesty in common with all other Nations —French and Dutch Ships resort to these Ports, and at times french Ships of War and Privateers. The Protection of His Majesty's Subjects and the Service require that these should be captured — American Ships navigated by Americans or men of any other Nation save British Subjects pass our Ships of War without molestation —At this moment the Americans have one hundred British Seamen in their Service, for every American by accident impressed on board His Majesty's Ships of War, and I aver the fact that a great proportion of the Crews of the American Frigates are Subjects of His Majesty's. It is also a matter of Notoriety that Certificates of Citizenship (commonly called Protections) are issued to English, Irish, and Scotch men, many of whom have not been a month in these States.

TO CAPTAIN BRADLEY.

New York 22[d] July 1804.

SIR,

When I communicated to you the possibility of the French Frigates attempting a passage through Hellgate to avoid an action with His Majestys Ships under your command, and of the means of giving you notice in such an event, I calculated on the least possibly favorable moment on our part, when the attempt could be made, and under these circumstances stated that it might take from ten to eighteen hours.   This was under an impression that you might be four or five leagues without the Hook. I am still of opinion that with a gale from the Southwest and the very first of the tide of flood, those ships will be under weigh, many hours before I can give you notice. A Pilot Boat with the wind from that quarter can make no head way against the tide: nor can a cutter or row boat do much better, particularly after they get below the narrows and have a heavy sea or swell to obstruct them.   In calculations of every kind, it is most safe to take the worst that can happen — ordinarily it is probable the notice could be conveyed to you in eight hours at farthest.

On my part you may rest assured of every attention to their motions, and of my using the best means to give you the earliest notice. They have been up in their barges, and sounded Hellgate, on their return they expressed their opinion of the difficulty of the navigation. I am therefore rather of opinion that they will not hazard it — One of the most experienced Pilots assures me it is an hundred to one but they get on there in the attempt.

The best manner to be adopted, will be to have Stevenson with his boat laying below the Narrows, with an officer from one of your ships always with him: at every slack tide during the day he can take a look at the Ships, and if they are not in motion go down with letters from me to you, or bring back dispatches from you, so as to be at his station before the next low water. This will be the best mode because below the narrows there is but little tide to obstruct a boat. I would not however have the boat to go down to you when the french Ships get under way: from the improbability of their being able to get through Hell gate, but to wait my orders. I will immediately cross to long Island and watch their motions; the instant they are through Hellgate, ride express to the Narrows and dispatch the boat to you. This cannot take more than an hour from the time they pass Hellgate. If you approve of the plan, let me know, send up an officer, and I will go and station them. Let the officer be dressed either in plain cloth, or as an ordinary seaman to prevent suspicion.

You must not think of again coming above the narrows — From private letters dated at Balltown Springs about 190 Miles up the Hudson river, Jerome Bonaparte and his Lady were there a few days since — I cannot therefore think they have it in contemplation to attempt an escape — still they may, their measures are very secret.

TO ADMIRAL SIR ANDREW MITCHELL.

New York 1ˢᵗ August 1804.

SIR.

The boat which returned this morning from the Cambrian brought me your letter of the 18ᵗʰ of July, and another from Captain Skene announcing his arrival off Sandy Hook in His Majestys Ship Leander. I am happy to learn that Captain Bradleys conduct meets your approbation. He is a very worthy, zealous officer and a gentleman for whom I have a sincere regard. I am however apprehensive you are under a mistake in supposing the officers commanding ships of War of belligerent Powers, having a right in a neutral Port to board ships of their own nation and to impress men from them. But this is a point for Mʳ Merry to maintain with the American Government, and unnecessary for me to discuss with you. I shall only add that I am clear His Majestys ministers will coincide with me. The conduct of French ships of War in this Port and in Virginia, may be used as a collateral argument in defence of Captain Bradleys measure; but never in justification — because two Wrongs will not make one right — I am rather apprehensive you have been misinformed respecting the "French Frigates now in this Port having boarded a French Schooner or Brig and impressed the whole of the crew." On an enquiry, all that I could learn, was that they had taken from a French Vessel four men, who they stated to have de-

12*

serted from them — The Conduct however of the Poursuivant this year, and of the Semilaute two or three years since in the Chesepeak was shamefully outrageous, and I have possessed Mr Merry of the facts to be used as an offset to the complaints of the French Minister against the Ships under your command now off this Port.

I have heretofore stated to you that the conduct of the Mayor and Port Wardens of this place was in my opinion violent, illegal, and highly expressive of their partiality to the French; and I have represented their measures in that point of view to Mr Merry and Lord Hawkesbury. Allow me however to answer the two Questions in your Letter — 1st, Why was not the Pilots taken from the French Frigates who was of superior force to the British? Answer — Because no requisition was made on the part of the Officers of His Majestys Ships for this purpose. I am rather inclined to believe that under similar circumstances, on application on the part of His Majesty to the American Government, an order would have issued inhibiting of French ships of War sailing until 24 hours had elapsed from the sailing of British Ships. I have in several instances made such an application in favor of Montreal ships to have Privateers detained, and always met a ready compliance.

2^d — Had any accident happened to the Pitt, who would the Master have applied to for assistance, the Mayor of New York, or the British Frigates? Answer. Undoubtedly to the Commander of the Frigates — I do not however see that this answer will in the least lead to a justification of Captain Bradleys conduct — On the part of Captain Campbell of the Pitt, there was no complaint against Captain Bradley, all he wanted was his ship to be admitted to an entry — he over and again said to Captain Bradley, if that could be effected he cared not for the men, because he supposed the greater part would leave him. It is the United States who complain of an infringement of their Laws within their Jurisdiction. Accept my best thanks for your complying with my request to take Robert Kelly on board your ship, I shall write Captain Keen respecting his wife who I believe a very decent woman.

In the Brig Jefferson sent to Halifax for adjudication, Captain Bradley sent as part of the prize crew, a man named Billings, who has been proved to Captain Bradley to be an American — I intreat you will have the goodness to order him to be discharged — in addition to every other reason, I am prejudiced in his favor from there having been no application to the American Government for his release, but only to me.

It is with much regret I inform you of the capture of His Majestys Ship Lilly, and the death of Captain Compton and the first Lieutenant. The inclosed packet from Consul Hamilton will give you the particulars.[1]

TO MR. MERRY.

New York 10ᵗʰ August 1804

SIR.

Captain Skene of His Majestys Ship Leander on Saturday the 4ᵗʰ Current boarded some Leagues from Sandy Hook the American Ship Eugenia John Mansfield Master from Bourdeaux to New York. On examining the Ship and her papers he was satisfied that Enemies property was on board. Under this conviction he took possession of the Ship put a prize Master and Seamen on board and ordered her for Halifax in Nova Scotia for trial in the Court of Vice Admiralty in that port. In consequence of Easterly Winds and the State of the Ships sails the prize master was obliged to come to an anchor under Fisher's Island near New London Light House; John Mansfield the late Master and Robert Parry the mate of the Eugenia who had been permitted by Captain Skene to remain

---

[1] The Lilly was captured on July 15, 1804, off the Carolina coast, by a French privateer. Captain Compton and the first lieutenant were killed early in the action, and the Lilly was afterward carried by boarding. The New-York Gazette of July 30 adds, "The French had 180 to 200 men, the Lilly about 78. The French had the evening before captured an English ship from Africa to Charleston with slaves, which the Frenchman took out, and gave the ship to her crew and that of the Lilly." The two English crews, with the captured slave-ship, reached Norfolk some days after the action.

on board that ship, to see that there was no embezzlement of
the cargo, improperly left the Ship, went on shore at New
London collected a number of persons, armed them and themselves, and in a fast sailing sloop over took the Eugenia,
boarded her by violence, took possession of her, turned the
prize master and British Seamen on Shore at New London,
and proceeded immediately to New York where she arrived
late on the Evening of the 8ᵗʰ Instant.   The ship was yesterday admitted to an entry —

At four oClock yesterday afternoon Mʳ Yates the Prize Master arrived in this City and stated the above facts. I have
taken his affidavit, herewith inclosed, to enable you, Sir, to
make a proper representation to the American Government of
this illegal act of violence and piracy committed by Citizens of
these States.

I have transmitted to the Collector and Naval Officer of this
Port a copy of Mʳ Yeat's affidavit, and requested them to demand all the original papers of the Eugenia from Mʳ Patrick
the owner and John Mansfield the Master, and to take immediate possession of the Ship and prevent any part of her cargo
being taken out or removed until they receive orders from
Mʳ Madison the American Secretary of State.

I forbear making any comments on this outrageous act on
the part of Captain Mansfield, his Mate and others, and trust
on a representation from you, that the American Government
will take such measures as justice and a wish to preserve the
present good understanding which subsist between His Majesty and the United States of America require.

TO MR. MERRY.

New York 14 August 1804

SIR,

It was not in my power to give you more information respecting the American Ship Eugenia than on the tenth of this
month, because she did not arrive until late in the Evening of
the 8ᵗʰ, on the ninth there were many contradictory reports in

circulation respecting her escape, to not any of which the least credit, could attach. I therefore waited the arrival of the prize Master, and lost not a moment to give you his Statement under oath —

Captain Skene of His Majestys Ship Leander pressed a British Seaman from the American Ship Swift, Murphy Master — He also has taken one British Seaman, and fifteen Irish Emigrants from the American Ship Live Oak, but both these ships were far beyond the line of demarcation, a League from Shore.— Indeed the Live Oak was subject to heavy pains and penalties for bringing out more men, than by her Tonage she was entitled by act of Parliament. I know of no other impressments: but I have this day written to Captain Bradley acquainting him, that I have fortunately suppressed the publication of the affidavits of three Masters of Ships, who deposed that they had been boarded from the Leander within three miles of the Shore, and I have requested him to prevent in future a similar breach of neutrality.

TO ADMIRAL SIR ANDREW MITCHELL.

New York 14 August 1804

SIR.

As it is uncertain that the Letters from Captⁿ Bradley and Captain Skene will arrive in time to go by this conveyance, and you may be anxious to know the particulars of the case of the American ship Eugenia, John Mansfield Master from Bourdeaux to New York, detained by Captain Skene on the 4 Instant and ordered to Halifax, I have the Honor to communicate the following facts collected from the testimony of Mr Yeates the Prize Master —

On the 4th of August Mr Yeates Master's Mate, Mr Masters Midshipman 8 Seamen and two marines were sent by Captain Skene from the Leander on board the Eugenia, with orders to Mr Yates the prize Master to take that Ship to Halifax Nova Scotia. Light Winds and those from the Eastward, together with the miserable situation of the Eugenia in sails, pre-

vented M[r] Yeates getting to the South East so as to double
Nantucket Shoals; and finding himself near to the Easternmost part of Long Island he resolved to go over the Shoals.
On the 6th he took a Pilot on board for that purpose, but the
Wind soon after coming to E S E blowing fresh, with thick
hazy weather, and being unable on either tack to weather the
land, by the advice of the Pilot he bore away for Fisher's
Island, and anchored about a mile from the New London
Light House.— Captain Mansfield and his mate who had been
sent in the Ship for Halifax, made their escape from her on the
7th Instant while M[r] Yeates was below, and went on shore,
where they hired an armed Banditte to retake the Ship, and
came out from New London in a sloop for that purpose.
Suspicious of this, and the Wind having changed a few
points, M[r] Yeates had cut his cable and got under way, and
had proceeded some leagues, when he was overtaken, boarded
and carried by twenty-five men from the Sloop —M[r] Yeates and
the Leanders men were put on shore at New London, and the
Eugenia proceeded direct to this place through the Sound
where she arrived on the 8th Instant.

M[r] Yeates, M[r] Masters three Seamen and the two Marines
come here late in the afternoon of the 9th — The other five
Seamen deserted at New London — I immediately took his
affidavit and transmitted it the next morning, with a letter
from me detailing the particulars and requesting M[r] Merry to
make spirited remonstrances with respect to the Conduct of
Captain Mansfield his Mate and the armed men hired at New
London, and to demand a restitution of the Ship.— As the
Ship altho' admitted to an entry had not yet commenced the
discharge of her Cargo, I also wrote on the morning of the
10th a Letter to the proper officers of the Customs on the Subject, inclosing a copy of M[r] Yeates' affidavit, and required of
them, to regain the possession of the Ship's papers, and to
take the said Ship into their custody and not permit an Article to be landed or removed from her, until they received orders from the American Secretary of State to whom M[r] Merry
would make a formal representation —

I have the Honor to inclose you copies of the answer to the

above — On Mr Merry's opinion, I shall make no other communication than that it does not correspond with mine. From his situation and experience however he must be the best judge.—I am pained to add he has been very unwell for some time past.

TO MR. MERRY.

New York Aug' 18th 1804

SIR.

I have the Honor to enclose you a letter from Captain Skene of His Majesty's Ship Leander, and a copy of a letter from Captain Bradley of the Cambrian to me received this Morning.

I have to acquaint you that the Ship Little Cornelia detained by the Leander and sent to Halifax for adjudication was retaken by the Master Mate & Cook and carried into New London. No act of Violence attending the Measure — Mr Juhel the Owner has very handsomely disavowed his approbation of the Measure, returned Captain Skene the papers, and offers to abide the Sentence of the Vice Court of Admiralty at Halifax.[1]

TO MR. HAMMOND.

New York 23^d August 1804.

SIR.

I was informed a few days since that the second instalment due by these states to His Majesty had not yet been paid, owing to Mr Merry not having received an order for that purpose — It may be of moment that Lord Harrowby should be made acquainted that Spanish dollars are not to be obtained at any premium; and bills of exchange bear an advance of two and one half per Cent, but would rise to five if £200,000 Sterling is to be purchased. Besides with every precaution there is much risque in buying bills from Merchants — Under

---

[1] Notwithstanding Mr. Juhel's handsome offer, it does not appear that the Little Cornelia was ever, in fact, surrendered. Mr. Juhel was a French merchant, living in New-York, who had married Cornelia Livingston, sister to Schuyler Livingston, Barclay's son-in-law.

these impressions and not knowing whether any mode has been adopted for advantageously remitting this Sum or making a convenient application of it; I am led to offer through you my opinion to his Lordship.—

The six hundred thousand pounds is to be paid by the American States as a gross Sum in satisfaction of British Debts due to American Loyalists — Whenever the Commissioners appointed to certify the Sums due each Loyalist report. I think it would be most for His Majestys Service to give drafts for the respective Sums awarded them payable in America. This mode will save the Government much trouble and expense and free it from the possibility of danger from protested Bills — The individuals who are to be paid will find ways of getting their money to Great Britain, indeed many will want it in this country.— A conviction of the prudence of this measure has led me to take the liberty of offering my opinion, and if no more proper person can be found to receive the money and pay the drafts, I beg leave to tender my Services —

It is with pain I mention to you Mr Merry having had a second severe attack — It is of the apoplectic kind — His mind since his arrival in America has been much perplexed by untoward events of which you are not ignorant.

His Majestys Ships Leander and Cambrian still continue off this Port, watching the French Frigates within — It is said the latter intend going to Sea in a few days. Many complaints from the American Government against the conduct of the commanders of the British Ships of War; but all of them unfounded, save that of the 17th of June, respecting the Ship Pitt, and treatment of the American officers.

TO MR. MERRY.

New York 24 August 1804.

(*Private.*)

DEAR SIR.

I am greatly pained to learn by your private letter that you have experienced a relapse and continue weak and indisposed.

The information in your own hand writing has been communicated to the Commanders of His Majestys Ships of War off this Port.— By the news papers you will see there are many charges against them of impressments within the American Waters, maltreatment and imprudent expressions, most if not the whole of them are without foundation : but four instances have come to my knowledge, neither of which have been made the subject of complaint, in which I am well assured the American ships were boarded within three miles of the Shore. I have repeatedly stated this to Captains Bradley and Skene, and requested them to be more careful in future that the American Ships are more than a League from Shore when Boarded—I added my opinion that a small relaxation in boarding and impressment would in my opinion be politic.— It is whispered, and I have reason to suspect it, that the two French Frigates will attempt their escape in a few days.

The Editor of the American Citizen has made a violent attack upon the President of the Marine insurance company, wherein he states that that Gentleman had written to you on the Subject of French Privateers being on the American coasts, and in consequence of his representations our Ships of war had been sent hither.[1] This we know to be false — But he has learnt from a confidential person, that you shewed to Mr Galatin my letter of the 12th of May, wherein I informed you

---

[1] The article appeared in the Citizen of August 22. The following extracts exhibit the substance of Cheetham's attack:

"THE LEANDER & CO.

"It is communicated to me by good authority that Mr. William Neilson Sen. of this city, merchant wrote to Mr. Merry immediately after his arrival in this country, requesting him to order a naval force off the Hook, to protect American Commerce. It is added that Mr. Neilson's letter is now in the hands of the Sec. of State communicated by Mr. Merry himself. As the Revolution which severed the colonies from the crown of Great Britain never altered, as we are informed, Mr. Neilson's attachment to it, Mr. Merry could not but comply with his request *to protect American Commerce*, and accordingly the Cambrian and the Driver, the Boston and the Leander were graciously sent for that purpose. . . . They have exhibited their protecting care over our commerce, in the capture of our vessels, the violation of our territory, the maltreatment of our fellow citizens."

that I had that day received a letter from the President of the Marine insurance Company in this City, stating a French Cruizer being off Georgia and South Carolina committing depredations on British and American Ships: and that I had notified Captain Douglas of it.— Mr Galatin has communicated this to several persons, and probably to the Editor of the Citizen, and by this means a shameful use has been made of that which was honorably and prudently intended, and the unfair conclusion has been drawn that on this information you applied to the Admiral for the Ships now off this port, and that the present blockade of this port is owing to Mr Neilson the President of the Marine insurance office. You will do me a favor by acquainting me with what passed between you and Mr Galatin, and whether you showed him the letter.

As my proposed ride to Philadelphia was intended as a visit of respect and regard to you and M^{ra} Merry, I shall postpone it until I am informed you are recovered — I sincerely hope soon to hear this from you. Present my best respects to M^{ra} Merry. I wish you was farther Northward where the air is more cool, and the country more pleasant.

TO VICE-ADMIRAL SIR ANDREW MITCHELL.

New York 25th August 1804.

SIR.

Captain Bradley and Captain Skene (particularly the latter) having written to you fully by this Conveyance renders it unnecessary for me to state any thing further either respecting the Eugenia or the little Cornelia. They are both very mortifying circumstances to me; and I have in a private letter to Captain Skene recommended while off this place in the event of ordering a Vessel to Halifax for examination to send only their Master or Mate in her, and to forward the two other principal Officers of the Vessel by the first private conveyance. This measure might be attended with an Expense of fifty to an hundred dollars, but what is that to insure the safe arrival of the Vessel.

It is rather singular Mr Merry and myself should differ in opinion on the only two questions of moment that have occurred since the arrival of His Majesty's Ships off Port.— In the case of the Ship Pitt, Mr Merry appears to have been rather in doubt that the Conduct of the officers of the Cambrian amounted to an infraction of Neutral Rights.— On that point I am most clear, notwithstanding the tacit consent of Portugal Hamburgh &c &c &c in similar cases. Their suffering British Ships of War to impress British Seamen in their ports can never alter the old established Laws of Nations, or take away the rights of other neutral powers.— In the regaining possession of the Eugenia by violence and recruiting an armed Body of Men on shore for that purpose, Mr Merry appears of opinion that it is not an Act that will admit of a remonstrance — There again I am so unfortunate as to be of a contrary opinion, which I have stated to him at large with my reasons.

I have notified Capt. Bradley of the probability of the French Frigates attempting their escape either through the Sound or by the Hook: If the latter they will wait the first fresh Gale from the N W and I have cautioned him to keep well to the Northward of Sandy Hook, so to have the Bay open to him up to the Narrows, that he may see the Ships coming down, and be ready to meet them, because in less than two hours from their getting under way they will be at Sea and if our Ships run to the Southward of the Hook they will be to leeward and never overtake them.

I am sorry to acquaint you that Mr Merry has had two or three very disagreeable attacks, which entre nous, are evidently apoplective. He is very nervous, and dejected weak and almost incapable of doing Business. His Life I consider very precarious, and I have pressed him to permit me to send for Mr. Chipman the Solicitor General of New Brunswick to assist him until his Health, if ever is re-established. Mr. Chipman is the best qualified Character in this State.

In one of my last letters I mentioned Samuel Billings an American Seaman who had been sent in a prize to Halifax — Captain Bradley told me he would be discharged there by you, and I requested you that he might, as he has been unequivocally proved to be a native American — If he has not been discharged when you receive this I intreat he may as I stand pledged that he will be.

TO MR. MERRY.

New York 30ᵗʰ August 1804.

SIR.

I did myself the Honor yesterday to communicate to you in a private letter that the French Frigates Sybil and Didon, had about 6 of the clock in the morning of that day got under way and proceeded towards Sandy Hook.   The Wind being light and part of the tide expended before they were in motion prevented their getting farther than Gravesend Bay, distant about eleven miles from this city where they came to an anchor and where they remained at dark last Evening — As the Ebb made very early this morning, boats have been prevented getting up, so that we remain ignorant whether they remain at Gravesend or have gone to the Hook with the morning tide — It is more than probable I shall hear before this letter goes to the Post Office.   The best opinion I can form, is that these ships will attempt getting to Sea the first favorable moment, when our Ships are to leeward to this port.

TO WILLIAM NEILSON.[1]

New York 7ᵗʰ September 1804.

SIR.

I have this moment received your letter of yesterday, and in compliance with your request inclose a Copy of the letter you wrote me on the 11ᵗʰ of May last as President of the Marine

[1] The American Citizen renewed its attacks on Mr. Neilson on August 28 and September 5. Barclay's letter was intended to afford an answer to these articles.

Insurance Company — Having seen an Extract of my letter to
the Mayor of this City of the 18th of June published in the
American Citizen, I was induced to examine that letter, as
well as the one you wrote to me, and I find that in giving my
reasons to the Mayor, for apprehending it would not be in the
power of the Commander of His Majesty's Ships of War to
comply with his request, I have been guilty of a mistake, in
stating to him that your letter to me, expressed the American
as well as British Commerce — My recital to the Mayor was
from Memory, and not from a reference to your letter. I am
extremely sorry for having unguardedly made use of two
words not in your letter, and can only account for it on this principle, that the Newspapers at that time contained information
of several American, as well as British Vessels having been
captured to the Southward by French Privateers, and from
my mind being impressed with these reports, led me, when
I wrote to the Mayor to suppose it was so expressed in your
letter.

I have never received any other letter from you than the
one herein mentioned.

TO MR. MERRY.

New York 13 Sept[r] 1804.

SIR.

I did not receive satisfactory proof that Jerome Bonaparte
and his Lady were still in these States until last Evening.
Two days since M[r] Wood told me that on the 5th Instant he
had met them in a common stage coach near Trenton; but so
universally was his, and his Wife's departure credited in this
place, that I apprehended M[r] Wood had made a mistake.   In
addition to every other report, a confidential man assured me
he saw her in a Barge with Monsieur Du Pont the French
agent going from Staten Island to the Ship that General Armstrong was in.   I also knew to a certainty that M[r] Du Pont
had borrowed money from a gentleman for the express pur-

13

pose of an advance to Bonaparte at his departure. There can be no doubt that every thing was arranged for their (especially his Ladys) going to Bordeaux in the Thomas, and I cannot but believe that General Armstrong must have had some knowledge of it.—As the Thomas passed Staten Island M^r Du Pont and Mrs Bonaparte in a Barge attempted to gain the Ship, but no notice was taken of them, nor would the Captain heave the Ship too for them, I cannot learn whether Jerome Bonaparte was in the Barge — M^r Du Pont has since mentioned his and their disappointment and insinuated that they had been unhandsomely treated.—The Gentleman who lent M^r Du Pont the money, mentioned yesterday to a friend, who I requested to interrogate him, the above particulars.— I have it also from another person to the same effect.[1] — The Didon will attempt her escape the first favorable moment. Pilots are engaged for the Sound as well as Sandy Hook. Captain Bradley although satisfied of the necessity appears unwilling to incur the expense of keeping a boat on pay at Gravesend to give him notice if she attempts a passage through the Sound. This in my opinion is necessary, because the same Wind and Tide which carries the Didon through Hell Gate and the Sound, will prevent a boat getting to Captain Bradley, and give the Didon at least nine hours start. Whereas a boat stationed at Gravesend, in one hour after the Didon got under way, would leave

---

[1] Barclay was correctly informed. On September 5, Mme. Bonaparte wrote to her father from New-York: "We have made the journey here for nothing, as General Armstrong, the Ambassador, after writing to Mr. Bonaparte that he would be delighted at taking me to France with him, changed his mind and went off without me. To-morrow we are to leave this place for Philadelphia, and from thence we go to Springfield immediately; so that, as I shall see you soon, it is unnecessary to say more. I thought the opportunity of going with an Ambassador too good to be missed, and Mr. Bonaparte was to have gone in the frigates a few days after me." In October, 1804, Jerome Bonaparte and his wife sailed from Philadelphia, but were wrecked off the Capes of the Delaware and returned. In November, they embarked in the French frigate Le Président, late Poursuivant; but disembarked on learning of the arrival of H. M. S. Révolutionnaire on the coast. This ended their attempts for the winter. In December they were in Washington.

that for His Majestys Ships. I have no authority to employ
such a Boat, unless you think proper to order it — The Syble
it is said will remain here until our Ships are compelled to
leave the coast; perhaps this is mere report.

TO VICE-ADMIRAL SIR A. MITCHELL.

New York 22ᵈ Sept' 1804.

(Private.)

DEAR SIR.

Through the intervention of a friend of Mʳ Pichon and
mine, I have this 'day requested you would send him any
private familiar letters of his which may have been forwarded
to you from Captⁿ Bradley or Skene — and informed you that
he would consider himself under an obligation if you feel
yourself at liberty to favor him with copies of his official letters, which were taken on board the Eugenia or little Cornelia, provided they contained nothing which can injure His
Majestys Service — This last request I should not have made,
had not Captain Skene informed me of the Contents of those
letters, and that they merely respected Jerome Bonaparte
going home — I am satisfied had Mʳ Pichon received those letters in Season, Jerome would before this have embarked on
board one of the Frigates, and attempted his Escape from
your Ships: and I am further of opinion that Mʳ Pichon will
hurry him off on receiving official copies of them.[1] — The Cambrian and Leander are now within the Hook, to avoid the effects of an equinoctial Gale and to complete their Water.

[1] The official letters referred to
were written by Decrès, the French
Minister of Marine, to Pichon and
Jerome Bonaparte, conveying the
orders of the First Consul for Jerome's return, but prohibiting the
coming of "the young person" with
whom he had formed a connection.
The letters are dated the 30th Ger-
minal in the year XII(April 19, 1804).
Translations are printed with other
original documents, in an otherwise
worthless little book, "The Bona-
parte-Patterson Marriage," Philadelphia, 1873.

The French Frigates remain moored near the City. The Syble has had her ballast overhauled and her rigging set, both Ships have been completed with Water, and their Coops filled with Poultry &c &c &c so that every thing indicates an intention of going to Sea speedily. Hell Gate (the only difficult part of the navigation through the Sound) has been repeatedly examined by the officers of their Ships, and Pilots have been examined as to the feasibility of taking them through and ordered to hold themselves in readiness — still I have it from unquestionable authority that they do not intend going to Sea that way, but will barely make the attempt, a ruse de guerre, in the hope that Captain Bradley on hearing that one of them has gone up, will send one of his Ships to the East end of Long Island to intercept her; in which case the french Frigate will return and both Ships put to Sea. The truth is, that what they intend as a feint, ought in reality to be carried into effect. By sending one of the French Ships to New Port Rhode Island Capt Bradley must have detached the Leander or Cambrian to watch her motions. If the Leander was the Ship, the French Frigate might easily escape, and if the Cambrian went off Rhode Island, then the Ship here might put to Sea — all they aim at present is to get Bonaparte off in either Ship. From receiving their complement of Provisions and Water the French Frigates swim very deep — The Syble draws twenty four feet Water — I have had private information, but on which no dependance can be placed, because the man is a Stranger to me, and I have reason to suspect him to be a spy, and treat him accordingly, until I am satisfied he is the reverse, that both the Ships are to remain where they are until our Ships retire, and that the Commodore will embark for France next week in a Merchant Ship — Time will develop this, and if the report proves true, induce me hereafter to afford to this man a grain more of credibility; I however very much doubt my being authorized to place confidence in him. I say enough when I add that he is a Dutch Jew, who has travelled over the Globe, knows every Body and every thing. —If he was honest, he would be serviceable as he daily visits the French Ships.

TO CAPTAIN BRADLEY.

New York 31ˢᵗ Octʳ 1804.

You have noticed from the papers that a french Frigate is expected here from France, which report is confirmed to me this day by Mʳ Merry. I have reason to believe she was yesterday off this port and communicated with one of the pilot boats. The French Chancellor mentioned this last Evening and the Gentleman to whom he stated it came and told me of it. White the pilot (who it appears is about to be turned out of his boat) came this morning to Peacock and told him, that both the French Frigates had taken Williams and Minugh and two Hell Gate Pilots on board, and would certainly pass through Hell Gate the first fair wind. You will therefore take your measures accordingly — It is added by White that the french frigates will go through this next flood if the wind will admit, and that you cannot go out until next tide — Perhaps the whole may be a finesse to put you out.

What fortifies me in the Idea that they are on the wing, is that they have lately had a press-gang on Shore, who took off six men that came to my knowledge and perhaps many more — Four of them they have been compelled to restore, and measures are taking for the other two — I wait only until matters are ripe to develope this act of violence to the public — I send this by an express, that you may be ready at a moment — Rely on my attention.

TO CAPTAIN BRADLEY.

New York 3ʳᵈ November 1804.

SIR.

By Bushat at 12 O'Clock A M this morning I received your three letters of yesterday and I am happy to learn from my Son that he saw both your ships out at day light this morning — The Breeze is light and favorable and I hope you will be at Montock Point in time to intercept them. It is said

13*

both French ships touched in going through, & that they anchored last night, but this is not confirmed.

Both Bushat and myself have been all over to hire a dispatch Boat but without success. At day Break I was on Long Island to procure one of the Block Island fishing Boats and offered three hundred dollars per Week to go and communicate with you. The men refused and said no money would induce them, as they could never again return to New York. I am convinced every boat has been bribed, or threatened not to go.

Bushat therefore goes himself in his own boat—He and Stevenson have been unremitted in their exertions and merit everything from us; should I learn anything of moment I will give it to you. If you once get sight of these ships, keep it, go where they will.

TO VICE-ADMIRAL SIR A. MITCHELL.

New York 7 Nov' 1804.

SIR.

I have the Honor to inform you that the French Frigates Didon and Cyble, proceeded through Hell Gate for Sea at half past four P M on the 2ᵈ of this month, with a fair Wind, and from the best accounts yet received, they were seen on Saturday[1] at 5 O Clock P M between Block and Long Island standing to Sea — It was then nearly calm and continued so all night early Sunday Morning the Wind was from the S E, light airs and thick foggy Weather—on Monday Morning at 2 o Clock A M the Wind came round to N N West and blowed fresh—

Captain Bradley received notice from me on the 31ˢᵗ of October of the intended departure of those ships by the way of Hell Gate, and was kept constantly informed from that day until they sailed—There was reason to suspect the French Ships intended merely the measure as a feint to draw His Majestys Ships to sea—It was therefore resolved by Captain Bradley not to proceed in pursuit until they had got through Hell Gate. For this purpose I had a confidential person posted

[1] November 3d.

at Brooklyn Heights to ride down to Gravesend the instant he saw the French Ship beyond Hell Gate, and to acquaint my son with it, who waited there to communicate by signal with Captain Bradley —At half past five o Clock in the Evening of that day he arrived at Gravesend, but it was then between day light and dark so that the Ensign hoisted on a flagstaff could not be distinguished from His Majestys Ships laying in Sandy Hook Bay, distant about twelve miles — Mr Henry Barclay therefore dispatched a boat to Captain Bradley with a letter confirming the departure of the French Ships, and immediately lighted a fire the night Signal, the Captain of the Packet by my orders informed Captain Bradley would be made. The light was observed on board ship, but not so satisfactorily as to induce Capt Bradley to go to Sea —At 8 o Clock however the light was distinctly seen, and some blue light also which Capt Porteous of the Packet had brought from the Cambrian, and the boat from my Son arrived at the same time — There was then about two hours flood remaining, and I had hoped His Majestys Ships would have gone out, as there was a very fine leading Wind.

His Majestys Ships however did not get under way until near day light of the next day (the 3d of November), early that Morning my Son saw them standing to the Eastward with every sail and a leading but light breeze — I dispatched a Schooner to watch the Enemy and communicate with His Majestys Ships off the East end of Long Island — We have had no report respecting either Ships, nor has the Pilot Boat which attended the French Frigates, or the one by me sent to Capt Bradley returned.

I fear there is little probability of His Majestys Ships meeting the French Frigates.

TO MR. HAMMOND.

New York 9th Novr 1804.

SIR.

I received on the 2d of this month a letter from William Bradley Esqr Commanding His Majestys Ship Cambrian, on the subject of his being superseded in the command of that ship in consequence of my letter to you of the 27th of June last, and that the Secretary of the Admiralty had by order of the Lords Commissioners transmitted a copy of my Letter to Vice Admiral Sir Andrew Mitchell Commander in Chief of His Majestys Ships of War on the Halifax Station, as the ground work of their order.[1]

I am particularly pained that such serious consequences have followed a detail of facts, by me intended only for the information of His Majestys Ministers — It is true I differed in opinion with Captain Bradley on his impressment of the Men at Staten Island from on board the British Ship Pitt, and urged him to restore them in which event every other complaint might have been happily got over with the American Government; but Captain Bradley could not persuade himself that he had acted improperly, and the situation His Majestys ships were then in, expecting any moment to come to action with a greatly superior force of the Enemy, I am convinced induced Captain Bradley to consider he was advancing His Majestys Service by retaining the men.

In justice to Captain Bradley I feel bound further to state that from his arrival with His Majestys Ships in June last to their departure on the third of this month, I know not an instance (save the one before mentioned) in which blame can attach to him, on any of the complaints which may have been made by the American Secretary of State, on the subject of impressment of men, breach of neutrality, or infringing the Limits of American Jurisdiction. The zeal and unwearied attention with which he has supported a tedious and difficult

---

[1] On the first of September, Lord Harrowby informed Mr. Monroe that the British Government had disapproved Captain Bradley's conduct and censured it by removing him from the command and ordering him home to account for it. Lord Harrowby said, adds Mr. Monroe, "that as this step had been taken before any complaint had been received from our Government, it could not be viewed otherwise than as a strong proof of the desire of His Majesty to cultivate the friendship of the United States; to which I readily assented." A year later Monroe learned that Captain Bradley had been appointed, immediately on his return, to the command of a ship of the line. Amer. State Papers, For. Rel., III, 90, 100.

blockade of five months, are proofs of his merit as a Seaman and an officer. I have the utmost respect for him, and will consider myself under an obligation by your acquainting the Lords Commissioners of the Admiralty, that my letter of the 27th of June was not intended by any means as a complaint against Captain Bradley, but for the information of His Majestys Ministers, that they might be possessed of the facts, whenever a representation was made by the American Government.

TO MR. MERRY.

New York 10 Nov[r] 1804.

SIR.

I yesterday by the return of the dispatch Boat, received a letter from Captain Bradley the officer commanding His Majestys Ships Cambrian and Leander dated at Sea the 7th Instant, wherein he informs me that he arrived at ten O Clock on the night of the third instant off the East End of Long Island, but that the weather was so very thick, that they could not see twice the length of the Ship, and that during the prevalence of this fogg the Enemy had passed him. He had therefore resolved to proceed immediately to Halifax Nova Scotia with both Ships.[1]

I cannot but regret that His Majestys Ships did not go to Sea, from six in the Evening of the 2[d] until 10 oClock that night during all which time the signal fire, which I had informed Captain Bradley would be lighted when the Enemy had passed Hell Gate, was burning, and seen from the Ships. At 8 oClock that night Captain Bradley received a letter from M[r] Barclay my Son, at the Signal Port, giving him notice of the departure of the French Ships, at which time, there was yet near two hours flood tide. Had he then proceeded His Majestys Ships would have doubled Montock point, the East End of Long Island, before sunset on Saturday, and as

[1] The French ships reached L'Orient in December, after a fine passage, and this in spite of their having sailed on a Friday. Was Bradley's failure to start promptly in pursuit due to superstition?

the weather was then clear must have seen the Enemys ships. From Captain Bradleys letter it appears, the pilot of the Cambrian made some demur about taking the Ship out at night, but I understand from Captain Skene of the Leander, that his Pilot was not only ready to carry her over the Bar, but return and conduct the Cambrian also.

CHAPTER V

FROM June 18 to November 3, 1804, the port of New-York had been practically blockaded by the little British squadron which had been kept to watch the *Didon* and *Cybèle*. Barclay's correspondence shows, beyond a doubt, that the original purpose of their visit was purely military, and therefore perfectly legitimate; but they improved the occasion by inflicting injuries and insults upon the commerce of a neutral port—one can hardly describe it as a friendly one—which are almost past belief. Basil Hall's account of his service as a midshipman aboard the *Leander* in this summer of 1804 is well known. "Every morning at daybreak," he writes, "we set about arresting the progress of all the vessels we saw, firing off guns to the right and left to make every ship that was running in heave to, or wait until we had leisure to send a boat on board 'to see,' in our lingo, 'what she was made of.' I have frequently known a dozen, and sometimes a couple of dozen, ships lying a league or two off the port, losing their fair wind, their tide, and worse than all their market, for many hours, sometimes the whole day, before our search was completed."[1] The search might result in ordering off the vessel to Halifax for adjudication, and it almost invariably did result in adding two or three likely men to the crew aboard his Majesty's ship. The guesses or

---

[1] Fragments of Voyages and Travels, Chap. V.

suspicions of British lieutenants as to the true ownership of goods, or the nationality of a seaman, were practically decisive; for redress came but seldom, and it
almost always came too late. The sense of wrong felt
by ship-owners and mariners was immensely aggravated
by the circumstance that all this was taking place in
full sight of American soil, and probably in many instances within American jurisdiction.

But now, for a time, the annoyance of a blockade
was over; and, indeed, it was never renewed in any
time of peace for more than a very brief period. The
chorus of complaints in regard to " impressment within
American waters, maltreatment, and imprudent expressions " had produced its effect even on the minds of
British naval officers. Since the latter part of August
they had exhibited little activity. During September
and October the *Leander* and *Cambrian* had, for the
most part, been lying snugly at anchor within the Hook,
partly because of protests and remonstrances, and partly
because the advancing season greatly multiplied the
difficulties of an effective blockade.

The coasts of New Jersey and Long Island trend
away to the southward and eastward, nearly at right
angles to each other, and deep water is generally to
be found close inshore. A wide opening and a broad
stretch of sea was thus left to be patroled by vessels
that watched outside the bar; and if the British
cruisers were strictly to observe American neutrality, and confine their efforts to points distant three
miles from either shore, the task of intercepting vessels
that chose to hug the beaches became almost hopeless.
The longer nights and stormier weather of autumn also
greatly facilitated the escape of outward-bound ships,
whether American traders or French frigates. No

square-rigged vessel could safely keep her station close outside the bar of New-York, in an easterly gale, so as to intercept all incoming vessels; and the northwesterly gales of winter would prevent her from lying to under canvas, a league or more offshore, in such a position as to arrest vessels who had the choice of running out either to the southward or eastward.

As soon, therefore, as the French frigates had sailed, the English gave up their watch on the port. For many months there was no further serious cause of complaint. But the reckless proceedings of the summer of 1804 had not been forgotten, and they were to bear bitter fruit in the increasing ill-will with which the American people regarded the Government of Great Britain.

All through the year 1805, while the great strategic movements which culminated at Trafalgar were going on in other waters, British squadrons had ample occupation elsewhere. In the month of June the *Cambrian* and *Leander* were once more for a few days off New-York, accompanied by the sloop-of-war *Busy;* but, with this exception, there were only brief visits from single ships. The *Révolutionnaire* called for Spanish dollars on February 3; the *Busy* came from Bermuda on March 6, with despatches, and sailed within a week for Halifax; an armed schooner was off Sandy Hook for a few days in May; the *Indian* arrived in August, and the *Cambrian* early in November, remaining each but a short time; and the *Busy* called again on December 6, with despatches. There was no attempt at a repetition of the blockade of 1804, and the year passed here without special incident. American vessels were, indeed, searched and seamen impressed, but it would be a mistake to suppose that there was, in 1805, anything like a continuous watch kept by the British upon the commerce of this port.[1]

In the spring of 1806, the *Cambrian* and *Leander* a third time appeared off Sandy Hook, this time in company with the sloop-of-war *Driver*. Their unwelcome presence was tragically signalized by the killing of an American citizen by a shot from the *Leander*, and their visit was brought to a sudden end.

Meanwhile, during these years of 1805 and 1806, Barclay's domestic affairs were prosperous. Henry, his eldest son, entered into partnership with a Mr. Henry C. Rumsey, "a wholesale Silk mercer." De Lancey left the 17th Dragoons and got a commission as Captain in the 56th Regiment of Foot. Thomas, after serving in the *Boston* and *Impétueux* under Captain Douglas, was promoted to the rank of Lieutenant, and joined the *Northumberland* under Admiral Cochrane.[2] George and Anthony were still at school in Nova Scotia.

One sad event occurred. Susan, who had married Mr. Stuyvesant in the summer of 1803, died within eighteen months of her marriage, when not quite twenty years old, in her new house in Partition (Fulton) street. Her death threw a great shadow over this period of Barclay's career; and it made a deep and lasting impression on his mind.

. His home, until the summer of 1806, continued to be in New-York, except when the yellow fever again drove him for a few weeks into the country. This time he found refuge at Elizabeth, in New Jersey, and he re-

---

[1] Into this mistake both Mr. Adams and Professor McMaster have fallen. Adams's Hist. of the U. S., Vol. III, pp. 91, 92; McMaster's Hist. of the U. S., Vol. III, pp. 236, 246.

[2] De Lancey Barclay's commission as Captain in H. M. Army bore date April 24, 1805; Thomas's as Lieutenant in the navy, September 11, 1805.

mained there from about September 12 to October 22, 1805. In June, 1806, Barclay gave up his Greenwich street residence and moved into the country, in the Town of Harlaem, about seven miles from the city; and there, for the next ten years, his family continued to live. His house, with its ten acres of ground, lay in a pleasant suburb near the East River. It was situated on both sides of the present line of First Avenue, and extended from about 108th to 113th street. It cost £5500 New-York currency, or $13,750.

These two peaceful years in New-York were eventful enough in the world's history. Jefferson was reëlected President. Burr's term as Vice-President ended, and he fell to hatching his mad conspiracy. Pitt died. The victories of Austerlitz and Jena gave Napoleon the mastery of Europe. The victory of Trafalgar gave England the absolute control of the sea.

TO THE COLLECTOR, NAVAL OFFICER, AND SURVEYOR OF THE PORT OF NEW-YORK.

New York 19ᵗʰ Novʳ 1804

GENTLEMEN.

The Lords of the Admiralty having ordered Captain Beresford of the Royal Navy to proceed to America to take the command of His Britannic Majestys Ship of War Cambrian, Captain Beresford in obedience to those orders arrived not long since at Norfolk in Virginia in His Majestys Ship of War Revolutionnaire. At the time of his arrival at Norfolk, the Cambrian was off and on this Port, and Captain Beresfords baggage and Stores were put on board an American coaster in Hampton Roads for the purpose of being conveyed to the Cambrian. Previous to the arrival of the coaster off this Port, not only the Cambrian but the Leander had sailed for

Halifax in Nova Scotia, and Captain Beresfords Baggage and Stores in which are included seven hogsheads, one quarter cask and thirty dozen of Madeira Wine, were brought up to this city, and are now on board the coaster. Captain Beresford wishes to have permission to remove them from thence on board a schooner which he has chartered to carry his baggage and stores to Halifax, free from the American duties to which the Wines have undoubtedly become liable by the unexpected departure of the Cambrian. — Permit me to request you Gentlemen will be pleased to grant a permit for the above purpose: The liberality of the American Government I trust will prevent an exaction of duties on articles composing the Stores of a naval officer casually arriving in transit within its Jurisdiction.[1]

TO MR. MERRY.

New York 20th November 1804

SIR.

By this day's post I have received your No 37, covering a draft made by G. Simpson Cashier of the Bank of the United States on the Cashier of the office of discount and deposit in this City in your favor for seven hundred and fifty thousand dollars and by you indorsed to me, also a form of the receipt I am to take in triplicate on delivering the above amount in gold to Captain Hotham Commander of His Majesty's Ship Revolutionnaire —

I have had a confidential communication with the Cashier of the office of discount & deposit in this City, who purposes if it meets your approbation to pay the whole in British and Portugal Gold, but by far the greater proportion in British — There is very little French Gold in the Bank here.—

[1] Captain Beresford did not go to Halifax, but remained in New-York until about December 23, when the Cambrian arrived here. Captain Beresford and his Madeira then joined her and proceeded at once to the West Indies.

TO MR. MERRY.

New York 6ᵗʰ Dec' 1804.

SIR.

The Spanish and French coins, as I have before noticed are in very good order, having suffered little or no mutilation, the proportion of French is very trifling.— The British Gold is also tolerably good, the one half at least standard weight, but the Portugal Gold is abominably clipped, sweated, and mutilated, and at least one fourth part of it consists of half Johannes made from Spanish Gold, for the West India market or plugged half Johannes.— These are returned and other good gold given in their place.— The selection of these is difficult and occupies much time. I however hope the whole will be examined and packed by Tuesday or Wednesday next.— Mʳ Burrell is very polite and accommodating.

I have by two conveyances notified Vice Admiral Sir Andrew Mitchell of the arrival of the Poursuivante (now called the President) in the Chesepeak — and shall by the next opportunity acquaint him with Captain Hothams situation.— Captain Beresford who is still here, has requested the Admiral to send the Cambrian to this place for him, and also notified him of the Poursuivante: he tells me he expects her here in the course of a few days.

TO MRS. MARGARET DE LANCEY.

New York 31 Jan' 1805.

DEAR MADAM.

The inclosed letter I received yesterday from the Attorney employed to collect the Debts due the late General Hamilton, who I retained as your Counsel against this State.— This charge stands in the Generals books in addition to the hundred dollars originally paid him by me; and of course ought to be paid. I have therefore discharged it, and will thank you to pay my draft in favor of Messrs. Brook Watson & Co: for that amount on you.

14

Mrs. Barclay, myself and family, are in extreme distress by the death of my lovely and most amiable daughter Mrs. Stuyvesant who died on the 14 of this month — She had not yet attained her twentieth year.— I do not say too much when I add that she was in mind and appearance one of the first of Women, and in duty and affection the best of Children.— You my dear Madam can and I am sure will feel for us.

TO JAMES FAIRLIE, DEPUTY MAYOR.

New York 7 March 1805.

SIR.

I have received your letter of this day, on the subject of James Smith, Richard Jenkins, James Stokely, James Bailey, James Woodworth and many other Citizens of the United States of America composing the crew of the American Ship Manhattan bound from Batavia to this Port having been impressed in February last at Sea by the Commander of His Britannic Majestys Sloop of War Busy, and that they are unlawfully detained on board the said Sloop now in this Harbour; and that these facts have been verified to you under oath.[1]

Permit me to assure you that it is not only contrary to the orders of the Lords of the Admiralty to impress, but to the wishes of the Commanders of His Majestys Ships of War to detain an American Seaman. But it is a fact too notorious to have escaped your knowledge, that many of His Majestys Subjects are furnished with American Protection, to which they have no right or title —

[1] The Manhattan belonged to Frederick and Philip Rhinelander, and was chartered by Minturn & Champlin for a voyage to Batavia and back. On her return, with a cargo of sugar, coffee, indigo, and spices, she was captured by H. M. brig Busy, on the alleged ground that she carried a Dutch passenger from the Cape of Good Hope. She was sent in to Bermuda, but ordered to be restored by the Vice-Admiralty Court. See Amer. State Papers, For. Rel., Vol. II, p. 765.

Capt Biam of the British Sloop of War now in this Port has on board, I believe, thirteen men of the Crew which sailed in the Manhattan from Batavia, and which he took out of that Ship when he sent her to the Vice Court of Admiralty at Bermuda for adjudication. There can be no question at present as to these men, because the owners, or rather the Gentlemen who chartered the Ship Messrs Minturn and Champlin have requested Capt Biam to take these men with him to Bermuda, in order that they may navigate the Manhattan from thence to this Port in the event of her being released by the Vice Court of Admiralty, which in their and my opinion is probable, although a part of the cargo may be condemned — These men are bound to perform the Voyage, and Captain Biam is equally bound to see them forth coming if the ship is restored — under these circumstances you will I trust be of opinion that they cannot be discharged here — Still Sir to insure the readiness of Captain Biam to comply with your request — He is willing in the event of a regular release to him from the owners of the Manhattan, the Underwriters and the freighters of that ship, to discharge forthwith such of the men as are bona fide Americans.

TO MR. HAMMOND.

New York 13th March 1805.
SIR.

By this days southern mail I have received information that Jerome Bonaparte his Lady & a female companion of hers, with several Servants, will or rather have embarked on board the Ship Erin Capt Stephenson ladened with flour, & was to sail about the 10th Inst from Baltimore probably for Lisbon.[1] The Erin sails very fast, & was lately employed by the Span-

---

[1] The Erin sailed from Baltimore on March 11, and arrived at Lisbon safely on April 2. Jerome Bonaparte there parted from his wife, who sailed in the Erin again to Amster- dam; but not being permitted to land, went to London, where her child was born July 7. She returned with the child to the United States in the autumn of this year.

ish minister at Lisbon to carry dispatches to Cuba & Porto Rico, from whence she came to Baltimore & has been hastily prepared to carry Bonaparte & his family —

I have thought proper to give you this information in the Event of its being thought necessary by His Majesty's Minister to have an attempt made to intercept him — Will you do me the honor to lay the above before Lord Mulgrave?[1]

TO VICE-ADMIRAL SIR JOHN ORDE.[2]

BRITISH CONSUL GENERALS OFFICE

New York 13th March 1805.

SIR.

I have this day received information, that Jerome Bonaparte, Brother to the Emperor, his Lady, a female companion and his domestics, were on the 10th Instant to embark on board the Ship Erin, Stephenson Master, at Baltimore for Lisbon; but possibly for some other European Port.

It is not long since that the Erin was chartered by the Spanish Minister at Lisbon to carry out dispatches to the Havannah and Porto Rico, having delivered them, she came to Baltimore, where she has taken a cargo, or part cargo of flour, and has been hurried to sail with all speed with Bonaparte.

She is a fine small Ship, sails very fast, bright sides, white bottom, black Wales, yellow Gun wale, dead eyes yellow, no bull work a midship, and a figure head.[3]

I have thought it proper to give you this information, that you may have it in your power to intercept them.—

[1] Lord Mulgrave had succeeded Lord Harrowby as Foreign Secretary upon Addington's joining Pitt's Ministry, January 11, 1805.

[2] Commanding the British Squadron blockading Cadiz.

[3] The Erin was captured a year or so later by H. M. S. Leopard, and Basil Hall put aboard of her as prize-master. "I certainly never saw a more perfect model of a merchant vessel," he wrote, "or one more commodiously fitted up." Fragments of Voyages and Travels, Chap. xvii.

TO MR. MERRY.

New York 18th March 1805

The Collector of the Customs informed me on Saturday that he had not officially received a copy of the "Act for the more " effectual preservation of Peace in the Ports and Harbours of "the United States and in the Waters under their Jurisdic-"tion": nor any rules, instructions, orders, or directions for the carrying the objects of this act into effect from the President of the United States, or otherwise.[1] He has assured me that on receiving any communication on this Subject he will give me the earliest notice, and permit me to peruse them, unless they are of a nature not to be divulged —

I shall take occasion from time to time to enquire of him whether he has received any instructions, and give you the earliest notice of their extent —

There will be no conveyance from hence to Bermuda in less than eighteen or twenty days; so that it is more than probable that Vice Admiral Sir Andrew Mitchell with his whole Squadron will have left that place for the Season, before your letter for him arrives — You will have time to give me further directions with respect to it. In the interval, I shall by every vessel going to the West Indies, write a line addressed to the Admiral or any of the Commanders of His Majestys Ships of War and desire them not to come within Sandy Hook, until they first communicate with me. There can be little doubt,

[1] This act was approved March 3, 1805. A brief summary of its provisions will be found in Adams's Hist. of the U. S., Vol. II, p. 397. Among other things, the act authorized the arrest of offenders against American laws when found on board foreign armed vessels, and required such vessels to report to the Collector of the port and obey his directions; and the President was required to give, "as soon as may be," instructions to all Collectors, U. S. Marshals, and other officers, as to their duties under this act. Mr. Merry's "inquietudo" with regard to the clause of the act permitting the arrest of foreign officers for "any tort or trespass" on an American vessel on the high seas, or "any unlawful interruption or vexation of trading vessels," is described in Mr. Madison's instructions to Mr. Monroe of March 6, 1805. Amer. State Papers, For. Rel., Vol. III, p. 100.

14*

but one of my letters will be received in the course of ten days or a fortnight —

TO VICE-ADMIRAL SIR ANDREW MITCHELL.

New York, 25 March 1805

SIR,

I take it for granted Mr. Merry has mentioned to you the very extraordinary act passed at the last session of Congress, with his opinion on it — You will perceive from the general tenor of this act, particularly the 4, 5, 6, 7 and last Sections, that it will be hazarding too much to permit His Majestys Ships of War to enter any of the American Ports until an explanation has taken place between the two Governments — By several conveyances to the West Indies I have addressed letters to you or any of the Commanders of His Majestys Ships of War advising them of this act, and recommending the laying off and on an American Port until you or they communicated with His Majestys Minister at Washington, or the resident British Consul, where the Ship may arrive — I have taken the liberty to inclose you the act, as I have reason to believe it is not in either of Mr. Merry's letters.

I also inclose you this day's paper by which you will learn the unpleasant account of the arrival of a French Squadron in the West Indies.[1]

TO JOHN McKENZIE.

New York 2ᵈ April 1805

DEAR SIR,

You will naturally be surprized at my Silence, which has even exceeded the limit I wished, but the situation of my mind for some months past has prevented my writing except in cases of emergency ; and as your cause before the Chancel-

---

[1] This was Missiessy's squadron, which reached Martinique February 20.

lor was not decided until Thursday last I deferred writing having nothing satisfactory to communicate.[1]

The chancellor has not without difficulty at last decreed the lands to me in trust to be sold for your benefit. I shall offer them immediately for sale, but Lands are so low and money scarce that I fear they cannot be disposed of to advantage.

Mrs. Barclay, myself and family are under the deepest affliction for the loss of my lovely and most amiable daughter Mrs. Stuyvesant who died in January, and before she had attained her twentieth year.— Her death was occasioned by a premature delivery of her first child, still born. She died four days after, but suffered inexpressible pain — To lose such a child, with such flattering prospects, and in such a manner is more than human nature can support — Within the short period of 18 months, two most beloved children have expired in my arms.— Parents never were blessed with more dutiful, correct and every way promising children — You who are a father can and as a friend I am sure will feel for me — God grant you may never taste of that cup of which so large a portion has been mine.

When you go up to London, I wish you would take occasion to say to some of the principal underwriters at Lloyds, that they are shamefully defrauded in this City, under the excuse of an averaged loss upon damaged goods — That nothing is more easy than to procure the Port Wardens to mark the goods as damaged — It is the daily practise when merchandize arrives to a bad market, or the importer is in want of cash — the very importer often buys them in at 50 per Cent under first costs — If one bale is injured ten others not injured are sold under the averaged loss — Every merchant of respectabil-

---

[1] Mr. McKenzie was a merchant in England who had a claim against the estate of Colonel McGregor. McKenzie authorized John Munro, of New-York, to collect or settle the debt, which he did by taking a conveyance of certain lands from Mc-Gregor's trustees; but Munro dying soon after, intestate, the title to the lands vested in his heirs, and the suit in question was brought to have a trust declared in respect to the property and to have a new trustee appointed.

ity in this City speaks of the impositions practised on the British underwriters — The Evil will continue while there is no person authorized to counteract the conduct of the Port Wardens, and to act as the agent for the underwriters.   You will perceive that it is the interest of the Port Wardens to condemn goods whenever they can, because they receive two per Cent on the sales, which constitutes the principal profits of their office.

Do me the favor to communicate this to the Gentlemen at Lloyds and to Mr. John Gladstone and the other merchants at Liverpool.

TO CAPTAIN CHAUNCEY.[1]

New York 2ᵈ April 1805

SIR,

Samuel Balfour master of the British Brig Culmar and Peter Brown master of the British Ship Cecilia have represented to me that an apprentice Boy of Capt. Balfour named John Garnly, and an articled Boy of Capt. Brown, named John Hamilton both British Subjects have entered and now are on board the United States Ship of War John Adams in this Port and under your command — That they have applied for the re-delivery of their Boys and are told by Lieut. Maxwell that they would not be restored until all expenses were paid.— It is unnecessary for me to make a remark on the impropriety of such an answer.— That the American Government have a right to receive on board their ships British Seamen who desert from British Ships, is a position that can never be maintained; and it follows, that on discovery they ought to be restored — Permit me therefore to request you will be pleased to direct that the Boys above mentioned may be delivered to

---

[1] Isaac Chauncey, at this time commanding the sloop John Adams, had already distinguished himself before Tripoli, and was to attain wider distinction in the War of 1812 by his services on Lake Ontario.

their respective masters, without any charge, as that rule cannot be admitted: nor is it ever practised in the British Navy —

I am under the necessity to acquaint you further that four Boys have deserted from His Majesty's Packet Queen Charlotte now in this Port and ready to sail to-morrow, and that they have been entered on board your Ship. Be pleased to inform me whether you will deliver them to the captain or master of the Packet if they wait on you for that purpose. They are assuredly on board your ship, the fact has been proved to me —

TO CAPTAIN CHAUNCEY.

New York 4ᵗʰ April 1805.

SIR.

I have the Honor to acknowledge the receipt of your letter of yesterday and beg your acceptance of my best acknowledgements for your ready compliance with my request —

I should certainly have made my first application to you respecting the British Seamen, had not Captain Balfour of the Culmar and Capt. Brown of the Cecilia told me that the officer commanding on board the United States Ship John Adams had referred them to Lieut. Maxwell the regulating officer at the Rendezvous here of that Ship, and that Lieut. Maxwell had told them, the men would not be given up until the advance money and all other expenses were paid. On this information I thought it unnecessary to apply to you, under a supposition that you were under such orders from the American Secretary of the Navy — The speedy departure of His Majesty's Packet rendered it necessary for me to apply to the Mayor as well as yourself, because in the event of their not being restored, I should have been obliged to have taken affidavits of the Facts — I took it for granted that the Mayor had no control over you or in Naval matters, yet it appeared probable to me that his recommendation would add weight to my application.

Your experience in every instance where you have met with Officers of His Britannic Majesty's Navy, renders it unnecessary for me to say with what pleasure they render the American Naval Officers every aid in their power and I am gratified by the very handsome and polite manner in which you have been pleased to express similar sentiments toward them, and your readiness to support a continuance of the present good Understanding which subsists between our respective Governments.

TO MR. MERRY.

New York, 16ᵗʰ April 1805.

(*Private.*)

DEAR SIR,

I am much obliged by your private letter of the 13ᵗʰ of this Month, and for your general justification of my proceedings respecting the Crew of the Manhattan, and my Correspondence with the Deputy Mayor of this City on the Subject, to which it appears the American Secretary of State has thought proper to except, and to transmit you a formal Complaint.— Wherever His Majesty's Interest, and that of the Nation are involved, I shall always consider it my duty to speak the truth, however unpleasant it may be to those who hear or feel it; an opposite line of Conduct will gain little in this Country, where politeness is too generally supposed to originate in timidity, & accommodation in Servility. The French know better how to treat the Americans.

You will be pleased to observe that, that point of my letter which appears to have given the greatest offence and of which you have given me an extract, was in reply to the demand of the Deputy Mayor, that every Seaman on board His Majesty's Sloop Busy from the Manhattan possessed of a Certificate of American Citizenship should immediately be set at liberty: upon this principle, that these Certificates were evidence of their being American Citizens, until the Contrary was proved. It became necessary to resist this position, & in my opinion, not improper in my reply, to state the above abuses in the granting of these Certificates. The Doctrine set up by the Deputy Mayor would be productive of serious consequences to His Majesty's Service, & effectually preclude the Commanders of Ships of War from recovering a British Seaman possessed of one of these Certificates. It is a claim admirably adapted to the carrying into effect the act for the better preservation of Peace in the Ports of the United States and the Waters within their Jurisdiction.— Let the Scotch accent or Irish Brogue, be ever so strong it is to have no weight, where opposed to a Certificate of Citizenship. Passing over in silence the innumerable instances where British Subjects within a month after their arrival in these States obtain Certificates, permit me to remind you, that by a Law of these States, a residence of five years entitles a man to a Certificate of Citizenship. The United States have a right to enact what laws they please, but it rests with His Majesty whether he will suffer them to operate in violation of his rights. If Congress have a right to say five years residence shall create a foreigner a Citizen, in such an absolute manner as not to be reclaimed by the power to which he originally belonged — They may with the same propriety enact the moment a foreigner sets foot in these States, he becomes ipso facto, an American Citizen & to be protected as such — The Documents which I have already furnished you prove the indiscriminate use of those Certificates, and I might appeal to the Commander of the American Ships of War whether the major part of their crews have not been natives of Great Britain or Ireland. The fact is notorious, and the truth of my remark was the only cause of offence. Perhaps my objection was too broad, I wish it had been more qualified, but will Mr Madison venture to say that there have not been great and innumerable abuses in granting of these Certificates — If this is the Case, really he should not have found fault with an assertion which possibly may have applied too extensive limits, to what is exceeded as extension. I shall studiously avoid in all my communications with the officers of the American Government using expressions which may in the most remote manner give pain or offence unless indispensable in asserting the Rights of my Sovereign. I have the Collector's assurances that he has not yet received any order for carrying the Act for the better preservation of Peace &c &c into effect —

TO VICE-ADMIRAL SIR ANDREW MITCHELL.

New York 3ᵈ May 1805.
SIR.

I understand Mʳ Le Blanc who commanded an armed tender attached to the Cambrian has left the position off Sandy Hook and returned to Halifax; in which event he will have been with you some time before this is received; and have informed you of the desertion of his sailing Master and eight Seamen with the Cutter.— Every exertion in my power has been made to regain the men, but no traces could be found of any of them, save the sailing Master and a man dressed in a black coat, white trousers and vest, about twenty-five years old, dark hair and about 5 feet 10 Inches. — They were discovered by a man who I had employed, but before I could get a peace officer to the house, they were off and have not been since seen. From the best legal advice I am however told that nothing could have been done with these men, because the taking of the Boat would not be adjudged a felony, as they left her on a beach, but merely as a means of their escape — That it has been so adjudged in the case of men who affected their escape from an American Ship in the same way.

I forwarded to you at Bermuda the act of Congress for the better preservation of peace in the harbours and ports of the United States and the Waters thereof — and I have since forwarded several letters from Mʳ Merry to you which I suppose to be on the same subject — No instructions have yet been received by the Collector of the Customs of this Port, as he assures me, from the President for carrying this law into effect —And it is not only my opinion but that of many of the best informed Gentlemen of this place, that the President will not

send any instructions, or if he does they will be so guardedly
expressed, as to give no power to the Collectors until each particular case is reported — If necessary I am therefore of opinion you may with safety send any of your ships here, I would
however recommend their not coming nearer town than Staten
Island —

TO VICE-ADMIRAL SIR ANDREW MITCHELL.

New York 4 May 1805.

SIR.

I have the Honor to inform you that several Vessels which
have arrived within these States from the West Indies, report
that they saw the french Squadron lately in the West Indies
on the 4th, 5th and 8th of last Month steering to the Northward,
on the last day they were in N. L. 24 : 14 — L. 66.

There is reason to suppose that they are bound for Newfoundland and possibly for Halifax.[1]

TO MR. MERRY.

New York 14th May 1805.

SIR.

I have the Honor to inform you that a french Privateer
Schooner of twelve Guns arrived here on the Evening of the
12th and came to an anchor between this and Staten Island;
but yesterday, Mail was closed, before I could learn her destination or object. — She belongs to Victor Hughes[2] the Governor of Cayenne and having sprung a leak has put in to this
place for repair, and I understand the Governor has granted
permission — I shall observe the nature of the repairs, and re-

---

[1] Missiessy, with the Rochefort Squadron, sailed from the West Indies
about the first of April, and reached Rochefort again on May 26.

[2] Hugues.

port them to you, if they appear more than necessary to carry
her back in safety to Cayenne —

I have received information this morning from a confidential
person who spoke a Spanish Privateer of 14 Guns on Sunday
a little to the Southward of this port, the Captain of which
said he should cruise some time between this and the Chesepeak — I shall give Vice-Admiral Sir Andrew Mitchell the
earliest information.

TO VICE-ADMIRAL SIR A. MITCHELL.

New York 16th May 1805

SIR

Since my letter to you of the 14th Current, I have received
information from the Master of an American Vessel, that he
was boarded about 50 Leagues to the Southward of Savannah
in Georgia by a french Privateer named the Grand Visiteur of
22 Guns and 150 Men, destined to cruise off Georgia — You
will perceive by the newspaper inclosed that there is also
another french Privateer off this Port — I take it for granted
they have heard of your having gone with the Squadron to
Nova Scotia, and have come on the American Coast to reap
while your Ships are in port — The President has not sent any
instructions to the Collector of the Customs for carrying into
effect the Law for the better preservation of Peace in the
Ports of the United States and the waters under their Jurisdiction: your ships may therefore for the present come with
safety within Sandy Hook — It may however not be amiss to
give particular orders to the Commanders, not to let the yawl
from the Pilot boat come along side, but send their own boat
to take him out, and when on board ship, that he is not permitted to speak to any of the Men — These Pilots invariably
bring letters from on board, and verbal complaints of Men
representing themselves to be Americans — as there is always
an officer on the Quarter Deck, it cannot in my opinion be
difficult to prevent the Pilot conversing with the Seamen —

TO DE WITT CLINTON.

New York 3ᵈ July 1805

SIR.

I am informed that the French Privateer Les Amie has more Guns on board than those she arrived with in this Port; her number of Guns being then eight and that she has increased her original complement of men, who were sixty four in number —

I have therefore to request that you will take the proper measures to prevent her leaving this Port with an increase of men or Guns, as it is inconsistent with the Laws of Nations — It is further stated to me, but this is a fact not in my power at present to prove but which ought to come within the knowledge of the Customs, that Powder has been put on board this Privateer in this Port — The Privateer will sail at daybreak to morrow morning, unless detained by you for examination —

TO MR. MERRY.

New York 6 July 1805

SIR.

I have the Honor to inclose to you my letter of the 3ᵈ current to the Mayor of this City on the Subject of the French Privateer Les Amie then in this Port, with his answer to me on the subject, which appears very positive, particularly when it is considered that his information from his own statement appears to have been drawn from the assurances of the French Commissary and the Agent of the Privateer. It is not for me to enter into a dispute with the Mayor on this subject, because I am not certain that it would be in my power to bring forward Witnesses to prove that the Privateer had received additional Guns while in this Port, or an increase of Powder and Shot; but I trust you will agree with me that his measures to ascertain the fact, should have been by an examination of the Ship by Custom House or other Civil officers, and not to build an answer on the assurances of the French Commissary or Agent of the Privateer.— I submit the case to your better judgement and hope you will be able to obtain from the American Secretary of State directions to the Mayor for his taking more satisfactory measures in future on similar occasions.

TO MR. MERRY.

New York, 22ᵈ July 1805

SIR.

On the subject of Mr. Madison's answer to your representation respecting the French Privateer Les Amie repaired in this Port, permit me to remark, that on her arrival here application was made to the Governor to allow her to come up to the City in order to undergo necessary repairs, to which he assented. I have since been informed by the Deputy Collector that on a supposition that she was a Commissioned Vessel the Custom House took no cognizance of her — an application therefore to the Collector would probably have proved unsatisfactory — But while that Privateer was in port, I privately called on the Surveyor of the Customs, and acquainted him that I had reason to believe that vessel would receive a repair beyond what was necessary under the treaty between France and the United States of America and contrary to the Laws of Nations, and that I had received information she would take on board Guns, powder and shot purchased in this City, and requested he would direct his officers to attend to her and report the facts — The Surveyor a few days before the sailing of the Privateer assured me that his officers had not been able to detect any thing which he considered illegal, but he added that as the Privateer lay in the Stream and he could not send an officer on board, that the Warlike articles by me mentioned might at night have been put on board without his knowledge or that of his officers.

TO MR. MERRY.

Elizabeth town New Jersey.

12ᵗʰ September 1805.

SIR.

I have in consequence of the yellow fever having extended itself over every part of New York, been obliged to remove with my family to this place until health is restored to that unfortunate City.

The symptoms of that fever and its mortality are stated by the faculty to be more violent and greater than in preceeding years.— You will for the present be pleased to address your letters for me at this place.

During the prevalence of the fever I shall be twice in each week, as near the City as possible to attend to the duties of my office.

TO MR. MERRY.

New York 7 Nov' 1805.

SIR.

It appears that Col: Williams of the Engineers some time since received orders to survey, and examine the Port of New York, and report the particular scite most proper for the erecting of Fortifications for the defence of that place, the extent and nature of these works, whether Islands might not be formed by art peculiarly adapted to defence, and to present an estimate of the aggregate expence which would attend the Works he should propose as necessary.[1]

[1] See as to Lt.-Col. Williams's Report, Amer. State Papers, Mil. Affairs, Vol. I, p. 193. Jonathan Williams, "the father of West Point," was born at Boston, May 26, 1750. He was a great-nephew of Benjamin Franklin, and was Franklin's secretary in Paris, where he studied the science of fortification. He returned to America after the peace, entered the Army, and became the first Superintendent of the Military Academy. He died May 16, 1815.

15

He attended the examination and survey for several days about the 20th of October, and a part of this duty was before that date and since committed to the Care of a Captain Macomb.[1] What his report was I cannot yet ascertain but hope to do it in the course of a week or ten days, but this is certain that while he was on this duty, he declared that as it was impossible to form any correct estimate, he would not therefore risque his reputation in reporting a Sum, that might exceed or fall short of the necessary expenditures.

The New York Gazette very incorrectly stated that a Pilot went down on the 5th to bring His Majesty's Ship Cambrian within the Hook — The Cambrian has not been within, on the sixth having agreed with Captain Beresford that he would be within a few miles of Sandy Hook, my son carried down some dollars in a Pilot Boat, and the Ship immediately got under way : and was to sail this day for Halifax, the limitation of the cruize being expired.

FROM MR. BROUGHTON.

Downing Street Jan' 3ᵈ 1806.
DEAR SIR,

I have just received your letter of the 5th ult? — The Anti Jacobin is stopped — The Gazette shall be commenced Tomorrow.   I delivered your letter to Capt Barclay whom I have requested to give me a few days previous notice should he desire to avail himself of your authority for him to draw upon me for a few Hundred Pounds to compleat the purchase of his Majority —

The Accounts from the Continent are so truly disastrous and afflicting that I will only say I consider the Good Cause as utterly hopeless — Bonaparte being absolute Master of the Continent.[2] The Southern Part of which he will carve and

[1] Alexander Macomb was at this time 23 years old. He was rapidly promoted during the war with England, attained the rank of Major-General in 1814, became Command-ing General of the Army, and died June 25, 1841.

[2] The battle of Austerlitz was fought December 2, 1805.

apportion in whatever manner he pleases. His Plan appears to me to be to reestablish The Empire of *The West* in his own Person.

There is little to look forward to with the smallest complacency. A protracted War will exhaust our pecuniary resources and a speedy Peace will release the Corsican's Sailors now in our Prisons and afford him the means of creating a Navy which may be able to dispute the Dominion of the Seas with that of Great Britain — until which, I hold all his Vaporing about Invasion as mere empty Gasconade — We never can be invaded with any prospect of Success on his Part until his descent is covered by a powerful Fleet.

Ever dear Sir
Very truly Yours
C. R. BROUGHTON.

TO VICE-ADMIRAL SIR ANDREW MITCHELL.

New York, 1ˢᵗ Feby 1806.

SIR.

Previous to your leaving Halifax for Bermuda, you must have heard that the Americans had warmly taken up the Doctrine advanced in a late British Pamphlet entitled war in Disguise;[1] and of what they termed a violation of their neutral Rights by recent captures on the Part of His Majesty and condemnations of property on board American Ships. The Merchants of the principal Cities in these States have memorialed Congress on this Subject in strong Languages — a Copy of one of these I have the Honor to inclose. Things appear to me to be approximating to an unpleasant Crisis between Great Britain and these States. On Wednesday last a resolution passed the lower house in Congress on the Subject of passing an Act to prohibit the importation of any goods wares merchandizes or any thing the Produce of Great Britain, its

---

[1] See Adams's Hist. of the U. S., Vol. III, pp. 50-53.

Dominions &c.— This resolution [1] you will find in one of the news Papers inclosed, and in another news paper the remonstrance of the Am[n] Minister at London to Lord Mulgrave on the general subject of violation of neutral rights. [2] It is doubtful whether Congress will eventually pass a law to prohibit importations from Great Britain and its dependencies, yet as they appear to grow daily more warm, in proportion as they debate on the question, I confess I should not be surprised if so imprudent a measure was carried. I have thought it my duty to give you this hint, that you may if you judge proper order some of the Ships under your command to touch more frequently here, than you originally intended.

I do not know what may have passed between you and Lieut General Gardner on the Subject of money now in my hands for the use of His Majestys Forces, and of its conveyance from hence to Halifax; but under the present appearances I much wish it was from this place; and could wish if it does not militate with more material parts of His Majestys Service that you would have the Goodness to send for it, as soon as it can be conveniently done.

TO ADMIRAL SIR ANDREW MITCHELL.

New York, 29 March 1806.

SIR.

I have the Honor to acknowledge the receipt of a dispatch from Captain Beresford of His Majestys Ship Cambrian of the 22[d] of February by His Majestys Sloop Driver, written by your

[1] The resolution referred to is apparently that introduced by Mr. Gregg of Pennsylvania on Wednesday, January 29, which was not adopted, but was merely referred to a Committee of the Whole on the State of the Union, and ordered to be printed. The resolution was subsequently debated from March 5 to March 17, and lost, a more moderate resolution, proposed by Mr. Nicholson of Maryland, being adopted as a substitute.

[2] Mr. Monroe's letter of September 23, 1805, is the one referred to. It was communicated to Congress by the President, together with memorials from the merchants of New-York, Philadelphia, Newburyport, Charleston, Baltimore, and Norfolk.

order in reply to my letter of the first of that month. I am sorry to inform you that neither the December, January or February Mails have arrived from England; by arrival from thence, I perceive it stated in the London papers that a Packet sailed from Falmouth on the 28th of January for New York. The Winds have since prevailed from the North Eastward, and as the Packets generally take a southern course during the Winter, the length of her passage is easily accounted for, while we have had numbers of Merchants Ships from England and France within the last ten days, in about thirty days passage — The Purser of the Driver came up about 8 oClock last Evening, and returned to the Hook this morning, it being Captain Simpsons intention as the Purser informs me to leave Sandy Hook this day on his return to Bermuda.—I think the packet must be in within 40 hours from this and I shall request the Purser to communicate my opinion to Captain Simpson, that he may wait that period if his orders will permit.—

The news papers herewith sent detail the proceedings in Congress since my last. You will perceive that a resolution has passed the House of Representatives to prohibit the importation of certain articles from Great Britain[1] and a Bill ordered to be brought in for that purpose. Many of the best informed Americans think that the bill will not pass the Senate; I confess, however I am of a different opinion. This Bill altho' not so extensive as M[r] Griggs original motion, cannot but be considered as a very unnecessarily strong measure.— M[r] Randolphs loose desultory speech,[2] will throw some light on the General Subject, it is in one of the News papers.— As most of the Ships that were detained in England last Autumn and early in the Winter, have since been returned and permitted to proceed on their respective Voyages; the American violence against Great Britain has in some measure subsided.

---

[1] Nicholson's resolution, adopted March 17, 1806, which, amended, passed the Senate April 15, 1806.

[2] Speech of March 5, 1806. It was with this speech, says Mr. Henry Adams, that Randolph "began his long public career of opposition.'' Adams's Randolph, pp. 173–181. The speech was reprinted as a pamphlet in London, with an introduction by James Stephen, the author of War in Disguise.

15*

TO MR. MERRY.

New York 24ᵗʰ April 1806

SIR.

The Purser of His Majestys Ship Leander has this day delivered me a letter from Captain Henry Whitby the Commander informing me of his arrival off Sandy Hook, that he was on his way from Bermuda to Halifax, and would proceed the moment the Purser returned with provisions—That he had made New York by order of the Commander in Chief for such dispatches as might be here for him. Captain Whitby will probably sail for Halifax on Sunday.[1]

TO MR. MERRY.

New York, 26ᵗʰ April 1806.

SIR.

I received last Evening a letter from Captain Nairne Commander of His Majesty's Ship Cambrian acquainting me of his arrival off Sandy Hook on his way to the Southward and of the Driver Sloop of War being in company with him. — It appears that the Cambrian went from Bermuda to Halifax, landed Captain Beresford the Senior Officer on that Station, refitted and sailed immediately on a cruise.

I am under the painful necessity to inform you that accounts have been received here last Evening, that the Leander in firing on an American Coaster coming into the Hook, killed the man at the Helm.— It is an accident much to be regretted and will occasion much ill will on the part of the Americans. I shall take occasion this day to recommend more caution to Captain Whitby the Commander of the Leander, and intreat that he and the two other ships of war, will not approach so near the American Coasts, or at least when in such a situation that they abstain from all acts which may give offence — The

[1] April 27.

Leander will proceed for Halifax the first fair Wind — The Cambrian on a cruize to the Southward — I am ignorant of the destination of the Driver.

TO CAPTAIN WHITBY.

New York, 26th April 1806.

SIR.

M[r] Gullet delivered your letter dated off Sandy Hook, which was written as he tells me on the 23[d] ins[t].

Three Mails from Falmouth and several other dispatches for the Naval Commander in chief at Halifax were forwarded some days since by the Princess Mary Packet to Halifax. I have not at present any dispatches —

It was my intention to have requested you to have carried some money for the use of his Majesty's Forces in Nova Scotia; but the accident which occurred to you last Evening in Killing by a Shot from the Leander, a man at the helm of a sloop coming into the Hook, has so irritated the minds of the people of this place, that I fear they will destroy the boat with provisions on board; and should she leave this in safety pursue and plunder her. In addition to this as the wind is from the Eastward attended with Rain and thick weather, you will Keep off shore, and consequently the Boat be obliged to wait within the Hook until it clears up — Under these Circumstances I think it would be imprudent to risque the money —

Your own good Sense will naturally point out to you that the death of this man (which I am sure on your part was unintentional) will occasion serious compl[ts] on the part of the American Government. The sooner therefore that you leave the Coast the better; and I think it advisable that the Cambrian and Driver also withdraw.

I shall not feel easy until I learn that M[r] Lawrence and Gullet are safe on board Ship — They will leave this privately — Be pleased to present my best regards to Captain Beresford.

TO MR. MERRY.

New York 27th April 1806.

SIR.

You have been informed by my letter of the 26th Instant that His Majestys Ships Leander Cambrian and Driver were off this Port, and that on the Evening of the 25th Instant a man belonging to a Sloop from the Delaware to this place had been killed by a shot from the Leander — I was made acquainted with this accident early in the morning of the 26th through the medium of the News Papers, and was convinced it would create much violence in this City.— A Boat which the Purser of the Leander had laden with Beef, Live Stock and other Refreshments and necessaries for the officers and men of that Ship, was therefore hurried from the Wharf, in the hope that she might get to the Leander before the public mind became so agitated as to prevent it. Her departure however was discovered and two fast sailing Boats were despatched to over take and bring her back. In this they succeeded and returned with her in Triumph about 3 oClock in the afternoon of that day. A mob was collected and the Articles placed on about twenty Carts, on the first of which I am informed the British colours were placed on a Pole round and under the American Flag. With Drums beating they paraded the City with the articles destined for the Leander and eventually deposited them in the Alms House for the use of the Poor. The Mob then proceeded some little distance towards St Pauls Church where they burnt the British Colours and after passing down Broadway to White Hall peaceably dispersed. — It was frequently urged by several of them both on the wharff, when they were loading the Carts and while parading the Streets, to go and ransack the British Consuls House — Others cried out, level it with the Ground, while the less violent proposed taking and detaining me a Prisoner until Captain Whitby was given up to be tried for the murder of this man. Through the prudence of some respectable Characters the mob were diverted from assailing my house or insulting my person.— This unfortunate accident has created much ill blood in this City. The

Body of the deceased has been exposed to public View, in order to inflame the minds of the Vulgar and to render the accident subservient to party views at the ensuing election which commences Tomorrow — The inclosed hand bill will give you an Idea of the violence which subsists here.

Under a conviction that that Commander of His Majestys Ship Leander is at this moment ignorant of the Circumstances, I have written to the Mayor for permission to go or send to him, that he may be made acquainted therewith. I have also requested his permission for the four officers of that Ship, who I understand are concealed in or near this City, to go and join her. A copy of my letter to the Mayor I have the Honor to inclose —

TO DE WITT CLINTON.

New York 27ᵗʰ April 1806.
SIR

No one more deeply regrets than I do the unfortunate and fatal accident that has so strongly excited the Sensibility of this City, a regard for whose peace, as well as a desire to apprize the Commander of His Majestys Ship Leander of this occurrence make it in my opinion highly expedient that I be permitted to transmit to this officer an account of what has happened, and of which at this moment, I believe, he remains uninformed —

It is proper likewise that I inform you, that four of His Majestys officers who came to this City two days before the Accident, and who are desirous of returning to the Leander are now in or near this City.

Under these circumstances it becomes my duty to request of you, as the first Magistrate of the City, that I may be permitted to go or send on board His Majestys Ship Leander for the purpose of informing the Commander of the unfortunate death occasioned by a shot from that Ship; and of the Sensibility and Resentment which the same has created throughout the City. It is also my duty to request that the four officers in question be allowed at the same time to go on board the Leander.

I am influenced on this occasion by an earnest desire to do my duty to the King my Master—to secure the Peace of this City and to promote the continuance of that good understanding and Harmony that happily subsists between our respective Countries—

TO MR. MERRY.

New York 29ᵗʰ April 1806

SIR

I have the Honor to inclose to you a copy of the Answer of the Mayor of New York to my letter of the 27ᵗʰ Instant—

You will perceive that the Mayor passes in silence that part of my letter which relates to the officers being permitted to return to their Ships, but his refusal to assent is contained in his general reply, "that he is unwilling to adopt any measures however inconsiderable until he has received orders from the Government"—With respect to my going or sending he adds that as the laws of these States permit it, there is no occasion for his authorization—This answer from the Mayor amounts to a refusal, because he Knows that the Citizens are prohibited by certain resolutions passed at a public meeting on the night of the 27ᵗʰ Instant from having any intercourse with His Majestys Ships—and at the time I delivered him my letter above mentioned, I explained fully to him, that the cause of my application for his permission was to remove the consequences of the Inhibition contained in those resolutions—

My object was to get the officers once more on board their Ships, to have forwarded the Affidavits respecting the death of Pearce, and to have recommended to the Commander the propriety of his Keeping at a greater distance from the American Line of marine Jurisdiction.—

I have been unwearied in my exertions to hire a Vessel to go down to the Ships—No man dares increase the public resentment by communicating with them. Captain Whitby is there-

fore kept in ignorance of the accident and of the public irritation of which you will perceive the Mayor partakes largely
from the expressions contained in his letter to me. I have already informed you in my private letter that I have reason to
believe the continuance of this inhibition, depends on the return of the Pilot Boat sent off on Saturday evening for the
purpose of retaking the American Vessels sent to Halifax for
adjudication. But there is reason to apprehend that the Commander of His Majesty's Ships will come up and enforce the
delivery of his officers — Such a measure would naturally produce very serious consequences — I have made up my mind not
to have any Agency in privately conveying the officers on
board their Ships, who came here on Business and who if they
are not allowed to transact that Business should at least be
permitted to return in safety —

TO CAPTAIN WHITBY.

New York 1ˢᵗ May 1806
SIR

I received at 10 oClock last night your letter of the 30ᵗʰ of
April, and went immediately to see Lieut Cowan who was the
Bearer of your dispatch, and had very properly stopped at Fort
Jay,[1] and to the Mayor of this City to enquire of him what answer he intended to make to your requisition and whether he
would permit the officers of your Ship and of the Cambrian
to return with Lieut Cowan. He replied that he never had
prevented those officers from returning to their Ships whenever
they thought fit to go.— I answered that I believe it true that
he never had publickly forbid them going, but his declining to
comply with my request of the 27ᵗʰ Instant to grant them leave,
was tantamount to a refusal, because he knew that by a set of
resolutions of the Merchants and other Citizens of the 26ᵗʰ Insᵗ
all intercourse had been prohibited between this City and His
Majesty's Ships, and therefore if I had sent those officers down

1 Governor's Island.

(admitting it possible to have procured a conveyance) I should have had the mortification to have seen them brought back, and probably subject to the violence and insult of a mob.— That he could not but know that the Pilot Boat had orders to intercept all Vessels attempting to make either of His Majestys Ships.—After some little further conversation the Mayor told me, he did agree to their going and that he would send me some time this day an answer to be forwarded to you.—

As I am anxious that the officers should be restored to you immediately, I have resolved to send them without the Mayor's reply to you, and shall forward it by the first Conveyance after it comes to hand, writing you more fully on this unpleasant subject. Had not Mr Cowan arrived, the officers were to have attempted getting on board for which purpose a Boat was in readiness — I shall write you more fully during the day. The appearance of rain & thick weather induces me to not to detain the Gentlemen —

I hope you rec'd during Yesterday letters from Mr Lawrence and myself which were put on board a Vessel for Martinique and which Mr Dupoy the owner of the Vessel promised me should be delivered to you —

TO DE WITT CLINTON.

New York 1st May 1806

SIR

I regret that I am under the necessity of again stating to you, that it is indispensably necessary that the officers of His Majesty's Ships of War Leander and Cambrian return to their respective Ships, and that without your Sanction and protection it is dangerous and impracticable for them to attempt it. I am well informed that there are persons in this City laying in wait to intercept those officers if they attempt to leave this City, and that there are Boats stationed near Sandy Hook to prevent any Vessels from communicating with either of His Majesty's Ships — I am also assured that if the officers are

taken in endeavouring to join their Ships, that they will be
brought back to this City, where their persons will be insulted
and their lives endangered.—

Under these assurances it is my duty to require of you, as
the chief Magistrate in this City, a safe conveyance for the officers from hence to one of His Majesty's Ships now laying off
the Bar at Sandy Hook waiting their return — Be pleased to
favor me with an answer.

TO MR. MERRY.

New York 3ᵈ May 1806.

SIR.

On the Evening of the 20ᵗʰ of April a cutter under the sanc-
tion of a Flag of Truce arrived from the Commander of His
Majestys Ships off Sandy Hook at Fort Jay or Governors
Island immediately opposite to this City. The officer who came
up in the Cutter placed himself under the protection of the
American officer at Fort Jay, and delivered him a letter from
Capᵗ Whitby the Commander of His Majestys Ships off Sandy
Hook to the Mayor of this City, and another for myself, en-
quiring as to the cause of the detention of his officers and requesting that they should be permitted to return to their ships.
Disavowing an intention to kill any man on board the Sloop,
of which I have already stated to you the circumstances and
stating that the cause of the accident was owing wholly to the
obstinacy of the master who would not bring to, to be examined.—

I waited that night in person on the Mayor on the subject
of this application, who assured me he would give every facility in his power to effect the return of the officers. At noon
of the following day, I again met him by appointment to confer with him and the officer Commanding at Fort Jay on the
mode to be adopted, when it was proposed by him, that the officer who came up with Capᵗ Whitbys letter should immediately return, and that an armed Boat from Fort Jay should

attend him until he had proceeded so far as to be in safety from any attack which might be made upon him from the Inhabitants of this City; and that he the Mayor would procure a Pilot Boat to take the officers, who arrived on the 23ᵈ of April, down to their ships during the ensuing night.— The Mayor then read to me a part of his answer to Captain Whitby, wherein he stated that the officers had never been detained, that they might have returned when they pleased; but if I thought their persons were in danger, he was ready to grant them safe conduct, on a request from me to that purport.

I told the Mayor, I could not but wonder at this statement to Capt. Whitby. That a prohibition to the Inhabitants of the City to have any communication with the Ships by resolves of a numerous meeting, and the placing of Pilot Boats to prevent any Vessel from going to His Majestys Ships, was in fact detaining the officers, by depriving them of a conveyance. That my letter to him of the 27ᵗʰ of April, a copy whereof I have sent to you, contained a request for his permission for those officers to return to their ships, and that his permission naturally would have included a protection. That the declaration contained in his answer to my letter of the 27ᵗʰ of April, towit that "he did not feel willing to adopt any steps however inconsiderable until he obtained instructions from the President of the United States," added to his passing over in silence that part of my letter which respected those officers appeared to me a refusal to grant them his permission to return to their Ships. However as he had stated to Captain Whitby that he would give the officers safe Conduct to their Ships, on an application from me, I would repeat my request for that purpose. A copy of this letter I have the Honor to inclose.

The Mayor then directed one of the Pilots to take the officers that night on board their Ships, and I understand they got on board about 3 o'Clock yesterday Morning, soon after which both Ships the Leander and Cambrian left the Station. The former for Halifax the latter on a cruize to the Southward.—

Much as I regret the accident of an American Seaman having been killed by a shot from His Majestys Ship Leander;

still I feel it my duty to add that a very improper use has been made of this unpleasant circumstance, by converting it into a political weapon, which the Federal and Republican Parties have used against each other, but at the same time has made the unhappy effort to influence the passions of the vulgar to an extravagant degree, against the British Government, and the officers of His Majestys Ships then near Sandy Hook.

TO CAPTAIN WHITBY.

New York 6th May 1806.

Sir.

Your letter of the 2[d] of May I have this moment received. M[r] Lawrence I had hoped would have informed you of every circumstance which occurred from his arrival in this City on the night of the 23[d] of April to that of his departure on the first of May.— On the morning of the 26th of April, I wrote to you, by the Boat that was to have taken down the Provisions, stating the accident which had happened and the improper use that had been made of it, by both Parties in this City then canvassing for a contested Election — The Boat, as M[r] Lawrence must have informed you, was pursued by a party of armed men and brought back — What became of the letter I know not, as it fell into the hands of some of the party. On the 27 of April I again wrote to you detailing every circumstance, but found it impracticable to procure a conveyance for the letter. On the 28 I wrote another letter in continuation to that of the preceeding day, but was equally unsuccessful as to the conveyance. On the 30th a M[r] Dupoy a Merchant in this city to whom I got a friend to make the proposal, agreed that on my becoming bound that his Brig should not be detained by yourself or the Captains of either of the Ships under your Command, that the Captain of His Brig (then going to the West Indies) should deliver my despatches to you at Sandy Hook — These dispatches contained three letters from myself, and from M[r] Lawrence, copies of the letters which had passed between the Mayor of this City and myself, on the subject of the officers detained here from your Ship, and a regular file of News papers from the 26th to the 30th of April. I have since understood that the Master of the Brig did not comply with his owners orders, but proceeded to sea while His Majestys Ships were at Anchor. To these circumstances you are to attribute not hearing from me, until Lieut. Cowan's return. In my letter to you of the first of May, I made mention of having sent those letters by the Brig.

I am confident Sir, that I have done my duty to His Majesty and to you, and that it was no more in my power to command conveyances, than it is in yours to control the Winds; and I had hoped you would have rested satisfied that every thing that could be effected, would have been done by me. My anxiety to give you notice was at least equal to yours to receive it. I have detailed the occurrence fully to Captain Beresford Commanding on the Halifax Station, and forwarded him Copies of the Communications between me and the Mayor of this City. These I have requested him to communicate to you.

You are perfectly at Liberty to make what comments you please on what you have thought proper to style my silence provided they are founded on reason and truth.

Hasty decisions are generally incorrect, and I trust you will after the perusal of this letter and the full communication I have made to the Naval Commander in Chief acquit me of inattention, and feel that your opinion with respect to myself was made up at a moment, when it was not in your power to judge correctly.

I was yesterday told by Peacok the Butcher, that he was to receive payment for the Articles forcibly taken from the Boat going down to you. Should he fail, an application shall be made by me.

TO MR. MERRY.

New York 13th May 1806.

SIR.

I have the Honor to inclose to you copies of a letter from Henry Whitby Esqr Commander of His Majestys Ship Lean-

der to me, with my answer, and a letter from me to Captain
Beresford the present Commander in Chief of His Majestys
Ships of War on the Halifax Station.—

From a perusal of these I trust you will be satisfied that
every exertion was made on my part to communicate with
Captain Whitby, while he was off this Port. Should this be
the case, I have to intreat you will fully acquit me of Captain
Whitbys charge of silence and inattention in your report to
His Majestys Ministers. The facts can be verified under the
Oaths of four or five persons of respectability, if deemed
necessary.

Between the 26th of April and second of May; it was almost
unsafe for me to leave my house, had I made my appearance
on the Wharves or at the Coffee House insult and probably
personal injury would have been the consequence.—I once
had it in contemplation to have sent the Pacquet with my letters to Captain Whitby, but not any of the Pilots would have
navigated her, and as the Ship was insured, her indemnity
would have been on my shoulders, in the event of a deviation;
besides as the time of her sailing was well known, had she attempted to move, she would have been arrested by the populace; indeed the Packet was more than once in danger during
this period.— You will from my communications to the Mayor
and his answer to me, observe that I requested from him and
the Collector the use of the Revenue Cutter, then lying at
Anchor in this port, for the purpose of going or sending
to Captain Whitby to inform him of the accident, and the
Mayor declining to allow that Vessel to go.— In truth every
means of communication was cut off; and I by accident discovered that a Man who I really believed a confidential person, and who I wished to hire to go down to His Majestys
Ships, went and laid my proposal before the Mayor, and when
he returned told me, he was afraid to undertake it, under
a conviction that it could not be effected, and that he should
be ever after odious to his fellow Citizens if detected.

16

TO CAPTAIN BERESFORD.

New York 28ᵗʰ May 1806.

(*Private.*)

MY DEAR SIR.

I received by the last Packet your affectionate letter of the 9ᵗʰ of May.— I am wholly ignorant of the correspondence between Capt Whitby and the Mayor, except that part of the Mayors answer which respected my not having applied to him for his protection, for the safe conveyance of the officers from hence to His Majesty's Ships near Sandy Hook. On this Point I have already fully informed you in my letter of the 2ᵈ of May and laid before you Copies of the letters that passed between me and the Mayor on that subject. It is probable however that Mʳ Merry has taken notice in his communications with you of this correspondence, as he stated some days since to me that in consequence of Captain Whitby's letter to the Mayor of this City, the President had resolved to put the whole of the Act of Congress of March 1805 into force — Mʳ Merry did not make any other remarks on the letter, nor has the President published a second proclamation.—

Great Britain at the present moment has a sufficiency of Enemies to contend without adding the Americans to the number, and the export of her manufactures in consequence of the late measures stands now in a great degree limited to America, a War therefore with these States would be very unpopular and prejudicial.— I do not from hence intend to infer either that I think a war probable, because I know it to be of all things what the Americans most deprecate, or that Great Britain to avoid a War, should cede a particle of her rights; but that we should if possible preserve an amicable intercourse with them.— In my last private letter, I took the Liberty to advise you until you was superseded in your command, or received explicit orders from Government, to consult with Judge Croke and the Chief Justice, on the subject of the orders you might give to the captains of the Ships under your Command, respecting neutral rights and Jurisdiction.— The Laws of Nations on this subject are vague and uncertain, and in most cases have been promulgated under the influence of temporary power. Reason however must assign a certain portion of the Sea, contiguous to the territory of every Government, as within their just Jurisdiction, and those limits on the narrowest possible Scale are a Gun shot from the Shore, (which taking a wide range may be called three miles) not from their Batteries, because it may so happen that the Government may have no Batteries near the Sea — I am sure my dear friend your intentions are right, and I have a perfect confidence that your orders will be dictated by sound sense and prudence —

TO VICE-ADMIRAL BERKELEY.

New York 30ᵗʰ Sept' 1806

SIR

By this day's Mail I have received letters from Baltimore and Norfolk, stating that the French Ship Patriot Capt Rochon of 74 Guns had arrived at Annapolis in Maryland and the Sybelle of 44 Guns at Norfolk in Virginia, both under Jury topmasts, much disabled, and that the Patriot has thrown many of her Guns overboard — These Ships with the remainder of the Squadron under Admiral Williams & Jerome Bonaparte, were on the 19ᵗʰ of August (after having been on this coast) about 100 Leagues to the Southward of Bermuda, when they encountered a Storm which lasted until the 21ˢᵗ — During the Gale the Squadron separated, and the officers of the Patriot have expressed their fears that some of the Ships have foundered. These two Ships after the Gale made for the Chesepeak, and such as have weathered the Storm will probably also make for that Bay.[1] The Jamaica fleet of Merchant Ships

---

[1] Willaumez sailed from Brest December 14, 1805, with a small squadron of six or seven vessels. His instructions were to proceed first to the Cape of Good Hope, and thence in such direction as he might deem most calculated to injure British commerce. The Cape of Good Hope surrendered before he could reach it, and on learning this fact he shaped his course for the coast of South America and the West Indies. His squadron was dispersed by a hurricane in August, 1806, as here

experienced the same Gale about 80 Leagues to the Eastward of Bermuda. The Captain of one that went down has arrived at Baltimore, who says he suspects many others shared the same fate.

I am sorry to learn the accident which has happened His Majestys Ship Chichester a Store Ship on going out the Chesepeak the Pilot run her on shore. She has sustained so much injury that it has been thought necessary for her to un-lode at Norfolk and to be hove down — Col: Hamilton the Consul there writes me many of her men have, and he appre-hends most of the others will desert — [1]

TO MR. FOX.[2]

New York 4th September 1806.

SIR.

I yesterday received a letter from Baltimore in Maryland of which the following is an extract.—

"The French Ship Patriot of 74 Guns Captain Rochon an-chored yesterday in Annapolis Road in a very shattered con-dition her Topmasts all gone, & a number of her Guns thrown overboard a French Frigate (said to be the Cybelle) of 44 Guns, has also arrived at Norfolk about the 30th August dis-masted."

"These Vessels are part of the Fleet under the Command of Williamez & Jerome Bonaparte which was dispersed on the 20th Augt about 150 Leagues to the Southward of Bermuda, the Gale commenced on the 19th & continued to the 21st & the

related — the flagship making a port in Havana, four vessels finding ref-uge in the Chesapeake, and one be-ing stranded on the Virginia beach. The Vétéran, commanded by Jerome Bonaparte, reached France in safety. It was the belief of Decrès that Je-rome had deliberately separated from the Admiral. See Du Casse, Les Rois Frères de Napoléon Ier, p. 195.

[1] Similar letters were sent to Ad-mirals Davies at Jamaica, and Coch-rane at Barbadoes.

[2] Charles James Fox became For-eign Secretary on February 7, 1806, after Mr. Pitt's death.

officers think some of the Ships must have gone down, none of the others had arrived in the Chesapeake on the 1st Instant."—

"They had made no Captures of any Consequence that I can learn, except one or two small Bermuda Vessels.— It is with much concern I have to inform you that the Fleet from Jamaica consisting of about 100 sail which left that Island about the 1st Augt experienced the Gale on the 20th 100 Leagues East of the Capes of Virginia one of them the Cumberland of Leith foundered & the Captain who has arrived here fears some of the others have gone down."

You must long since have been informed that this Fleet had been in the West Indies but very fortunately did little or no mischief.— Early in August they were seen near Charleston South Carolina and some days after that about 40 Leagues to the Southward of this Port. It was generally at that time supposed that they were on their way to Boston to refit, but from the Latitude and Longitude they were in on the 20th of August they must have shaped a South Easterly course either in the hope of meeting the Jamaica Convoy or to regain the West Indies.— I am happy to announce to you that they have hitherto done very little injury to British Ships. Some American Captains have been on board this fleet they all agree that they were wretchedly manned, their Masts, Spars and rigging in a miserable state, and short of Provisions and water.

TO MR. MERRY.

New York 6 Septr 1806.

SIR.

The British Letter of Marque Brig Fox, John Thomas Master arrived at this place from Jamaica on or about the 12th of August last past. On the 18th of that month Charles Mathews, George Robinson, John Reid and Edward Hicks four of the crew of the Brig: went before the officers of the Police of this
16*

City and made oath, that Thomas the Master had on the passage willfully murdered a negro man (one of the Ships Company) named John Good by cruelly and wickedly beating him. In consequence of their depositions Captain Thomas was apprehended and committed, a Bill of Indictment has since been found against him, and he has been arraigned — By advice of His Counsel he has pleaded to the Jurisdiction of the Court, stating that he is a subject of His Britannic Majesty, that the crime (if any) having been committed on board a British Ship on the high Seas is only cognizable in a British Court. This plea has been overruled by the district Judge of the district Court of the United States, and he has been ordered to plead in chief guilty or not guilty. The latter will be his plea, which he declares to me to be the truth. From the papers I have the Honor to inclose you will perceive that William Hearst the mate or first officer of the Brig and Charles Gauverneau the Passenger have deposed the reverse of the four Seamen; they are unquestionably more worthy of credit than the common Seamen, and under the circumstances I advised the master some days since to stand his trial, but Business having called Mr. Gauverneau to Canada, and having now only the testimony of the mate to oppose to the oaths of the four Seamen, his Counsel have advised him to apply to you, through me, to demand him as a British Subject, to be sent to Great Britain or Jamaica for his trial.— I inclose therefore the certified documents delivered to me by them. Under the late treaty of Amity Commerce and Navigation between his Majesty and the United States of America there could be no doubt of your right to demand him, as a person charged with murder: but as that treaty has expired, he can now only be demanded under the Laws of Nations. Captain Thomas' counsel are of opinion that the Prejudices of American Jurors against British Subjects are too great for him to risque his Life on their verdict. They hope to put off the trial until your answer can be obtained, by making an affidavit that Gauverneau is a material Witness.— No time however is to be lost, as the district court are now sitting.

TO MR. MERRY.

New York 9 Sept[r] 1806.

(*Private.*)

DEAR SIR.

I was all day yesterday employed in search of a fast sailing Vessel to carry the Letters to Admiral Berkeley, but did not find any that could be ready before Thursday; and as the Lark a very fine fast sailing British Schooner a constant Trader sails for Halifax tomorrow I have thought it best to send them by her, the master having promised to carry a press of sail to expedite the delivery of the letters. Two objections lay to the hiring a Pilot Boat. The Pilots of this Port are all Democrats and much attached to the French. Secondly the price per day of a Pilot Boat is twenty-five dollars. There is too much reason to suspect had I hired one, they would have delayed her passage to Halifax and possibly back again; at all events no confidence could have been placed in them; and before they engaged with me they would have consulted the Mayor[1] who is a Frenchman in Grain, who either would have prevented the contract, or rendered the letters nugatory.— I had written Admiral Berkeley on Saturday, notifying him of the arrival of the Patriot and the Sybelle in the Chesepeak which letter is now in the Lark. I also advise Admiral Cochrane of the circumstance. I hope you will approve of my having put the letters on board the Lark instead of a Pilot Boat —

TO MR. FOX.

New York, 29th Sept[r] 1806

SIR.

I have the Honor to inclose to you a duplicate of my letters of the 4th Instant, acquainting you with the Gale of Wind the French Fleet under Admiral Guillamez had encountered to the

[1] De Witt Clinton.

Southward of Bermuda on the 19, 20 & 21 of August, and of a Ship of the Line and a Frigate of that Fleet having got into the Chesepeak in a very wretched state, under jury topmasts and most of their Guns having been thrown overboard.— Since that the Valereux Frigate has got into the Delaware in a similar State, and the Eole a line of Battle Ship equally a wreck has arrived within the capes of Virginia — The Impetueux another of that fleet made the capes of Virginia some days since, but was discovered by the Melampus Frigate one of the Squadron who pursued and ran her on shore, took the officers and men out and burnt the Ship. I have understood that the officers and men were immediately landed and set at Liberty, having been taken within the American marine Jurisdiction — The Americans complain of the act of the burning of the French Line of Battle Ship within their Waters.

A British Squadron under Sir R Strahan arrived off the Capes of Virginia about the 12th of this month, from the best accounts this Squadron also suffered much during the Gale in August; and on the 20th Instant Sir John Borlase Warren with six sail of the Line also arrived there: and I suspect continue off and on the Capes in expectation of some of the French Ships arriving there. An American Captain who arrived here about a Week since states that he met Jerome Bonaparte in his Ship at Sea, on her way to France — It is generally supposed that the remainder of the French Ships foundered in the Gale — Those within the Capes, will probably remain some time, as they require great repairs, and it is said no merchant will advance money.

TO MR. MERRY.

New York 25 October 1806

SIR.

It was not until late last Evening that I received an answer from the Counsel of Captain Thomas of the Brig Fox to the Communication contained in your No 14 and the Copy of Mr Madisons letter accompanying it. They are of opinion that an appeal in Criminal Cases will not lay from the district Court to the Supreme Court of the United States; altho the Laws have provided for an appeal in such cases: And that therefore the remedy proposed by the American Secretary of State if attempted would meet with a negative on the part of the Supreme Court of the United States, and probably in the first instance be over ruled by the District Judge. The Counsel are further of opinion that in a similar case if application had been made by any nation in amity with Great Britain for the delivery of a Subject of such nation charged with murder, that the person so charged would be delivered up; and that a case can not be cited, wherein Great Britain has refused the application, and the Court proceeded to try and sentence the person so charged. They admit that applications have been made, and refused, but in such cases the murder was committed by the Foreigner on the high Seas on board a British Ship, upon the principle that the Ship constituted the Jurisdiction.— Mr Harison one of the Counsel for the Prisoner is allowed to be one of (if not) the soundest Lawyer in America.— Unless therefore you feel yourself at Liberty to make a second application for the delivery of Thomas, and it proves more successful than the former, the poor man must go to Trial early in November under all the disadvantages of the want of Witnesses and probably a prejudiced Jury.[1]

TO VICE-ADMIRAL BERKELEY.

New York 17th November, 1806.

SIR.

In consequence of Mr Merry's request for leave of absence; The Honorable David Erskine has arrived at Washington in these States as His Majestys Envoy Extraordinary and Minister Plenipotentiary and has been received as such by the President of the United States.[2] Mr Merry has taken leave and

[1] No record of this case can now be found in the Clerk's Office of the United States District Court. It is probable that Thomas was never brought to trial, the evidence against him being really very weak.

[2] Mr. Erskine arrived at Washington, November 4, 1806.

will sail from the Chesapeak in all this month. Mr Merry's state of health is unequal to a Winter voyage — I have a public dispatch from Mr Merry to you, but he has limited its conveyance to the Ship of War or armed Vessel you may send during the Winter for your dispatches. — The September Packet is not yet arrived, in a few days the October will be due.— Accounts by private Ships from England, state that Lord Howic has succeeded to foreign department vacant by Mr Fox's demise, and that M^r T Greville is first Lord of the Admiralty.[1] On the 26th of September Lord Lauderdale had not returned from Paris; yet there was no expectation of Peace.— Russia and Prussia appear condensing their forces and making every preparation for War with France; who is equally active in her measures.

The Valeureux French Frigate of 44 Guns which arrived after the August Gale in the Delaware and went up to Philadelphia for repairs, has on a survey been found unworthy of them.—A fine American Ship the George Washington of upwards of 400 Tons, with a figure head, quarter and Stern Gallaries and new main topmast has been taken up to carry to France the men, Guns and Stores of this Frigate, she will sail about the 25 of this month. The Indiana another American Ship was a few days since along side the Valeureux taking from her such part of her Guns, Stores and men, as were supposed more than the Washington could carry, this last named ship will sail in a few days. As either of these ships would in the event of capture prove good and valuable prizes, I have dispatched two letters on Saturday last to Halifax, one to Norfolk and two by Vessels bound to the West Indies to be given to any of the Commanders of His Majestys Ships of War. I have little hope that either of my letters will arrive at Halifax in time to have a ship (if any is there) off the Delaware to meet the George Washington. But that of Norfolk I trust will be delivered this Evening, and it is probable one of the others may be put on board one of your Ships on this coast.

[1] Mr. Thomas Grenville, a brother of the Lord Grenville who was Secretary for Foreign Affairs from 1791 to 1801.

TO LORD HOWICK.[1]

New York 6ᵗʰ Decʳ 1806.

MY LORD,

I have the Honor to inclose to your Lordship the Speech of the President of the United States on the opening of the present Session of Congress.—

It is asserted and generally believed that Mʳ Burr late vice President of the United States of America is at the head of that " great number of private Individuals who " (the President in his Speech observes) " were combining together arming and organizing themselves contrary to Law to carry on a military expedition against the territories of Spain."— The object of this combination is not known. What the President suggests may be correct; but it appears to be the opinion of the best informed in these States, that Mʳ Burr's views extend to a division of the United States of America, and creating a new Government in the Western part thereof —

[1] On Mr. Fox's death, September 13, 1806, the Foreign Office was committed to Earl Spencer *ad interim;* but on September 24, Lord Howick, afterward Earl Grey, became Secretary for Foreign Affairs.

THE same month of April that witnessed the killing of Pearce had witnessed also the beginning of that long and fruitless struggle which Jefferson and Madison carried on, in the vain hope of compelling the European belligerents to respect the just rights of the United States as a neutral nation. On April 15, 1806, Congress had passed the non-importation act, prohibiting the importation of a long list of British manufactures, and this had been immediately followed by the appointment of William Pinkney of Maryland as a special envoy to England. Pinkney was instructed to unite with Monroe, then American Minister to England, in one more effort to effect an amicable settlement of all differences; but they were to agree to no treaty which did not include a renunciation of the right of impressment, and which did not satisfactorily settle the questions connected with the West India trade. Pinkney had joined Monroe in London late in July, and negotiations had since been actively carried on with the government of which Mr. Fox was the head.

This was the situation at the beginning of the year 1807, so far as was known in America; but important events had, in fact, happened in Europe, of which the news had not yet arrived. On the last day of the year 1806 Monroe and Pinkney had succeeded in getting the British commissioners to sign a treaty of amity, commerce, and navigation. The negotiation had been greatly facilitated by the simple process of disregarding the positive instructions of the President. But even then the British negotiators were not entirely content with the terms of the treaty, and they accompanied their signatures by a written warning that the King would decline to ratify their act unless the United States should forcibly resist the operation of Napoleon's Berlin decree.

The Berlin decree, which was soon to become familiar throughout the United States, was dated November 21, 1806. It undertook, by a mere edict of the Emperor's, to prohibit all commerce, even in neutral vessels, between the British islands or colonies and any part of the European continent which was under the control of France; it declared the British islands to be in a state of blockade; and it directed the confiscation of any vessel which entered a continental port after having been in any British possession.

The English Government were not slow to reply. In addition to calling upon the United States to resist the decree, an order in council was issued on January 7, 1807, by which all trade was forbidden between any two ports on the continent of Europe. The doctrine that one nation could forbid another to trade peacefully between two foreign ports, was certainly novel. But the British authorities were still not satisfied. They went further, and by a second order in council, dated November 11, 1807, they forbade all trade with the continent wherever originating, unless the goods first passed through an English port and paid a duty at an English custom-house.

Napoleon, in his turn, retaliated by the Milan decree of December 17, 1807. Every neutral vessel was to be condemned which had submitted to be searched by a British ship, or had paid duty to the British Government, or had come from or was bound to any British possession.

Such were the arbitrary decrees and orders by which neutral commerce was attacked on every side. The British Government allowed no neutral ship to go to the continent but by way of England. The French seized every neutral ship that came from any British port. The British Government declared they would be friends with the United States only on condition of our forcibly resisting the Berlin decree. Napoleon declared that he would confiscate every American ship which did not forcibly resist any attempt of a British man-of-war to search her.

The news of this general assault upon American commerce — this declaration of both parties to the European contest that there should be no more neutrals — excited the deepest resentment in the United States. But it did not affect the action of the Government in regard to the British treaty. Before the news of the first order in council had reached Washington, Jefferson had peremptorily declined to consider the question of ratification, or even to submit the treaty to the Senate. But strangely enough, he was still hopeful of success. In spite of the difficulties which Monroe and Pinkney had already experienced, in spite of new obstacles to an adjustment, instructions were prepared looking to further negotiations with England. This second attempt came, however, too late. The growing ill-will between the two countries, and the fall of the Whig administration early in 1807, had already served to render negotiation practically impossible; when the attack of the *Leopard* upon the *Chesapeake* toward the latter part of June, aroused American feelings to a still higher pitch of an-ger. After months of discussion, and some idle attempts at obtaining satisfaction by diplomatic methods, public opinion at last found expression in the passage by Congress, on December 22, 1807, of the act of embargo, which absolutely closed the ports of the United States to foreign commerce of every kind.

The effect on the city of New-York was instantaneous. Ships were hurried to sea, wharves were left deserted, counting-houses were shut up, and the ordinary duties of the British Consul-General came very nearly to an end.

The United States comprised even then a great variety of resources within their borders, and were able — though doubtless at the expense of not a little suffering — to dispense with foreign markets either for selling or buying; but such a state of things could not long continue. Congress had never contemplated its duration beyond the time when loss of the American trade should make Europe more moderate in its views. But Europe was not to be moved by any peaceful arguments, and the experiment was of necessity abandoned after a patient trial. All through the year 1808 and the first two months of 1809, the heavy hand of the embargo was laid on American commerce. The close of Jefferson's administration was signalized by an important change in the policy of the American Government. Almost the last act which Jefferson performed as President was to sign the new law which repealed the embargo, and substituted non-intercourse — a law which instead of universal prohibition of trade, merely prohibited commerce with Great Britain and with the countries under French control. The statute further authorized the President to suspend this prohibition as to either Great Britain or France as soon as one or the other should desist from violating neutral rights.

An excuse for renewing commercial relations was not long delayed. On April 21, 1809, immediately upon the rather unexpected conclusion of a liberal and satisfactory diplomatic arrangement with Erskine, the British minister in Washington, the non-intercourse act was suspended as to Great Britain; and foreign trade, long dormant, suddenly sprang into excessive activity. This happy truce was short-lived. Erskine had effected his arrangement by a deliberate and almost defiant disregard of Canning's instructions; and his acts were promptly disavowed by his government. His recall was followed by a renewal of non-intercourse under a presidential proclamation of August 9, 1809.

But notwithstanding the disavowal of Erskine, the British Government had made an apparent concession to the United States by the adoption of new orders in council which revoked the stringent prohibitions of the orders of 1807, and substituted a paper blockade of all ports and places under the government of France — a distinction which, on the whole, was perhaps without any important difference. France, on the other hand, entered upon a course of further aggressions. Louis Bonaparte was driven from his kingdom of Holland because he refused to attack neutral commerce, and all American ships found lying at Amsterdam were seized. Finally, by the decree of Rambouillet, every American ship found in any French port was confiscated and ordered sold.

England and the United States thus seemed for the moment to be slowly drawing together in the presence of a common enemy, when suddenly the whole situation of affairs was changed by the formal announcement on August 5, 1810, of the Emperor's intended revocation of the decrees of Berlin and Milan, such revocation to take place on the first day of the following November, provided the British Government revoked their orders in council, or (and this was the important provision) the United States caused their rights to be respected. This promise, as Napoleon had privately pointed out a few days before, committed him to nothing; but it was accepted with all seriousness on the part of the United States.

In reliance upon the imperial word, commercial intercourse with Great Britain — which had been once more resumed in May, 1810 — was for the third time suspended. This, it was thought, was " causing American rights to be respected"; and although the condemnation of American ships went on without a pause in every continental port, the Government of the United States clung with the strangest pertinacity to the belief that Napoleon's declarations were sincere.

The practical effect of all this was to bar the door against any possible settlement with Great Britain. Commerce was now permanently suspended; there was a long list of grievances to be redressed, and negotiation was exhausted. In the month of February, 1811, Pinkney — who had become the sole American representative in London — took an " inamicable leave," and further efforts looking to a peaceful settlement of our accumulated difficulties with England were abandoned. On November 4, 1811, Congress met in a perplexed but somewhat warlike humor. Much tedious debate ensued. It was not until June 18, 1812, after many hesitations and misgivings, that war was actually declared against Great Britain.

On July 9, 1812, Colonel Barclay, accompanied by the British Minister, sailed from New-York on H. M. S. *Colibri* for England.

17

The six preceding years had been for Barclay a period of quiet prosperity. His life had been easy and happy. His fortune had increased through judicious investments and reasonable economy. His eldest son, Henry, was now well established as a merchant in New-York. De Lancey had been promoted to the rank of major in the British army on August 23, 1810, and lieutenant-colonel on February 28, 1812. Thomas, on June 8, 1808, had become Vice-Admiral Cochrane's flag-lieutenant, and on June 14, 1809, had been given a ship — commanding successively the *Epervier*, *Snap*, and *Peruvian* — with the rank of commander. George had left Nova Scotia in 1808 to join Henry in business in New-York; while Anthony had gone to England to complete his education and study for the bar. Only one break in the family had come by death. On July 8, 1809, Schuyler Livingston, the husband of Barclay's eldest daughter, died at Harlem.

TO VICE-ADMIRAL BERKELEY, BERMUDA.

New York 24 January 1807.

SIR

Several fast sailing pilot boat Schooners and perhaps other Vessels have been for some time past employed in bringing Spanish Dollars from Vera Cruz to these States a great proportion of which I understand has been landed at New Orleans, Savannah in Georgia, and Charleston South Carolina; large sums also at Baltimore in Maryland and perhaps two or three hundred thousand dollars in this City. It is said and I believe with truth that the house of Messrs Hope's of Amsterdam and an extensive house at Hamburg, have either purchased these Dollars from the King of Spain deliverable to them at Vera Cruz; or that they have contracted to bring them from thence and on their arrival in Europe, or the proceeds from them to pay the Spanish Goverpment — The Dollars when they arrive in these States I suspect are employed in purchasing Cotton Coffee Sugar &c &c &c which are remitted to Europe — The Schooner pilot Boats in which most if not all the money is brought, are low, long vessels, very sharp and sail fast. I thought it my duty to give you this information and hope you may be so fortunate as to intercept some of them. M[r] Parish one of the House at Hamburgh is in these States superintending the Business, but he has respectable merchants in the Ports mentioned acting as his Agents, or perhaps in their own names [1] —

TO MR. ERSKINE.

New York 2[d] February 1807

(*Private.*)

DEAR SIR.

I am this day honored with your private letter of the 30th of January covering two Proclamations from Sir Eyre Coote Lieut Governor of Jamaica which I will take care to have inserted in the News Papers of this city.[2]

Previous to the receipt of your letter I had noticed in the Aurora a newspaper published in Philadelphia a violent Philippic against me for the letter I had written in favor of Mess[rs] Rutgers and Seaman the owners of the American Ship Messenger, and of which M[r] Madison has complained to you.[3]

---

[1] Copies of the foregoing letter were also sent to Vice-Admiral Davies, Jamaica; and Rear-Admiral Cochrane, Barbadoes.

[2] They were proclamations permitting the importation and exportation of certain articles, for a limited period, in neutral vessels. This Sir Eyre Coote was a nephew of the better-known East Indian General of the same name. He had served in the American War from Long Island to Yorktown, and was appointed Governor of Jamaica in 1805 — a post he held till 1808. He died in obscurity and disgrace about 1824.

[3] The "violent Philippic" was published in the Aurora January 29, 1807. The following extracts will give a sufficient notion of its purport:

"WARMLY FEDERAL."

We promised to say something about the ship Messenger; we can say a *great*

Mess" Rutgers and Seaman of this City Merchants and owners of the Messenger on hearing that their Ship, on board of
which M' Herman Rutgers was super Cargo, had been sent to
Halifax for adjudication requested of me a letter of introduction and recommendation to some Gentleman of that place.
In compliance with their solicitation I wrote a private confidential Letter, which I understand has been improperly intercepted and published, to M' Hartshorne a merchant in Halifax,
and knowing M' Hartshorne so far to have taken an interest in
the Politics of these States as to have a predeliction for the
federal Party to induce him the more readily to act in favor of
these Gentlemen it is very probable I represented them, agreeable to their general characters, to be " warm Federalists "—
    With the Politics of this Country I never did nor will I ever
interfere — Mess" Rutgers and Seaman are Gentlemen of respectability in this City, of whom I have little personal Knowledge, we do not visit, nor have I ever met them in company.

deal more, than even what we now shall
say; and the new advocate of the "great
sea robber" may, perhaps before we
have done, wish that the thing had not
been meddled with.
    " Mr. Rutgers is a gentleman and
warmly federal" said Mr. Barclay.—
    Did you ever see a cat catch a mouse?
When a cat catches some kind of mice—
they are eat up—they are devoured at
once—smack—'tis gone!
    These are your democratic mice—we
recollect that a great noise was made in
congress some nine or ten years ago
about such things.
    But there are rats, which the cats
sometimes catch. Did you ever see a
cat play with a rat?
    One of your "warm federal" rats —
Puss, when she catches this species of
rats, lets them go a bit; — then she puts
out her nether paw and catches them
again — you would suppose that she became fond of them, from the fraternal
hugs she gives them, she tosses them
up — they are a little alarmed — the rats
then cry out that they are "warmly
federal."
    Puss lets them go then — but she sends
them off in a direction from their natu-

ral holes — and they fall into the proctor
traps, and the lawyer traps, and the
agency traps. There the rats again
squeak out that they are "warmly federal."
    They are then put under the great
Tom cat of the admiralty — Puss catches
them and tosses them and paws them,
and plays with them, and gives them
hopes of escaping.
    But at last Tom Puss after amusing
himself with them until he is tired of
play — notwithstanding all their protes-
tations of being "warmly federal rats
and gentleman rats," pounces upon
them, and devours and eats them, just
as she would the democratic mice — the
last squeak is all that is heard of them —
so of the ship Messenger.
    .   .   .   .
    The object of the British government
is to cramp your trade in order that they
may monopolize it — for this they plunder you, and care little whether federal,
quiddical or democratical. They may
not devour you at once, as hungry cats
swallow mice, but they will play with
you, and tantalize, and deceive you, as
federal rats — but they will devour you
all if they can at last.

But in describing a Gentleman, I suspect I am entitled to say he is a Federalist or an antifederalist as he and the person to whom he is recommended may happen to be without giving offense to the opposite Party. Had these Gentlemen been antifederal and Mr Hartshornes sentiments corresponded with theirs, I assuredly should have described them to him as such.

TO MR. ERSKINE.

New York 10th March 1807.

DEAR SIR

I am particularly indebted to you for your private letter of the 5th Instant, at a moment when you must have been more than ordinarily hurried & I shall bear in memory this flattering proof of your attention and regard, for which I intreat your acceptance of my warmest acknowledgments.   I am sorry that a treaty formed on the part of His Majesty with every wish for consideration should not meet the approbation or at least the acceptance of the President of these States.[1]

On the impressment of American Seamen, I feel assured that the Commissioners of both nations on debating the Subject found insuperable difficulties, and on mature reflection considered it best to pass it sub silentio.— The impressment has for years past been used as a political Engine, when in truth the number of bona fide American Seamen detained on board His Majestys Ships of War was trifling in the extreme when compared with those who were claimed by America as such.— The Note delivered by the British Comm^{rs} to the American Com^{rs} prior to the signing of the Treaty was dictated by imperious circumstances and necessary for

---

[1] This was the treaty negotiated by Monroe and Pinkney and signed December 31, 1806. Erskine's copy arrived in Washington on March 3, just as Congress was adjourning, and his unusual hurry was due to his unavailing efforts to induce the President to submit the treaty to the Senate. This Mr. Jefferson steadfastly refused to do. The treaty itself and accompanying correspondence is printed in Amer. State Papers, For. Rel., Vol. III, pp. 109-183.

17*

the security of the Interest of Britain, I might add for the interest of America.[1]

If upon reflection you feel yourself at Liberty to entrust to me a copy of the treaty in confidence that it shall not be made public, otherwise than in arguing on it, I think much good might be derived from an early development of the Articles attended with the natural remarks on the benefits or disadvantages accruing from each of them, and a candid enquiry into the purport of the note delivered with the Treaty. Should you concur in opinion with me, not a moment is to be lost in transmitting the Copy. The Public mind altho' much agitated is still in suspense for want of material to form an opinion. It is unnecessary to add that under these circumstances, a favorable impression is of great consequence.

TO VICE-ADMIRAL BERKELEY.

New York 31ˢᵗ March 1807.

SIR.

In the inclosed newspaper you will perceive a statement that the American Ship Brutus of this place bound for Gonaives a small Island near St Domingo, had exchanged some shots with His Majestys Sloop of War Squirrel.— If this should have been the case that ship has become a lawful prize, and I take it for granted you will be anxious to have her taken, in consequence of the very improper conduct of her Commander in firing upon one of His Majestys Ships. Mʳ Lewis the Supercargo or Agent on board this Ship, and who probably commanded her, is the very person who when he commanded the American Ship Leander fired into His Majestys Ship Fortunio and killed a seaman.[2]—What renders the conduct of Mʳ Lewis particularly

---

[1] This extraordinary note is in Amer. State Papers, For. Rel., Vol. III, p. 151. It was to the effect that unless the American Government should forcibly resist the enforcement of Bonaparte's Berlin decree, the King would not consider himself bound by the signature of his commissioners.

[2] The Leander, commanded by Thomas Lewis, carried Miranda's filibusters to South America in February, 1806.

blameable is his having promised me in the event of his meeting one of His Majestys Ships of War at sea, that he would deliver up a deserter from the Packet, who had entered on board the Brutus, in consequence of which I gave him a letter of introduction to the Commander of His Majestys Ships of War.

The Brutus was bound to St Domingo for the recovery of Debts due a Mr Ogden a Bankrupt, who also was on board that Ship, and to receive payment in Coffee and other articles. Capt Byam knows this Ship, as he saw her repeatedly when he was last here.— She is a french built Ship, figure head, Quarter galleries, but I do not recollect whether she has stern galleries.—When she arrived here from the Isle of France two years since her name was the James, since that the Emperor, and now the Brutus.— She will remain some time at the Island of Gonaives.

TO LORD HOWICK.

New York 2^d June 1807.

My Lord —

Mr Cazeaux a Frenchman who has resided as French Consul some years at Portsmouth in New Hampshire went last Autumn to France with an intention of remaining there. On his arrival he had an interview with the Emperor and several with Tallyrand in consequence of which he was sent out early this Spring to America, went to Washington to confer with the French Minister, and has proceeded to Portsmouth with a view of entering Canada by the State of Vermont.—He has acquired during his residence in America the English language and American manners to a degree which will enable him to pass as an American, and there can be no doubt but his object is to sound the dispositions of the Canadians in the event of an attempt on Canada. Of all this I have informed Mr Dunn administering the Government of Lower Canada, and gave him a particular description of his age, person and appearance, so that I hope he may be apprehended.— I have reason to expect he will endeavor to tamper with the inhabitants of Vermont and those parts of the State of New Hampshire and Massachusetts which lay nearest Canada, to induce them to cooperate with a French Force should they arrive in Canada. I have considered it my duty to communicate this to your Lordship, that it may be laid before His Majesty. Every means in my power shall be used to disclose the extent of Mr Cazeaux mission to America — He is to return to France this Autumn.

TO MR. CANNING.[1]

New York 2d July 1807.

SIR.

A very unpleasant occurrence has lately taken place at Sea off the Capes of Virginia between His Majestys Ship Leopard and the American Ship of War Chesapeak; of which you will undoubtedly receive much more correct information from M^r. Erskine His Majestys Minister to these States, and from M^r. Hamilton the British Consul, than it is at present in my power to give you.[2]

I shall only therefore state that the circumstance is viewed by the respectable part of the Inhabitants of this City and the United States of America in a very serious point of view, and that the lower order of the American are much irritated and inclined for violent measures.

I have the honor to inclose to you some of the American News Papers on the subject.

TO MR. CANNING.

New York 5th of August 1807.

SIR

You will naturally at the present moment be anxious to have any information from these States; and although it is not im-

[1] George Canning became Secretary for Foreign Affairs April 8, 1807, on the dismissal of the Whig Cabinet. Mr. Perceval and the Duke of Portland were at the head of the administration.

[2] The Leopard fired on the Chesapeake June 22, 1807.

mediately within the line of my duty to communicate with you on the present occasion perhaps it may not be disagreeable. The midshipman and seamen made prisoners on landing from one of His Majestys Ships in Hampton Roads have by order of the President been returned — Preparations are making for the fortifying of this and the other principal Ports in these States. About fifty Gun Boats laying in ordinary in this place have been got ready for service — and 100000 militia are drafted for service on short notice. Congress are called for the 26 of October about six weeks earlier than usual.

I am satisfied that the rencounter between His Majesty's Ship Leopard and the American Frigate Chesapeak, will by the American Government be made the instrument of pressing on His Majesty's Ministers that the American Flag shall protect all Seamen and passengers, other than Subjects of Powers at War with Great Britain. What confirms this opinion is a late publication at Boston of an official Letter on this subject in 1804 from M^r. Madison the Secretary of State to M^r. Monroe Minister at London. It must have been published at M^r. Madison's instance, and at Boston that it might appear to come from a different Source and to operate on the minds of persons, who think very widely perhaps from Mr Madison.—

The Eastern States are averse to a War with Great Britain. In this State a great proportion of the respectable characters are of similar sentiments, but as you progress to the Southward they are more warm, and in Maryland, Virginia and the Carolinas I suspect War would be a popular measure. It has been with great reluctance, that within these few weeks, I have been obliged to believe the present administration in these States are not averse to war. What the inducement can be it is impossible to say. They are without Ships, or Land Forces; and the Revenue drawn wholly from import duties dependant on Commerce.—

By an act of Congress a part of the funded Debt is ordered to be purchased in half yearly by the Cashier of the United States Bank. About a fortnight since an order was issued from the Government that he should purchase no stock standing in the name of a Foreigner, or which had been transfered by a foreigner to an American citizen subsequent to the first of July.— This measure is pointed to British Subjects, and evinces an inclination to sequester or confiscate their property should a war take place.

TO VICE-ADMIRAL BERKELEY.

New York 11ᵗʰ August 1807.

SIR.

I yesterday received your letter of the fourth of July, informing me that the transaction off the Capes of Virginia between His Majestys Ship Leopard and the United States Frigate Chesapeak had been much misrepresented in some of the American newspapers, which you was apprehensive might occasion animosity between the two Nations, that you thought it proper to inclose me a copy of the orders under which the Captain of the Leopard acted, which you had not issued until an application to restore the mutineers and Deserters from the British Ships had been made by His Majestys Minister Consuls and officers and had been rejected by the Government of the United States, and that I was at Liberty to promote the knowledge of their contents in whatever way I might think best calculated to preserve the good understanding which ought to subsist between Great Britain and America.

Your orders to the Commanders of His Majestys Ships of War under your command have been some days since published in most of the American News Papers, and the fact that a regular and formal demand for the delivery of the Mutineers and Deserters had been made by the officers of His Majestys Ships in Hampton Roads and Mʳ Consul Hamilton on the American officer who entered them as Seamen to serve on board the Chesapeak, and by Mʳ Erskine His Majestys Minister to these States, on the American Secretary of State to the same effect both which demands had respectively been refused, has also received every possible publicity through the Medium of the American Newspapers.

I shall however take every opportunity to state the transaction in its real colours and as you wish it.

TO VICE-ADMIRAL BERKELEY.

New York [August, 1807].

SIR.

I have received your original and duplicate letter of the 15th of July and the hand Bills which accompanied them. I had them posted up in the parts of this City, but they were the next day either mutilated or destroyed; since which I have had your Proclamation offering a Pardon to Deserters published in the Newspapers, but as the Period for their surrender (to wit the 31st of August) was so nearly expired I omitted putting that or any other day of limitation in it, because in your Proclamation you hold out a Pardon to those Seamen only who shall immediately return to their duty. Every means in my power shall be used to make your proclamation generally known, and to invite British Seamen to avail themselves of it. I am fearful however that but few will surrender themselves; because they get such enormous wages in the American Merchant Service. — Rendevous have been opened for entering Seamen for the American Navy. I understand very few here have entered, and those chiefly were of colour or Irish Lands men.—

I have obtained from Captain Crafts a copy of his letter to Mr Gallatin Secretary of the American Treasury respecting two men Deserters from the Melampus who were taken out of the Chesapeak by the Leopard, and who Commodore Barron of the Chesapeak had reported as our Newspapers state to be American Seamen impressed from the American Brig Neptune Crafts Master. I inclose a copy of this letter which I have had published in the newspapers you will perceive that the men deserted the Neptune and were not impressed and that Captain Crafts was pleased with the Treatment he received from Captain Poyntz — If any British Seamen offer to enter His Majestys Service, I will take care to forward them to you.

You will pardon me for advising you that if you send a Ship of War off this Harbour, it would at the present critical moment be prudent to direct that she should as little as possible interrupt Ships coming in or going out. The late violence is subsiding, the Eastern People are very moderate and opposed to a War with Great Britain. When Congress meet, they will strain every nerve to prevent it. I think it advisable therefore not to furnish their opponents with fresh arguments.

TO MR. CANNING.

New York 2ᵈ Sept 1807.

SIR.

Mʳ Gallatin the American Secretary of the Treasury having been lately in this City called on a Captain Crafts late Master of the American Brig Neptune for information respecting some Seamen who it was stated Commodore Barron had reported to have been impressed from the Neptune in the Bay of Biscay in the year 1805 by His Majestys Ship Melampus, two of which men Ware and Martin were taken from the American Frigate Chesapeak in June last as Deserters from His Majestys Service, by Capᵗ Humphreys of the Leopard.— As it is probable the American remonstrance by Mʳ Monro the Minister in London, may represent these men as impressed into His Majestys Service, I inclose you a copy of Captain Crafts letters to Mʳ Gallatin and to me on this Subject, which state the reverse to have been the case. It is probable Mʳ Monro is not furnished with this information as Captain Crafts told me, when he delivered the letter to Mʳ Gallatin and he had read it, Mʳ Gallatin desired him to keep the facts to himself, or not to make them publick. Crafts is now gone up the Mediterranean, but told me he was ready at any time to verify under oath the letter and what Mr. Gallatin said to him.

TO SIR ROBERT LAURIE.[1]

New York 5 Sep" 1807.

SIR.

I have received your letter of the 25th of August by Captain Bradshaw of His Majestys Sloop Columbine, informing me that the Honorable Vice Admiral Berkeley Commander in Chief upon this Station, having understood that many British Seamen had expressed their wishes to join the Standard of their Sovereign and that several men had applied to me for that purpose, he had directed you to send His Majestys Sloop of War Columbine to anchor at Sandy Hook for the purpose of receiving any men that may offer; that Captain Bradshaw was to acquaint me of his arrival and to remain on that service, as long as he shall think it necessary after consulting with me.— That as the Columbine was in want of water and provisions you had desired her Commander to demand through me such supplies as he may stand in need of, and as the Presidents Proclamation does not seclude Ships of War carrying dispatches, from every privilege of neutrality, you had no doubt I would forward them without delay.

I did not receive Captain Bradshaws letter of the 2d Instant until late last Evening owing to the Pilots refusing to bring it up; my son Mr Henry Barclay therefore went down for it.— Admiral Berkeley I suspect has been misinformed respecting British Seamen and Landmen in this Port wishing to return to the Service of their King as a few instances have occurred in which the applicants have been sent on to Halifax or England, as they wished, in the Pacquets. I really cannot think it an object for the Columbine to remain at Sandy Hook for the purpose she has been sent for, and I shall so express myself to Captain Bradshaw. There is generally a Packet in this Port, which can always receive ten times the number of men who will offer.

<hr />

1 Sir Robert Laurie was captain of H. M. S. Milan, and senior officer of the British ships in the Chesapeake. The Milan was formerly the French ship Ville de Milan, captured in the West Indies. An account of her capture is given in Basil Hall's Fragments of Voyages, etc.

Monday 7th Sep[r]

I had proceeded thus far in my letter to you on Saturday and was going to add that the Collector of this Port had in a very handsome manner consented to my sending down to the Columbine the provisions of which Cap[t] Bradshaw represented he was in need, when I received a note from the Collector informing me that he was under the painful necessity of retracting his permission and that he was compelled to require Captain Bradshaw immediately to depart from Sandy Hook.

It appears that a Revenue Cutter lay at no great distance from the Columbine, that a man deserted from the latter who Captain Bradshaw supposed had gone on board this Cutter, that a Boat with an officer from the Columbine was sent to the Cutter to enquire about this man. That the officer was told he was not on board, but that he was not satisfied with this assurance, but declared he would search the Cutter. That the Revenue officer who commanded the Cutter remonstrated against the measure and forbid it, notwithstanding which the search was made, but the Deserter was not found. This is the substance of the Report of the Revenue officer to the Collector, who considers it an act of violence committed on an American national vessel within the Jurisdiction of the United States, which justifies and renders it his duty to order the immediate departure of the Columbine. I hope this report of the Revenue officer may be exaggerated — I have not yet heard whether Capt Bradshaw has gone to Sea — On Saturday I made him acquainted with the above report, and I hope this day to hear from him.[1]

TO GENERAL SIR JAMES CRAIG, GOVERNOR-GENERAL OF CANADA.

New York, 22[d] Nov[r] 1807

SIR.

I some time since informed M[r] Dunn then administering the Government of Lower Canada, that a M[r] Cazeaux late French

---

[1] An account of this affair, taken from the newspapers of the day, will be found in McMaster's History of the U. S., Vol. III, pp. 267, 268.

Consul at Portsmouth New Hampshire had arrived from France charged by the French Government to visit Canada for the purpose of alienating the affections of the Canadians from His Majesty and the Government and other traitorous purposes — I beg leave to refer you to the letter to Mr Dunn for the particulars —

I have lately heard that Cazeaux will not return to France this Winter but remain in Canada in disguise — His abilities are equal to his cunning, and as he speaks English remarkably well it will be difficult to discover him. He will probably assume the dress of a Peasant. It is of the utmost consequence he should be apprehended. The plan must be well laid to discover him, as the Canadians will naturally incline to conceal him —

TO THE GOVERNOR OF BARBADOES.

New York 28th Dec, 1807

SIR

I have the honor to inclose you a News Paper of this day, containing an Act of Congress passed the 22^d Current laying an Embargo on all Vessels within the Ports of the United States, with a provisional clause in favor of Foreign merchant vessels, and another in favor of Foreign Ships of War.

I am requested by Mr Erskine His Majestys Minister Plenipotentiary to these States, to inform you that the American Government have declared that the Embargo is not intended as a measure of Hostility against Great Britain, but only of Precaution against the Risk of Capture by the Belligerents Powers in the present extraordinary State of things.[1]

TO VICE-ADMIRAL BERKELEY.

New York 26th December 1807.

SIR.

I have the Honor to inclose to you the act of Congress passed a few days since laying an Embargo, and to inform

[1] Similar letters were sent to the Governors of Jamaica, the Bahamas, Bermuda, and Nova Scotia.

you that the act of congress prohibiting the importation of
the greater part of the merchandize usually imported from His
Majestys United Kingdom, went into operation on the 14th Instant — It is certain that these measures have been adopted in
consequence of the present unpleasant position of affairs between Great Britain and America; but I suspect the Embargo
has taken place rather from the present relative situation of
France and America.   By the National Schooner Revenge
dispatches were received from the American Minister at Paris,
the precise purport of which has not yet transpired, but it is
stated that Bonaparte has declared there shall be no neutrals,
and that these States must take part with G. Britain or France
— Congress have sat since the 19th Instant, the day the President sent them a communication on the subject of the resolution
of Bonaparte, with closed doors.   The Embargo was the result
of their deliberation, during which letters from Washington
state, the disputes with G Britain was never mentioned —
The presumption is therefore that the Embargo was ordered
to prevent Am[n] Ships going to France — A letter however
from a sensible, respectable member in Congress, opposed to
French measures,[1] dated the 19th of December, says that notwithstanding matters can be amicably adjusted between G
Britain and America, he fears through french influence a War
between them will take place, to avoid a War with France —
M[r] Rose has not yet arrived, and I begin to fear some accident
has occurred to the Statira.[2]

TO SIR ROBERT LAURIE.

New York Dec[r] 29th 1807.
SIR.

His Majesty's Schooner Chubb under the command of Lieut :
Crooke arrived last night at the quarrantine ground about
nine miles from this City, and Lieut Crooke came up in the

---

[1] Barent Gardenier (?).

[2] George Henry Rose, the special envoy sent over to treat of the Chesapeake
affair, arrived at Norfolk the same day this letter was written.

Pilot boat the Collector however hearing of his Landing immediately ordered the Pilot to take him again on board the Chubb, as his landing was in the face of the presidents proclamation, so that I have not seen M[r] Crooke.

The Collector however immediately sent me your and Govvernor Hodgsons dispatches, with a polite message that a boat was always ready from the customs for me to communicate with the Commander of the Chubb. I shall send the dispatches on board the Chubb at high water tomorrow and request Lieut Crooke to sail the first wind, at present the wind is at S. E. and every appearance of a gale.

TO MR. ERSKINE.

New York 3[d] Feb[ry] 1808.

SIR.

By yesterday's mail I had the Honor to receive your letter of the 28th of January covering a Statement respecting circumstances which have occurred on board His Majestys Ship Statira near Norfolk and which has been much misrepresented in the American News Papers.—This statement will be published in the Evening Post this day, and in the New York Gazette tomorrow, with a few remarks.[1]

[1] The Norfolk Herald of January 12th stated that a boat had gone alongside the Statira with provisions; that they were "saluted with the groans of prisoners who appeared to be suffering the most excruciating torture"; that the passengers on the boat wished to proceed, but were "treated in the most brutal manner"; that "the groans were those of an American citizen writhing under the lash of a petty tyrant, and their crime having declared they were American citizens and having sent letters on shore by the pilot." The Baltimore Whig republished this under the heading, "Peace is now Disgrace."

The answer published by the New-York papers stated that when the boat came alongside a seaman was being flogged "for having falsely accused his officers"; that he did claim to be an American, but had given no proof of it; that he had volunteered at Portsmouth in England and received the bounty as such; that during the punishment the boat was requested to keep off a few minutes; that a "verbal altercation" ensued; but that the boat's crew carried their point, although they "wished some inconvenience to the Frigate."|

18

TO CAPT. BROMLEY, H. M. S. STATIRA.

New York 15 Feb' 1808.

SIR :

I am this day honored with your letter of the 1st Current on the Subject of British Seamen who may apply to me for passages to their native country in consequence of His Majestys late Proclamation or otherwise, with your request that I would forward such Seamen to His Majestys Ship Statira under your command, where you will receive them for His Majestys service for a passage to England on the return of the Statira with the British Mission —

Since the passing of the Act of Congress in December last laying an embargo on American Vessels, British Seamen to the number of about forty have applied for passages to Great Britain or other parts of His Majestys dominions, some of whom have been sent in Packets to Falmouth, others to Halifax in Nova Scotia, and two to Rear Admiral Sir Alx' Cochrane at Barbadoes. I have also made it known at all the houses where British Seamen resort, that I was ready to furnish them with passages to His Majestys Dominions on their application; I am sorry to add that no others have availed themselves of His Majestys Proclamation.

If any British Seamen hereafter apply, and a conveyance offers for the Chesapeak, I shall assuredly send them to you; but if there should be no such conveyance, and a vessel ready for Halifax, I shall feel it my duty to send them thither.—Had the Statira arrived here instead of the Chesapeak, I have no doubt, two or three hundred able British Seamen would have entered on board her for His Majestys Service, and even at this late day, was your station removed to this City, I feel confident, provided the embargo continues, you would more than complete your complement.

TO GENERAL SIR JAMES CRAIG.

New York 4th April 1808.

SIR.

I have received your letters of the 6th and 12th of March the former per Post, the latter by John Wyatt on his return to this City. I have also received from M^r McKenzie of the Northwest Company one hundred dollars advanced to defray Porteous' expenses in going to you; and a draft from Mr Richardson on Mess^n McVicker and Co; which was paid, for the hundred dollars given to Wyatt on account of his expenses in going with dispatches for you.— I am happy to learn you are possessed of sufficient information to counteract the Designs of those Persons respecting whom I have given you notice.

Mr Rose His Majestys Special Envoy to these States, sailed in the Statira Frigate on the 27th ulto. from Hampton Roads for England his mission to these States having failed of its friendly object. Within the last Fortnight however a great change it is said has taken place in the disposition of Congress and the American Government, and that there is every reason to believe we shall continue on Terms of Amity. In proof of this, the President has stated in conversation that the dispatches lately received from Mr Pinckney the American Minister in London were expressive of the most conciliatory disposition on the part of His Majesty; and the Presidents laying before Congress the official documents received from France, so long with held and wrapped in secrecy. — The present state of suspense cannot long continue; nor will the Americans remain much longer silent under the inconvenience and ruinous consequences of the Embargo.

TO MR. ERSKINE.

New York 9th April 1808.

SIR:

I have the Honor to inclose to you a copy of my letter to Commodore Rodgers Commanding the American Ships of War in this Port, requesting him to discharge from the

American Ship of War Wasp a subject of His Majestys named James Grady. Also Commodore Rodgers answer to me, wherein he recommends my applying to the Secretary of the American Navy on the subject; and impliedly contradicts my assertion that Grady is a Subject of His Majesty.

Grady avers that he was born in Ireland, and was a Gardner several years with Lady Connolly, daughter of the late Duke of Richmond. In addition to which the Irish dialect is so broad on his Tongue, that every person who hears him speak, would .at once pronounce him an Irishman. — I am therefore positive that I was correct in saying he was a subject of His Majesty; nor can I imagine Commodore Rodgers can have any Ground for denying it, unless he sets up the plea of Grady being a Citizen of these States or having taken the Oath of allegiance. Grady assures me he has not been made a citizen or taken the Oath of allegiance. He is anxious for his discharge and desirous to enter into His Majestys Service. I hope you will feel yourself at Liberty to make an application for him. — It is time to ascertain whether the Amⁿ Government intend retaining in their Service British Subjects.

TO GENERAL HISLOP, GOVERNOR OF TRINIDAD.

New York 5ᵗʰ May 1808.

Sir.

I am this moment honored with your Excel⁷ⁱ letter of the 29ᵗʰ of March covering your Proclamation respecting the loss of a great number of Houses and other Buildings at the Port of Spain, the distress of the Inhabitants, and inviting all friendly neutrals to export to that place Provisions and Lumber and that they shall be permitted to carry away in return Sugar, Rum, Molasses, Cocoa and Coffee.—

I most sincerely participate with you and the Sufferers in the losses they have sustained and the inconveniences they must experience; and it adds much to my mortification that I cannot officially make public your proclamation, in consequence of the continuance of the Embargo Law — I will however if possible get it a place in some of the News Papers edited in this City.— Mr Erskine His Majestys Minister at Washington I fear will not succeed in obtaining any indulgence from the Am^n Government, for two reasons, first because I suspect they are not inclined to grant them to His Majestys Subjects, and secondly if they do, they cannot refuse similar applications from the French and Spanish Governments. At this moment there are two officers at Washington deputed by the Governor of the City of St Domingo requesting permission to export flour from these States to that place to prevent the Inhabitants from perishing.— There is at present not the least probability of the Embargo being taken off.

TO REAR-ADMIRAL COCHRANE.

New York 2^d May 1808

SIR.

A french built Ship formerly sailing out of this Port under an American Sea letter under the name of the Eliza, has during this Winter been cut down in France and everyway fitted for a Privateer, she arrived here some weeks since with a Cargo of Brandy and has cleared out for the Isle of France under the name of the Constant, Vauvage Master. This is not the fact. Vauvage is the owner of this Ship and on board of her : but an American of the name of Waterman is the real Captain. She is not bound for the Isle of France but the West Indies, or that part of the Continent which comprehends Surinam, Demarara and Berbice. She has three or four Guns mounted, but the remainder to equip her to 18 Guns are in her hold, the weight or length of which I have not been able to ascertain. She sails uncommonly fast, and will probably make many Captures unless taken.— Waterman and such others of her Crew as are Americans will merit particular care and treatment being found on board an Enemy's Ship of War.— She may assume the name of the Eliza, Waterman Master and show an American Sea letter; or that of the Constant, Vauvage Master with some other Custom House document — It will be proper for you to forward this to the Commander in Chief of the Jamaica Station.

18*

TO ADMIRAL SIR JOHN BORLASE WARREN.[1]

New York 19th July 1808

SIR.

The day before yesterday it was announced in the News Papers of this City and mentioned in private letters that a French National Brig of 20 Guns had arrived in the Chesepeak from Brest with dispatches from the French Government. By letters received from Baltimore & Alexandria by this days mail it appears that a French National Brig of 20 Guns and 150 men had arrived in the Chesepeak (not from Brest but) from Guadeloupe. It is generally supposed her object is to obtain provisions.—

I am aware that under present circumstances it is not His Majestys Wish that the Squadron under your command should give even a shadow of offence to this Government; still with submission to your better Judgment, I should suppose some of the Frigates and Sloops under your command might be off and on these Ports, and occasionally capture Enemies Ships. The French are apprised that British Ships of War seldom cruise off the Am[n] Ports and avail themselves of their absence.—I have advised Sir Alexander Cochrane of the Brig being here and that she will probably return in a month or six Weeks to Guadeloupe or Martinico. Should a conveyance offer for Barbadoes or contiguous from Halifax permit me to recommend your repeating the information.

TO MR. ERSKINE.

New York 1st August 1808

SIR,

I am at this moment honored with your letter of the 29th of July requesting me as His Majestys Com[r] under the 5th Article of the Treaty of Amity Commerce and Navigation between

[1] Nephew of Sir Peter Warren. Born in 1754, died 1822. Sir John was not only a sailor, but a diplo- matist, having been British Ambassador to Russia in 1802.

His M: & the United States of America to inform you whether Moose Island in Passamaquoddy Bay is within His Majestys Limits or those of the United States.

For the more ready comprehending the conduct of the Comⁿ with respect to the Islands in that Bay permit me to give you two extracts, the first from the second Article of the definitive Treaty of Peace between His Majesty and the United States, the other from the fifth Article of the Treaty of Amity Commerce and Navigation above mentioned.— In describing the boundaries which are to divide His Majestys (then) Province of Nova Scotia from the United States, the definitive Treaty declares — "East by a Line to be drawn along the middle of the *River St Croix from its mouth in the Bay of Fundy to its source.*" The same Article grants all Islands within twenty Leagues of any part of the Shores of the United States and lying between lines to be drawn due East from the Points where the aforesaid Boundaries between Nova Scotia on the one part, and East Florida on the other shall respectively touch the Bay of Fundy and the Atlantic Ocean, "*excepting such Islands as now are, or heretofore have been within the Limits of the said Province of Nova Scotia.*" The treaty of Amity Commerce and Navigation directs that the three Commissioners appointed under the 5th Article of that Treaty, "shall by a declaration under their hands and Seals decide what River is the River intended by the" (definitive) "Treaty," and "that the said declaration shall contain a description of the said River, and shall particularize the Latitude and Longitude *of its mouth and of its Source.*"

You will perceive from these extracts that the Commissioners under the definitive Treaty in 1783 contemplated and described the mouth of the River St Croix to be in the Bay of Fundy — and that the 5th Article of the Treaty makes mention only of its mouth, without reference to the Bay of Fundy, indeed the Bay of Fundy is not mentioned in the Article.— It was the wish of the Commissioners under the 5th Article of the Treaty of Amity Commerce and Navigation to have if possible carried the mouth of the River St Croix into the Bay of Fundy; but on a fair examination of the River St Croix we were of opinion that the mouth of the River St Croix was at a place called Joe's Point nearly opposite to the Town of St Andrews in the Westernmost Part of the Bay of Passamaquoddy, and left the Boundary from thence to the Bay of Fundy to be arranged by His Majesty and the United States of America at some future Period. The Commissioners however agreed that they would recommend to their respective Governments that the Centre of the Main Channel which leads from Joe's Point into the Bay of Fundy should be the dividing Line. This Line has never been confirmed, if it had Moose Island would have been on the American Side of it, but this would not have affected His Majestys Right to that Island, because by the exception in the second Article of the definitive Treaty such Islands as then were or theretofore had been within the limits of the Province of Nova Scotia were not to appertain to the United States.— Mr Chipman His Majestys Agent was prepared to show on the part of His Majesty that Moose Island then was and had been within the Limits of the Province of Nova Scotia; but the Commissioners refused to hear him, having no power or direction to decide with respect to those Islands.— Mr Chipman is His Majestys Solicitor General at St John in the Province of New Brunswick, and will readily furnish the Admiral and General with copies of the documents he had prepared to lay before the Com^{rs} had they conceived themselves authorized to receive them —

As it may at a future day be urged on the part of the United States of America that His Majesty in the year 1802 or 1803 had agreed to yield Moose Island to these States, permit me to add, what I by no means hold to be material, but to avoid a charge of suppression. That when I was in London in 1802 and 1803, Lord Hawkesbury then Secretary of State for foreign affairs informed me that Mr King the American Minister in London, had in conversing on the Subject of the Islands in the Bay of Fundy and on the establishing a boundary Line from the mouth of the River St Croix (Joes Point) to the Bay of Fundy, mentioned that several of those Islands appertained to the United States of America.— In reply I told his Lordship I considered the reverse the fact and that every Island in Pas-

samaquoddy Bay had appertained to the Province of Nova
Scotia; I however added that if a full and compleat settlement of Boundaries took place between His Majesty and the
United States of America, which was then under his Lordships and M[r] Kings consideration, that it was my opinion
Moose Island should be granted ex gratis by His Majesty to
the United States of America, as they had possessed it since
1783 and used it as a Port of Entry.— His Lordship directed
me to confer with M[r] King on the Subject.   M[r] King and myself met twice or three times, and he finally agreed to accept
Moose Island in full of all claims for Islands in the Bay of
Passamaquoddy, as an eventual arrangement of the Boundary Lines[1]— Soon after this I understood M[r] King received
instructions from his Government not to proceed any further
in the proposed Commission for running the remainder of the
unascertained Lines between His Majesty and these States.—

TO ADMIRAL SIR JOHN BORLASE WARREN.

New York 3[d] Sept[r] 1808.

SIR.

I have the Honor to acknowledge the receipt of your three
several letters to me of the 28th of July.— I regret that the five
Seamen I sent to the officer Commanding His Majestys Ships
of War at Passamaquoddy, have not been delivered.   At the
time I put them on board there was no conveyance for Halifax.   The masters of Merchant Vessels cannot be confided in:
and the Captains of Packets, in consequence of the number of
Passengers they carry to Falmouth, since the Embargo, are
averse to be troubled with Seamen, intended for the Navy.—
Captain Davis of the Manchester on his arrival told me he
would take fifty Seamen for you, if I had them; prior however to his departure he complained of his Ship being much
crowded and eventually received very few.— The next (the
October Packet) will be the last which touches at Halifax
from hence until March next, after her there will be no con-

1 See ante, page 146.

veyance for Seamen.   Perhaps it would not be amiss for you to send a small armed vessel occasionally between the middle of October and March to take such men as may wish to return to His Majestys Dominions.   The ostensible reason for the arrival of an armed Ship from you, must be dispatches, and the Officer Commanding on his arrival at Sandy Hook or Staten Island is directed by Law to report his arrival and the cause (towit that he is charged with dispatches) to the Collector of the Customs, who will then if requested grant him Provisions, &c.

TO ADMIRAL SIR JOHN BORLASE WARREN.

New York 3ᵈ Sept' 1808.

(Private.)

DEAR SIR:

The incidents which have occurred in Europe, and in the Spanish Colonies in North and South America, are events of such general importance and so peculiarly fortunate for Great Britain that I cannot refrain offering you my sincere congratulations.— I cannot say I am very sanguine in my expectations of the consequences of the revolutions in Spain and Portugal, unless they are supported by what we have had hints to expect, a revolution in Italy, and a cooperation of the Northern Powers.   Should these take place, and unanimity, decision and energy actuate the allies, the Tyrant must fall.— At all events if the Spaniards and Portugese act with prudence and promptness, and carry on merely a defensive and desultory war, avoiding at least for two years any thing like a general action, there is work cut out to occupy Bonaparte the remainder of his Life — Where ever the French main Body appears only Women children and old men should be found.   The elite of the Spanish and Portugese Troops, of which the greater part ought to be cavalry, should hang on the rear and flanks of the Enemy, oppose them in front at every strong pass, harass them night and day by partial and occasionally

more extensive attacks, and cut up all their foraging parties
and escorts. Such a mode would make Soldiers of them, while
it rendered the French discontented from constant duty and
scanty supplies. You will perhaps smile and remark that it is
easier to prescribe the mode, than to carry it into effect. I
grant it, but beg leave to add that Troops in their own country, having every man their Friend have incredible advantages
over an Enemy who is ignorant of the country, and of local
information.— The immediate consequences of these revolutions are singular fortunate to Great Britain during the operation of the American non importation and embargo Laws.
The Spanish Colonies in the West Indies and on the Continent
of America will now take from our manufacturers all that
their Industry can supply; and I am at times in doubt whether
a continuance of the American Embargo will not operate bene-
ficially to Britain. — Whether the occurrences in Europe have
had any effect on Mr Jefferson and his Ministers has not yet
transpired. I have no hesitation to say, but for these events,
they would have gone to War with us, and united themselves
more closely with France. — For this purpose they have pursued every measure which could give offence to His Majesty
and His Ministers in the hopes of inducing them to some act
which would be generally offensive to the Americans and give
colour to a War. — A large proportion of the Americans perhaps a major part are averse to War with Britain. If therefore Britain could have been so goaded as to commit the first
aggression, the American Government believed many if not
most of those who were opposed to a War, would become advocates for it.— It was under this conviction that I some time
since took the Liberty to give you my opinion, with respect to
Moose Island in Passamaquoddy Bay, possessed by the Americans, but appertaining to His Majesty; and to recommend the
avoiding all acts of violence to gain the possession, indeed not
even to make a demand at present, for it. — My reasons were
given at length and shall not now be repeated — Vermont
Massachusetts and Connecticut are decidedly favorable to
Britain in opposition to France. In this State and in Jersey
and Pennsylvania they are nearly divided, and in consequence

of the Embargo the federal party are daily gaining strength throughout the Union. — Petitions or rather Memorials are sending from the Eastern and Northern States to the President for a repeal of the Embargo, and should it not be raised in November or December, I should not be surprised if violence was opposed to Law.   Orders have been issued by the President for building two large Armed Brigs and some gun boats on the Lakes; and large depots of small arms, ordnance and military Stores have been lately established as I am informed in those parts of this State which are contiguous to Canada.—These are strongly indicative measures. — Daily experience adds moreover to past conviction that admitting we are to be at War with America it is of immense moment, we should avoid giving the American Government a pretext for it; because should they wantonly unite with France against His Majesty, we will have three of the most powerful States with respect to men, and great numbers also in the other States, our Friends so as to impede, if not frustrate all offensive operations; and possibly to occasion a civil war among themselves.   The jealousy of the Eastern & Northern States of the influence in Council and preponderance in Congress of Virginia is great, and they live under them with an impatience, bordering on a determination to shake them off.

You will perceive in the News Papers, that the French official dispatches to the Governors of the Spanish Colonies in America of the resignation of the crown of Spain in favor of Bonaparte, were forwarded by the American Consul under cover to M[r] Madison Secretary of State.   They have happily been intercepted; but M[r] Madison owes it to his own reputation, and to these States as a power at present in Amity with Britain to disavow all knowledge of the act, and that no part of his conduct had or could have given the American Consul in Spain reason to believe he would have approved of receiving such dispatches to forward — The day I hope will arrive when His Majesty may notice this act of perfidy with prudence and demand a satisfactory explanation and apology.

The period I trust is not distant when we shall be on more friendly terms with America, in which case you may with propriety visit this place, which you will find wonderfully extended and improved, most of the lands which belonged at Greenwich to the Heirs of the late Sir Peter Warren are now included in this City. — Your Cousin Lady Southampton is also a first Cousin to Mrs Barclays; who was a Delancey, niece to and named after the late Lady Warren.[1] — I think Lady Warren, & yourself, would be pleased by a summer excursion hither. I shall only add we should be most happy to see you.

FROM JUDGE BENSON.

MY DEAR SIR,

I have reflected on what passed in the confidential Conversation between Us a few days since; and am perfectly satisfied the British Government can never justify taking Possession of Moose Island on the ground either of *better Title*, as it regards *Boundary*, or as not within the Boundary of any of the Grants under which the Territory there has been claimed and so, as it were, *vacant;* for in the latter Case the American Government would be intitled to it by Right of *prior Occupancy,* the Fact I presume being, that from the Beginning, and certainly since the Decision by the Commissioners in 1798, actual Jurisdiction has been exercised over the Island as appertaining to Massachusetts —

The Treaty of 1783, and the subsequent one of 1794, both assume it, that the River St. Croix was the Boundary of Massachusetts, and as such the eastern Boundary of the United States, and the only Question which discovered itself after the first Treaty was which is the *true* River? This Question was submitted to Commissioners who between the [Schoodic] claimed on part of the King of G. B. and [Magaguadavic] claimed on the part of the U. S. decided in favor of the former. The Treaties also suppose, that whichever might be the true River, it emptied immediately into the Bay of Fundy or *Sea* in that Quarter, whereas both the Rivers claimed empty into the Bay

---

[1] Lady Southampton was a daughter of Sir Peter Warren, whose wife was Susan De Lancey, daughter of the first Stephen De Lancey.

of Passamaquoddy, a Bay, if it may be so expressed, of the Bay of Fundy; and it being only submitted to the Commissioners to ascertain the true River, and with it it's Head or Source and it's Mouth or Confluence with other waters, and they having ascertained the latter to be at [Joe's Point] there would seem to be a Defect in the Boundary of Massachusetts as to the Space or Distance between the Mouth of the River and the Bay of Fundy, and the Parties being independent Sovereignties and therefore not amenable to any common Tribunal the Doubt or Question arising from it was necessarily left as the Subject of further Convention — I speak of it as a *seeming* Defect only being perswaded the Law would *constructively* supply it by declaring the *Filum Aquae* the middle of the Channel of the nearest Passage fit for the ordinary Navigation between the Mouth of the River and the Bay of Fundy to be the Boundary — The Necessity of this Construction will be more obviously discerned if we suppose the [Magaguadavic] to have been decided to be the River, the Mouth of it being just within the northern Headland of the Bay of Passamaquoddy; so that without some such *closing* Line as I have suggested this most incongruous Consequence would follow, that the Nation, having the main Land forming the shores of the Bay of Passamaquoddy in nearly the whole of its Circumference, would still be without a Right to any of the Islands in it, or even to the Use of it's Waters —

You may communicate this Letter as you may think proper trusting that my Motives to it will not be misconceived,

Yours sincerely

EGB^T BENSON.

Octr 26, 1808.

TO MR. ERSKINE.

New York 28th October 1808.

(*Private.*)

SIR.

The late confidential communications respecting Moose Island, which you have been pleased to transmit to me, and the refusal of the American Government to deliver that Island to His Majesty, have led me to reconsider the Subject and I feel it my duty to inform you of the result.

I fear I have heretofore been led into an error by giving the Treaty of 1783 between His Majesty and the United States of America too confined a construction.— On mature deliberation I am inclined to believe it was the intention of His Majesty and the Government of the United States of America in 1783 that the Eastern Boundary of the then Province of Massachusetts, should be the Line to divide His Majestys Colony of Nova Scotia from the Territory he was about to cede to the United States of America; and as the River St Croix had originally been the Eastern Boundary which divided Massachusetts from Nova Scotia it was agreed by the Treaty that "a line drawn along the middle of the River St Croix from its mouth in the Bay of Fundy to its Source, and from its Source directly North to the aforesaid Highlands which divide the Rivers that fall into the Atlantic Ocean from those which fall into the River St Lawrence" should be the Eastern Boundary.—

Then follow the words under which His Majestys present claim to Moose Island is founded towit "comprehending all Islands within twenty leagues of the Shores of the United States, and lying between Lines to be drawn due East from the Points where the aforesaid Boundaries between Nova Scotia on the one part and East Florida on the other shall respectively touch the Bay of Fundy and the Atlantic Ocean, excepting such Islands as now are or heretofore have been within the Limits of the said Province of Nova Scotia."

It appears to me that His Majesty cannot justify taking possession of Moose Island.

[*Here Colonel Barclay repeats the arguments used in the foregoing letter from Judge Benson.*]

It is also evident that the Treaty of 1783 which gave to the United States "all Islands within twenty leagues of the Shores of the United States except those which then were or theretofore had been within the Limits of the Province of Nova Scotia," intended only Islands laying in the Bay of Fundy and in the

Ocean; because it expressly defines them to be, "lying between Lines to be drawn *due East* from the points where the aforesaid Boundaries between Nova Scotia on the one part and East Florida on the other shall respectively touch the Bay of Fundy and the Atlantic Ocean." — Now a Line drawn *due East*, from the middle of the River St Croix, supposing its mouth to be in the Bay of Fundy, would run in an opposite direction from a Line, which is to include Moose Island.

I have in a former letter to you observed that I did not think Moose Island worth five hundred Guineas to an Individual. I consider it of no consequence to His Majesty for Fortifications. Campo Bello an adjacent and much larger Island is better adapted either for defense or annoyance.—

TO MR. ERSKINE.

New York 23 December 1808

SIR.

Finch the Courier who left this on the 12th of November with your dispatch for General Sir James Craig returned last Evening with the letter I have now the Honor to inclose—Major Thornton Military Secretary to the General has not informed me of the day he arrived; by the date of his letter to me, it must have been on or before the 28th of November, so that the Courier was not more than 16 days in going, which was very expeditious particularly as Lake Champlain was impassable —

The small letter you sent me on the 11th Instant to forward and which came too late for the second Courier, was put under a cover and despatched on the 20th Instant by a very reputable character who will be punctual in the Delivery of it —

TO MR. ERSKINE.

New York, 9th March 1809

SIR.

I have the honor to inclose herewith a copy of the instructions of the Secretary of the Treasury of the United States to the Collectors of the different Ports for their rule of conduct under the Non intercourse Act.[1] —

These instructions appear to me to comport neither with the letter or spirit of that Act; and pregnant with serious inconvenience and probable loss to His Majestys Subjects. Should they appear in the same light to you, I take it for granted you will endeavor to obtain a reasonable alteration. I take the liberty to inclose my private remarks on the instructions.

Permit me to notice that it will be necessary to obtain from the Secretary of the Treasury an additional instruction to the Commanders of the American Ships of War, and Gun Boats, and to the Collectors of the Customs to enjoin the Pilots and Masters of Revenue Cutters to give notice to the Masters of all foreign Ships and Vessels attempting to enter the harbours and Waters of the United States of the forfeiture they will incur under the Non intercourse act by entering the Harbours and Waters of these States. Such a notice to persons ignorant of the act is reasonable, and may eventually save the unpleasant circumstance of remonstrance for want of due notice —

TO DOCTOR CROKE.[2]

April (?) 1809

SIR.

By the Brig General Prevost, Tupper Master, I did myself the Honor to inclose to you a copy of the Non intercourse Act passed in the late Session of Congress; together with an abstract of Mr Gallatin the Secretary of the Treasury of the United States, his circular letter of instructions to the Collectors of the Customs, explanatory of the Act and directing the manner in which they were to conform their conduct under it.—I informed you at the same time, that I had stated to His Majestys Minister at Washington, the objections to the instructions contained in the circular letter before mentioned; and took the liberty to recommend to him in the Event of his concurring in opinion with me, a remonstrance on the part of

---

[1] The act of March 1, 1809.

[2] Dr. Croke at this time was Acting Governor of Nova Scotia.

19

His Majesty.— I am happy to inform you that M[r] Erskine His Majestys Minister made such a representation to the Secretary of the Treasury, and that he on the reconsideration of his instructions has thought proper to make the alterations suggested. I inclose you the circular on this subject, whereby foreign Vessels are now permitted to clear out until the 20th of May next in ballast, or with the Cargoes they brought into Port, provided they have not been landed, for any port whatever.

TO CAPTAIN HAWKES, H. M. S. MELAMPUS.

New York 31st May 1809

SIR

I have this moment received your letter of yesterday acquainting me with your being off Sandy Hook with His majestys Ships Melampus and Euridice under your Command, in cruizing along this coast to endeavor to intercept a French Frigate supposed to be in Boston or some other Port in these States, and requesting me to furnish you with any intelligence of which I may be possessed.

I have not heard of any French Frigate or other Ship of War having arrived for months past or now being in any Port within the United States of America nor do I believe there is; nor have I any local or foreign news to communicate. I regret that my last file of papers were forwarded on Monday to R. Admiral Sir Alexander Cochrane.— On the 10th of June the intercourse between Great Britain and these States is to be renewed, and His Majestys orders in Council revoked as to American Ships.   Congress are now sitting, and an act has passed the House of Representatives and will probably pass the Senate and President opening the Ports to British Ships immediately.   This act, I have some reason to believe, will be on tomorrow or next day.— Should either of the Ships of War under your command be in want of supplies, perhaps it would be as well to remain off and on a day or two to know the fate of this Act, of this however you are the best Judge.—

TO MR. HAMMOND.

New York 16ᵗʰ Nov' 1809

(Private.)

SIR.

As I am ignorant whether Mʳ Jackson His Majestys Minister to these States did communicate by the Africaine Frigate to His Majestys Secretary of State for the foreign Department the unpleasant event detailed in the inclosed letter; or even whether it had occurred prior to the departure of the Africaine from the Chesepeak, I consider it my duty to send to you a copy of a circular Letter received by me this day from Mʳ Jackson, which you will have the Goodness to lay before the Secretary of the foreign Department, provided he has not been advised by Mʳ Jackson on the Subject —[1]

TO MR. JACKSON.

New York 24ᵗʰ November 1809

SIR.

I regret that it is not in my power to return you a satisfactory answer to the first of your Questions respecting the number of Militia men assembled in the States belonging to my district in consequence of the Presidents orders for 100000 men to hold themselves in readiness.— It appears, from correct information, that the American Secretary of War, sent an order to the Governor of each State, specifying the number of men the State he commanded was to furnish, but that he did not communicate to such Governor the Contingent to be furnished by each of the other States. I can therefore only give the number this State furnished, and I inclose you Mʳ Skin-

---

[1] The "unpleasant event" was the refusal of the United States Government on November 8 to receive further communications from Mr. Jackson. The circular letter addressed by Mr. Jackson to the British consuls is printed in American State Papers, For. Rel., Vol. III, p. 323. Mr. Erskine had been recalled upon the disavowal by the British Government of the arrangements made by him, and Francis James Jackson was appointed his successor. He arrived in Washington September 8, 1809.

ner, the Consul ad interim, during the absence of Mr Alton who is His Majestys Consul for Massachusetts, New Hampshire and Vermont, his report of the Quota promised by Massachusetts, and the report of Mr Gilpin; Vice Consul for Connecticut and Rhode Island. The Governor of Connecticut refused to obey the order of the President, no militia therefore were embodied under that order in that State. I inclose for your information a copy of the return of the Militia of the United States; contained in Mr Jeffersons letter to Congress of the 25 of March 1808, this return was the Scale on which the relative quotas of each state was graduated. You will perceive by contrasting New York with Massachusetts, that the proportions are not arithmetically correct, still perhaps sufficiently so to take either of them to resolve the probable number furnished by Vermont and New Hampshire, the two States from which it is impracticable without expense and great trouble to obtain returns.— The State of New York furnished 14339 Militia men under the order of the President.— They never were assembled at the same time and place. Each county in this State furnished its proportion of the 14339 Men, under the order of the Governor of this State. They were drafted; and in some Counties, the men were three times assembled, in others only once, and in a few of the Counties they never were assembled. In the County of New York they assembled once: but on legal advice being taken, it was discovered, their attendance could not be compelled, and the two subsequent meetings of the drafted Militia for that City and County were very incomplete.— The Drafts were generally officered, in some Counties formed into Companies — The Governors order specified the respective divisions which were to form each Battalion but these Divisions never united so as in reality to form Battalions. They did not receive clothing. They were all armed with their own Arms, which were of different Calibres, and various lengths, some with Bayonets, others without, and not a fourth with Cartouch boxes. The Arms generally speaking the reverse of serviceable.— Not any proficiency was made in their Military Exercise and Movements. The drafted men were exempt from assembling with the Vol-

unteer Corps and common Militia on the ordinary days prescribed by Law; until they were discharged from the Special
duty for which they had been drafted.

TO MR. MORIER.[1]

New York 10ᵗʰ October 1810

SIR.

By the Sandwich Packet I received a letter from Mʳ Hamilton the Under Secretary of State for foreign Affairs acquainting
me that he had sent to me in that Packet a Box containing
several copies of Mʳ Goldsmiths Book upon the secret History
of the Cabinet of Buonaparte:[2] and that he was directed by
the Marquis of Wellesley[3] to desire that I would forward a
dozen copies of it to you, and take your opinion respecting the
manner in which I should distribute the remainder.

By this days Mail I forward you one of these copies, and beg
your directions whether I shall send the remainder in a Box
by the mail, or by water.— Permit me to request your opinion
in what manner I shall distribute the rest, so as to render
their contents generally known in these States.

[1] John Philip Morier, British Secretary of Legation, and Chargé d'Affaires *ad interim.*

[2] Lewis Goldsmith was a Portu-
guese Jew by descent, an Englishman by birth, and a journalist by
profession. He lived many years in
France, and was the father-in-law
of Lord Lyndhurst. According to
his own account, he was on intimate
terms with Napoleon, who trusted
him with large sums of money and
employed him as a secret agent in
various dishonorable transactions —
among other things in an attempt to
kidnap Louis XVIII. In 1809 he
escaped to England, and in 1811
started a subscription for setting a
price on Napoleon's head. This matter being brought to the notice of
Parliament on June 24, 1811, the
Government expressed great indignation, and promised to punish the
author. Their indignation did not,
however, lead them to take any effective steps, nor did it prevent
their using strenuous efforts to continue circulating his scurrilous Secret History of the Cabinet of Bonaparte. He died in extreme old age
at Paris in 1846.

[3] The Marquis of Wellesley, elder
brother of the Duke of Wellington,
was appointed Foreign Secretary on
December 6, 1809, upon Canning's
withdrawal from Perceval's administration.

19*

Some delay occurred in getting leave from the Custom House to Land the Box, as it was not included in the mails, to which cause you are to attribute your not having received the copy more early.

TO MR. HAMILTON.[1]

New York 6 Nov' 1810.

SIR.

I beg leave to acquaint you for the information of the Marquis of Wellesley, that M' Morier having given me his opinion that the most eligible mode to distribute the copies of Goldsmiths Secret History of the Cabinet of Buonaparte, sent by you to me, was to forward some sets to each of His Majestys Consuls resident in these States, I have in compliance with his directions sent six sets to M' Bond His Majestys Consul General for the middle and Southern States, an equal Number to M' Allen Consul for Massachusetts, New Hampshire and Rhode Island, and three sets to each of His Majestys Consuls for Maryland, Virginia and North Carolina — The remainder after forwarding a dozen copies to M' Morier, I have given to well disposed Individuals, who have promised me to circulate the contents to the utmost of their power — One copy I gave to M' Sargeant a Bookseller, who has now in the press 2000 Copies which will be ready for sale in a few days.[2]

TO THE COMMANDER OF HIS BRITANNIC MAJESTY'S
SHIP OF WAR OFF SANDY HOOK.

BRITISH CONSUL GENERALS OFFICE

New York 2ᵈ May 1811.

SIR.

I have the honor to inclose to you a letter received from the Mayor of this City, respecting the impressment yesterday of

[1] William Richard Hamilton, Under Secretary of State for Foreign Affairs from October 16, 1809, to January 22, 1822.

[2] Sergeant's edition is in two volumes, 18mo, and is accompanied by "Notes by a Gentleman of New-York."

John Deggins,[1] a native Citizen of the United States of America from the American Brig Spitfire, and now on board His Majestys Ship under your command off this Port. I also inclose three affidavits taken before the Mayor, which fully prove that Diggins is a native Citizen of these States, forcibly taken yesterday from the Spitfire and carried on board H: M: Ship under your command; and your refusal to restore him to Josiah Fichett, his master, who was a passenger on board the Spitfire.

In addition to the Arguments which the inclosed depositions naturally suggest for the discharge of this man, permit me to remark, that the impressment of a native American at this moment is peculiarly unfortunate as the two Nations are far from being on friendly Terms; and one of the points most obstinately persevered in on the part of these States in their negotiations with Great Britain, and which at present forms the principal objection to a Treaty, is " that the Commanders of His Majestys Ships of War shall not be permitted to impress men from American Vessels." Now notwithstanding His Majesty can never surrender his right to take His Subjects when found at Sea on board neutral Ships, still every instance of an illegal, unjustifiable impressment tends to weaken this right and to furnish an argument for its being given up —

I flatter myself on a perusal of the inclosed papers, you will readily deliver up the young man to the Person, who is the Bearer of this letter, and who is authorized by M[r] Fichett to receive him. Allow me to assure you that the good of the Service requires that you should at present refrain to make impressments on the coasts of these States.

I am under the awkward necessity of addressing this letter to you, simply, as " the Commander of His Majestys Ship of War off Sandy Hook," not knowing either your name, or that of your Ship.[2] For several days past we have had accounts of your being off and on this Port, but not a person has ar-

---

[1] Deggins, Digo, or Diggio, has obtained a certain historical importance, because it was while seeking to investigate his case that the President met and fired upon the Little Belt on May 16. See further as to his impressment, page 297, below.

[2] The ship was the Guerrière, afterward destroyed in action by the Constitution.

rived who has been able to give the name of the Ship or her Commander—

TO REAR ADMIRAL SIR FRANCIS LAFNEY, LEEWARD ISLANDS.

BRITISH CONSUL GENERALS OFFICE

New York 11ᵗʰ May 1811.

SIR.

It may not be improper in me to explain to you my inducement for occasionally making to the Lords of the Admiralty, and to the Commanders in Chief of His Majestys Ships of War on foreign Stations applications of the nature I am now about to make to you, as in addition to reasons of more consequence; I shall acquit myself of the imputation of improper interference.—You are not unacquainted, that the American Government are loud in their complaints and remonstrances that Citizens of these States are frequently impressed and detained on board His Majestys Ships of War; and if I am not misinformed, one of the principal present difficulties in effecting a treaty between His Majesty and these States, arises from impressments of American Seamen, to prevent which the American Government require that no Seamen shall be impressed from American Ships—A point that can never be agreed to on the part of His Majesty.— From these remarks, I trust you will agree with me, that if any instances occur in which the Commanders of any of His Majestys Ships of War have through mistake or otherwise impressed a Native Citizen of these States, it is for the benefit of His Majestys Service, that the circumstance should remain unreported to the American Government, and thereby an official representation and remonstrance prevented.— Under this conviction I have made it a rule to receive private applications, and after making due inquiry to transmit either to the Lords of the Admiralty or the Commander in Chief of the Squadron wherein such Seaman is, the necessary documents to prove him a native Citizen and to identify his person — Allow me to add that by this mode the Parties are less irritated, and generally satisfied with what I say to them.

I am now requested by Mr Spook the father of James Spook both of whom are native Citizens of these States to intreat you will have the goodness to order James Spook to be discharged from whatever ships he may be in under your command — He was originally impressed on board His Majestys Brig Frolick, T Whingates Esqr Commander: and I inclose for your satisfaction, the Certificate of his Citizenship, the deposition of the Father, and certain Questions to be put to the Youth, with the answers he ought to make, to entitle him to his discharge. Certificates of Citizenship, are evidence I place little confidence in; the intention on the part of Congress was correct; but the Certificates have been issued to all descriptions of persons, from the native American to the Irish and Scotsman not two months from his native Country.—

TO REAR-ADMIRAL SAWYER, HALIFAX.

BRITISH CONSUL GENERALS OFFICE

New York 20th May 1811.

SIR —

I am under the necessity of calling your attention to the two following cases of impressment by Captain Pashell of His Majestys Ship Guerriere. On the first of these I wrote to Captain Pashell while he was off this Port, and a Pilot Boat was despatched to deliver it, the Boat returned without being able to meet the Guerriere and the letter is on board the Revenue Cutter now at Sea for the purpose of delivering it.— On the first instant John Digo a native citizen of the United States of America, and an apprentice to Josiah Fichet of Portland Ship Carpenter was impressed off this Port from on board the American Brig Spitfire of Portland in the Province of Main, a new Vessel built by Mr Fichet coming to this place for sale, by His Majestys Frigate Guerriere. Mr Fichet went on board the Gueriere claimed the young man, but Captain

Pashell refused to deliver him — I have examined Mr Fichett and the Captain of the Brig as well as several other persons, and there is no doubt that Digeo is a Native Citizen of these States — He was born at Cape Elizabeth in the Province of Main and has a Scar on the back of one of his hands —

On the fifth of May off Long Island to the N: E of this Port, Captain Pashell also impressed another American Seaman from the American Sloop George named Gideon Caprion, the documents respecting whom I have the Honor to inclose — At the present moment such impressments off the mouths of American Ports are peculiarly unfortunate, and what adds to the disagreeableness of the circumstances, is that both these men belong to Eastern States who are not in the habit of giving Certificates of Citizenship to His Majestys Subjects; have few of their men impressed through mistake, and are therefore more sensibly hurt, whenever such accidents occur in addition to which the people of the Eastern States are more Friendly to the English than all the other States.— Permit me therefore to request you will have the Goodness to order these two young men to be discharged, and when discharged to direct them to be delivered to Mr Lawrence Hartshorne, who has my directions to supply them with money to carry them to their Homes.

I have stated these impressments to have been made by Capt Pashell of H. M. S. Gueriere; yet I am not positive this is the case. The Commander of the Frigate which has been for some days off this Coast concealed his own and his Ships name. But several Vessels which came into Port have Stated that the name of the Frigate was Gueriere. Yet I observe in the News Paper which I inclose to you that the name of the Ship on board of which Digo or Diggio was impressed, is said to be the Pizarro. This you can easily ascertain.

TO THE MARQUIS OF WELLESLEY.

B: C: G: Office New York 16 Augt 1811.

My Lord —

I received by the last Pacquet a letter from Mr Hamilton under Secretary for the foreign department of State dated the

17th of June, in which he informs me that your Lordship had directed him to transmit to me an extract of a letter from Rear Admiral Sir Francis Lafney Bar[t]: Commander in Chief in the Leeward Islands, representing that the French Privateer La Diligente had captured several English and Spanish Vessels, and that she was reported to be in part owned by persons in New York whither she was bound; and that your Lordship desired me to enquire into the truth of the above statement and to report to your Lordship the result of my enquiries and also to communicate the same to His Majestys Minister at Washington —

In obedience to your Lordships directions I have made an attentive search through the Books of the Customs in this City, and in the different Insurance offices here, in which registers are left of any Vessel which arrives in this Port; but not a Vestige is to be found, that a Privateer, or any other Vessel, of the name of La Diligente has been in this Port or is owned by a Person in this City; nor have the officers of the Customs, or of the Insurance offices any recollection of such a vessel having entered or departed this Port. I have extended my enquiries to the Pilots and other Individuals who it was probable might recollect the Circumstance, all of whom assure me they believe such a vessel never was here of that name —

La Diligente, Grassin Commander is a French Privateer well known throughout these States, in consequence of the great number of English Spanish and American Vessels which she has captured, plundered, in some instances allowed to be ransomed, but generally destroyed. The number of American Vessels by her captured far exceeds, that of English and Spanish United. Captain Grassin arrived in La Diligente this last Spring at Philadelphia, where he and his Schooner still remain. The American News papers have been filled with details of American Ships by him captured and destroyed. The Populace in Philadelphia meditated to burn this Schooner, at the instance however of Captain Grassin the Governor of the State of Pennsylvania issued a Proclamation inhibiting under heavy penalties any person or persons from injuring or molesting the person or property of Captain Grassin in consequence of which the Vessel remains safe at Philadelphia — Several actions have been commenced against Captain Grassin by Citizens of these States, not any of which have yet been tried —

It is said a Frenchman named Guier who lately removed from Baltimore to this City and who I understand is not a respectable Character is a part owner of the La Diligente. It has also been suggested that Guier is merely the nominal owner — I sent a Frenchman in whom I could confide to endeavour to draw from him whether he was really the owner or in any way interested in the Vessel. The inquiry was well managed the subject introduced as if by accident and he was asked whether he had made any insurance on his Vessel in Philadelphia against any acts of violence which might there be committed against her — He replied he had no interest in the Vessel and was merely Agent to Captain Grassin —

There is at present a small French Privateer from L'Orient cruizing off this Port, named the Marengo, Ordonaux Master — Captain Lawrence of His Majestys Packet the Duke of Kent is under no apprehension of danger from her.

TO MR. FOSTER.[1]

New York 28ᵗʰ August 1811

SIR.

I have the Honor to send addressed to you the Evening Paper of this day, from which you will perceive that the British Merchant Ship Tottenham, Young Master, arrived in this Port at 3 oClock this afternoon, a Prize to the French Privateer the Duke of Dantzic, Arregnaudic Commander, member of the Legion of Honor. The Tottenham was captured off Barbadoes the 3ᵈ instant — The Captain and Crew, three men and two Boys excepted who were left on Board her, were taken on board the Privateer.— I have seen the Tottenham, She appears a Ship of 600 Tons, I am told is laden with Coals, the British Flag hoisted under that of France —

[1] Augustus J. Foster was appointed as Minister to the United States in April, 1811, and arrived in Washington July 1. He had already been here as secretary to Mr. Merry.

The above information I have thought necessary to give you, as I do not know of any Law of nations, which allows the Prizes of Belligerents to be brought in and receive protection and comforts in a Port of a nation at peace with both the Belligerents — The Collector here can do nothing, consequently an application from you to the American Secretary of State for the restoration of this Ship is the only possible mode by which possession can be obtained — I am told by a man who was on board the Tottenham that all the Prize Crew are British or American Seamen as they spoke the English language with great fluency.

TO MR. FOSTER.

New York 2ᵈ December, 1811.

DEAR SIR.

Having some days since discovered that the collector of the customs in this port, had granted permission to the captors of the British Ship Tottenham, a prize now here, taken by a French Privateer in the West Indies, to sell the cargo of that ship, for the purpose of repairing her; and being convinced that the captors did not intend to repair the ship, and that their object was only to realize the amount of the cargo, I considered it my duty to remonstrate against it, and wrote to the collector a Letter to that effect, a copy of which I have the Honor to enclose. You are the best judge, Sir, how far such a License, operates in violation of those principles of neutrality which the United States of America uniformly assert they scrupulously maintain towards Great Britain and France. Permit me to make this one remark, that the sale of the whole was incorrect, because it was uncertain what the amount of repairs and other incidental charges would be; I am further of opinion that the repairs should have been made before the permission for the sale was granted. The cargo though not amounting to a large sum, I am of opinion will pay more than double the expense of repairs and charges.

Permissions like this will induce the Commanders of French Privateers to send their prizes to these States, as the proceeds of the cargo sold here under a Custom House License, will amount to something of consequence; and while it is so much saved to the captors, it takes from His Majestys subjects the possibility of recapture.

FROM SIR GEORGE PREVOST.[1]

Quebec 4th. January, 1812.
DEAR SIR: —

I have been waiting for the arrival of the September and October letters to announce to you my appointment to the Chief Command, Civil and Military, in the British American provinces, but from some cause, hitherto unknown, neither the one or the other of those mails has yet reached Quebec — However I will no longer delay acquainting you that under a special Instruction from the Prince Regent I assumed the administration of the Government of Lower Canada, until a Commission of Captain General could be sent to me, and that I received about the same time His Royal Highness's appointment as Commander of the Forces in British America.—

Considering the spirit of hostility shewn to England by the United States no longer likely to be confined to a paper and commercial warfare, and that therefore it is of importance I should receive a correct account of the disposition and views of the American Government, I have sent Capt. Coore one of my Aids de Camp to Mr. Forster for that purpose, who is instructed to communicate with you as he passes through New York. As great confidence may be placed in Captain Coore's

[1] Sir George Prevost, born in New York in 1767, was the son of Augustine Prevost, an officer in the British Army, and Theodosia de Visme, his wife. Augustine Prevost having died in the West Indies about 1776, his widow married Aaron Burr and became the mother of Theodosia Alston. George Prevost entered the British Army, served with some credit, became a Baronet and Lieutenant-General, and succeeded Sir James Craig as Commander of the Forces in British North America — a post he held all through the war with the United States. His military career came to an end with the failure of his attack on Plattsburgh in September, 1814. He died in London in January, 1816.

discretion, I beg leave to refer you to him for any further particulars respecting his present mission.

I have etc.
GEORGE PREVOST.

FROM SIR JOHN SHERBROOKE.[1]

Halifax, 13th Jany, 1812.

MY DEAR SIR:—

As the Packets going home do not touch here at this season of the year and as some of the Merchants are very desirous of sending letters to England I have for the public accommodation ordered a Government Schooner to New York in the expectation that She will arrive there before the next packet will sail from thence for Falmouth and as we are very much in the dark here with respect to the State of Public Affairs in your part of the world, I shall hope to be favoured with a letter from you by this Vessel when She returns.

I beg to offer you my best thanks for some New York Gazettes to 3rd. Dec. last which you were so obliging as to send me Via Eastport & which were particularly acceptable.

As I think it probable that Mr. Forster may wish to communicate with Admiral Sawyer or with me, I enclose a letter which I beg you will forward to Him, and I should wish the Schooner to remain at New York until you receive Mr. Forsters answer in case He should have any letter to send.

The Commander of the Schooner has received orders to report himself to you on his arrival at New York, & to attend to any directions which you may think proper to give Him. If you have not already forwarded the Articles which your Son was so good as to request you would purchase for me some time ago, I beg they may be sent by this Conveyance and as I have desired the Commander of the Vessel to buy several other things for me at New York I shall be indebted to you if you will afford him every assistance in making these purchases.

I have etc.
J. C. SHERBROOKE.

[1] Commander of the Forces at Halifax.

TO SIR GEORGE PREVOST.

New York, 22nd January, 1812.

DEAR SIR.

Captain Coore a few days since delivered me your private
Letter of the 4th of this month, announcing your appointment
to the chief command, civil and military in the British American Provinces. Permit me to congratulate you on this additional Testimony of His Majestys gracious confidence in
you, and His Royal approbation of your conduct. Mr. Foster
whose residence at Washington affords him peculiar advantages in obtaining correct information of the intentions of
this Government, will naturally possess Captain Coore with
all that he knows on this subject, to be communicated to you.
On Captain Coores return to this place, I shall learn from
him; what Mr. Fosters opinion is, and should it materially
differ from mine, I will give him my Sentiments and the reason whereon they are founded, that you may form a correct
Judgment. I agree with you that the period is fast approaching when these States will take active hostile measures against
Great Britain. And it is apparent that their first military
operations will be directed against His Majestys Provinces of
lower and upper Canada. I am satisfied also that attempts
will be made to seduce the Inhabitants of upper Canada generally, and the French Canadians in lower Canada from their
allegiance. You will pardon therefore the liberty I take in
recommending the utmost attention in admitting persons
within cities of these provinces, as attempts will be made to
introduce characters fitted to persuade and delude the ignorant. There is a man who lives on the Line (45) between these
States and Lower Canada, Col. Armstrong knows him, his
name is Rous. Of him particular care should be taken, and
of those who have communications with him. He is a sensible, intriguing cunning man, eminently qualified for such purposes, and well acquainted with all the disaffected Canadians.
His movements require special care.

FROM CAPTAIN THOMSON, H. M. S. COLIBRI.

H. M. Sloop Colibri, Staten Island.
Jany. 31st. 1812.

SIR:

I beg leave to acquaint you for the information of the American government of the arrival of his Majestys Sloop under my command with dispatches for the British Minister at Washington, which require an answer and which I am to be the bearer of, I have therefore to request you will be pleased to forward them without delay — They will be delivered to you by Lieut. Stephens, he will inform you of our sad disaster at Amelia, where we had run from us no less than thirteen men, eight of whom took a boat & went to St. Marys on the American side. I waited on Commodore Campbell and the public Authorities requesting them to grant a warrant for their apprehension but without effect, altho' I met my men walking the streets I dared not apprehend them, without I was on the eve of being mob'd for only speaking to them and I consider myself fortunate to have escaped without a broken head, o hopeful Land of liberty, you will perceive Sir how disagreeable it must be to a British officer to enter any of the Ports of the United States at this critical period, when we are in dayly apprehension of our men deserting, and when they once touch the shore laugh at us, and are then protected by the public Authorities. For my own part I think perfect Harmony can never exist between the two countrys until all deserters are given up on both sides and this settled by treaty.

I am informed there are a number of distressed British seamen in New York, and as I am considerably short of complement I have to request you will use your exertions to procure me some of them as we will make some stay here. I have sent the Purser to procure Fresh Beef & vegetables whom I will thank you to assist, we shall allso want before we sail four live Bullocks with a proportion of Fodder and about ten or fiveteen Tons of water.

I have etc.

JNO. THOMSON, Captain.

20

FROM MR. FOSTER.

Washington, March 26, 1812.

MY DEAR SIR

I have not urged this Government again with regard to the Tottenham, nor do I mean to do so until you shall have heard of the result of your application for leave to ransom her.

The Conduct of Sir James Craig, should the papers produced by Henry prove authentic, in my opinion, admits of little Justification.[1] It seems to have been dangerous impolitic and imprudent. I have not asked to look at the papers nor could I compare his Signature with any Letters in his hand writing which you may have, without incurring the Risk of being obliged to acknowledge a Resemblance, therefore I would not trouble you to send them to me.

Should any flagrant Case of French Violation of the Rights of America come under your knowledge, I should be much obliged to you if you would send me an authentic Copy of any document which you might be able to lay your hands on. I regret that Mr. Stewart of New London has not sent me a Copy of the Protest of Captain Chew.[2]

I am &c

AUG. J. FOSTER

I heard of one Cask of apples arriving safely for Mr. Hamilton the Un. Sec[y] who says they are excellent — so good he wishes for some more.

---

[1] James Henry's secret correspondence with Sir James Craig was sent to Congress on March 9, 1812.

[2] The brig Thames, Samuel Chew, master, had been searched by a French frigate, and brought news of the burning of two American merchantmen by a French squadron. Adams' Hist. of the U. S., Vol. VI, p. 193.

FROM MR. FOSTER.

Washington April 10, 1812

MY DEAR SIR,

I believe the U. S. Act will be soon suspended or even repealed. You see it is brought on in Congress.[1] I believe the Congress talk of adjourning to the 20 June. There is a report credited by many that de W. Clinton will coalesce with Mr. Madison and be V. President. Your New York politics are becoming interesting.[2] If you hear of anything decisive in that way pray let me know. Do you know what Mr. Villiers Mansel is come to this country about. He is a young man I believe of about 31 years of age — I am told he is coming on here. I am &c

AUG. J. FOSTER.

Is there any way of writing to England from New York. I return you many thanks for your trouble in trying to get me the documents about ships captured &c. A. J. F.

FROM MR. FOSTER.

Washington April 24, 1812

MY DEAR SIR,

I thank you for your letter of the 19th inst. The Senate read twice a bill for adjourning to-day, time in blank, supposed will be to the 2[d] June, it is uncertain if it will pass in the house. Indeed everything is uncertain here. Last week, we should have all sworn there would be war, to-day it's adjournment. Don't be surprised if I fear committing myself in giving an opinion when such changes are constantly taking place.

I will be much obliged to you to give me the Character of de Wit Clinton how he lives at New York, what fortune he has, his age & friends.

[1] A bill to suspend the non-importation act was considered in the House of Representatives on April 9. It did not pass.

[2] An election was to take place in May; and it resulted in a Federalist success.

I shall also thank you to give me any information you may possess as to the State of defences of New York Harbor & as to the manufactures lately established in the State.

Ever yours &c

AUG. J. FOSTER.

FROM VICE-ADMIRAL SAWYER.

Bermuda May 7, 1812

(*Private.*)

MY DEAR SIR,

The Bramble is charged with Despatches for Mr. Foster, and has brought two Seamen late of the Chesapeake, which I retain here 'till the pleasure of the U. S. Government is known, as to where they are to be sent — with which information the Bramble will call here on her *way home* — when I hope at the same time to hear, matters at Washington, are from the late aggressions of the French, putting on a more favourable aspect — His R. H. the Regent appears to have great difficulties in forming an Administration, but we still trust the good sense of all parties will prevail, and the general good be the ultimate object of all — in Spain all looks well,[1] and in the North, it is to be hoped Buonaparte will find his hands full.

I have very much to thank you for your attention to all my little Commissions, and will take care you receive the amount in *specie*, as soon as I reach Halifax,— my departure for which will not be (if no unforeseen occurrence arises) till after I again hear from Mr. Foster.

We have ships on the look out for the French Frigates, who seem to spare their *friends* as little as their foes — which is perhaps at this moment very fortunate.

Will Mr. Madison in any shape avow or countenance the late transaction at Amelia?[2]

I am &c

H. SAWYER.

[1] Ciudad Rodrigo, January 19; Badajoz, April 6, 1812.
[2] General Matthews seized Amelia Island on March 19, 1812; and though his action was disapproved, possession of the island was retained by the United States.

P. S. I have just got hold of 130 Dollars which I send in part payment of my *debts* — perhaps you can send me a few Pots of *very superior* french Pomatum — and two Half Chests of Tea by this same Bramble — or to Halifax at some future time.

FROM MR. FOSTER.

Washington May 10, 1812

(Private.)

DEAR SIR,

It was a Map that might include a general outline of the harbour of New York with its Islands & batteries that I wished, but I should rather have a good plan of the harbour.

I am obliged to you for all your hints & for your Information about Emigrants to the U. S. I fear the sending back some of the Irish unless done with great Circonspection might tend in a degree to hold forth an idea that returning would be a Matter of little difficulty & encourage many to come over on speculation to look about them in the hopes of getting back for nothing if they did not succeed — tho' the Welsh case you cite is certainly a strong one. Perhaps the promising to send their Letters free of Expence to their friends might have the same effect as their being sent back by holding to them an inducement to write their sentiments freely & at full length. It must be seldom that a Man who has once broke up his Establishment & the ties which attach him to a Country can be an acquisition to it in returning.

It is now thought that the Restrictive System is all the rage and that the plan of war is but a Mask to the continuance of it, — so absolutely are they here without Chart or Compass that I really am at a loss to give you news — or accounts of any kind.

When I see such unstable proceedings I think more than ever on the value of the sentiments of Horace *justum* et tenacem propositi virum &c — but then the justum is as it should be the first word & Condition of all the rest.

20*

Be assured we work for friendly relations with America but then it is necessary they should be more impartial &·less ungracious to us than they have hitherto been.

What is become of Mr. Villiers—it was said he was at Baltimore — is it not strange L⁴ Jersey's Brother should be here & have no letter for me who know L⁴ and Lʸ Jersey very well?

Ever Yours &c

AUG. J. FOSTER.

I am glad to see you have sent on my Letters to Halifax — where can the V. Admiral be. I much fear some Collision with the American frigates — they have taken in 6 months water & provisions I hear and are gone Southward.

A. J. F.

FROM MR. FOSTER.

Washington June 20, 1812

MY DEAR SIR,

I am not yet able to send you officially the decision of the American Government respecting your Consular functions nor the act declaring War. I shall, however, be able to do so to-morrow.

I pray you to send off Coasters in every Direction to apprize H. M. Ships of the State of things that they may keep together and join the admiral. The American frigates have no orders as I have been informed to go far to Sea in Search of our Ships, and no Privateers will be yet allowed to go to Sea.

Mr. Baker[1] does not go on to-morrow but a Mr. Hamilton

[1] Anthony St. John Baker, the British Secretary of Legation. He remained for some time in the United States acting as agent for prisoners of war. The Government finally refused to hold further communication with him, and he returned to England about the beginning of the year 1813. He was Secretary of the British Commissioners at Ghent, brought the ratified treaty to Washington, and was then received as Chargé d'Affaires, in which office he continued until the arrival of Mr. Charles Bagot as Minister, in 1817.

who will take Dispatches for me to England by way of Halifax will set out in Monday's mail stage. I beg you will endeavour to procure a Conveyance for him either to drop him at Halifax or conditionally to take him the whole way to England should the Adm^l have no vessel for him.

I am &c

AUG. J. FOSTER

CHAPTER VII

H M. S. COLIBRI, sailing away from New-York with
the British Minister and the British Consul-
General, touched at Halifax, and was there met by the
news that Great Britain—just too late—had suspended
the orders in council. Foster forwarded the despatches
to Baker, his Secretary of Legation, at Washington,[1]
and the *Colibri* continued on to England, arriving
about August 22, 1812. If Barclay landed at Portsmouth, as is most likely, he must have been welcomed
there by his naval son, who had just been appointed to
command H. M. S. *Success,* then lying at Portsmouth
under orders for Halifax and Bermuda.

On reaching London, Barclay, like many an American traveler since his day, took lodgings in Clarges
street, near Piccadilly; and later removed to Queen
street just out of Curzon street in Mayfair.

A month after his departure from New-York the war
had fairly begun, with its two unpleasant surprises —
defeat for the Americans on land and for the British at
sea. Hull had surrendered at Detroit on August 16,
and three days later the *Constitution* had utterly destroyed the *Guerrière*, after less than thirty minutes of
fierce cannonading.

The news of both events reached London on Octo-

---

[1] American State Papers, For. Rel., Vol. III, p. 587.

ber 6. On September 1, Jonathan Russell, the American Chargé, had notified Lord Castlereagh of his departure for the United States, and of the appointment of Mr. Beasley as American agent for prisoners of war in Great Britain; and three weeks later he had sailed for New-York. It had thus become evident that the American Government was in earnest in its prosecution of the war; that each party had failed where it might reasonably have felt a confidence of success; that the combatants were not unequally matched; and that the struggle promised to be long and doubtful.

Prisoners on each side were rapidly accumulating. What with the naval and military forces that had surrendered, and the crews of merchant ships taken by privateers or national vessels, the numbers were already large. In England, and at Quebec, Halifax, and Jamaica, American prisoners were confined in barracks or on shipboard. At Salem, Pittsfield, Worcester, Albany, Savannah and Chillicothe, British soldiers and sailors were detained,—often with inadequate food and clothing, in unsuitable quarters, and not infrequently in the common jail. The appointment of a British agent for prisoners of war, to reside in the United States, was thus an obvious necessity, and the choice very naturally fell upon Barclay. The formal mode of his appointment is not a little singular, as illustrating the methods of circumlocution which prevailed in the British public service. On November 13, 1812, the Lords of the Admiralty issued their order to "the commissioners for conducting his Majesty's transport service," directing them to appoint Colonel Barclay their accredited agent in the United States for the purpose of attending to the relief of British prisoners, with a salary of two pounds a day, and allowances for clerk hire and traveling expenses; and thereupon the transport board in turn issued their warrant to Barclay, and gave him the necessary authority and instructions. Having obtained leave from the Foreign Office to accept this appointment, Barclay sailed from Portsmouth early in January for Bermuda, where he met and consulted with Sir John Borlase Warren, the admiral in command of the station, who had been vested with extensive powers to treat with the American Government. From Bermuda Barclay proceeded to New-York, where he arrived on April 1, 1813, and immediately went to Washington to present his credentials to the Secretary of State. The President had appointed as Commissary-General of prisoners, General John Mason, who lived near Georgetown on the pleasant island of Analostan;[1] and with him Barclay at once proceeded to business. The first step was to frame a cartel for regulating exchanges of prisoners. A preliminary agreement had been concluded at Halifax in November, but it was defective and unsatisfactory in many respects, and after much discussion a revised agreement was prepared and signed at Washington on May 12, 1813. It provides for the humane treatment and speedy exchange of prison-

[1] John Mason was the fourth son of the well-known Virginia statesman, George Mason of Gunston Hall. He was born in the spring of 1766, and spent several of the earlier years of his life as a merchant at Bordeaux, in France. He married a Miss Murray of Annapolis, Md., and thus became connected with Richard Rush, whose wife was a sister of Mrs. Mason's. Another sister was the wife of Governor Lloyd of Maryland. Mason was a man of means and entertained largely, and at the time of the war with England, Analostan Island (which lies in the Potomac, opposite Georgetown) was one of the chief attractions of the District of Columbia. A charming account of the house and grounds, as also incidentally of Mrs. Mason and her nine children, will be found in Warden's District of Columbia (1816), pp. 134–150. "We walked to the Mansion house," says the writer, "under a delicious shade, the blossoms of the cherry, apple and peach trees, of the hawthorn and aromatic

ers of war; defines what persons are to be considered non-combatant, and declares that they shall not be held as prisoners; authorizes the appointment by each party of sub-agents at the several depots; establishes the forms of paroles for officers, the allowances for subsistence of prisoners in health, and the care to be given to the sick; specifies what punishments may be inflicted in case of disorderly conduct; prescribes the number of cartel-ships to be employed, and how they shall be fitted and supplied; and in general regulates with great precision the rights of prisoners and the powers and duties of prison guards.

This task completed, and the troublesome business of verifying the number and rank of the prisoners on each side being put in a fair way of settlement, Barclay left Washington about the middle of May, and once more found himself in the rural seclusion of Harlem. New-York was considered a military post and he was forbidden to come within it, so that his activities were necessarily confined to a very sustained and vigorous correspondence with General Mason and with the various British sub-agents throughout the country. The correspondence with Mason, extending over a period

shrubs, filling the air with their fragrance. . . . The house, of a simple and neat form, is situated near that side of the island which commands a view of the Potomac, the President's house, the Capitol, and other buildings. The garden, the sides of which are washed by the waters of the river, is ornamented with a variety of trees and shrubs, and in the midst, there is a lawn covered with a beautiful verdure." At a later period Mason built another house, which was modeled after the style of a French château, and was known as Clermont, in Fairfax County, Virginia; and there he died on March 19, 1849. One of his sons, John Murray Mason, sat in the United States Senate, and, in connection with his colleague, Mr. Slidell of Louisiana, acquired international notoriety in 1861. See as to the Mason Family, Miss Rowland's Life, Correspondence, and Speeches of George Mason.

of nearly eighteen months, embraced a multiplicity of topics. The rights of non-combatants, the effect of paroles, the carrying away of slaves, the alleged seduction by one nation or the other of prisoners in its custody, were constant subjects of discussion. The sending to England of some Irish soldiers captured on the Niagara River, whom it was believed the British Government intended to try upon charges of treason, led to retaliation and counter-retaliation; and the escape of certain British officers held as hostages at Worcester, Massachusetts, gave still further occasion for endless exchange of letters. In addition, there were the daily questions of detail — the giving of a parole by this officer and the surrender of his parole by that; the status of the crew of the *Essex*, captured at Valparaiso and paroled by Capt. Hillyar, R. N., of whom a certain midshipman Farragut was one; the sailing and arrival of cartel-ships; the verification of lists of prisoners; the physical condition of the men at the various depots as reported by the sub-agents: all of which needed incessant attention.[1]

For a time matters went forward smoothly enough; but toward the autumn of 1813 the letters began to assume a more acrimonious tone, each of the correspondents being engaged in the fascinating but somewhat futile pursuit of trying to put his adversary in the wrong. Mason, however, had at least the advantage of physical force on his side, and he sought to cut the correspondence short by bringing Barclay to the neighborhood of Washington. An order was issued designating Bladensburg as his place of residence. Barclay protested in vain. He was assured that "Bladensburg is

---

[1] The correspondence was, in part, laid before Congress, and will be found in Amer. State Papers, For. Rel., Vol. III, pp. 630–684, 728–730.

a comfortable village, inhabited by a respectable people, among whom are several opulent and genteel Families, supplied by a plentiful adjacent country, and affording for occupancy not only decent, but convenient and respectable houses," and the order to proceed thither was repeated. Barclay despatched to London his resignation as agent for prisoners, to take effect on the arrival of his successor, and about February 22, 1814, he reluctantly set out over the all but impassable roads of retreating winter for the "comfortable village" which was to be his residence.

His residence at Bladensburg was brought to a sudden close by causes over which neither he nor the American Government had any control. On August 17 Admiral Cochrane's squadron anchored at the mouth of the Patuxent, and landed upward of 4000 British troops. Two days later Mason wrote that a "residence at a place in the interior more remote from the waters" was considered suitable under the existing circumstances, and Barclay was required to remove at once to Hagerstown. On the morning of August 24— the day of the battle of Bladensburg—Barclay departed.

A week later Mason wrote again. The purport of his letter this time was to inform Colonel Barclay that the American Government declined to hold any further correspondence with him. Two grounds were assigned for this determination. The first, that Barclay had not left Bladensburg until the very day of the battle; the second, that he had attempted to communicate secretly with Admiral Cochrane. Barclay's reply was brief. He had remained at Bladensburg because he could find no vehicle to carry him away; and though he had given Mr. Edward Calvert a letter to Admiral Cochrane, it was merely to request him to release two of Mr. Calvert's servants who had been made prisoners. This explanation was never disputed, and subsequent events showed that the authorities at Washington were satisfied there was no dishonorable purpose in Barclay's conduct. But a natural irritation lingered after the burning of Washington, and Barclay, at his own request, was furnished with a passport to leave the country.

About the middle of October, 1814, he sailed from New-York in the American ship *Fingal*, accompanied by his youngest son Anthony, who had come back with him from England. Barclay had intended taking with him his wife and his unmarried daughter, Ann; but for some reason they were left behind.

The war was nearly over when Barclay for the third time landed in England. For three months the commissioners of the two belligerent nations had been sitting at Ghent, and by the end of November negotiations had so far progressed that the sole remaining questions had been reduced to two points — the fisheries and the possession of Moose Island in Passamaquoddy Bay. On December 24, 1814, the treaty of peace was signed.

Barclay found both his elder sons again promoted. De Lancey had been appointed to the First Foot Guards on July 25. Thomas had been made a post captain on June 7, upon the signing of the treaty of peace with France, and had retired on half pay September 30, 1814.

TO MR. HAMILTON.

No. 4 Clarges Street, London,
21st November, 1812.

SIR.

In a conversation some days since with Sir Rupert George of the Transport Board, he mentioned to me the necessity of sending to America an Agent for Prisoners of War. I informed him that if it met with the approbation of Lord Castlereagh,[1] I had no objection to go in that character, as I was at present without any immediate consular employment, and considered it probable under cloak of the superintendance of British Prisoners of War, I might from time to time have it in my power, from the extensive acquaintance which fourteen years residence in the United States had given me, to furnish not only His Majesty's ministers, but the Governor General of Canada and His Majesty's naval and military Commanders in Nova Scotia with early information.

I am now called on for my answer, or rather the Lords Commissioners of the Admiralty without any further communication have ordered me to be appointed. I cannot however think of accepting this appointment without Lord Castlereagh's entire approbation, and under an assurance that it shall not interfere with the consular appointment, I have for many years held under His Majesty.

Employment to me is preferable to Idleness, and I feel assured, that if the War with America is protracted, it will be in my power from holding the proposed appointment to communicate to His Majesty's ministers early intelligence of what occurs in the states. Under this impression permit me to request, you will be pleased to communicate the purport of this letter to Lord Castlereagh and to add that if it is his pleasure I should go to America under the present temporary proposed appointment, that I am ready to obey his commands; if not that I will immediately decline the proposal.

FROM MR. HAMILTON.

Foreign Office,
Nov. 27, 1812.

DEAR SIR,

I did not omit to lay before Lord Castlereagh your letter of the 21st inst acquainting His Lordship of your nomination by

---

[1] Lord Castlereagh became Foreign Secretary on February 22, 1812, on the retirement of the Marquis of Wellesley.

the Lords of the Admiralty to reside as Agent for Prisoners of War in the United States of America and requesting his Sanction to your acceptance of that Appointment. I have the Satisfaction to assure you that Lord Castlereagh perfectly approves of your Intention to accept it if not objectionable to yourself, and that it will in no way interfere with the renewal of your late Appointment under this office.

I am &c

W. HAMILTON.

FROM THE TRANSPORT BOARD.

Transport office 11ᵗʰ December 1812.

SIR.

Having by our warrant under this date appointed you to be an Agent to reside in the United States of America for the relief of British Prisoners of War in those States, and for carrying on under our direction a general exchange of Prisoners upon such Principles as may hereafter be settled between the two Countries, we direct you upon the receipt of this letter to proceed with all convenient dispatch to the United States for the purpose of taking upon yourself the Functions of your employment accordingly; and immediately after your arrival there you are to present yourself to Admiral Sir John B. Warren, or the Flag officer Commanding in Chief, or senior officer on that Station, and to communicate to him your warrant and instructions consulting with him as to the fittest place for you to take up your residence.

You will lose no time in demanding of the American Government, through the proper Channel, permission to visit all the depots for British Prisoners of War as often as you may judge necessary, taking care to inform the American Government, that whatever Privileges and Indulgencies may be allowed to you the same will be granted to Mr R. G. Beasley who is accredited here as the American Agent for Prisoners of War.

You are further with as little delay as possible to endeavour to procure from such department of the American Government as the Business may immediately concern (and to transmit to us) a list of all the British Subjects who are detained as Prisoners of War in the United States, specifying their names, quality, time of capture, in what Ship captured, the place of their detention and whether on parole or not respectively, as also lists of all such, as shall have been released since the commencement of the War.

For your information and guidance we herewith transmit to you Copies of the several instructions and regulations relative to the treatment of American Prisoners of War in Health in this Country, and of the allowance made to them, whether in confinement or on Parole, and with respect to sick Prisoners it is only necessary to inform you, that they are treated in all respects the same, as Seamen of His Majestys Navy. There is no part of the Treatment of American Prisoners here, that we are not desirous to be open to every proper inspection, and the most humane and generous means are established for affording them every reasonable comfort that their State of Captivity will admit of. We therefore flatter ourselves that upon your application, the American Government will issue such orders, as may be necessary for your having communication with all the British Prisoners either personally, or through the medium of such Sub-Agents, as you may find it necessary to appoint, and generally give you every assistance in the execution of the Service entrusted to your case.

You are to report to us as soon as possible, the exact quantities and nature of the allowances, whether in provisions, or money, which the British Prisoners may be entitled to from the American Government, and you are always to be particularly attentive that those allowances be fully distributed.— You will also take care to inform yourself, whether there are any British Prisoners entitled from their Rank and Qualities to the indulgence of Parole, who do not enjoy it; and in the event of any case of this kind or improper treatment of any other nature coming to your knowledge, you are to make a becoming remonstrance to the proper department of the American Government on the Subject.

21

You are to lose no time, in obtaining information, respecting the State of the clothing of the Prisoners, and to report the same to us, in order that we may be enabled to give you directions on the subject. In the mean time we authorize you to purchase on the best terms in your power, such articles as any of the Prisoners may be in absolute want of.

Besides the allowances which may be made to the Prisoners by the American Government, we authorize you to cause to be paid to them the several allowances specified in the enclosed paper according to their respective qualities, on account of this department, taking care that such payments be made according to the par of exchange.

If British Prisoners carried into the Ports of the United States by French cruizers be delivered up to your Sub Agents, and no objection to their release be made on the part of the American Government, you are to cause all Prisoners of that description to be subsisted at the charge of this department from the time of their being so delivered up, and we authorize you to pay to such Prisoners the daily allowances specified in the above mentioned Paper according to their respective Ranks.

With respect to the Hire of Vessels for the removal of Prisoners of War from the United States, you are to consult the Admiral if there be time; and also to apply to the Boards Agents at Halifax and Bermuda in case they should have any Vessels at their disposal, transmitting Lists &c &c to those Agents of the Prisoners embarked; and it is expected you will pay every attention in your power to the most strict Economy in this, as well as every other matter respecting which it is impossible to give you any definite instructions. We think it proper however to observe to you, that all Vessels ought to be hired at a certain rate per man or per Ton for the Voyage or Run; and not for time, and that no Prisoners be sent to Europe without the order of the Commander in Chief or Flag officer, but be conveyed to Halifax, Bermuda, and the West India Islands, including the Bahamas. The proportion of the Prisoners to the Tonnage of a cartel Vessel, must depend upon the length of the Voyage, and the particular construction of the Vessel,

but between this Country and France, it is usual to embark
not less than three men for every two Tons. The daily ration which you are to order for British Prisoners while on
their voyage from the United States is to be, one pound of
Bread, one pound of Beef (or two-thirds of a pound of Pork)
and one quarter of a pint of Rum for all Prisoners without
distinction, and no more.—The Passports to be given to such
Vessels must of course be from the American Government,
and all Vessels conveying American Prisoners from hence
will be furnished with Passports from us in the annexed form,
nevertheless each Vessel having British Prisoners on Board,
should be furnished with a certificate from you, or one of your
Sub Agents, stating the Service on which she is employed,
and in order to prevent misconceptions it will be proper for
you to communicate with the American Government on the
subject of such Instructions. Vessels hired for the conveyance of Prisoners must always be supplied with a proper
quantity of Water at the expense of the owner, and it will be
adviseable to agree with the owners of such Vessels at a certain rate per day for the Prisoners victualling.

Your sub Agents will be allowed after the rate of five Shillings per day for every day on which any British Prisoners
are under their care.

We enclose for your further information a copy of a letter
from the Lords Commissioners of the Admiralty by which you
will perceive that no British released Seamen, not belonging
to His Majestys Navy are to be impressed until 48 Hours
shall have expired after their arrival at a British Port, which
you are to cause to be made known to all British Seamen who
may embark on board Cartels.

The printed copies of instructions to Agents for Prisoners
of War are sent to you for your information respecting the
manner in which Prisoners of War are treated by us, but you
must be well aware that no specific Instructions to Agents
of British Prisoners in Enemies Countries can be prepared in
a similar manner, because the nature and details of Instructions in such cases must depend entirely upon the way in
which such Prisoners are treated by the Government of the

Country in which they are detained. For this reason when any particular point occurs to you upon which you may wish to have our directions, it is proper that you should communicate it to us from time to time with as little delay as possible, and in the mean time to procure and follow the directions of the Admiral or Flag officer, with whom you are also generally to communicate respecting the duties which you are entrusted to perform under this department.

We enclose for your information a copy of an order from the Right Honorable the Lords Commissioners of the Admiralty relative to a proposed Cartel for the exchange of Prisoners of War between this Country and the United States of America, together with a project for such Cartel which we have also transmitted to Admiral The Right Honorable Sir John Borlase Warren and requested that he would through you, or any other Channel make the necessary communication on the Subject to the American Government.

You are to transmit to us quarterly accounts of your expenses and to draw upon us from time to time for such Sums as you may require for carrying on the service entrusted to you — For your further information we annex a list of our several Agents in the West Indies and America

We are
Sir
your most humble Servants
J. BOWEN
JNO. HARNESS
J. BOOTHBY

FROM THE TRANSPORT BOARD.

(*Secret.*)

Transport Office,—
5th January, 1813.

SIR,

In pursuance of Instructions from the Right Honorable the Lords Commissioners of the Admiralty, we direct you to

proceed to Portsmouth, so as to be there before the 7th instant, waiting on Admiral Sir Richard Bickerton immediately
on your Arrival, who has Orders to provide you with a Passage to your Destination; and you are, for very particular
Reasons, to avoid, if possible, making either your Name, or
Destination, known to any other Person than the Admiral.

We are, &c.

J. BOWEN
JNO. HARNESS
W. BOOTHBY.

TO THE TRANSPORT BOARD.

Washington City 15th April 1813.

SIRS.

I have the honor to inform you that I arrived at New York
on the first of this month from Bermuda, and at this place on
the 5th Instant, I immediately waited on the Secretary of State
and delivered to him my warrant and Instructions from you
to be laid before the President of the United States, in order
to my being accredited as His Majesty's Agent for the relief
of British Prisoners of War and for carrying on under your
directions a general exchange of Prisoners.

The President has been pleased to receive me in that
character, and has since appointed General John Mason of
George Town in Columbia Commissary General of Prisoners of War throughout the United States of America; with
whom I am directed to confer on all points relating to my
mission.

General Mason and myself have had three conferences and
have made some progress in the arrangement of a system for
the future subsistence and clothing of Prisoners, and their
accommodations. Preparations have also commenced on
the part of this government to draw together the British
Prisoners now in these States, in order to their being sent as
speedily as possible to Bermuda and the West Indies, and

21*

the cartels which convey them are to bring back a corresponding number of Americans. The President not having ratified the provisional agreement for the exchange of Prisoners made at Halifax in Nova Scotia on the 28th of November last; some small alterations have been proposed by him, which in my opinion are not of moment to oppose, and which I shall, with an amendment on the part of his Majesty conditionally agree to, subject to your and Sir John Borlase Warren's ratification. These when prepared shall be forwarded.

I have reason to believe, from the assurances of the Secretary of State, and General Mason, that this Government is desirous that every facility shall be given to the exchange of Prisoners of War, and to their comfort while Prisoners.

I enclose for your information a copy of a letter addressed to General Mason on the subject of British Prisoners being enticed to enter into the service of the United States, to which I have not yet received an answer. I have however his and the Secretary of States verbal assurances, that if any such irregularities have occurred at the commencement of the War they were without the knowledge of the Government and that they shall not hereafter be permitted.

Sir John B. Warren having coincided in opinion with me that New York, being a central position, was best adapted for my residence, I have obtained the President's leave to reside there for the present.

I learn with regret that a difference in opinion exists between Lieut. General Sir George Prevost, Governor General and commanding His Majesty's Forces in the Canadas, and this Government on the Subject of Exchanges made last Autumn. A case on the part of these States is now preparing for me, which I shall transmit to Sir George Prevost, and request his answer. Of both these I shall avail myself of the earliest conveyance to forward you copies, with my remarks thereon, to enable you to more readily to give me your orders on the Subject.

All letters coming to or going from this country are opened and read by persons appointed for that purpose, and when

considered of importance transmitted to the Secretary of State
at this place.

TO SIR JOHN BORLASE WARREN.

(*Private and confidential.*)

Washington 14ᵗʰ April 1813.
DEAR SIR.

I took occasion to observe to Mr. Monroe my surprise that
this Government had not acceded to the proposal of Rear Admiral Cockburn, to receive from him American Prisoners and
return British by the same conveyances. In reply Mr. Monroe
did not acknowledge the fact, but made this remark, that if
anything unpleasant or apparently unreasonable had occurred,
it was wholly to be attributed to the conduct of Mr. Baker who
had been left here, as pro tempore Agent for Prisoners of War
by Mr. Foster. That he had given great offense, and would
have been indicted, had not the President interfered, who was
averse to such strong measures against a Gentleman, who had
lately held.the appointment of Secretary of Legation, that in
consequence of Mr. Baker's conduct he had for some time past
refused all communication with him. I discovered a principle
cause of complaint against him was his having after his Functions as Secretary of Legation ceased, and while he acted
merely as Agent for Prisoners of War, delivered a number of
Licenses (to protect Cargoes) left with him by Mr. Foster.
Mr. Monroe expressed his satisfaction on my arrival, and
added that I should find every disposition on the part of this
Government to carry on exchanges on principles of reciprocity
and liberality. In the amendments to the provisional agreement for the exchange of Prisoners, it will be proposed that Bermuda is made a depot; or possibly that it should be substituted in the place of Bridge Town Barbadoes. To the former,
I think you will have no objection. I notice in the American
papers that the Masters and Crews of several vessels captured
by the Brig Atalanta have been sent into these States and,
from the manner in which it is stated apprehend proper re-

ceipts have not been obtained. It is therefore advisable until
I make the necessary arrangements, not to send them on shore
in this irregular manner. I will thank you to direct your Secretary to order Lieut. Miller of Halifax to forward to me correct returns of all American Prisoners sent from Halifax, and
copies of the receipts taken when delivered — also returns of
all British Prisoners received from these states in exchange.
I have reason to believe this Government intend to put a stop
to the present communications by Packets, and I informed
Mr. Monroe, that I suspected that mode of communication was
far from agreeable to you.

TO SIR THOMAS HARDY.[1]

Washington 21 April 1813.
SIR.

Your letter of the 11th of this month dated off Block Island,
I received last evening. I arrived here from Bermuda on the
6th Instant and was much surprised to learn from Mr. Monroe
the American Secretary of State that the provisional agreement executed in November last at Halifax, had not been ratified by the President of the United States, or measures taken
by this Government, with Mr. Baker, to amend the agreement
and to send it to Admiral Sir John Warren for his approval.
On expressing my surprise Mr. Monroe informed me, the delay
had been occasioned by the improper Conduct of Mr. Baker,
and with whom he had declined having further communications. I did not think proper to enter on the merits of the
dispute.

This Government received me with politeness and have assured me of every disposition on their part to facilitate a general exchange, and to continue exchanges on liberal and humane principles. General John Mason has been appointed
Commissary General of Prisoners of War, and I am directed

[1] Nelson's Captain Hardy, the commander of the Victory at Trafalgar, and
who was now in command of the squadron blockading New London.

to confer with him on all matters relating to my mission to these States.

One of our first objects has been to amend the provisional Agreement, so as to meet the convenience of the President, and of the Admiral and final ratification on the part of His Majesty. It includes Land Forces. This day it is to be laid before the President. Until he ratifies it, I cannot give you any directions on the subject of receipts for Prisoners whom you may land in the United States. In the meantime I beg leave to recommend your continuing the mode you have already used, and obtain receipts from the Chief Justice or some other Magistrate of Respectability. I doubt however the propriety of making use of this mode in the event of your capturing any American Ship or Vessel of War; in such a case a more formal exchange and delivery would be necessary. In addition to my communicating with the Admiral, I shall take the earliest means to transmit to you the Agreement as amended.

TO SIR JOHN BORLASE WARREN.

George Town 26th April 1813.
SIR.

In my despatch of the 14th current I stated to you that the provisional Agreement for the exchange of Prisoners entered into at Halifax by Mr. Uniacke and Lieut. Miller on the part of his Majesty and Mr. Michell on the part of the United States of America in November last had not met the approbation of the President, and that he had directed General John Mason the American Commissary General of Prisoners to confer with me on the subject of amending the provisional agreement so as to meet the wishes of both parties.

General Mason and myself have therefore altered several of the Articles and added two to the original number. They have been laid before the President who is ready to ratify them on the part of the United States in order that they may be sent to England for the necessary ratification on the part of His Majesty. I informed this Government, that it was my duty prior to ratification to submit the agreement as amended to your consideration. I now enclose it and hope it will meet your approbation: but should this not be the case, I will thank you to be distinct and full on the Subject to which you may dissent, or require an amendment, so that I may fully comprehend your wishes.

As this agreement comprehends Prisoners taken on Land and Sea and extends to all His Majesty's Dominions, your signature of approval to it becomes unnecessary, perhaps improper because in that case it must also be sent not only to Lt. General Sir George Prevost at Quebec, but to all other Commanders in Chief. I therefore submit it to you for your approval, and when amended agreeably to what may comport with your Ideas, the instrument will be signed by General Mason and myself and ratified by the President, after which I will transmit it to the Commissioners for Transport and Prisoners of War to be by them laid before His Royal Highness The Prince Regent for his Royal Pleasure thereon.

TO THE TRANSPORT BOARD.

Harlaem near New York

20ᵗʰ May 1813.

SIRS,

Referring you to my letter of the 15th of April of which a duplicate is enclosed I have the Honor to enclose to you the Agreement entered into between John Mason Esqr. Commissary General of Prisoners on the part of the United States and myself as His Majesty's Agent for Prisoners of War. I forward it for your consideration and to be laid before the Lords of the Admiralty and the other proper departments of State.

As this Agreement is of a nature not of sufficient magnitude

to require the ratification of His Royal Highness the Prince
Regent it was proposed by the President of the United States
that it should be ratified upon the part of the United States
by the American Secretary of State and on the part of His Majesty by the Lords of the Admiralty. A copy of this agreement with the ratification by Mr. Munroe the American Secretary of State will be forwarded by him to their Lordships,
and if no objection lays to the agreement their Lordships will
be pleased to transmit a copy ratified by them to this Government. It may however be prudent to delay the ratification
until Sir George Prevost communicates to his Secretary of
State his opinion, to whom I send a copy, and I have submitted it to Admiral Sir John Warren who approves thereof.

I am sending the British Prisoners from hence as fast as the
cartels arrive; and the instant I am in possession of all the
Lists and receipts of American Prisoners delivered or sent to
America, I shall proceed to a general exchange.

On my arrival here on the first of April, I was informed that
a number of respectable British Subjects, principally merchants, whose affairs at the declaration of war by these states
compelled them to remain here, and who continued in America
after the six months leave given them by these States for their
departure, had been ordered by this Government to remove
from the Sea Port Towns, their former residences and reside
on parole forty miles from Tide Water in the interior of the
Country. Many of them were desirous to return to His Majesty's Dominions and all the others to their former abodes.
With respect to the latter I did not conceive myself entitled
during the War to interfere, but with regard to the former, I
applied to the American Commissary General of Prisoners,
and required their delivery to me as Non-Combatants and for
two Flags of Truce to carry them from these States. During
the correspondence on this subject on an application by the
American Commissary to the President for instructions, he directed him to cease any further communications with me on
this subject and to inform me, he was of opinion my appointment did not extend to this description of Persons: but that
if I had anything to communicate on the subject, I must ad-

dress myself to the Secretary of State, who would return me an answer. I therefore wrote him a letter whereof the enclosed document is a copy: to which I received his answer a copy whereof is also enclosed.

You will perceive the Secretary of States refuses to consider them Prisoners of War, and that he hints at detaining them as fit Subjects to be hereafter used for retaliatory measures, should this Government think proper to resort to them; and that he denies my authority to interfere. On reverting to your warrant of my appointment, I think you will agree with me, that words cannot be more appropriate to express my superintendance and care of these Gentlemen: but you will notice that in my letter to the Secretary of State, I do not press this point, but take a stronger and more extensive ground, to wit that every man deprived of his Liberty was a Prisoner.— My right to act in this instance being denied by this Government, I have returned Mr. Monroe, a general answer, informing him I had submitted the correspondence to my Government for their consideration and directions, I shall therefore wait your orders. It remains with His Majesty's Government whether they will not treat the Citizens of the United States and in the united Kingdoms in a similar manner, and hold them Prisoners, to respond the treatment the British Subjects now here may receive from the United States.

The President has thought proper for the present not to allow me to come within less than two miles of the City of New York, it being considered a military Post. I am not otherwise restricted. This limitation will not be attended with inconvenience.

I have made an exchange of the officers and men of the American Sloop Viper for the officers and men of His Majesty's late Sloop Peacock, and a few officers and men of other British Ships to make the exchange equal, but as the Peacock's men are not yet embarked, and casualties may occur, I do not send you the exchange by the present conveyance, as alterations may be necessary, which is provided for in the Receipts.

TO THE TRANSPORT BOARD.

Harlem, New York, 5th June 1813.

SIRS.

I have the Honor to inform you that I received from this Government repeated assurances that it will do all in its power, to prevent British Prisoners of War being received into the American Naval or Land Service. These declarations I have reasons to believe are sincere. I lament however to add, that the measures hitherto adopted have proved ineffectual; and that His Majesty's Subjects, Prisoners, have since my arrival in these states, been taken into the American service: and that in the case of some men of His Majesty's late Sloop Peacock, I applied to Commodore Decatur but he did not think proper to restore them at my request, and although he did not defend the practice of receiving British Prisoners of War into the American Service in express terms : he did it equivocally by stating that similar conduct had been used towards American Prisoners by the officers of His Majesty's Ship Africa.

An unpleasant occurence has taken place with respect to an arrangement between General Mason and myself with the concurrence of Admiral Sir John Borlase Warren. The American Government had purchased the Brig Analostan as a National Cartel, laying at Washington, subsequent to the blockade of the Chesepeak; and was desirous to send this Cartel to Jamaica for American Prisoners, reported to be in a sickly state. I communicated this to Sir John B. Warren and requested his consent that the Cartel might leave the blockaded waters for the above purpose. In reply the Admiral informed me he would consent on Condition that this Government delivered on board one of His Majesty's ships in Lynnhaven Bay all the British Prisoners at Norfolk and in its vicinity, and he added that on this being agreed to upon the part of the United States he would instantly deliver from on board the Ships up the Chesepeak near 300 American Prisoners, on their parole. This was assented to on the part of this Government, and there is no disagreement between General Mason and myself on the Terms.

Sir John Warren according to promise delivered 296 American Prisoners at Annapolis and received the usual receipts which he transmitted to me.

I was apprehensive that notwithstanding General Mason intended to execute the agreement with good faith, still that from want of energy in the Government, and from many other causes, the whole of the British Prisoners would not be sent by the American Cartel on board His Majesty's Ships of War in Lynnhaven Bay. As Sir John Borlase Warren was at that time some hundred miles from thence, I considered it my duty to inform the officer commanding H. M. Ships in Lynnhaven Bay to whom the British Prisoners were to be delivered, of the round number he was to receive and added, that I submitted to his better Judgement, whether in the event of a defalcation in the number delivered, it would not be prudent to detain the Cartel. It appears that little more than $3/5$ of the British Prisoners were delivered, and no reasons assigned for not delivering the remainder, the Cartel has in consequence been detained.

Until I can induce this Government to compel more attention to its orders and business gets into a regular Train, I beg leave to recommend, that American Prisoners may not be sent to these States until exchanged. There are other strong reasons for adopting this rule. I wish you would write to the several agents abroad to this effect, and direct them not to send Prisoners, unless ordered by your Board, or by Admiral Sir John Warren, or requested by myself.

I have not been able to obtain an answer to my letter of the 12th of April addressed to the American Commissary of Prisoners on the various points contained in your instructions to me, and on which I can only procure the necessary information from him. I have repeatedly reminded him and requested his answer not only to that, but to most of my other Letters to him. General Mason holds several other public appointments, which probably occasions these delays. In the agreement which accompanies this you will observe the allowance of food or money per day to each Prisoner. The British Prisoners have been liberally fed hitherto by the United States, and the humane treatment of the Marshalls in each State towards them is universally acknowledged.

TO THE TRANSPORT BOARD.

New York 22nd June 1813.

SIRS.

After repeated applications to the American Commissary General of Prisoners, I have received his answer to my letter of the 12th of April respecting certain points on which by your instructions of the 1st of December last I was directed to request information from this Government and to report to you.

You will perceive that the President has not thought proper to permit me to visit all the American Stations and Depots as often as I judge necessary; on the contrary I am only to visit them on special occasions, having previously assigned my reasons and obtained his permission. Nor are the Sub-Agents, from the tenor of General Mason's letter, to have leave to visit any other Station or Depot except the one at or near which each of them respectively resides. I have noticed this in my reply of the 20th current to General Mason a copy whereof is also enclosed. His answer when received shall be transmitted to you.

It is for you Sirs to determine whether it is necessary to restrict in a similar manner the American Agents in England and other parts of His Majesty's Dominions. Distrust and jealousy mark the conduct of the members of the present American Administration. This is not without some reason. It is well known that from Pennsylvania North all the Gentlemen of respectability and property are opposed to them and to their measures, and that in every State, South of the Delaware there are many characters of equal property and respectability who entertain the same sentiments. They are therefore unwilling that His Majesty's Subjects, myself and the sub-agents, in particular, should have an opportunity of communicating with Gentlemen so essentially differing in Sentiment with them. In addition to which they are apprehensive a more liberal indulgence to British Agents would give offence to their Friends and Supporters.

TO LORD CASTLEREAGH.[1]

(*Private.*)

New York,

Sept. 30, 1813.

My Lord,

The continued success of the American Ships of War in actions with those of His Majesty, added to the inequality in the numbers killed and wounded on board the American if we compare with them the numbers lost on board the British ships, and the generally trivial injury to the bodies and rigging of the former, contrasted with the damage received by the latter, are events respecting which your Lordship will naturally be desirous of a solution. A residence of 14 years in the United States has afforded me an opportunity for information and I hope your Lordship will not consider it impertinent to offer you my sentiments on so important a subject.

I shall divide it under three heads. The ships, officers and men, and discipline. The American ships of War are not only much larger than those of His Majesty of the same class, but the materials contain more cubic feet and inches, hence they are less liable to injury from shot, and impenetrable to grape: When therefore ships of the same class come in contact, the American has the advantage.

In sailing if there is a difference, it is in favour of the American ships. They are brave and aspiring, able seamen, and manœuvre a few ships admirably. With respect to the Warrant and Petty officers and men on board the ships of the respective nations, the superiority is greatly in favour of the United States.

In the American Navy at least one half are British Seamen. The remainder are subjects of Sweden, Denmark, Prussia, &c.,

[1] This letter was sent in cipher.

&c., and a few Americans. From the great influx of seamen, the commanders of American Ships of War have had it in their power to select young well-made prime seamen. Those who are subjects of His Majesty fight with desperation, most of them being deserters. Thus manned the American officer has an evident superiority over the British Commander, whose crew are the reverse of select, and by far the greater proportion not able seamen. It is a lamentable truth that our seamen are tired and dissatisfied with their success, and long confinement on board ship in consequence of 20 years' war, and I fear capture by the Americans is not disagreeable to many of them.

I forbear touching on the present discipline of H. M. Navy. That it is not what it was, I appeal to every officer of experience. The mutiny in the Fleet and other causes may have rendered some relaxation necessary : whether it has not been carried too far merits enquiry.

The discipline which formerly prevailed in our Navy is now practised in the American service on British seamen with good effect.

The seamen in the American service are practised for hours at the great guns, small arms, & in sham boarding, and as the complement of men is $\frac{1}{4}$ more than in our service, an additional number of men are appointed to serve as marines in the tops: also there are howitzers with men appointed to them. From these, with the musketry in the tops, and the quarter-deck well manned with marines, a destructive fire is kept up during an action. From the before remarks, your Lordship will perceive that in every particular officers excepted, the American ship has the advantage over the British. It is an abuse of words to call the crews of the U. S. Ships American. They are British crews commanded by American officers.

The complement of men on board our largest frigates does not exceed 350, while the American frigates carry 500; of these, 250 are superlatively able and strong British Seamen. I sincerely believe the 250 British on Board an American ship are an equal to 350 of the men who ordinarily compose our

22

ship's company. It follows that with the addition of 250 men on board the American ship, many of whom are equal to the British, victory must attend the former.

I have omitted to inform your Lordship that the guns on board the American ships are elevated or depressed by a scale on the screw and on the coign. When therefore the proper elevation is ascertained, in consequence of the shot from any particular gun having struck the enemy, an order is issued and all the other guns are graduated accordingly.

What I have submitted to yr. Lp. is in perfect confidence. I beg my name may not be mentioned.

FROM GENERAL MASON.

Office of Commissary General of Prisoners
Washington Oct. 5th, 1813.

SIR.

It is intended to give answers in this letter to the letters accumulated from you during the late short absence, I made from the seat of Government, to which I have not already replied, and about which I find you are beginning to complain.

I did not fail to remark your frequent complaints, on the same subject, last summer: I am not conscious that I have at any time permitted a communication of yours to remain unanswered, more than a few days, an early reply to which, was a matter of any consequence to either Government; it is very true that I often did delay answers to those of the very numerous letters, which you were constantly in the habit of addressing to me, that were considered of minor importance, from the necessity of making them occasionally yield to the more essential avocations, which the various duties of this office daily produce; and such, Sir, must inevitably be the case, while it is attempted to conduct all the business of your Government, in connection with this office, with which you are entrusted, at the distance, at which we are placed, through the medium of correspondence only. During the six months that you, and I have now been in official intercourse, you have al-

ready addressed me about one hundred and twenty-five public
letters, not unfrequently two, or three, on a day the subjects
of many of which might have been settled, by a personal interview in a few moments; nor is this all; it has several times
happened and it must often happen again, that while with
every possible promptness in answering letters, it requires at
least one week to communicate by mail a business of importance to the two nations, demanding despatch, must stand, un-
till a discussion takes place by letter, that will produce, perhaps, the interchange of several communications. It was apprehended, when your request, at the time of your reception-
that your Residence should be taken near New York, was as,
sented to, that inconvenience would be experienced from the
remoteness, at which you would be located from the Seat of
Government; from a desire that you should be accommodated,
in your personal arrangements, I made myself no objection to
it; but now that experience has proved to me that it is impossible to conduct the Intercourse relative to Prisoners, with
proper advantage to either Government (and more particularly as the war advances, and that intercourse will necessarily
become more complex) at the distance, at which their agents
are now placed from each other, I have considered it incumbent on me to apprise you of my conviction on this point, and
to recommend it to your serious consideration.

I have &c
J. MASON.

FROM THE TRANSPORT BOARD.

Transport Office,
6th November 1813.

SIR.

In reference to our letter of the 18th of August last, in answer to yours of the 20th of May, relative to the Cartel Agreement entered into by yourself and General Mason, for the
Exchange of Prisoners of War, we now transmit, for your Information and Guidance, the Copies of an Order of the Right

Honorable the Lords Commissioners of the Admiralty, dated the 30th of September and of its Inclosure from Colonel Bunbury, signifying the Opinion of the Earl Bathurst, on the several Articles of the said Cartel Agreement, and desiring that the same might be ratified with the Alterations suggested by His Lordship, in consequence of our Observations thereon, a Copy of which you will also receive herewith and we direct you to propose such alterations to the American Government. For your further Information, we enclose a Draft of a Cartel which you are to propose in lieu of the one transmitted by you, and we desire that in any discussion which may take place on the several Points therein, you will conduct yourself in conformity to the Suggestions contained in Colonel Bunbury's letter abovementioned.

You will observe that, in the Draft above referred to no Mention has been made of the Ration, as no Alteration can be made in the Rations at present allowed to American Prisoners of War either in this country or on Foreign Stations, of which a Statement was contained in our Letter of the 1st December 1812.

With respect to the subsistence of Parole Prisoners, we acquaint you that the Allowance to American Prisoners in this Country has been augmented to Two Shillings Per Diem for Commissioned Officers, and One Shilling and Six Pence per Diem for all inferior Parole Prisoners, the Allowance to those on Foreign Stations to remain as at present.

You will also observe, that in the Names of Places at which American Prisoners are to be stationed for Exchange, Liverpool and Falmouth have been omitted, there being no means of accommodating Prisoners of War at those Places; and we consider that the Insertion of them in the Cartel Agreement entered into by you arose from a misapprehension of our Letter of the 5th January last, wherein we acquainted you that Liverpool and Falmouth were Ports appointed for the Reception of American Cartels.

We are &c

Rup^t George

J. Bowen

Jno. Harness.

FROM MR. MONROE.

Department of State,
Dec' 28, 1813.

SIR,

For reasons which every day become more evident, the President has determined that you should reside near the seat of government.

You will be pleased, as soon after the reception of this letter as your convenience will permit, to take your residence at Bladensburg, in the vicinity of this city. A passport to travel thither is sent you.

Such regulations will be made, as to your visits to the office of the Commissary General, or other places, required by your functions, as are observed towards our agents in the country of the enemy.

I remain &c

JAS. MONROE.

TO MR. MONROE.

Harlem, New York, 4ᵗʰ Jan! 1814.

(Private.)

SIR,

I beg leave to inform you the order of the President communicated to me in your official letter of the 28ᵗʰ was not unexpected, General Mason having more than once mentioned to me that my residence at this distance from the seat of Govᵗ was inconvenient to him, as he was obliged to devote a greater part of his time to writing, than his other duties would permit, and that by my removal, this inconvenience would be remedied, as most of our communications would be verbal.

If Genˡ Mason's conclusions were correct, I would readily have concurred with his original proposal — the contrary is the fact, at least as it respects myself. I should hold myself guilty of extreme negligence in conducting the business of the

22*

office I hold by verbal communications liable to different constructions, mistakes and want of memory.— Wherever I reside, while I execute the Office I hold, I shall feel bound to make and receive all official propositions and suggestions in writing — Gen' Mason will therefore derive no additional convenience from my residence at Bladensburg; and he was in full possession of my sentiments, that in the event of my being ordered to or near Washington, I should apply to his Majesty's Ministers for leave to resign my appointment. From my official letter to you Sir of this day you will observe that I have done this. In April, I hope my Successor will arrive.

Altho' I do not consider myself entitled to request your good Offices in my favor, still I trust you will have the goodness to state in the most respectful manner to the President, what I have stated to you and to aid my request with your personal interest that I may be permitted to remain in my present situation until a Successor arrives.

FROM MR. MONROE.

Department of State,
February 2, 1814.
SIR,

In answer to your solicitation, under date of the 4th ultimo, for a postponement of your removal from the place of your present residence, respecting which the President's determination was communicated to you from this Department on the 28th of December last, I have to state to you, that Bladensburg is a post town, affording an opportunity of daily communication with other parts of the United States; and that you will be thereby enabled as promptly to fulfil the appropriate duties of your agency for prisoners in that situation, as if you were to remain in the vicinity of the City of New York. The President has always been disposed to grant the most liberal indulgences that the conduct of individuals and the circumstances of the war would justify; but the British Government cannot reasonably expect for its agents in this country, a greater latitude of personal convenience than that which those of the United States enjoy in the dominions of Great Britain. The rigor exercised towards the American Agents for prisoners at Quebec and Halifax, in particular, requires a corresponding treatment of British Agents by this government. I am, therefore, constrained to renew to you the request contained in my letter of the 28th of December, and to refer you to the passport which accompanied it.

I remain &c.

JAS. MONROE.

TO THE TRANSPORT BOARD.

Harlem, 13th February 1814.

SIRS,

In December last I received a letter from Mr. Monroe, the American Secretary of State, acquainting me that the President had determined for reasons which every day became more evident, that I should reside near the Seat of Government; and that as soon as my convenience would permit it was directed by the President that I should remove to a place called Bladensburg within nine miles of the City of Washington. In my answer, I informed Mr. Monroe I should obey the order of the President, but that my removal to Bladensburgh would place it wholly out of my power to do my duty to the British Prisoners of War, and that under this conviction, I should write to you Gentlemen and request you to accept of my resignation, and to send out a person to succeed me in Office and I submitted for the consideration of the President, whether under the circumstance of my having requested you to send out a Gentleman to succeed me in office, he might not leave me in my present situation, where I could execute the duties of my office for a period not exceeding five months, within which period, my successor would arrive.[1]

[1] The letter to Monroe which is here abstracted is the official letter of January 4. Barclay wrote to the Transport Board on January 5, briefly, on the subject.

On the 3rd of this month I received Mr. Monroe's reply in which the original order of the President for my removal was repeated, and he informed me that the restrictions imposed on Mr. Mitchell the American Agent for Prisoners at Halifax Nova Scotia, and Col. Gardner the American Agent at Quebec, were in the number of reasons which had induced the President to order my removal.

I request you will be pleased to appoint an Agent to succeed me in the Office I hold under you, and that he may be sent to America with all convenient dispatch. I cannot think of holding an Office when I am placed in a situation which will prevent my performing the duties assigned me.

Should the negotiations to be carried on at Gottenburg between Great Britain and the United States promise a peace, I have no objection to continue in Office until the result is known; but should they be broken off and the war continued, I entreat you will be pleased to supersede me.[1]

FROM THE TRANSPORT BOARD.

Transport Office
9th June 1814..

SIR.

We have received your letters of the 13th and 18th of February last, and having communicated the same to the Lords Commissioners of the Admiralty we have received their Lordships directions to appoint Mr. Gilbert Robertson to succeed you as Agent for Prisoners of War in the United States of America — you will accordingly deliver up to Mr. Gilbert Robertson on his arrival, all the Public Papers in your possession belonging to this Department, and transmit your final Accounts to this Office, with as little delay as possible.

We are &c
RUPT. W. GEORGE
J. DOUGLASS
A. BOYLE.

[1] These were the negotiations proposed to be undertaken under the mediation of Russia.

FROM GENERAL MASON.

Office of Commissary General of Prisoners.
Washington August 19, 1814.

SIR.

At the time it was determined that your residence should be nearer the Seat of Government than that at Harlem in the State of New York, for the purpose of giving facility and expedition to the Communications in which you are engaged with the Government, Bladensburg was named because of its immediate vicinity.

In the present state of the war, considerations present themselves which will readily occur to you, to make that place or any other in the neighborhood of our waters occupied or which may probably be occupied by the hostile forces, no longer a proper residence for an Agent of the Enemy. Troops have already arrived, and a camp as you will have observed, is forming at Bladensburg.

Under these circumstances, I am instructed by the Secretary of State to inform you it has been determined that you take your residence at a place in the interior more remote from the waters; that Hagerstown in Maryland has been fixed on for that purpose; and that in consequence of the menacing movements of the enemy, you are requested to remove with the least possible delay from Bladensburg to that place, for which end I have the honor to enclose a Passport.

I have &c
J. MASON.

TO GENERAL MASON.

Hagers Town Washington County Maryland
Sept' 2nd 1814.

SIR.

Mr. Barton on his arrival here the day before yesterday, laid before me your Letter of the 28th of last month in which you express your astonishment that he still remained in Bladensburg, and acquainted him that you were instructed to require him to leave that place for Hagers Town within two hours after the receipt of your Letter.

On Monday the 22nd of August I had the Honor to receive your Letter of the 19th of that month containing an order for my immediate removal from Bladensburg to this place, in consequence of which I sent Mr. Barton on the 22nd of August to acquaint you, and to request you would supply me with carriages for the removal of myself and office papers; at the same time I did all in my power to procure a conveyance for my office papers and baggage and a carriage for Mr. Barton and myself, my inquiries were continued Tuesday and Wednesday morning, but without effect. At 10 o'clock on Wednesday the 24 inst. a small Coachee was sent by Mr. Gantt of your office with directions for my immediately leaving Bladensburg. The vehicle was too small to take even a part of my office papers, in order therefore to comply as far as lay in my power with the directions of your Government, I stepped into the Coachee with a small trunk and left Bladensburg at 11 o'clock for this place, leaving Mr. Barton in charge of the papers and baggage, with directions to follow me as soon as possible. You must be sensible, Sir, of the importance of the papers belonging to my office, and I cannot entertain an Idea, that it was the intention of this Government or yourself, that they should have been left at Bladensburg without either Mr. Barton or myself to protect them. Such however has been the case from your positive injunction to Mr. Barton. It could not, or ought not, to have escaped the notice of this Government and yourself that at the time I was ordered to leave Bladensburg to the day Mr. Barton was compelled to remove from thence, every Waggon, cart and other carriage were either impressed into the military service of the United States or hired by Individuals removing from Washington and George Town, consequently compelling Mr. Barton and myself to leave Bladensburg, was reducing us to the necessity of abandoning the public documents belonging to my office; under these circumstances, permit me to say, it became your duty to have provided a mode for conveying the office papers, when myself, and Mr. Barton afterwards were compelled to leave Bladensburg. I feel it my duty to add that I protest against my having been obliged to remove without my papers, and in still stronger Terms, that Mr. Barton, who I had left in charge of them, was forced to leave them, unprotected, in compliance with your mandatory injunction of the 28 ulto. I regret that Mr. Barton obeyed your order, at the risque of the loss of the papers; and would rather at this moment he was placed in confinement for disobedience of orders, than to have deserted his charge, to obey those orders. During the late long war on the Continent of Europe, or in any preceding Wars, I suspect no instance occurred where a public civil officer of one of the Nations at war, recognized as such by the other nation and residing within its jurisdiction, was compelled to remove from one place to another, without his official papers, or being permitted to leave his Secretary or Clerk to take charge of them. Should an accident occur to the papers, His Majesty will have just cause of complaint against this Government.

If the office papers do not arrive in a day or two, I shall feel it my duty at all hazard to send Mr. Barton with a Waggon or cart from hence for them, as it would be imprudent to entrust them to a Servant or common carrier.

FROM GENERAL MASON.

Office of Commissary General of Prisoners.
Washington August 31st 1814.

SIR,

I am in possession, by the honourable conduct of a Gentleman whose character you have greatly mistaken, of a letter addressed by you on the 21st instant to Admiral Sir Alexander Cochrane, and which you attempted to convey under seal (secreted in the foot of a stocking) contrary to an arrangement made with you on principles of reciprocity, and against the injunctions of this Government, as admitted by you in your note of the same date, to the Gentleman you expected to have made the bearer of that letter.

These have been submitted to the Secretary of State, as have been the facts, that although notified from this Office of his requisition that you should leave Bladensburg, so that your retiring would have taken place at least three days before the approach of the Enemy, you did not leave it by as many hours before a battle was fought on the spot ; and that your Secretary remained not only in a situation to communicate personally with the Officers of the Army of the Enemy, but continued there several days after, and until a peremptory order addressed to himself, was sent for his removal.

I am instructed to state to you that this course of conduct, so incompatible with your obvious duty, and more especially with the confidence belonging to your station makes it necessary to declare that all correspondence with you on the part of the Government is to cease; and that as an alien enemy you are required to remain for the present at Hagerstown.

I have &c
J. MASON.

TO GENERAL MASON.

Hagers Town, Maryland 5th Septr. 1814.
SIR.

Your letter of the 31st of August, informing me you was instructed to state that all correspondence with me was to cease on the part of this Government, I have had the Honor to receive.

It appears that three exceptions to my conduct are suggested as the cause of the above mentioned determination. With respect to the first, the intercepted Note from me to Vice Admiral Sir Alexander Cochrane, found on the person of Mr. Edward Calvert, I have only to remark that the purport of the letter was perfectly innocent, and related only to the release of his overseer and a domestic made Prisoners by a detachment of His Majesty's Naval Forces in the Patuxent. It is true I did recommend Mr. Calvert to conceal the Letter, not from an unwillingness that it should be examined, but to prevent delay in his application, and from an apprehension the Prisoners would in a day or two be sent to Halifax. It is with surprise I now learn, this act of mine, which was intended to accommodate a citizen of these States, is considered exceptionable by your Government.

With regard to the two other exceptions, I beg leave to refer you to my Letter of the 2d Instant, which I trust contains a full answer; in which I consider myself, with just cause, the person aggrieved.

In consequence of the determination of this Government, I now enclose a Letter to Mr. Monroe the Secretary of State, requesting him to furnish me with usual Passports for myself, Clerk, and Family. Be pleased to deliver it, and obtain an answer as early as convenient.

FROM GENERAL MASON.

Office of Commissary General of Prisoners.
Washington Sept' 16 1814.

SIR

I have received your letters of the 2ᵈ, 5ᵗʰ and 12ᵗʰ of September. The letter for the Secretary of State covered by yours of the 5ᵗʰ Sept', has been sent to him, accompanied by such a statement from this office, as the case required.

I am instructed by the Secretary of State to inform you, that a Cartel Ship owned by Mr. Astor of New York, is now advertised by the permission of the Government, to go to Europe; that she will land passengers in the British Channel; that she will sail from New York in fifteen days from this time, and that if you think proper to avail yourself of this opportunity to return to England, passports will be sent you for yourself and family to embark from Amboy in Jersey, and to go on board Ship in the outer harbour of New York, and an Officer will be sent to accompany you from Hagerstown to Amboy; that on account of the military works now prosecuting at Harlem, permission cannot be granted you to go to that place, nor can any excursions from Hagerstown be permitted, previous to your departure from that place for embarkation; that Mr. Barton, your Secretary, will be permitted to remain there for the present, in charge of your papers, and may correspond, through this Office, with your Sub-agents, and when he shall require it, if no reasons, personal to him, in the mean time occur against it, he will have a passport, and permission to return to England.

I have etc.

J. MASON.

FROM GENERAL MASON.

Office of Commissary General of Prisoners.
Washington Sept' 23rd 1814.

SIR

This letter will be handed you by Col? Gardner, the Officer who has been designated to accompany you, in a route prescribed to him, to Amboy in Jersey, and to remain with you until your embarkation. Your passport will be sent to you, to meet you at Amboy. You will be pleased to name, to me, the persons of your Family, whom you wish to embark with you, and to be inserted in your passport.

I am instructed to inform you, that it is expected you will come under an engagement, to this Government, not to leave the ship, in which you will sail, until you arrive on the coast of England; that you will not be the Bearer of any letters or packets, which have not been submitted for examination, and that while Col? Gardner is with you, all letters which you may write, or receive, except those to, or from, your family, shall be inspected by him.

As the information to you may be useful to the service of your Government, in the disposition of your Official Papers, I am authorized to inform you, that if the Mr. Robertson, whom you mention in your letter of the 5th of Sept' to the Secretary of State, as having been appointed your successor, is the Mr. Gilbert Robertson, lately residing in the State of New York, he will not be received or permitted to land. It must be presumed, if this is the person, that the British Government was not apprized of his conduct here, and of the circumstances, under which he left the Country.

I shall notify this determination to Admiral Cochrane, and

inform him, that if he is disposed to send an Agent for Prisoners to reside here, until his government has an opportunity of making a more permanent appointment, he shall be received and respected.

I have etc.

J. Mason.

TO GENERAL MASON.

Hagers Town Maryland 26ᵗʰ Septʳ. 1814.

Sir

Your letter of the 23ʳᵈ Instant was delivered to me last evening by Col. Gardner, who will acquaint you of the delay he has experienced on the road by which my departure will be delayed three days. I shall certainly not leave the Ship on which I depart from the Port of New York until my arrival in England, unless by some accident she become unsafe. I do not think I shall be the Bearer of any letter, but should I take charge of some, I will lay them before Col. Gardner for his inspection. Mr. Gilbert Robertson who is appointed to succeed me, is the Gentleman who lately resided in these States; and who unquestionably had a right to leave them, he not being under any parole or other promise to the contrary. I have to request you will be pleased to transmit the enclosed letter to Vice Admiral The Honorable Sir Alexander Cochrane; and you will oblige me by acquainting him, with the determination of your Government, whether it will receive Mr. George Barton as Agent for Prisoners, ad interim, should the Admiral wish to appoint him.—

At the foot hereof are the names of my family to be included in the passport.

Mrs. Barclay.
Miss Barclay.
Mr. Anthony Barclay.
John McDonald, Servant.
Mrs. Barclay's Maid Servant, name not known, as she is endeavoring to procure one who is accustomed to the Sea.

TO VICE-ADMIRAL SIR ALEXANDER COCHRANE.

Hagers Town Maryland 26ᵃ September 1814.

SIR,

I have the Honor to enclose herewith the copy of a letter received from the American Commissary General of Prisoners of War, from which you will perceive that it is the determination of this Government, on the arrival of Mr. Gilbert Robertson, off any of the American Ports [not] to permit him to land, or to accredit him, as His Majesty's Agent for the Relief of British Subjects detained in the United States and for carrying of exchanges of prisoners. That if you are disposed to send an Agent for Prisoners to reside in these States, until His Majesty's Government has an opportunity of making a more permanent appointment, he will be received and respected.

I beg leave to acquaint you, that I leave Mr. George Barton, my Clerk, here to settle the present Quarterly accounts to the 30 of this month. Mr. Barton was to have followed me to England the moment this business was completed: if however he can be of service, he will remain in these States, until an Agent is sent out by the Commissioners of Transports, but no longer. I mention this, that you may avail yourself of his services in the event of your wishing to appoint an Agent and being at a loss for a character competent to the Duties. Mr. Barton has been in my office upwards of a year, and is thoroughly acquainted with the routine of Business. He is a Gentleman of most respectable Connections in England and in my opinion every way trustworthy. You will be pleased to recollect that Mr. Barton has no wish to be appointed; but will act to accommodate the Service until a successor arrives. His allowances will of course be similar to those I have received. Be pleased to acquaint him with your determination, and should you desire him to act, as my Successor, it will be proper to send him a commission or warrant for the purpose. I leave this to-morrow for Perth Amboy (there being no conveyance this day) and shall immediately embark on board the American Ship Fingal for England.

CHAPTER VIII

THE NORTHEAST BOUNDARY

THE third article of the Treaty of Ghent provided that all prisoners of war taken on either side, as well by land as by sea, should be restored as soon as practicable after the ratification of the treaty; and that each of the two contracting parties should discharge in specie the advances made by the other for the sustenance and maintenance of such prisoners. The making up and verification of the accounts under this article no doubt proved a troublesome business, and Barclay, who was now in London at No. 12 Tavistock Square, and later at 64 South Molton Street, must have had abundant occupation in consequence all through the famous cold winter of 1815.

But more important duties were to be devolved upon him under the succeeding articles, which related to the ever vexatious question of the Canadian boundary. The commission under Jay's treaty had done no more than fix the starting-point; and, except the line of the River St. Croix, not another foot of the boundary had been ascertained in the thirty-one years which had elapsed since the treaty of 1783. Rufus King in 1803 had indeed succeeded in negotiating a convention which defined the boundary through the several islands of Passamaquoddy Bay, and provided for the appointment of a commission to run the remainder of the line;

but the convention failed of ratification, owing to a doubt as to the effect the purchase of Louisiana might have upon the boundary near its western end.[1]

Monroe and Pinkney in 1807 had also labored to adjust the terms of a boundary convention,. which was to follow closely King's treaty of 1803; but this business was broken off by the fall of the Whig government after Mr. Fox's death, and the accession of the Duke of Portland's administration.[2]

From the very beginning of the negotiations at Ghent, the settlement of the boundary question had been kept in view. The British commissioners had tried, in the earlier stages of the discussion, to obtain something more than a mere tracing of the lines laid down in the treaty of 1783, and to gain some accession of territory. They desired, especially, to "revise" the frontier so as to secure a direct communication between Quebec and Halifax.[3] This demand was, however, withdrawn, and the negotiation proceeded on the basis of the *status quo ante bellum*. On November 10, 1814, the American commissioners presented the draft of a treaty in which five articles were devoted to a plan for the complete ascertainment of the boundary from Eastport to the Lake of the Woods, which lies in the western half of the present State of Minnesota; and with comparatively trifling modifications their draft of these five articles was adopted.

A single question relating to the boundaries was a cause of much hesitation and difficulty. The British had seized Eastport during the war, and they declined

[1] Amer. State Papers, For. Rel., Vol. II, pp. 584-591.
[2] Amer. State Papers, For. Rel., Vol. III, pp. 162-165.
[3] Note of British commissioners, August 19, 1814; Amer. State Papers, For. Rel., Vol. III, p. 710.

to restore Moose Island, on which it stands — although their title was in dispute. It was finally agreed that both parties should at once restore all territory taken during the war, *except* the islands in the Bay of Passamaquoddy; but that the retention of these islands by the British should not affect the rights of either party.

In the treaty as actually signed, Articles IV., V., VI., VII., and VIII. related to the boundaries. By the fourth article two commissioners were to be appointed — one by each nation — to decide upon the title to Grand Menan and the islands of Passamaquoddy Bay; and, in case of a disagreement, the question was to be referred to the decision of some friendly sovereign. By the fifth article a similar board was to determine the line from the source of the St. Croix round the northern frontiers of Maine, New Hampshire, Vermont, and New-York to the point where the boundary reached the St. Lawrence. A third board was to be appointed under the sixth article to ascertain the boundary westward from the point where the commissioners under the fifth article left it, up the St. Lawrence, through the Thousand Islands, through Lake Ontario, the Niagara River, Lake Erie, the Detroit River, the Lake and River of St. Clair, and so through Lake Huron and on to the Sault Ste. Marie. And finally, by the seventh article, the same commissioners were further to trace the line through Lake Superior and on to the Lake of the Woods. The eighth article prescribed general regulations affecting all the boards of commissioners.

The British Government selected its representatives without much delay. Thomas Barclay was appointed His Majesty's Commissioner under the fourth and fifth articles; John Ogilvy, of Montreal, was appointed Commissioner under Articles VI. and VII.[1]

Barclay's appointment was announced to him by Lord Castlereagh June 25, 1815, while London streets were still echoing to the shouts that greeted the news from Waterloo. To Barclay himself the tidings of that momentous event had brought mingled emotions. His own son had passed unhurt through the varying fortunes of the day; but his sister's son, Sir William Howe De Lancey, Wellington's chief of staff, had fallen, mortally wounded, at the commander's side.[2]

Three weeks later Barclay sailed once more for America, landing at Boston. He reached New-York August 29, 1815, and at once resumed the duties of the Consul-General's office, pending the arrival of his new commission. That instrument bears date September 4, 1815, although, for some quite unaccountable reason, it did not reach New-York till eleven months later.

In the mean time, the President of the United States had appointed the American commissioners — John Holmes, of Maine,[3] under the fourth article; Cornelius

[1] Mr. Ogilvy fell a victim to the dangers incident to his employment. He died at Amherstburgh, near Detroit, on September 28, 1819, of a bilious fever contracted among the marshes of the St. Clair. He was succeeded as Commissioner under the sixth and seventh articles by Anthony Barclay, Thomas Barclay's youngest son.

[2] See Ropes's Waterloo Campaign. De Lancey had married Captain Basil Hall's sister only two months before — and hence the allusion in Sir Walter Scott's dull lines on The Field of Waterloo:

Thou saw'st in seas of gore expire
Redoubted Picton's soul of fire —
De Lancey change Love's bridal wreath
For laurels from the hand of Death.

An account of De Lancey's death, in the Duke's own words, will be found in Samuel Rogers's Recollections.

[3] John Holmes was born at Kingston, Mass., in March, 1773; graduated at Brown University in 1796; was admitted to the bar in 1799; and settled at Alfred, the county town of York County, Maine. He was a member of the Massachusetts Legislature for some years, and was

P. Van Ness, of Vermont,[1] under the fifth article; and Peter B. Porter, of New-York,[2] under the sixth and seventh articles.

Barclay's commission had no sooner arrived than he set about the business with which he was intrusted. The American commissioners under the fourth and fifth articles were notified, and meetings were held at St. Andrews, New Brunswick, the place specified in the treaty, on September 23, 1816.

Affairs under the fourth article progressed rapidly. The sole question, as we have seen, related to the title to the Island of Grand Menan and the islands in the Bay of Passamaquoddy — all of which lie far to the southward of the mouth of the River St. Croix.

Coming from the westward, every vessel bound up the Bay of Fundy follows along the picturesque coast of Maine and passes through the deep and secure channel of which Grand Menan forms the eastern and southern side. The bold and rugged cliffs of the island extend for twenty-two miles opposite the American shore,

---

elected to Congress, as we shall see, in 1817. When Maine was admitted as a State, in 1820, he was elected to the U. S. Senate, and served obscurely until 1833. He was afterward U. S. District-Attorney, and died in 1843. An extended sketch of his life will be found in Willis's "Law, the Courts, and Lawyers in Maine."

[1] Cornelius Peter Van Ness was born at Kinderhook, N. Y., January 26, 1782, and was only thirty-four years old when appointed on the boundary commission. He was a persistent office-holder. He had been already U. S. District-Attorney for Ver-

mont, and was subsequently Collector of the Port of Burlington, Chief Justice of Vermont, Governor of that State, U. S. Minister to Spain under both of Jackson's administrations, and Collector of the Port of New-York under Tyler. He died in Philadelphia December 15, 1852.

[2] Peter Buel Porter was the founder of the well-known family who owned so much of the land about Niagara Falls. He was a native of Connecticut, was for two terms a member of Congress, and served with some credit in the War of 1812. He was active in promoting the Erie Canal, and died in 1844.

23*

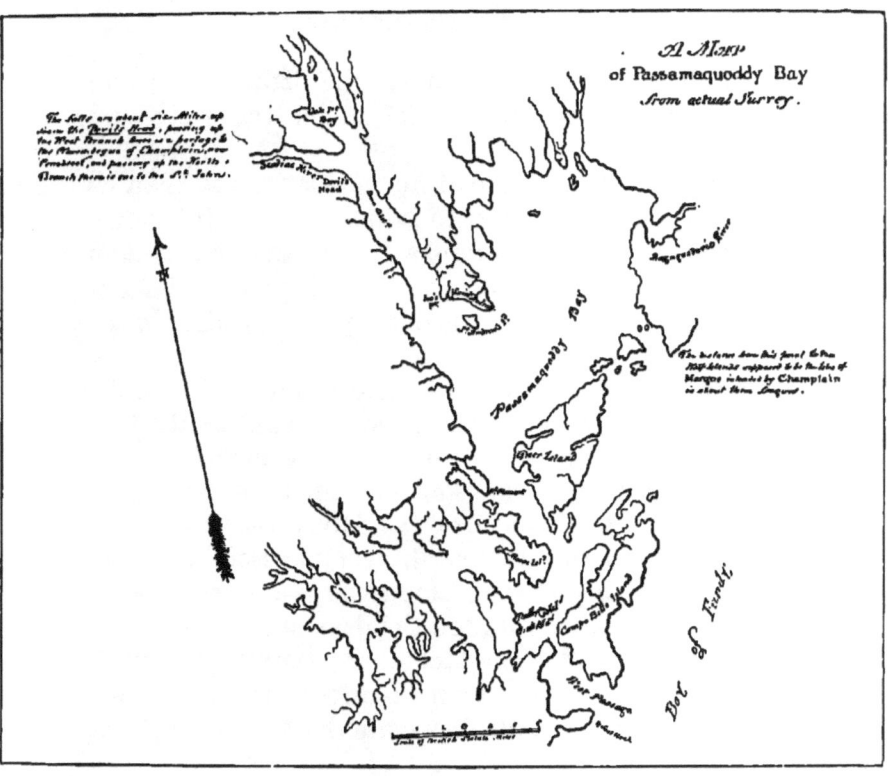

A Map
of Passamaquoddy Bay
from actual Survey.

terminating in a lofty headland just in front of that
difficult entrance into Passamaquoddy Bay which is
known as the West Passage, or Lubec Narrows. The
southern shore of this entrance is formed by the mainland; the northern shore by the romantic island of
Campobello — now chiefly known as the site of a couple
of summer hotels. Across the pretty bay lies Eastport,
famous for its fisheries; and further north are Deer
Island and the smaller rocky islets of Passamaquoddy.

By their position and means of communication with
the mainland, these islands are all naturally within the
territory of the United States; but the controversy in
1816 did not at all relate to what ought to be their ownership. The dispute was the purely legal one whether
these islands, or any of them, came within the exception mentioned in the second article of the treaty of
1783. By that article all islands along the coast, south
of the River St. Croix, were to belong to the United
States, " *excepting such islands as now are, or heretofore
have been, within the limits of the said province of Nova
Scotia.*" The inquiry turned, therefore, upon a historical examination of the ancient charters of Nova Scotia
and Massachusetts Bay; and upon this point interesting arguments were submitted to the Commissioners
by the respective agents. Ward Chipman — who had
served in a similar capacity in 1796 — appeared on the
British side; James T. Austin on the American.[1] The
board met at Boston in June, 1817, to hear argument,
and adjourned until September to allow the preparation of replies. A long debate ensued, but on October

[1] James T. Austin was born in
Boston January 7, 1784; married a
daughter of Elbridge Gerry; became
a leader of the Massachusetts Bar;
was Attorney-General of Massachusetts from 1832 to 1843; and died
May 8, 1870.

9th a final conclusion was reached, under which Deer Island, Campobello, and Grand Menan were awarded to Great Britain, and Moose Island (Eastport) and two smaller islands to the United States. The formal award, engrossed on parchment, was executed at New-York on November 24, 1817.

Far less satisfactory was the fate of the inquiry under the fifth article of the Treaty of Ghent. The boundary had been defined in the treaty of 1783 as running due north from the source of the St. Croix to the northwest angle of Nova Scotia, at " the highlands which divide those rivers that empty themselves into the River St. Lawrence, from those which fall into the Atlantic Ocean "; thence along the " highlands " to the " north-westernmost head of the Connecticut River "; thence down that river to the forty-fifth parallel of latitude; and thence due west to the St. Lawrence, and so up the St. Lawrence and through the lakes.

From the very first Barclay doubted whether it would be possible to come to any agreement as to the two important points,— the northwest angle of Nova Scotia and the head of the Connecticut,— although the British Foreign Office, in cheerful ignorance of all the facts, regarded it as a " mere operation of survey." Barclay was right. The question remained unsettled for twenty-seven years, and when it was finally compromised by the Webster-Ashburton Treaty, in 1842, the conduct of each of the negotiators was vehemently denounced by his own countrymen as a surrender.

Barclay not only knew the facts of the case, so far as anybody knew them in that day, but he was also deeply conscious of the delicate position in which he was placed. He was a native of New-York, he had married his wife in New-York, his family had their home there,

A Northwest angle of Nova Scotia as
   contended for by the United States.
B Northwest angle of Nova Scotia as
   contended for by Great Britain.
C Northwesternmost head of Connecticut River
   as contended for by Great Britain.
D Northwesternmost head of Connecticut R.
   as contended for by the United States.

his sons were New-York merchants, his daughters had
married Livingstons and Stuyvesants, and he was a
cousin of half the people in the place. Nova Scotia
and Canada were sensitive on the subject, and if Lord
Ashburton was attacked and discredited because he had
married an American wife, we may guess what sort of
a storm would have been raised if Barclay had yielded
to American demands. Far more stubbornly, probably, than any native Englishman, Barclay stood firm
for the extremest British claims.

The Commissioners met for the first time at St. Andrews on September 23, 1816, and obviously no more
could then be done than to appoint surveyors to explore
the unknown wilderness about the head waters of the
St. John, the Restigouche, the Penobscot, the Kennebec and the Connecticut. The summer of 1817 passed
in preliminary exploration, which was followed the next
season by more detailed surveys, and as the season
of 1818 drew to an end, the facts of the case in their
general outlines became perfectly and unmistakably
clear.

The north line, as it runs from the monument at the
source of the St. Croix, dips down into the broad basin
drained by the River St. John, whose waters empty
into the Bay of Fundy. The country is rough and
hilly, and at Mars Hill, about forty miles from the monument, the line reaches its highest elevation. Not quite
forty miles further on the River St. John is crossed,
and then the line rises to the ridge dividing the waters
of the St. John and the Restigouche, the latter a stream
emptying into the Gulf of St. Lawrence. Crossing the
basin of the Restigouche the line finally — at a distance
of 143 miles from the St. Croix monument — reaches
waters flowing into the River St. Lawrence.

Now the treaty of 1783 required the line to end at "Highlands," dividing rivers running into the River St. Lawrence from rivers "which fall into the Atlantic Ocean." Did "Highlands" mean mountains? If it did, there was nothing to answer that description north of Mars Hill. Did it mean merely a watershed,— a dividing ridge? If so, there was the choice between two such ridges,— that between the St. John and the Restigouche, and that between the Restigouche and the St. Lawrence. But the St. John fell into the Bay of Fundy, and the Restigouche into the Gulf of St. Lawrence; and the British representatives contended that neither of these could be held to be rivers "which fall into the Atlantic Ocean," within the meaning of the treaty. Their argument was precisely that used by Mr. Blaine in 1890, when he urged that the Bering Sea was not included in the terms of a treaty which related to the Pacific Ocean. The American reply anticipated Lord Salisbury's retorts and illustrations. The Bay of Fundy and the Gulf of St. Lawrence, it was said, were just as much a part of the Atlantic Ocean as the Bay of Biscay; and they were much more clearly a part of the ocean than Long Island Sound, into which flowed the Connecticut River,— a stream conceded on all hands to be one of those which were wholly within the territory of the United States.

But the Americans drew a stronger argument from a historical examination of the circumstances attending the framing of the treaty of 1783. The purpose of that treaty, they contended, was unmistakable. Its purpose was to confirm to the United States all of the territory of the thirteen colonies, and to leave to Great Britain the whole of Canada and Nova Scotia. If this were admitted, the rest followed at once; for the southern boundary of Canada had been fixed by a royal proclamation of October 7, 1763,— just after the conquest from the French,— as a line "crossing the river St. Lawrence and Lake Champlain in forty five degrees of North latitude," and then passing "along the Highlands which divide the rivers that empty themselves into the said River St. Lawrence from those which fall into THE SEA, and also along the north of the coast of the Bay des Chaleurs," etc. The treaty of 1783 only varied the language by substituting THE ATLANTIC OCEAN for THE SEA. If this was not meant to vary the meaning (and there was no evidence of any purpose to enlarge the boundaries of Canada), then it was plain that the head waters of both the St. John and the Restigouche must be within American soil, and that the north line must run its 143 miles up to a point almost within sight of the St. Lawrence.

For a quarter of a century the debate dragged on with much wearisome iteration, and without any more satisfactory conclusion than that the treaty of 1783 was "inexplicable and impracticable." The controversy has long since been compromised, and looking back at it now, free from the passion and prejudice which it aroused while still unsettled, one sees no difficulty either in explaining or enforcing the treaty. The British Government in 1763 had deliberately intended to include in Canada only the basin of the St. Lawrence, to which the French population was confined. The confirmation of existing bounds, which was the simple principle underlying the whole of the treaty of 1783, plainly required the same line to be run. How near that line might come to the St. Lawrence was not known to any of the negotiators, and it can hardly have been a circumstance which they took into account. No one to-day can doubt that in this dispute the United States had right on their side.[1]

The controversy about the northwesternmost head of the Connecticut River was of minor importance. It turned upon surveys of several rivulets, any one of which might perhaps fairly be looked upon as furnishing the important source.

A third point arose, most fortunately for British interests, based this time upon perfectly indisputable facts. The line of 45° north latitude had been run, about 1766, from the St. Lawrence to the Connecticut, and the monuments then set up had always been looked upon as fixing the unquestioned northern boundary of New-York and Vermont. Just where the line crossed Lake Champlain lay Rouse's Point, and there the Government of the United States had gone to great expense in fortifying what was considered in that day a most valuable strategic position. It was worth a whole wilderness of pine timber, and no one had ever doubted that it lay within the limits of the United States. The fact was, however,—and it was first ascertained in 1818,— that the line run in 1766 was grievously in error, and every stone in the fortifications was really upon British soil.[2] Nor was this all; for the old line, diverging as it ran eastward from the true parallel of latitude, added to New-York and Vermont some hundred thousand acres which, under the plain words of the treaty, belonged, without a doubt, to Canada.

And so, at the beginning of 1819, the northeastern boundary question stood thus: The line had been run

---

[1] See "The Boundaries Formerly in Dispute," by Sir Francis Hincks (Montreal, 1885), wherein the justice of the American claim is fully con- ceded, so far as the northwest angle of Nova Scotia is concerned.

[2] See map in Winsor's Narrative and Critical History, Vol. VII.

from the Atlantic Ocean through the islands of Passamaquoddy Bay to the mouth of the St. Croix, and up
the St. Croix to its source. The north line had been so
far surveyed as to show that at least an argument might
be made to reduce the American claims in that quarter. The northwestern source of the Connecticut River
was in doubt. And the old and long-recognized line
west of the Connecticut had been shown to be grossly
incorrect.

The years that had elapsed since the close of the War
of 1812 had wrought many changes in Barclay's family.
His youngest daughter, Ann, had married Mr. W. B.
Parsons, a retired officer of the Royal Navy,— a marriage not approved by her parents, but which, nevertheless, turned out well. Of the sons, Henry and
Anthony had also married. George at the beginning
of 1819 was in England, where he had recently married
— having gone there with the purpose of establishing
himself in business. Mrs. Livingston, the eldest daughter, had died. The house at Harlem had been sold, and
Barclay and his wife, with Mrs. Livingston's children,
— now the only members of their household,— had
again taken up their residence in New-York; this time
at No. 386 Greenwich Street, which was thenceforward
to be their home.

FROM LORD CASTLEREAGH.

Foreign Office, Sept. 4th, 1815.

SIR:

His Royal Highness The Prince Regent having been graciously pleased to name you to act as His Majesty's Commissioner
for the purposes specified in the 4th and 5th Articles of the Treaty
of Peace and Amity concluded at Ghent on the 24th December

last, with the United States of America, I herewith transmit to you His Majesty's Commission under the Great Seal appointing you to that office.

You will lose no time in proceding to St. Andrews in Nova Scotia where the Commissioners of both Parties are by the said Treaty appointed to meet.

On your arrival there you will be joined by Mr. Chipman who has received orders to accompany you in the capacity of Agent on the part of His Majesty's Government. M. la Bouchette [1] will accompany you as Surveyor of the boundaries which it is intended to define and establish by the Commission entrusted to you.

In case the Commissioner who is to act with you on the part of the American Government should not have proceeded to his destination, His Majesty's Chargé d'Affaires at Washington will be instructed to press his departure, so that no time may be lost in the execution of your respective Duties.

Your commission embraces Two distinct Objects the Nature of which the enclosed copy of the 4th and 5th Articles of the Treaty will demonstrate as well as the mode in which the Questions at issue are to be finally arranged between you and the American Commission.

With regard to the regulation of your conduct in bringing to a favorable issue the first question namely, whether the several Islands in the Bay of Passamaquoddy and in the Bay of Fundy belong of right to the United States or to Great Britain; it may be necessary that you keep in mind (altho' in deciding upon it you are solely to be led by the Evidence that will be adduced in favour of the Claims of other countries) that His Majesty's right to those Islands is supposed to be founded on the Second Article of the Treaty of Peace of 1783 which excepted from the line of 20 leagues from the line of Coast, by which it was then agreed to fix that side of the

[1] The person intended was Joseph Bouchette, the Surveyor-General of Canada, who was at this time in England superintending the publication of one of his books. He proved most unsatisfactory as a Surveyor to the Commission. He died in 1841, having published several valuable works on the topography and statistics of Canada.

Boundary of the United States, such Islands as now are or heretofore have been within the Limits of Nova Scotia.—And that the Islands in question did come within the Limits of that Province, will be proved not only from the Circumstance of the Jurisdiction which the Government of Nova Scotia always was in the habit of exercising over the Inhabitants up to the Peace of 1783, but more forcibly from the fact that the original Patent or Grant (an Extract of which I inclose) of the said Province made by King James the 5th. to Sir William Alexander in 1621, after tracing the Boundaries of the United States [sic] in it's circumference proceeds to include in it all Islands &c., within Six Leagues of any part of that circumference.[1]

[1] The original patent is in Latin. The important parts of it may be thus translated: "We have given, granted and conveyed and by the tenor of this our present Charter we do give, grant and convey, unto the said Sir William Alexander, his heirs or assigns whomsoever in inheritance, all and singular the lands, continents or islands situate and lying in America within the headland or promontory commonly called Cap de Sable, lying near the latitude of 43 degrees or thereabouts north of the equinoctial line; from which promontory stretching westwardly along the seashore to the harbor of Saint Mary, and thence toward the North by a straight line crossing the entrance or mouth of that great bay which runs into the Eastern tract of land between the countries of the Suriquois and Etchemins to the river commonly called St. Croix; and to the most remote spring or source which from the western part of the same first mingles itself with the said river; thence by an imaginary straight line which may be conceived to go through the land or to run toward the North to the nearest harbor, river or spring emptying itself into the great river of Canada; and from thence extending toward the East along the shores of the same river of Canada to the river, harbor, port or shore commonly called and known by the name of Gashcpe or Gaspe; and from thence toward the South East to the islands called Baccalaos or Cap Breton, leaving those islands on the right, and the gulf of the said river of Canada or great bay, and the lands of Newfoundland with the islands to the said lands belonging, on the left; and thence to the headland or promontory of Cap Breton aforesaid, lying near the latitude of 45 degrees, or thereabouts; and from the said promontory of Cap Breton toward the South and West to the said Cap de Sable, where the perambulation began; including and comprehending within the aforesaid seashores and their circumferences from sea to sea, all lands and continents with the rivers, streams, bays, shores, islands or seas lying near or within six leagues of any part of the same on the Western, Northern or

It cannot also have escaped your recollection that in the discussion in which you were engaged with the United States in 1796 and which terminated in your fixing the Mouth of the River St. Croix at Joes Point, the point now at issue was in some degree decided, a reference to the Proceedings of the Commissioners at that period will prove that the objection made to that decision on the part of the American Agent was that he [sic] conferred upon Great Britain the possession of the very Islands now under dispute, and he on that ground argued tho' ineffectually the impropriety of the decision itself.

The Second object to which you are to direct your attention relates to the Boundary which is to be determined according to the 5th Art. of the present Treaty, also in conformity to the Provisions of the Treaty of 1783.

In a former commission with which you were charged, you determined one of the doubtful Points connected with this part of the Boundary now to be fixed, namely, which was the true River of St. Croix: so that your labours will now begin from the source of this River with a view of continuing and terminating the survey as therein detailed to the River Iroquois or Cataraguy.

This being a mere operation of Survey, it will not be necessary to give you any specific Instructions for the regulation of your Conduct on this head. It will therefore only remain in general to enjoin you to use the utmost diligence in the discharge of the important Trust now committed to your Care,

Eastern parts of the said shores and precincts. . . . Moreover we of our certain knowledge, mere motion, regal authority and royal power, have made, united, annexed, created and incorporated; and by the tenor of this our present charter we do make, unite, annex, erect, create and incorporate the whole and entire Province and lands of Nova Scotia aforesaid with all their limits, seas, &c, offices and jurisdictions and all other things generally and particularly above mentioned, into one entire and free dominion and barony to be called in all future time by the aforesaid name, Nova Scotia. . . . And even if any questions or doubts touching the interpretation or construction of any clause in this our present Charter should arise, all such are to be taken and interpreted in the most ample form and in favor of the said Sir William Alexander and his heirs."

A line drawn from the mouth of St. Mary's Bay to the mouth of the St. Croix just touches Grand Menan.

as well as the nicest and most minute accuracy in fixing and determining the Lines of the said Boundaries, so that no room may remain for any doubts in future on that Matter.

You will keep me regularly informed of the progress of the Commission with which you are charged as well as of any occurrences which may come within your knowledge and which it may be material that His Majesty's Government should have cognizance and you will not fail to communicate with His Majesty's Minister at Washington on any Matters that may be for the good of His Majesty's Service.

I am &c.

CASTLEREAGH.

FROM LORD CASTLEREAGH.

Foreign Office Septr. 4, 1815.

SIR,

In consequence of your having received the appointment of which a communication has been made to you in my Instruction No. 1 of this date, I am to inform you that it is His Royal Highness The Prince Regent's Pleasure that your appointment as His Majesty's Consul General in the State of New York should cease on the Quarter ending the 5th of July next: But that the same allowance be continued to you from that Period in your new capacity of His Majesty's Commissioner for the Execution of the 4th and 5th Articles of the Treaty of Ghent.[1]

In addition to your regular Allowances, you will be authorized to draw upon this office for the actual expense of Journies to which you may be exposed by moving from Place to place in the Execution of your Functions taking care to transmit to this Office the proper Vouchers for such Expenditure.

Should it however be understood between you and the Commissioner on the part of America that such Expenses as well as all others attending the said Commission are to be defrayed

---

[1] The salary was at this time £1600 a year; and it appears to have been paid more regularly and with fewer deductions than during the stress of the Napoleonic wars.

24

equally by the two Parties in pursuance of the Provision which
is made in the 8th Art. of the said Treaty you will conform to
that arrangement.

For the further regulation of your conduct on this subject,
I herewith inclose a Copy of the receipt signed by Mr. Munroe
on the exchange of the Ratifications of the Treaty of Ghent in
which is inserted a declaration that the Principles which were
observed in carrying into Execution the Treaty of 1794, are to
be followed in this Instance.

I am &c.,

CASTLEREAGH.

TO LORD CASTLEREAGH.

New York 10th August 1816.

MY LORD,

It was not before the 7th of this month, by the June Packet
from Falmouth that I had the Honor to receive your Lordships Letters Nos. 1 and 2 of the 4th of September last informing me that His Royal Highness The Prince Regent had been
graciously pleased to name me to act as His Majesty's Commissioner for the purposes specified in the 4th and 5th Articles of
the Treaty of Peace and Amity concluded at Ghent on the 24th
of December 1814 with the United States of America, and that
your Lordship had by the same conveyance transmitted to me
His Majesty's Commission under the Great Seal appointing
me to that office.

I beg leave respectfully to assure your Lordship that I am
duly sensible of this further mark of His Majesty's most gracious condescencion and favor, and I intreat you will be pleased
to lay my most humble acknowledgement at the Feet of His
Royal Highness The Prince Regent for this gracious Testimony
of His Royal Confidence. It shall be my study not to render
myself unworthy of it.

The instant I received your Lordships Letters and my Commission, I transmitted copies of your No. 1 and of the Commission to His Majestys Minister at Washington and requested

him to communicate the purport thereof to the American Government, and to propose that a meeting should take place between the American Commissioner or Commissioners and myself at St. Andrews in New Brunswick on the 16th of September. This was as early a day as could with safety be named, under the circumstances of my being obliged to notify the American Government of my appointments, and for it to send directions for the American Commissioner to proceed without delay so as to meet me at St. Andrews on the 16th of next month. I have in like manner requested Mr. Chipman the Agent on the part of His Majesty to be at St. Andrews on that day. I have not yet heard of Mr. La Bouchette's arrival in America. His presence however is not indispensibly necessary at the first meeting of the Commissioners. Your Lordships remarks with respect to the Islands in Passamaquoddy Bay and the Principles on which His Majesty's claim to those Islands is founded are in my opinion perfectly correct, and such as cannot be controverted. I am apprehensive it will be difficult for His Majestys Agent to support with equal evidence His Majesty's claim to the Island of Grand Manan in the Bay of Fundy, an island of far more national importance, than any of the others. On this point and on the 5th Article of the Treaty I shall take the Liberty of communicating more fully with your Lordship.

TO LORD CASTLEREAGH.

New York 12th August 1816.

MY LORD,

In my Letter No. 1 of the 10th Current, I stated, that I should do myself the Honor more fully to communicate with your Lordship on His Majesty's claim to the Island of Grand Manan, and on the 5th Article of the Treaty of Ghent.

By the Treaty of Peace in 1783 between His Majesty and the United States of America all Islands that were at the time of that Treaty, or theretofore had been within the Limits of the Province of Nova Scotia were reserved to His Majesty.

In order to support His Majestys claim to Grand Manan, the most valuable of these Islands it is necessary to ascertain and establish the most extensive westerly Bounds at any time heretofore prescribed to the Province of Nova Scotia. The Boundaries of this Province have from time to time been variously described from the original Grant to Sir William Alexander to the year 1773.

The Grant of the Province of Nova Scotia to Sir William Alexander in the year 1621 is the most ancient and contains the most formal Description of the Limits of Nova Scotia, and in point of authority is superior to any subsequent act of His Majesty or His Royal Predecessors in which the Limits of that Province are defined.

In His Majestys Commission to Montague Wilmot Esqr as Governor of Nova Scotia the ancient Western limits of the Province of Nova Scotia are described, and it appears an alteration was then made with respect to the western Boundary Line, in the words following, "and to the Westward although our said Province hath anciently extended and doth of right extend as far as the River Pentagoet or Penobscot it shall be bounded by a line drawn from Cape Sable across the entrance of the Bay of Fundy to the mouth of the River St. Croix" &c., &c. I understand this alteration was made by His Majesty in council in the year 1763. The order I have not seen. It cannot be doubted, but that His Majesty in council at the period of altering the Western Bounds of Nova Scotia, had before him some legal documents by which the original Bounds of Nova Scotia, to which the order refers, had been established, to wit Westward to the River Penobscot. What appears in the order of council however is merely by way of preamble. It is therefore of moment that His Majestys Agent should if possible be possessed of the instrument by which the Western limits of Nova Scotia were, as is stated in the preamble originally established at and by the River Penobscot. Perhaps upon a search in the Council Books and papers or in the proper offices, some clue may be found which would lead to the discovery of this important document. As there is no trace of any Grant having been made by His Majesty or His Predecessors of the

Island of Grand Manan other than that to Sir William Alexander, and which is constructive and in some measure defective, it will be necessary to produce the next best evidence that Grand Manan heretofore was within the Province of Nova Scotia. This can be done by showing that the Governor and Council of that Province so far exercised a right over that Island as to grant a reservation of it to Lord William Campbell until His Majestys pleasure should be known, this reservation was made in the year 1773, and is an evident proof that the Government of Nova Scotia then considered it, as appertaining to that Province. Unless therefore it is shown, that Massachusetts at that time or previously exercised a jurisdiction over or laid claim to this Island, the act of the Governor and Council, I humbly conceive must be considered as conclusive. As the above reservation was made until His Majestys pleasure was known, it is to be presumed his Lordship petitioned His Majesty to grant him this Island, and that something was done upon the petition. If the petition and the minutes of what was ordered thereupon, can at this remote day be found, they would perhaps greatly strengthen the present claim.

I have reason to believe it will be attempted to support the claim of the United States to Grand Manan and the Islands in the Bay of Passamaquoddy by the limits of Nova Scotia as described in His Majestys Commission to Lord William Campbell in 1766 and to Francis Legge Esqr. in 1773 as Governor of that Province. In the commission of the latter, the following is a description of the Boundaries of Nova Scotia: "Bounded on the Westward by a Line drawn from Cape Sable across the entrance of the Bay of Fundy to the mouth of the River St. Croix, by the said River to its source and by a Line drawn due North from thence to the Southern Boundary of our colony of Quebec to the Northward by the same Boundary as far as the Western extremity of the Bay des Chaleurs to the Eastward by the said Bay and the Gulph of St. Lawrence to the Cape or Promontory called Breton in the Island of that name including that Island and all the other Islands within six leagues of the coast excepting our said Island of St. John

24*

which we have thought fit to erect into a separate Government
and to the Southward by the Atlantic Ocean from the said
Cape to Cape Sable aforesaid including the Islands of that
name and all other Islands within forty leagues of the Coast."
I have not seen an extract of the Commission to Lord William
Campbell, but Mr. Chipman His Majesty's Agent writes me,
the Boundaries described therein are the same with those in
Sir Francis Legge's commission. From these commissions it
would appear that the Islands within six leagues of the coast are
confined to the coast on the Eastern side of the Province
of Nova Scotia. The Commissions refer to Islands on the
East and South sides of the Province, but are silent with respect to those on the West Side. I attribute this to inattention
in those who framed the commissions. At that period it was
not perhaps considered necessary to be critically particular in
such descriptions in commissions to Governors, the Limits and
appendages of the respective Provinces had been declared, but
had never been surveyed and defined by actual measurement.
His Majesty's Ministers could not have intended to take these
Islands from the jurisdiction of Nova Scotia without either
erecting them into a distinct colony, which would have been
ridiculous, or annexing them to the, then, Province of Massachusetts. Neither of these was the case, it therefore follows
that they remained part or parcel of Nova Scotia under the
Grant to Sir William Alexander. Besides it required express
words to take those Islands formerly declared to appertain to
Nova Scotia, from it: and your Lordship will presently perceive that on a nearly similar occasion in contracting the
Western Limits of Nova Scotia express words were used in
the commission to Governor Wilmot.

In the latter part of your No. 1 your Lordship is pleased to
notice in reference to the 5th Article of the Treaty of Ghent,
that this being a mere operation of survey, it will not be necessary to give me any specific instructions for the regulation of
my conduct on this head. The running of a Line due North
from the source of the River St. Croix is certainly a simple
operation, but from all that I have been able to learn, it is very
doubtful, whether Highlands, such as will satisfy, the second

Article of the Treaty of Peace in 1783, and to which the Treaty of Ghent refers, will be found on running this line. I am not less apprehensive admitting that such Highlands corresponding with the Treaty are found, that a question of no small difficulty will arise with respect to which rivulet or little stream the appellation of the North Westermost Head of Connecticut River is most applicable. These difficulties removed, the remainder of the execution of the 5th Article would be plain and easy. I cannot however refrain expressing my fears to your Lordship that one or both of the above named points will prove insuperable to the Commissioners, and that recourse must be had by a referance, on the reports of the Commissioners, to some friendly Sovereign or State; or some amicable adjustment of the line take place between His Majesty and the United States. The latter, if practicable would unquestionably be most eligible.

TO LORD CASTLEREAGH.

New York 2 October 1816.
MY LORD.

In my No. 1 of the 10th of August, I stated to your Lordship that I had requested Mr. Bagot His Majesty's Minister Plenipotentiary at Washington[1] to propose to the American Government that the American Commissioners under the 4th and 5th Articles of the Treaty of Ghent should be directed to meet me at St. Andrews on the 16th of September in order to proceed on the Duties expressed in our respective Commissions, and the proposition having met the concurrence of this Government, I proceeded from hence to Portland in the Dis-

---

[1] Charles Bagot was born September 23, 1781; held the post of British Minister in Washington from the spring of 1816 to the spring of 1819; became Governor-General of Canada; and died there May 19, 1843. "Bagot," wrote John Quincy Adams, " is tall, well proportioned, and with a remarkably handsome face; perfectly well-bred, and of dignified and gentlemanly deportment. . . . No English Minister has ever been so popular; and the mediocrity of his talents has been one of the principal causes of his success." Diary, Vol. IV, p. 338.

trict of Maine to meet Mr. Holmes the American Commissioner under the 4th and Mr. Van Ness the American Commissioner under the 5th Article of that Treaty, from whence we were to take passage for St. Andrews. Owing to adverse winds and calms we were delayed several Days at Portland, and it was not before the 22^d of September that we landed at St. Andrews, where Mr. Chipman His Majesty's Agent had been several days waiting our arrival. Mr. Austin the American Agent came with the Commissioners. On the 23rd of September the commissions were opened and copies under both Articles interchanged. The Commissioners were also sworn agreeably to the Treaty. The Agents under the 4th Article were then called upon to exhibit their claims, and produce their credentials. The American Agent delivered a formal commission from the President of the United States, but Mr. Chipman exhibited only a letter from Lord Bathurst His Majesty's Principal Secretary of State for the Colonial Department. The American commissioner objected to the Letter as insufficient, first because there was no official seal, and secondly that His Lordship had not expressed his official character after his signature to the Letter. I endeavored to remove both these objections and so far succeeded as to obtain the consent of the American Commissioners to proceed to business, under a promise that Mr. Chipman should at the next meeting of the Board produce a more official appointment. Mr. Chipman will write Earl Bathurst on the Subject. On the 24th of September the Agents delivered to the commissioners the claims of their respective Governments to the Islands in the Bay of Passamaquoddy and Bay of Fundy, copies of which I have the Honor to enclose. The Commissioners requested to know whether they were prepared to argue and prove their claims, and if not, when they would be. The Agents answered that they thought the 28th of May as early a day as could consistently be named for these purposes. The Commissioners acceded and adjourned from St. Andrews to meet at Boston in the State of Massachusetts on the 28th of May 1817.

No Agent appeared on the part of the United States under the 5th Article of the Treaty of Ghent, nor Surveyor for either nation. By the words of the Treaty I should have considered the Commissioners authorized to appoint Surveyors but as your Lordship had signified to me that Earl Bathurst had appointed Colonel Bouchette Surveyor on the part of His Majesty, I declined doing so, and represented to Mr. Van Ness, the American Commissioner, that Col. Bouchette was momently expected from England as the British Surveyor. Mr. Van Ness was also equally convinced with myself that the Season was too far advanced for the Surveyors to commence any operations this Autumn. The best informed Inhabitants at St. Andrews and Robbins Town (the American side of the River St. Croix) agreed in opinion that the Surveyors could not commence their operations before the month of June next, owing to the Bodies of snow remaining in the Woods and the Brooks and other streams being overcharged with water. It was therefore agreed by the Commissioners under the 5th Article to meet at Boston on the 4th of June, and to direct that the Surveyors attend them on that day, at that place. The Agents are to be directed to provide Chain Bearers, ax men, and persons to carry Provisions &c. &c. also to purchase the necessary provisions. The conveyance of Provisions will I fear be a matter of no small difficulty, increasing as the surveys recede from the Rivers St. Croix and St. John. I have received no information of Colonel Bouchette's arrival in America. Should he still remain in England, I beg leave to suggest to your Lordship the necessity of his being ordered to repair to Boston without delay, or rather to St. Johns, New Brunswick, so that he may confer with Mr. Chipman, and be made acquainted with the merits of the Question, previous to his attending the Commissioners on the 4th of June. The Surveyors are to receive precise instructions from the Agents, and general Instructions from the Commissioners.

FROM MR. GOULBURN.[1]

Downing Street
March 14th 1817.

(*Private & Confidential.*)

DEAR SIR,

By desire of Lord Bathurst I take this opportunity of acquainting you that in consequence of the representations which have been made both of the talents of the persons selected by the American Government to make the survey of the Boundary and of the incompetence of Mr. Bouchette to undertake an accurate astronomical survey His Lordship has entered into communication with Sir Jos. Banks[2] for the purpose of procuring the assistance of some Gentleman of great science and consequently more able to check the proceedings of the American Surveyors. He was in hopes that such a person would have been ready to proceed by the present packet but as this is unfortunately not the case I am desired to suggest to you the propriety of deferring if it be possible the astronomical part of the survey until time can be given for the arrival of such a Gentleman in America. The proceedings of the Commissioners need not be deferred on this account as the other parts of the survey may be proceeded in without waiting his arrival.

I have &c.

HENRY GOULBURN.

TO LORD CASTLEREAGH.

Boston, State of Massachusetts, 5ᵗʰ June, 1817.

MY LORD.

During the preceeding Winter I requested Mr. Chipman, His Majestys Agent, who resides at St. John in the Province of

---

[1] Henry Goulburn was one of the British Commissioners at Ghent, where his manner and tone seem to have been particularly offensive to the Americans. J. Q. Adams, in his diary, repeatedly refers to Goulburn's entire want of control over his temper, and the insulting manner of his speech. He was Under-Secretary for the Colonies.

[2] The President of the Royal Society.

New Brunswick to meet me at this place on the 20th of May, one week prior to the meeting of the Commissioners under the 4th Article of the Treaty of Ghent, that I might examine the Arguments and evidence he had prepared to deliver to the Board in support of His Majestys claim to the Islands in the Bays of Fundy and Passamaquoddy. A severe fit of the Gout prevented his arriving at the time appointed and subsequent to his recovery contrary winds detained him until the second instant. The succeeding day the Board proceeded to Business, and is now progressing with industry. The arguments on the part of both nations will I hope be read over by the 12th current, that on the part of the United States is unnecessarily diffuse; after which the Agents will require some time to prepare replies each to the others arguments, so that a short adjournment will probably take place. Mr. Chipman has at my request introduced in his memorial the Arguments used by Comrs. Shirley and Milday in their negotiations at Paris in 1750 and the extract of the council minutes in 1763, although he is of opinion, in which I concur, that the claim on the part of His Majesty, must and will eventually rest on the Grant to Sir Wm. Alexander in 1621. I confess my principal inducement for incorporating in the present case, the Arguments used by the Commissioners at Paris in 1750, is founded more on the effect it may produce on the friendly Power to whom the case may be referred, in the event of the Commissioners not being able to agree in a decision, than on the Commissioners in the first Instance.— I am satisfied that your Lordship is Master of the Subject and will not therefore trouble you suggesting my reasons on this point.

On the 4th of June the Commissioners under the 5th Article of the Treaty met agreeably to adjournment in September; and the Agents are preparing instructions for the Surveyors, who will leave this in a few days for the Source of the River St. Croix and commence running the due North Line and endeavor to establish the North West Angle of Nova Scotia. It is proposed that an exploring party be sent forward to endeavor to discover the Highlands, while the Surveyors are proceeding under the more dillatory process of actual admeasurement. The American Commissioner was anxious that the ascertaining of the Boundaries should commence at the River Cataraqui on the parallel of the 45 Degree of North Latitude; but having received directions from Earl Bathurst to delay astronomical observations until a Gentleman who he would send from England for that particular service arrived, I opposed his proposition and succeeded in limiting the operations to commence at the Source of the St. Croix where simple surveying alone be necessary. I fear the survey and entire observation will occupy much time, and I am not less apprehensive of great difficulty in establishing the real Highlands and North-westermost Source of the Connecticut River named in the Treaty.

TO LORD CASTLEREAGH.

New York 25ᵗʰ June 1817.

MY LORD.

Referring your Lordship to my No. 4 of the 5ᵗʰ Current, I have the honor to acquaint you that after the Agents of both nations under the 4ᵗʰ Article of the Treaty of Ghent had respectively read their agreements to the Commissioners and delivered them to the Secretary His Majesty's Agent requested an adjournment of the Board to the 25ᵗʰ of September, to enable him to reply to the case made out by the Agent of the United States, in consequence of which the Commissioners on the 13ᵗʰ Instant adjourned to meet at Boston on the 25ᵗʰ of September to hear the Agents of both nations in reply each to the other.

The Commissioners under the 5ᵗʰ Article of that Treaty, under an impression that it would expedite the Business, have appointed two sets of Surveyors as suggested in my No. 4 to your Lordship, who were to leave Boston with their respective chain Bearers and ax men &c. &c on the 22ᵈ Instant for the source of the River St. Croix, from whence they are to commence their operations. They are furnished with such instructions as the Commissioners and Agents considered necessary. On the 14ᵗʰ instant the commissioners under this Article adjourned to the 5th of May next to New York, unless an intervening meeting may be necessary, when the commissioners of either nation (by agreement) may name a day and place for such meeting. This I am led to think is improbable, as the Surveyors will not have progressed so far as to render such meeting necessary, before winter will impede all Field operations, there being little more than four months in that part of America, wherein Surveyors can be employed.

TO MR. OGILVY.

New York 27th June 1817.
My DEAR SIR.

By this morning's Post, I received a Packet of Letters from Boston, (which arrived there after I had left it) in which was your favor of the 10th instant. I will cheerfully give you my sentiments on the subject you have suggested, and beg you will at all times freely command my best services. General Porter is in part right in saying that it is customary with Ambassadors, Ministers Plenipotentiary, Commissioners and all other official characters, while transacting business with Gentlemen of the same official Denomination belonging to other nations invariably to name their own King or Government first. For instance in official letters of any other official acts emanating from General Porter to you wherein he makes mention of both nations, it is due to his own to name it first. With respect to the Journal (which appears to be the object of the present difference of opinion between you and him) I am of opinion both you and he are under an error and that neither of you are to keep the Journal or a duplicate of it, but that the Journal is to remain with the Secretary who is the proper officer and in whose custody all papers filed are to remain. There can be but one Journal. You may have as many copies as you please of it, but if any of them vary from the original Journal they must be corrected by it. It is usual with Commissioners to have the proceedings of the day entered on loose paper, and every day the last thing the Board does before adjournment is to make the Secretary read the proceedings to prevent omissions or mistakes, or correct the mode of expression. On the adjournment of the Board, the Secretary immediately enters the proceedings of the day in his Journal, verbatim from the loose minutes, and at the next meeting of the Board before they proceed to Business, one of the Commissioners examines the Journal of the preceding day with the Secretary who reads aloud the proceedings from the minutes. If this mode is adhered to no mistake can be made. The Secretary should carefully file all these loose minutes.

I come now to the main object stated in your Letter, to wit, the alternately or occasionally naming the United States of America before His Britannic Majesty in the Journal, for as I have before noticed there can be but one Journal. It will be best answered by two or three Questions and answers. Ques. ? Under what authority did His Majesty and the President of the United States of America nominate you Gentlemen Commissioners. Answer. Under the Treaty of Peace and Amity concluded at Ghent the 24th of December 1814. Q. In the caption of that Treaty and throughout the whole of the Treaty, who is first named, His Britannic Majesty, or the United States of America. A. His Britannic Majesty without an exception. Q. If the Commissioners who drew up and concluded the Treaty of Ghent invariably named His Britannic Majesty, before the United States of America, ought not the Commissioners who are now acting under the 6th and 7th Articles of that Treaty to adopt the same rule. A. Unquestionably.— Is it not customary to name the older first, especially when he stands as Parent. A. Certainly.—

In the Journals of the Commissioners under the 4 and 5 Articles of the Treaty of Ghent, His Majesty's Commissioner is always first named. It was so also under the Commission of 1796. It never became a Question, because the Language of the Treaty was adopted.

TO THE COMMISSIONERS UNDER THE SIXTH AND SEVENTH
ARTICLES OF THE TREATY OF GHENT.

New York 14 July 1817.

SIRS.

I yesterday received a Letter from Mr. Orne, Secretary to
the Commissioners under the 5th Article of the Treaty concluded at Ghent in December 1814, between His Britannick
Majesty and the United States of America, enclosing a copy
of a resolution passed by your Board on the 3[d] of June, on
the subject of ascertaining the point at which the 45 degree
of North Latitude, continued West from the Northwestermost
head of the Connecticut river strikes the River Iroquois, or
Cataraquy. That as the establishing this was an object equally
the duty of the Commissioners under the 5th Article of the
Treaty, as well of you Gentlemen Commissioners under the
6th & 7th Articles, it was desirable that they cooperated with
you in ascertaining and establishing the same; and that you
proposed " a joint meeting of the Boards with the Astronomers employed by them respectively should be held at or in
the vicinity of S[t] Regis as early as it may suit the convenience
of the Commissioners under the 5th Article for the purpose of
comparing the results of the several observations made under
the direction of the respective Boards and awarding thereon";
also that you hoped the meeting, if acceded to might not be
delayed beyond the month of September.

I have the Honor to acquaint you that early in May, I received a Letter from His Majesty's Colonial Department of
State dated the 14th of March last informing me that a Gentleman would without loss of time be sent to me from London to
execute the Astronomical Parts of the Service enjoined by the
5th Article of the Treaty, and directing me to proceed in the
meantime on the surveys which form another part of the service.
In June therefore when the Board (under the 5th Article) met
at Boston, I communicated to Mr. Van Ness, my brother Commissioner, the purport of the Letter, in consequence of which,
we immediately detached the Surveyor to the Source of the
River St. Croix with directions to commence and proceed in

running the due North Line, and it was agreed by Mr. Van Ness and myself, that on the arrival of the Astronomer from London, he and the Astronomer on the part of the United States of America, should forthwith proceed to establish the Parallel of Latitude directed in the 5th Article of the Treaty. The Gentleman has not yet arrived, but is momently expected.

I feel assured that Mr. Van Ness will, as well as myself, accept the polite proposal contained in your resolution of a joint co operation of the two boards in ascertaining a point necessary to be established under the 5th and 6 articles of the Treaty.— I shall by this days mail write him on the Subject and request him to communicate to you his determination. If he acceeds, which I take for granted he will, on the arrival of the Astronomer from England I will immediately proceed with him to St. Regis, there to meet you Gentlemen and Mr. Van Ness with the four Astronomers finally to establish the Point where the 45th degree of North Latitude extended from the North Westermost head of Connecticut River intersects the River Cateraquy.— It is proper for me to add, that if the arrival of the astronomer, should be delayed beyond the 1st of September (an event by no means probable) it will not be in my power personally to attend, because the Board of Commissioners under the 4th Article of the Treaty are to meet at Boston on the 25th of that month; but I will notwithstanding send on the astronomer to unite with Mr. Ellicott[1] in ascertaining the parallel of Latitude, which will in all probability be confirmed by Mr. Van Ness and myself, particularly if it accords with the observations and results of the two Gentlemen now employed by you for the same purpose — It will naturally occur to you, that it will be prudent for Mr. Ellicott to remain in the vicinity of St. Regis, ready to commence the astronomical observations.

[1] Andrew Ellicott was born in Pennsylvania in 1754. He was employed as a surveyor by the U. S. Government on various occasions, notably in the work of laying out the Federal City. In 1813 he was appointed Professor of Mathematics at West Point, a post he held until his death in 1820.

TO MR. VAN NESS.

New York 25 August 1817.

SIR

I have the Honor to acquaint you with the arrival of Dr. Tiarks His Majestys Astronomer under the 5th, 6th and 7th Articles of the Treaty of Ghent, at this place in the last Packet from England. [1] — Mr. Ellicott the Astronomer on the part of the United States is also at present in this City, who informs me that he has by his observations established the point where the parallel of the 45 Degree of Latitude strikes the River Cataraquy,[2] and that his duty at West Point at present prevents his attending Dr. Tiarks to St. Regis; he adds that even was it in his power it would be unnecessary, because he is satisfied his observations and their results are correct, and that the Season is so far advanced, as to prevent Dr. Tiarks doing anything more until next Spring, than ascertaining whether the point established by him (Mr. Ellicott) at the River Cataraquy is correct or not.

Dr. Tiarks will proceed in the morning for St. Regis for this purpose; should you differ in opinion with Mr. Ellicott, and prefer having an Astronomer to observe at the same time with Dr. Tiarks, to proceed to send him to St. Regis, perhaps you may wish to be there in person. It is not in my power to go thither, as the Commissioners under the 4th Article of the Treaty meet at Boston on the 25 of September.

Mr. Ellicott also told me, that at the request of the President, he should hold himself in readiness to establish and run the parallel of the 45 Degree of North Latitude as early in the Spring as the weather will permit. I beg leave to add that Dr. Tiarks will be ready to accompany him.

---

[1] This gentleman was a Swiss by birth. Little seems to be known of him. He died about 1830.

[2] The point thus established by Mr. Ellicott was adopted by the Commissioners under the sixth article as the starting-point of their part of the line. See their award published in Treaties and Conventions of the United States.

25

TO LORD CASTLEREAGH.

New York 2ᵈ September 1817.

MY LORD,

Your Lordships Letter of the 6th of June, announcing that I should shortly be joined by Dr. Tiarks, His Majesty astronomer under the 5th and 6th Articles of the Treaty of Ghent, I have had the Honor to receive.— Dr. Tiarks has since arrived, and gone to St. Regis on that part of the River St. Lawrence designated under the Treaty of 1783, by the name of the Iroquois or Cataraquy, in order to ascertain whether the parallel of the 45 Degree of North Latitude which strikes that River, as reported a few weeks since by the American Astronomer Mr. Ellicott is correct, who makes to correspond within two or three feet of Hollands parallel in 1768, or thereabout. I regret to add from Mr. Ellicott's information that this operation will occupy the whole of the remainder of the season in that cold climate. As early in the Spring however as the weather will permit, I will take care to have the astronomers employed in establishing the parallel of Latitude towards the North Westermost head of the Connecticut River. The Surveyors are now engaged in running the due North Line, and searching for the Highlands from the Source of the River St. Croix.—I have every reason to hope the Arguments of the Agents appointed under the 4th Article of the Treaty of Ghent, will be closed at the meeting of the Commissioners at Boston on the 25th instant, and I am sanguine in my expectation that the result will prove favorable to the claims of His Majesty. However, as it is possible I may be disappointed in my expectation, I shall be prepared, as far as anticipation will permit, with my report in the event of our disagreeing. The report I am fearful will be more than ordinarily long, as it will contain no small part of the arguments of the Agents, as well as my own remarks.

TO MR. OGILVY.

New York 22 October, 1817.

MY DEAR SIR,

Your letter of the 22nd ult° and private letter of the same date from Rapid Plat Upper Canada, I had the pleasure to receive while at Boston from whence I returned to this place yesterday. I was so much engaged while there during a short Session as not to have it in my power to reply to your favor, I therefore avail myself of the first moment on my return.

It was certainly desirable that Dr. Tiarks should have brought out with him all the instruments necessary for the accurate observations committed to him by His Majestys Government, indeed he did bring all with the exception of the Refracting Circle, and I should have detained him at this place until its arrival, had not Mr. Ellicott, the American Astronomer told Dr. Tiarks that there was at St. Regis such an instrument appertaining to the American Government, much at his Service, and that he would write to General Porter, (or some other Gentleman who had the charge of it, I do not recall which) to allow Dr. Tiarks the use of it. I am happy to learn that General Porter has politely directed it to be delivered to him, and hope before this he has completed his observations at St. Regis. As he is engaged under the 5 Article, it is proper that all sums necessary for that Service and his expenses should be paid by me, his drafts therefore on me will be honored. If you have advanced him money, let him draw in your favor on me for it.

Scientific men are generally absent in character, I was therefore not surprised that Dr. Tiarks had forgotten he had a letter for you from me, nor that he had placed it, in so safe a place as to be out of sight. As matters have turned out, it was not material. He appears an amiable correct character: of his abilities I have no doubt, yet let me add I am not competent to decide.

I have the pleasure to inform you that contrary to my expectation, Mr. Holmes the American Commissioner and myself under the 4th Article of the Treaty of Ghent have come to a decision, an event I little expected. It is due to Mr. Holmes to add that throughout the whole of the Business committed to him and me, he has conducted himself with candor and Liberality, and although much argument has taken place between him and me previous to our coming to a decision, it was conducted with courtesy, impartiality and perfect good humour. The decision is executed on paper at present, for fear of accident by death or otherwise to him or me, but we meet here on the 24th of November to execute it when engrossed on parchment when it will be transmitted to both Governments, and duplicates delivered to the Agents. I may safely add that no commission of similar magnitude has been gone through and decided in so short a period and at so trifling an expense. The Agents of both Governments memorialed the Board to be further heard and for an adjournment to next Spring for them to prepare their Arguments by way of rejoinder. The Commissioners declined acceding to their request, under a conviction that they were fully possessed of the merits of the case submitted to them. An adjournment of the Board for six days took place, during which Mr. Holmes and myself conferred in private and eventually agreed upon a decision. In doing this some little has been yielded on both sides. This in my opinion was preferable to our reporting the Grounds of our differing in opinion and by that means rendering a reference to some friendly Sovereign to decide necessary, whose decision in all probability would not have been as agreeable to both nations; and a measure pregnant with delay and expense.

On the opposite page is the copy of a letter from the foreign office, from which you will perceive Col. Bouchette is no longer to act as surveyor under the 6th & 7th Articles of the Treaty of Ghent.

TO LORD CASTLEREAGH.

New York 25 October 1817.

My Lord.

I have the Honor to inform your Lordship, that the Commissioners appointed by virtue of the 4th Article of the Treaty

of Ghent met at Boston in the State of Massachusetts, pursu-
ant to adjournment, on the 25th of September last past, to hear
the Agents of both Nations, each in reply to the others Arguments delivered to the Board at its Session in June last. On
the first of October the agents concluded reading their Arguments and on the 2^d the Commissioners agreed to adjourn to
the 8th of the same Month, under an impression that from
the Evidence already exhibited by the Agents, they were fully
possessed of the merits of the Question submitted to them, and
for the purpose of attempting to come to a decision thereon.

I had previously conferred with His Majestys Agent on this
point; who concurred in opinion with me, that a further hearing of the Agents by rejoinder, would be useless, and tend
only.to prolong the discussion and create expense. In addition to this I was aware that if a decision was not made on or
before the 1st of December ensuing, another Commissioner
on the part of the United States must be appointed, as Mr.
Holmes, the present Commissioner had been elected a member
of Congress, and by the Constitution of these States, he would
be obliged to resign his appointment as Commissioner prior to
his taking his seat in the House of Representatives. In such
an Event the case must have been reargued, and the proceedings necessarily drawn out to a greater length. I had also
reason to believe, from the general tenor of Mr. Holmes' conduct, that it was more than doubtful, whether another Commissioner would possess that candor and Discrimination, I had
in every instance experienced in this Gentleman.

In the discussion which took place between the Commissioner on the part of the United States and myself, in the
interval from the 2nd to the 9th of October, I endeavored to
convince him, that by the express words used in the Grant of
King James to Sir William Alexander in 1621, to wit, "in-
cludens et comprehendens intra praedictas maris oras littorales *ac earum circumferentias*, a mari ad mare, omnes terras
continentes cum fluminibus, torrentibus, sinibus, littoribus,
insulis, aut maribus jacentibus *prope* aut infra sex leucas ad
aliquam earundem partem ex occidentali, boreali, vel orientali
partibus orarum littoralium et *praecinctuum earundem*," all the

25*

Islands in the Bay of Passamaquoddy and the Island of Grand
Manan in the Bay of Fundy were included within the Limits
of that Grant. For that although a line drawn from Cape St.
Marys (one of the boundary Lines described in the Grant to
Sir William Alexander) to the River St. Croix would not include all the Islands within it; still a parallel Line six leagues
distant to the South West would embrace them — and that the
Words "sex leucas" referred to "earum circumferentias" and
"praecinctuum earundem," and not to "oras littorales" nor
"orarum littoralium."— That the Line from St. Marys Bay to
the River St. Croix was the "circumferentias" and the "praecinctuum" mentioned in the Grant, and that the "sex leucas"
was to be extended from that Line and not from the Coasts or
Shores of Nova Scotia.— To this the American Commissioner
replied, that it was unnecessary for him and me to enter upon
the construction given by me on the Words of the Grant, as
the Crown had decided it repeatedly in the Commissions to the
Governors of Nova Scotia, wherein the Limits of Nova Scotia
were defined; and he referred to the Commission to Montague
Wilmot Esqr. in 1763, wherein all Islands on the North and
East within six Leagues of the *Coasts*, are declared to be
within the Limits of Nova Scotia, and to the Southward all
Islands within forty leagues of the *Coast*, but that to the
Westward no mention was made of Islands in the Commission to Mr. Wilmot, nor in any other of the Commissions to
the Governors of Nova Scotia; if, therefore, he were to allow
this as an accidental omission, I could not in justice require
him to admit more than was given on the North and East,
which would be all Islands within six leagues of the Western
part of the *Coast* of Nova Scotia, and that this would comport
with the Words of Sir William Alexanders Grant "infra
sex leucas ad aliquam earundem partem ex occidentali, boreali vel orientali partibus " &c &c &c,— but that the six Leagues
must be measured from the Shores and Coasts, and not from
the circumferences of the Boundaries.— I suggested that the
Commissions were generally penned in haste, by Clerks in the
public offices, and intended merely as instructions to Governors, not as Acts which were to bind his Majesty on other

points and the foreign Powers; because, if Declarations contained in such Commissions could not bind foreign Powers, it was unreasonable, that the Power making such Declarations, and possibly with private views, confined to its own Subjects, should be bound thereby. In support of this Doctrine, I stated several cases, and in some measure brought the American Commissioner to think there was not so much weight in his objection, as he originally imagined. I assured, and endeavored to convince him, that from the Evidence before the Board, it was manifest, that all Islands in question were included in the Grant to Sir William Alexander, and consequently appertained to His Majesty; and called on him to unite with me in decision to that effect. This he of course declined; remarking that such a decision would deprive the United States of Moose Island and the two adjoining small Islands, named Dudley and Frederick, which had been decided to them by the Convention or Treaty in 1803 and by the Supplemental Treaty in 1807, neither of which it was true had been ratified on the part of the United States, but that they were evidence, that Great Britain either considered these Islands to belong to the United States, or was willing to acknowledge them as such, provided the United States would relinquish claim to all the other Islands in the Bay of Passamaquoddy. He added that although he was determined not to execute a decision whereby all the Islands in question were to be adjudged to belong to His Majesty, yet he was willing to come to a determination which should comport with the principles agreed upon by Earl Liverpool, then Lord Hawkesbury, and Mr. King in 1803, and by Lord Holland and Lord Auckland and Mr. Monroe and Mr. Pinkney in 1807. That if I would not consent to this, he was ready to report, jointly or separately, stating the points on which we differed, and the grounds on which our respective opinions had been formed, and to leave it to the two Governments to refer the report to some friendly Sovereign or State for decision,— which decision could not possibly be more adverse to the claims of the United States and might be more favorable, than that I had proposed. That where nothing more could be lost, and something might be gained, it was his duty to refer the question to the Tribunal pointed out by the Treaty in the event of the Commissioners not coming to a decision. In adjourning for that day (the 5th of October) I communicated the substance of the conferences, which had taken place between the Commissioner on the part of the United States and myself, to His Majesty's Agent. His opinion coincided with mine in the following particulars.—That in the event of the report being referred to a friendly Sovereign, it would naturally be placed by him, in the hands of one of His Ministers, or Law officers, with directions to examine the reports, and to recommend the decision which ought to be made. — That it was probable that either from want of time, or other cause, the attention necessary to form a correct opinion might not be given, or that the Arguments in the report might not be fully comprehended; and that such Sovereign being called upon by both nations, in the character of a Friend, would probably adopt the Terms agreed upon (though not ratified) by the two nations, in the Convention of 1803 and supplemental convention in 1807. That if this should be the Line pursued by such friendly Power, still it would remain a matter of doubt to whom it would decide the Island of Grand Manan to belong.— That this Island was of more value to His Majesty, in point of Territory, than all the Islands in the Bay of Passamaquoddy; and in a military and naval Point of View of much greater importance.— That it commands the North West Side the Bay of Fundy, is immediately opposite that part of the American Coast, where the waters which pass into and out of the Bay of Passamaquoddy at a place called West-quoddy passage and — that His Majesty by being possessed of this Island, would have it in his power, in the event of a War, to prevent American Privateers from sheltering themselves in that Passage and to protect the Province of New Brunswick and that part of Nova Scotia which lies in the Bay of Fundy — That unless the six leagues should be measured from the line described in the Grant to Sir William Alexander, from St. Marys Bay to the River St. Croix, this Island would not be comprehended within the Limits of Nova Scotia, but only a small part of it,— and that the friendly power might possibly decide in favor of the United States, or that the small portion of it belonged to His Majesty, and the remainder to those States — that either event would be extremely prejudicial to His Majesty's Interest — that in the number of unpleasant consequences which would attend a reference to a friendly Sovereign or State, independantly of the uncertainty of the decision, are the time it would occupy, and the expense attending such an appeal.

His Majestys Agent further agreed with me, that Moose Island is of no moment to His Majesty. It had never been granted by him to any of his Subjects: on the contrary the State of Massachusetts had granted it to citizens of the United States — admitting that the friendly Sovereign should decide, that this Island did belong to His Majesty, the present Possessors would, on taking the Oaths of Allegiance, be confirmed in their titles to the Lands they held, while their sentiments would probably remain favorable to the Interests of the United States, and from their having access to His Majestys other Territories, would in time of War have it in their power to communicate information to His Majestys Enemies. That this Island lay within less than half a mile of the American Shores, and consequently was at any moment liable to be taken possession of, unless defended by strong works, and a competent Garrison — That it was not worth this expense, nor, indeed either in an agricultural point of view, or for a fishery, of any value to the Crown.—That Frederick and Dudley Islands, adjacent thereto, were merely Rocks in the Bay of Passamaquoddy, extremely small and incapable of improvement, or, indeed, of being made useful in any manner whatever. If an amicable decision could be effected by giving Moose Island with Dudley and Frederick Islands, its natural appendages to the United States, his Majestys Agent thought it would be an advantageous adjustment on the part of His Majesty, and infinitely preferable to leaving the question to be decided by a friendly Sovereign. Accordingly when I met the American Commissioner on the 6th of October, I stated to him, that I had reflected on what he had suggested, and notwithstanding my conviction, that His Majesty's claim to all the Islands was supported by incontrovertible evidence, that I was willing, in order that a decision might be made in preference to a report, to yield up a part of the Islands claimed by His Majesty, to wit, Moose Island and Dudley and Frederick Islands, on condition that all the other Islands in the Bay of Passamaquoddy, and Grand Manan, should be decided to belong to His Majesty. He appeared astonished that either myself, or his Majestys Agent, had ever been serious in the claim for Grand Manan: represented its lying directly opposite the American Shores, and without the Limits of Sir William Alexanders Grant, except a fractional part of it; and that he never could consent to decide that this Island belonged to His Majesty. To these remarks I replied, by declaring, that unless he acceded to my last proposal, the appeal should be made to a friendly Sovereign or State. Eventually he agreed to give up Grand Manan, provided I would add the Island of Campo Bello to the three I had offered to give to the United States. I told him he had my ultimatum, an ultimatum I had brought myself with much difficulty to offer, while under a conviction that His Majesty's Title to Moose, Dudley and Frederick Islands was beyond dispute — It was not until the morning of the 9th, that I could induce the Commissioner on the part of the United States to agree to the Terms I had proposed, and then with great reluctance and apparent Hesitation, and only on condition that I would unite with him in a Letter to both Governments, expressive of our opinion that the Eastern Passage from the Bay of Passamaquoddy was common to both nations. This letter he penned while I wrote the decision, but the Letter was so corrected by me, as to render it a mere matter of opinion, not official, on the part of the Commissioners and consequently not binding on either of the nations. Still I beg leave to observe to your Lordship, that I think the United States, in justice, and for preserving harmony between the two nations, should be permitted the use of this Eastern Passage, or outlet into the Bay of Fundy.

I have the Honor to enclose herewith a copy of that Letter, and of the decision, at present executed on paper. As the copying of the Arguments of the Agents, and of other papers required some Weeks, we adjourned to the 24th of November, then to re-execute the decision, to be engrossed on Parchment, and to deliver to the Agents the documents directed by the Treaty: all which will be done before the close of that month.

It would be withholding a Tribute justly due to the Talents, Industry, and unremitted attention, of Mr. Chipman, His Majestys Agent, throughout the discussion which has taken place, and to his prudence in securing some valuable papers used under the Commission to which he was Agent in 1796, did I not state to your Lordship how ably he has advocated His Majestys claim. This declaration in his favor would be unnecessary, if it were in your Lordship's power to spare the time which a perusal of his two arguments would require.

I trust your Lordship and His Majestys other Ministers, will approve of the decision, whereby the United States acquire only the same three small Islands, intended for them by the unratified conventions of 1803 and 1807, while not only the Title to all the other Islands in the Bay of Passamaquoddy, in like manner secured to His Majesty by those Conventions, is confirmed, but the Island of Grand Manan is declared to belong to His Majesty; — an Island justly remarked, in a preceding part of this Letter, to be of more intrinsic value and national importance, than all the Islands in the Bay of Passamaquoddy.

TO MR. CHIPMAN.

New York 8th November 1817.

DEAR SIR,

I have read with no little pain, your sons Letter to you of the 24th of October. It is distressing to think that a person, so unequal to the duty, as Col. Bouchette appears from his representation to be, should have been appointed to a service, which required Talents, as well as professional knowledge with respect to the practical parts of the Surveys. Independent of every other objection, he is unfit for his office, if he is the timid Character represented by your Son and bullied by the American Surveyor. Ascertain the fact, and give me the earliest information, that I may acquaint Government.— I was not a little surprised to find, your Son attached incompetency to Mr. Campbell, as well as Col: Bouchette, having always understood from you, that he was fully equal to running a plain, simple North line. If the fact is so, another must be procured by you to supply his place. Is young Mr. Odell as clever and competent, as your Son represents, if so write me officially recommending him, and I will request Lord Castlereagh to appoint him in the place of Col: Bouchette. If Odell looks forward to succeed his Father, or to the future countenance of Government, he will not refuse the appointment. No time is to be lost, let me therefore hear from you as early as possible.— I know so little of this North Line, or the consequences which will follow if the Restigouche is adopted as the River, whose waters empty into the River St. Lawrence, that I can form no opinion. I observe what you notice at the foot of your Letter to me of the 30' ult°, namely that the River Restigouche empties into the Gulf of St Lawrence by the Bay of Chaleurs, and not into the River. This is a decisive objection, should it hereafter become necessary to avail ourselves of it.— Col. Bouchette however, in his Letter to your Son, speaks of the intersection of the Line with this River four miles North of the little Wagansis, as advantageous to His Majesty, as Great Britain will partake in all the advantages of the Portage.— Is he correct on this point.— All must be left, and I cheerfully do submit it, to you, who are as it were on the spot, and can acquire important information and advice from the Surveyor General and other Gentlemen well informed on the Subject.— On this Article we must exert ourselves, and do our Government the Justice it merits. I feel assured it is unnecessary to urge you or your Son to increased exertions.

TO MR. VAN NESS.

New York, 3^d December 1817.

SIR,

Although it scarce admits of a doubt, that the Secretary of the Board of Commissioners under the 6th & 7th Articles of the

Treaty of Ghent has addressed a letter to you containing a resolution of that Board on the 29th of October, still to prevent the possibility of your not having received it, I do myself the Honor to enclose you a copy. — By the resolution you will perceive that these Commissioners are to meet at Hamilton on the 15th of May next and that they are in the interval ready to receive any communications from you and me relating to the joint meeting of the two Boards to establish at the River Cateraquy tħe precise point where the parallel of the 45 Degree of North Latitude intersects that River.

If I recollect, in a letter I received from you during last Summer, you hinted an opinion that neither the Treaty of Ghent, nor the Treaty of Peace in 1783 to which it refers gave any directions to these Commissioners to establish this precise point. In this I agree in opinion with you: but as they are to proceed (under the 5th Article of the Treaty of Ghent) from the middle of that part of the River Iroquois or Cateraquy where the parallel of the 45 Degree of North Latitude strikes that River, it becomes important to them to know the precise spot as a locus a quo from which their surveys commence. If this parallel is ascertained by the Astronomers under the two Commissions separately, it is probable there may be a difference of a few feet in the results of the astronomical observations in which event there would be two points established by the respective Boards as the parallel where the 45th degree of North Latitude where it strikes the River Cateraquy. This if possible should be avoided, and by a joint meeting of the two Boards prevented. Our Board stands adjourned to meet at New York early in May, at which time and place I take for granted the Surveyors of the exploring Party will attend as well as the Agents. It appears to me, that if we were to change the place of our meeting to Hamilton, or some other convenient place near St. Regis, and direct the Secretary, Agents, Dr. Tiarks and Mr. Ellicott the Astronomers and Mr. Bouchette and Mr. Johnson the Surveyors to meet us there, it would be attended with little trouble or difficulty to them, indeed I conceive that I will be the only person materially inconvenienced. By this measure we shall be on the spot, and can arrange with the other commissioners the point of intersection, while we can at the same time receive the reports of the Surveyors with respect to what has been done this Summer and give them such further directions as may appear necessary. These are my sentiments, but I am by no means tenacious of them, if they coincide with yours I shall be happy, if not favor me with your reasons, so that we may return an answer to the Commissioners under the 6 and 7 Articles; and in the former event notify our Secretary, Agents, Astronomers and Surveyors, where and when to attend. Any day between the first and 10th day of May will suit me to meet our own Board, and the Board of the other Comm".

TO MR. CHIPMAN.

New York 6ᵗʰ Dec. 1817.

MY DEAR SIR,

I received a few days since your Letter of the 17ᵗʰ of November together with its enclosures, seven in number, for which accept my thanks. I am pleased to find, notwithstanding an expression contained in one of your Sons Letters, that you continue satisfied with the conduct of Mr. Campbell the Surveyor, as it corresponds with the character you had invariably given me of that Gentleman. I know not sufficient of the Country to form any Idea of the consequences which will follow adopting the Restigouche for the River whose waters empty into the River St. Lawrence, or how it will comport with a River to be found the Waters of which discharge into the Atlantic Ocean. This point, as I suggested to you in my Letter of the 8th ult. I leave wholly to your better information and judgment, with this one remark, that if adopting this river will tend to His Majestys Interest there can be no objection to falling in with the wishes of the American Surveyor, and on the contrary should it be found prejudicial we may easily prevent the adoption of it, because it empties into the Bay of Chaleurs in the Gulf St. Lawrence, and not into the River of that name. If a Stream can be found whose waters empty into any River which discharges itself into the Atlantic Ocean, (nay I am not certain but even a Stream which unites with a River which pours its Waters into the Atlantic Ocean by the Bay of Fundy) such River, if it accords with the Interest of His Majesty should be pressed on the Surveyors as the River. If you are satisfied with Bouchette, all is well. In justice to our government, I beg leave to say, that it would have left the appointment of Astronomers and Surveyors to me, but as I did not know of any really able ones in America, and did not wish to assume that responsibility which would attach to my appointment, I requested the Foreign office to provide the Commission with adequate Astronomers and Surveyors. Still if necessary I am of opinion, and shall have no reluctance to appoint others, and supersede those now on that service. I enclose herewith the engrossed Decision of the Commissioners under the 4th Article of the Treaty also the sheets of the Journal to complete those you took on from Boston; and the Presidents message to Congress. You will notice the manner in which he informs Congress of the decision of the Commissioners. He tells the truth but not the whole Truth. Not a word of the Bay of Fundy or Island of Grand Manan.—I think this augurs he feels sore on the point, otherwise he would have added to which of the two Nations that Island had been decided.[1] Although the Commission under the 5th Article stands adjourned to meet here in May, I think it rather probable that we shall change the place of meeting to St Regis on the St Lawrence, near the point of intersection of the Parallel of the 45th Degree of North Latitude with that River. Should it be so agreed upon between Mr. Van Ness and myself, you shall have the earliest Notice.

---

[1] "I have also the satisfaction to state that the Commissioners under the fourth article of the treaty of Ghent, to whom it was referred to decide to which party the several islands in the Bay of Passamaquod-dy belonged, under the treaty of 1783, have agreed in a report, by which all the islands in the possession of each party before the late war have been decreed to it."—*Pres. Monroe's Message, December 2, 1817.*

TO LORD CASTLEREAGH.

New York 1st January 1818.

MY LORD.

In my Letters to your Lordship of the 5th and 25th of June on the Subject of the Surveys then about to be commenced from the source of the River St. Croix to the Highlands, one of the objects directed by the 3^d Article of the Treaty of Ghent, I acquainted your Lordship, that the Commissioners under that Article had appointed two sets of Surveyors, the one to run the due North Line and admeasure the distance, the other to precede them and endeavor to discover that point of the Highlands described in the Treaty of Ghent and in the Treaty of 1783 as forming the North West Angle of Nova Scotia. The last named party was denominated the exploring Surveyors, and consisted of Mr. Bouchette on the part of His Majesty and Mr. Johnson on the part of the United States, the principal Surveyors of both nations.—These Gentlemen have explored about one hundred miles north to a stream called the Wagunsis, which falls into the River Restigouche, which emptieth (not into the River St. Lawrence) but into the Gulf of St. Lawrence by the Bay of Chaleurs: It appears they consider this Stream to comport with the description in the second Article of the Treaty of 1783 respecting the Highlands, and the waters which empty into the River St. Lawrence. At present it is impossible to determine whether the adopting of this Stream will comport with His Majesty's interests. Waters falling into the Atlantic ocean corresponding with the words of the Treaty must be found before this result can be ascertained. Should the adoption of this Stream prove injurious, it can always be rejected on proof that the waters do not empty into the River, but into the Gulf of St. Lawrence. In the present uncertain state of the exploring survey, it was not my intention to have troubled your Lordship on the Subject. I have, however, been led to make the preceding remarks to show under what part of the Surveys Mr. Bouchette had been employed during the last Season, and to enable your Lordship the more readily to com-

prehend the enclosed copy of a Letter from Mr. Chipman, His
Majestys Agent to me.

Your Lordship will perceive from this Letter that Mr.
Chipman is dissatisfied with Mr. Bouchette, that he thinks
he wants at least practical professional knowledge, prudence,
nerve and constitution, and on the whole is not a character
in whom a matter of so much moment as ascertaining the
North West Angle of Nova Scotia can with safety be confided.
Yet as his opinion is formed in some measure from conjecture
and the reports of others, Mr. Chipman is unwilling that Mr.
Bouchette should be superceded in his appointment, he therefore recommends that I acceed at the meeting of the Board
in May next to the proposition of the American Commissioner
and Agent to commence running the parallel of the 45 Degree
of North Latitude from the River Cataraguay to the North-
westmost head of the Connecticut River, and to employ Mr.
Bouchette on this service, which will be simple and over a
tract of country generally under cultivation, in addition to
his remarks, I beg leave to add that Dr. Tiarks His Majestys
Astronomer and the American Astronomer Mr. Ellicott will
be always near the Surveyors to correct any error. Indeed
the Surveyors on this Line will have only to run and measure
on a due east course from one station to another of the parallel to be established by the Astronomers. If this proposal
meets your Lordships concurrence, I will in May assign to
Mr. Bouchette this part of the Service.—A Surveyor in this
event will be wanted to fill the place of Mr. Bouchette on the
exploring survey to ascertain the Highlands, North of the
Source of the River St. Croix, that divide those Rivers which
empty themselves into the River St. Lawrence, from those
which fall into the Atlantic Ocean. Mr. Chipman has named,
Mr. Odell the Present Secretary of the Province of New
Brunswick, Son of the late Secretary of that Province, as a
Gentleman every way qualified for this important Service, a
Service infinitely the most material under the 5th article of
the Treaty. He is however under an apprehension that Mr.
Odell will not feel inclined to undertake so laborious a task
on his or my request. I have no knowledge of Mr. Odell, but

the confidence I place in Mr. Chipmans prudence and judgment leads me to consider Mr. Odell as the most proper person to execute this duty. Should your Lordship think proper to adopt Mr. Chipmans recommendation it will be necessary for your Lordship, or Earl Bathurst to whose department as Secretary of New Brunswick he more immediately belongs, to write him a Letter, expressive of the Wishes of Government that he should undertake this Service, and that it is expected he will not decline doing it. The Letters on this Subject to Mr. Odell and to Mr. Chipman require dispatch. Mr. Chipmans Letter to me, whereof a copy is enclosed, is confidential, and I feel it my duty to request your Lordship will be pleased to consider it such, and that it may not be communicated to any person, other than His Majestys ministers.[1]

FROM DR. TIARKS.

On the Old Line east of Lake Champlain.
Oct. 15, 1818.

SIR.

Your letter of the 29th Sept. I had the honor of receiving to-day. I returned last Monday from the Station at Odelltown[2] and found Mr. Hassler[3] according to our agreement encamped on Lake Champlain on the Old Line nearly opposite the American fort. I had no time to calculate my observations

[1] Col. Bouchette never rendered any further service on the survey, declining, it would seem, to act under Dr. Tiarks; and he was finally discharged by an order of Lord Castlereagh, dated July 10, 1819. The commissioners under the 5th Article met this year (1818) at Burlington, Vermont, in the month of May, and there settled some matters relative to the survey of the line running north from the head of the St. Croix. From Burlington, the commissioners went to Montreal, and thence to St. Regis, where they gave instructions for running the line of latitude 45° eastward along the States of New-York and Vermont, and about the middle of June they adjourned to meet again in the spring of 1819.

[2] A small village in Canada, near Rouse's Point.

[3] Ferdinand R. Hassler was, like Dr. Tiarks, a native of Switzerland. He was the first superintendent of the Coast Survey, and planned and directed that great work until his death in 1843.

at Odelltown made with the instrument you lately sent to
me, but one which I had tried gave the Old Line about 3000
feet too far north. Lieut. Vinton calculated one in which he
placed great confidence and found the Old Line 35″ (about
3535 feet) north. Surprising as these results were yet their
agreement made me think that they are correct. When I arrived at the Camp and informed Mr. Hassler of what I had
found he expressed his belief that the Line was likewise too
far north at this place. You may easily imagine my ardent
desire to make observations with the repeating circle, but
neither the observatory was finished nor the circle placed. I
then took immediately the reflecting circle of Mr. Hassler and
to my astonishment two observations of the Sun which agreed
remarkably well gave my Latitude 45° 0′ 38″. That is about
3838′ North of the Parallel of 45° which I observed on the old
line. I communicated it to Mr. Hassler and to my still greater
surprise heard that the few observations he had calculated
brought the old Line still farther north, that is about 46″
(4646′) which had likewise been so unexpected to him that he
could at first not credit it. He then calculated some others
and obtained with little difference the same result. Most
anxious to get as quickly as possible at the truth he communicated to me an observation of the Pole Star, which I calculated
this morning. The result of the whole observation consisting
of two series of repetitions gave about 40″ nearly the same
which my own two Solar observations had given. Lieut Vinton yet ignorant of our result then began to calculate observations of his own made with a reflecting circle and obtained
only 12″ north; another however gave him 50″. These are all
the observations hitherto calculated. They are taken by three
different observers with three several instruments of two dif-
erent constructions on different celestial objects and leaving
out Mr. Vinton's one observation, which being a star observed
by the reflecting circle deserves naturally less credit, they
seem to indicate that the Old Line is about ¾ mile too far
north. The distance of the Fort built by Col Totten from
the Old Line is reckoned less than half a mile; the other now
building is very near it and there seems therefore, hardly to

remain any doubt but that both Forts are on *British* territory! I have been thus particular in detailing to you what knowledge I have and on what it is founded as this point is of extreme importance and as I thought it necessary that you should be informed of it as soon as possible. We have thought it advisable to keep this a profound secret; nobody knows it as yet except those who calculated themselves, and even most of our Assistants are still ignorant of it. Lieut Vinton goes tomorrow to the American Agent and Mr. Hassler has written to General Swift about it partly with a view of obtaining a Zenith Sector ordered in London which may be expected to have arrived as it will be his duty to insist on the most accurate determination of this point. It is Mr. Hassler's opinion that the success of our operations might be endangered if this matter became generally known by the irritation which such a thing may produce on the minds of the lower classes, and he has requested me to keep it secret as long as possible. Whether such fears are grounded or not I cannot say being too little acquainted with the inhabitants of this State.[1] As I have perfectly laid open to you whatever I know I think to have discharged my duty and shall quietly continue my operations and await the further results. I am, &c.,   T. L. TIARKS.

[1] "I was going to the President's, but was detained half an hour by Mr. Bagot, who came, in much agitation, wit a letter he had just received from Mr. Barclay, the British Commissioner under the fifth Article of the Treaty of Ghent. It appears that in running their forty-fifth parallel of latitude they find, by the observations of the astronomers on both sides, that the existing line touchin upon Lake Champlain is about three-quarters of a mile too far north, and that the new line will bring two forts lately built by us within the British territory. Hassler, the American astronomer, is so much alarmed at this result that he is afraid there will be a riot among the people there. . . . I told Bagot I thought it was nothing but a maggot in the brain of Hassler, and that there was no danger whatever. But I promised to mention it to the President and inform him of the result. I found Crawford and Calhoun with the President, and told them of Bagot's communication. Notice of the fact that the astronomical observations are likely to deprive us of our two new forts had been received yesterday from Colonel Totten by a letter from Hassler, but the President and Calhoun laughed at the idea of the apprehended rebellion against the astronomers in Vermont."—*Diary of John Quincy Adams, October* 28, 1818.

CHAPTER IX

LAST DAYS

FEW records exist of the last twelve years of Barclay's life; and, indeed, it was a quiet old age, disturbed by no unusual incidents and marked by no extremes of good or evil fortune.

The chief public duty which remained still to be performed was the closing up of the affairs of the commission under the fifth article of the Treaty of Ghent. It had become perfectly clear, as early as the beginning of the year 1819, that Barclay's first impressions were correct, and that the difficulties in the way of an adjustment of the northeast boundary were so great as to preclude all hope of the commissioners reaching an agreement. From that time on, the efforts of the representatives of both governments were strenuously devoted to collecting evidence favorable to their respective claims, and to making up a record for submission to an arbitrator.

The work of surveying progressed with exasperating slowness, and the public, on both sides of the Atlantic, condemned the commission for their delays and for the heavy expense which they incurred. But accurate surveys were indispensably necessary; and the country to be explored was extraordinarily difficult and the season for operations extremely short.

The commission sat in New-York in May, 1819, and again in Boston in May, 1820, but nothing beyond routine business could be transacted. Maps were filed, surveyors and astronomers were instructed, and accounts were audited. At length it was agreed that the surveys had so far progressed as to allow the commission to proceed to a discussion of the principles which were to be followed in running the line. A meeting for the purpose of hearing arguments was fixed for October 23, 1820; but Mr. Chipman, the British agent, was unable to attend, and an adjournment was taken until the spring.

The next year, 1821, the commission went industriously to work. They sat in New-York from May 14 to June 9; again from August 1 to August 14; and finally from September 20 to October 4, when the arguments of the agents were completed, and a long and ill-tempered discussion between them was finally brought to an end. The commissioners separated upon the understanding that separate reports were to be brought in, and that the winter was to be devoted to a preparation of all the reports, maps and papers in duplicate which the Treaty of Ghent required should be laid before each government.

On April 1, 1822, the final session of the commission was begun in New-York. The accounts were audited, the minor employees paid off, the reports were read, and finally, on April 13, the commissioners formally entered on their journal their failure to agree, and adjourned until the further pleasure of the two governments should be known. Their disagreement was complete. They did not even unite in reporting a general map of the region in dispute, but filed instead a mass of disconnected surveys. They differed as to the location of the northwest angle of Nova Scotia; as to the situation of the "highlands"; as to the source of the Connecticut River; and even as to the parallel of 45° north latitude.[1] The report of the American commissioner was comparatively brief, the copy filed in the State department at Washington covering only seventy folio pages of a rather small manuscript. Barclay's report was much more elaborate. Written in a very similar hand to that of his colleague's report, it extends to 322 folio pages, to which are added 177 pages of appendix. It is a complete review of the subject in all its phases, and contains, besides an historical account of the boundaries of the provinces of Nova Scotia, Quebec and Massachusetts, a discussion of every argument advanced on either side. These reports have never been printed in full, but liberal extracts were printed as appendices LIII. and LIV. (pp. 371–398) to the "American Case presented to the King of the Netherlands" (Washington, 1829), a volume not published, but which is to be found in some of the larger libraries.

The subsequent history of the northeast boundary question is not a little curious. The event of a disagreement between the commissioners, contemplated by the Treaty of Ghent, having thus arisen, it had now become the duty of the two governments to submit their dispute to "a friendly sovereign or State"; but the terms of the treaty were so vague in respect to methods of procedure that more than five years were consumed in desultory discussion before the needful arrangements could be made. At length, in September, 1827, Albert Gallatin, then United States Minister in London, negotiated a treaty by which all the points

---

[1] The U. S. agent claimed that geocentric instead of geographical latitude should be taken, the result of which would be to save Rouse's Point; but the commissioner, Mr. Van Ness, expressed no opinion on this point in his report.

were covered. This treaty recites that the reports of the commissioners and the annexed documents are "so voluminous and complicated as to render it improbable that any sovereign or State should be willing to undertake the office of investigating or arbitrating upon them," and it is thereupon agreed to submit instead a new statement of facts on each side, accompanied by a general map — which is annexed to the new treaty — showing the watercourses and the boundary lines as contended for by each party respectively.[1] The statements of the parties were to be exchanged within fifteen months of the ratification of the treaty, and replies thereto in six months thereafter; and the statements and replies were then to be submitted to the arbitrator.

If a hope was really entertained of shortening the arguments to be submitted, that hope must very soon have been dispelled. The case could not be presented briefly. An enormous mass of printed matter was prepared by the representatives of each party, and during the year 1830 this great bulk of assertion and argument was laid before the King of the Netherlands, who had consented, in a rash moment, to act as arbitrator.

On January 10, 1831, the arbitrator made his report. Instead of simply deciding the questions submitted to him, the King declared his inability to decide upon the line truly intended by the treaty of 1783, and he proposed instead a new line as a matter of compromise which—he suggested—it would be suitable (*il conviendra*) to adopt. Instead of following "highlands," the line was to run through a valley, proceeding along the middle of the rivers St. John and St. Francis. The difficulty in regard to the parallel of 45 north latitude was got around by proposing to run the line according

[1] See a copy of this map, which is known as Map A, *ante* page 44.

to the corrected observations, but to save Rouse's Point to the United States by describing a semicircle round the fort.

The award was satisfactory to neither party, and was rejected by both, and has never been published. Matters now seemed more unpromising than ever. Public feeling ran high, especially in Maine and New Brunswick. On one occasion, in 1838, certain British subjects having cut timber on the disputed territory, a Maine constable was sent with a posse to drive them off; but he was himself arrested and imprisoned by the provincial authorities. The militia were ordered out, and actual warfare seemed for a time to be close at hand, until good sense prevailed, and "the Restook War" became nothing but a local reminiscence.[1]

The Webster-Ashburton Treaty in 1842 finally put an end to the whole troublesome business, not without blustering from Benton in the United States Senate, and Palmerston in the House of Commons. The attempt to find the northwest angle of Nova Scotia was given up. A line intermediate between the extreme pretensions of the two parties was drawn. And the unquestionable British claim to the line of 45° north latitude was surrendered, the old incorrect line of 1763 being retained as the northern boundary of New-York and Vermont. Precisely twenty years and six months elapsed from the day the boundary commission adjourned *sine die* in New-York until the ratifications of the Webster-Ashburton Treaty were exchanged in London.

On that same day of the adjournment of the commission, Barclay paid Messrs. Isaac Wright & Son thir-

[1] Some account of the negotiations between the authorities on the border will be found in General Scott's Autobiography, Chap. xxiii.

ty-five guineas passage-money for a berth in the ship *James Cropper;* and a day or two later he sailed for England, accompanied by Mr. Chipman. They landed at Kinsale, in Ireland, crossed the channel from Cork, and posted to London, arriving there early in June. They took with them the reports and records of the commission to be filed in the Foreign Office. Their business was soon settled, and Barclay probably found less to attract him than when he had first visited England nearly twenty years earlier. Before the summer was over he was ready to return, and he sailed from Liverpool in the *James Thompson,* landing in New-York on September 7, 1822.[1]

On his return from this his last visit to England, Barclay was sixty-nine years of age, and the story of his remaining years may be told in few words. His work was done, and increasing infirmities put a peremptory stop to further activity.

In the summer of 1823 he hired a country place on Manhattan Island, which comprised a house and twelve acres of land. It lay on the Eastern Post Road, near the four-mile stone, sloping down to where a cove set in from the rocky shores of the East River. The waters of the little cove were shallow, and afforded a safe anchorage for small craft away from the swirling tides that set through the narrow passage between Manhattan and Blackwell's Islands; and Rock Harbor was the name which was given, appropriately enough, to the suburban villa. The site of it is covered to-day with breweries and tenement-houses, and it lies just east of

---

[1] He paid forty guineas for the westward trip, the rate of passage this way, according to the usual custom, being higher than to the eastward. Owing to the prevailing westerly winds the voyage from England was commonly the longer.

Third Avenue, between Forty-fifth and Forty-seventh streets in the city of New-York. Barclay was pleased with his modest country-seat, and in March, 1824, he bought it of the owner, paying $500 an acre for it, or $6000 in all. He remained in possession of the property until the summer before his death, when he sold it for $9000, thus realizing a profit of fifty per cent. on his investment.

His life was easy and uneventful. His grandchildren were multiplying and growing up about him, and his estate was prospering. He occupied himself with little household occupations, and noted with care the days of his migrations from town to country, and from country to town. A visit to Maryland, another to Newport, another to his son, Henry, on the Hudson River, were duly recorded; and with them the bottling of his Madeira, and the days when servants were engaged or discharged. One reads in his note-books how he paid his coachman fourteen dollars a month, his gardener ten, and "Cicely, a black cook," only seven; and one observes further down, without surprise, that Cicely was "dismissed for incompetence" at the end of a month. Lists were kept of the guests at his dinner-parties, and he made precise notes of his engagements to dine abroad. The old gentlemen, his friends, were mostly "warm Federalists," though Federalism, hot or cold, had ceased to be—Mr. Gracie, Mr. Ray, Dr. Hosack, Mr. Varick. Hours were earlier than at this end of the century. Mr. Waddington, and Mr. Jauncey, and Mr. Moses Rogers, we find, dined at five o'clock; but Mr. Low and Mr. H. Rogers dined at the less dissipated hour of four.

In October, 1825, the fiftieth anniversary of Barclay's wedding came round. All the surviving children were at hand, except Maria, who was away with her husband in British Guiana, and De Lancey in England. De Lancey had this year been made a colonel by brevet, and aide-de-camp to King George IV.; and he had now at last married, being forty-five years of age. George had given up his notions of settling in England, and was now established as a successful merchant in New-York.

The spring of the next year brought the ill news of De Lancey's death—of pneumonia, it would seem— only a very few days after the birth of his child, a little girl, who died young. His death was a bitter blow to his father, who had always cherished a peculiar affection for the handsome soldier. Financial worry came also through Henry, the eldest son, who had retired from business in New-York, and had embarked in rather ill-advised ventures at Saugerties, in Ulster County, where he established iron-works and a paper-mill that absorbed a great deal of money, and made no returns for a long time afterward.

But there were good days as well as evil, and time on the whole passed by not unhappily. Barclay's health, for the most part, continued good, though there were long intervals in winter when fear of cold weather kept him in his house. In particular, and most fortunately for him, his mental faculties and his eyesight were unimpaired, and letters written almost in the last month of his life show no change either in their style or in the small and rather difficult handwriting. From the summer of 1829, however, he began to fail rather rapidly. The end came at last on Wednesday, April 21, 1830. In the words of a book which he loved, he was gathered to his fathers, having the testimony of a good conscience; in the communion of the Catholic Church;

in the confidence of a certain faith; in the comfort of
a reasonable, religious and holy hope; and. in perfect
charity with the world.

His wife survived him a little over seven years, and
died May 2, 1837, being then nearly eighty-two years
of age. They are buried together, in the churchyard
of St. Mark's in the Bowery.

APPENDIX

CHILDREN OF THOMAS AND SUSAN BARCLAY

1. ELIZA BARCLAY, born at Flushing, N. Y., December 3, 1776; married Schuyler Livingston of New-York, June 17, 1796; died at Harlem, June 21, 1817.

2. HENRY BARCLAY, born in New-York, October 27, 1778; married Catherine Watts, August 13, 1817; died at Saugerties, N. Y., January 3, 1851.

3. DE LANCEY BARCLAY, born in New-York, June 16, 1780; married Mary, widow of Gurney Barclay, in 1825; died in England, March 29, 1826.

4. MARIA BARCLAY, born in New-York, June 27, 1782; married Simon Fraser of Berbice, British Guiana; died at New-York, August 7, 1862.

5. THOMAS EDMUND BARCLAY, born at Wilmot, Nova Scotia, December 4, 1783; married Catherine Channing, February 14, 1821; died at New-York, January 30, 1838.

6. SUSAN BARCLAY, born at Annapolis, Nova Scotia, February 5, 1785; married Peter Gerard Stuyvesant of New-York, August 20, 1803; died at New-York, January 14, 1805.

7. BEVERLEY ROBINSON BARCLAY, born at Annapolis, Nova Scotia, December 22, 1786; died at New-York, June 15, 1803.

8. ANN BARCLAY, born at Annapolis, Nova Scotia, December 7, 1788; married William B. Parsons, R. N., May 29, 1815; died at New-York, June 20, 1869.

9. GEORGE BARCLAY, born at Annapolis, Nova Scotia, July 4, 1790; married Anna Matilda Aufrère, December 8, 1818; died at New Hamburgh, N. Y., July 28, 1869.

10. ANTHONY BARCLAY, born at Annapolis, Nova Scotia, September 27, 1792; married Ann Waldberg Glenn; died at Hartford, Conn., March 21, 1877.

11. CLEMENT HORTON BARCLAY, born at Annapolis, Nova Scotia, August 3, 1796; and died there in September, 1797.

12. CORNELIA ELIZABETH STEWART BARCLAY, born in New-York, May 23, 1801; and died there, June 28, 1801.

INDEX

INDEX

ACT for the more effectual preservation of peace, etc., 213, 214, 219, 220, 222.

Adams, John; testimony as to map used at Paris in fixing Northeast Boundary, 66, 73-75; probably re-elected President, 115.

Adams, John Quincy, 375, 378, 404.

Admiralty, Courts of, American complaints concerning, 119; reform in, 120, 134.

Africaine, H. M. Ship, 291.

Albany. Rev. Thomas Barclay settled in (1707-1722), 4; Rev. Henry Barclay born in, 6; clergyman in (1738-1746), 7.

Alexander, Sir William, grant to, 55, 59, 71, 91, 367, 372, 374, 379, 389-392.

Alternate naming of Sovereigns in public documents, when rule to be followed, 381, 382.

Ambuscade, French Frigate, 173.

American Ships of War, reasons of their success in actions with British Ships, 336-338.

Analostan, American Brig, 333.

Analostan Island, residence of Gen. John Mason, 314.

Andromache, H. M. Ship, 126, 129, 154.

Annapolis, Nova Scotia, 25, 29, 35, 36.

Asia, H. M. Ship, 15.

Aurora, newspaper, attacks Col. Barclay, 259.

Austin, James T., American agent before the Commissioners under the fourth article of the Treaty of Ghent, 359, 376.

BAGOT, CHARLES, British Minister at Washington, 375, 404.

Banks, Sir Joseph, 378.

Baker, Anthony St. John, British Secretary of Legation at Washington, 310, 327, 328.

Barclay, Andrew (of Newtown, L.I.), 9, 11.

Barclay, Ann (daughter of Col. Thomas Barclay), 318, 351, 415; marries W. B. Parsons, 365.

Barclay, Anna Dorothea (wife of Beverly Robinson), 9.

Barclay, Anthony (of Albany), 6.

Barclay, Anthony (son of Col. Thomas Barclay), 416; at school in Nova Scotia, 96, 206; goes to England to study for the bar, 258; appointed British Commissioner under the sixth and seventh articles of the Treaty of Ghent, on the death of Mr. Ogilvy, 356; marries Ann Waldberg Glenn, 365.

Barclay, Beverley, 415; removes to New York, 96; death of, 146.

Barclay, Catharine, 9.

Barclay, Clement, 77, 416.

Barclay, Cornelia (wife of Stephen De Lancey), 9.

Barclay, Cornelia (daughter of Col. Thomas Barclay), 128, 416.

Barclay, David, emigrates to America and dies at sea, 2.

Barclay, De Lancey, 415; serves in a Nova Scotia regiment, 95; applies for commission in the regular army, 104; Ensign in 41st Foot, 105; goes to Montreal, 117; promoted, 135; goes to England, 145; promoted to be Captain, 206, 226; Major and Lieut.-Colonel, 258; appointed to the Guards, 318; promoted to be Colonel and marries Mary Barclay, 412; his death, 412.

Barclay, Eliza (wife of Schuyler Livingston), 61, 415; her death, 365.

Barclay, George, 415; at school in Nova Scotia, 96, 206; comes to New York in 1808 and goes into business with Henry Barclay, 258; marries Anna Matilda Aufrère, 365.

419